If You are Lucky

LESLIE D. STUART

Destiny Whispers Publishing, LLC
Tucson, Arizona
www.DestinyNovels.com

Copyright © 2017 by Destiny Whispers Publishing, LLC
LESLIE D. STUART, Author
IF YOU ARE LUCKY – Special Enhanced Publisher's Edition, August 17, 2017
ISBN-13 #978-1-943504-50-3
ISBN-10 #1-943504-50-4

1st Ed. "Touched by Sunlight"
Feb. 14, 2014 ISBN-13: #978-0-9892929-1-7
ALL RIGHTS ARE LEGAL PROPERTY OF THE AUTHOR

Author: Leslie D. Stuart
Destiny Rose Editorial Review, LLC / www.DestinyRose-Reads.com
Book Format Design: Leslie D. Stuart, CRDR, Destiny Whispers Publishing, LLC
Cover Art License: BigStock Photos / www.bigstockphoto.com
Cover Art Design: LadyDestiny, CleverKatCreations
www.CleverCatCreations.com

Destiny Whispers Publishing, LLC / Tucson, Arizona
AN ARCHER GUARDIAN EXTRAORDINARY JOURNEY
www.DestinyNovels.com
www.DestinyAuthor.us

Everything we do, even the slightest thing we do,
can have a ripple effect and repercussions that emanate.
If you throw a pebble into the water on one side of the ocean,
it can create a tidal wave on the other side.
~~ Victor Webster

My Wish for You

Live strong my Friend, with Truth and real Integrity.
May your moments in the sun outshine any rain.
Make memories to be proud of, without fear or regret,
Letting the days of your Life fill your heart with Love.
Until emotions overflow, brightening your eyes with tears of joy.
For without choosing to overlook bad, letting Love light the way,
The spirit never finds solace or peace, only pain.
So, open your eyes, my friend.
And open your heart.
See beauty in the world, everywhere you go.
In faces, in places, in small ordinary moments
For small things can become cherished memories.
Be kind, for everyone you meet needs a little compassion.
No heart is too hard, no soul too damaged to be tossed aside.
May the days of your Life be long, lovely, and lucky,
And may Love always shine upon your shoulders.

-- Leslie D. Stuart

Secrets in sunny San Diego.
One man dreams of danger, another haunts the shadows seeking redemption. A life built on lies is the only truth Solaris has ever known. A priceless ruby necklace holds her answers, but powerful corrupt people will destroy anyone who threatens to expose their secrets.

If you are lucky
life gives you one true friend.

Forever My Friend

When opportunity opens a new door in Life, spread your wings and fly.

~~ Solaris Anne Sullivan

The bayside coffee shop was crowded to almost overflowing today. As people took refuge from the rain, their robust tumult of friendly conversations became soaked in the welcoming aroma of dark roasted latte, sugary treats, and fresh baked bread. As Solaris stepped in, a couple passed her at the doorway. Before anyone else saw the empty space, she sat at a solitary table for two by the windows.

It was noisier than usual. But the warm atmosphere saturating every corner made her smile. Usually the café by the San Diego Bay was a quiet place. Today excited voices percolated. Metal chair legs scraped against ceramic tile floor. Spoons rhythmically tapped against ceramic mugs. The sounds were an aromatic blend that somehow made a room full of strangers feel cozy.

It must be the rain, she thought.

Silver-gray droplets streaked down the window beside her table. It seemed appropriate that the sky would cry today. Big changes were coming. Everything old was being washed away.

She just needed the courage to tell Tristan.

He would be here soon.

When the waitress came to her table she ordered a caramel macchiato. She loved the caffeinated treat. Waiting for her coffee and fiancé to arrive, she wondered which would appear first. She felt impatient. Her news for Tristan was important. Solaris tried not to worry about what he might say. The facts were set. No amount of argument on his part would change it.

But her stomach had a nervous knot.

Trying to relax, she gazed outside at the rainy day.

She loved the rain. It cleansed the soul.

As she watched, across the San Diego Harbor near Coronado Island the springtime storm clouds parted, just a little. Slender sunbeams quickly shot through the small opening, illuminating the blue steel arch of the Coronado Bridge. It formed a misty rainbow.

The sky isn't crying. It's raining sunlight.

The moment felt like a lucky sign.

Solaris wished she had her camera, but it was safe and dry inside her car. She loved capturing special moments. Photography was her life. She had recently graduated with an honors degree in photojournalism from the University of San Diego. Already, her articles and photos had appeared in a dozen travel magazines. But Solaris dreamed of exploring life far beyond her familiar Southern California world. Soon, her dreams would come true. The airline ticket in her purse was proof.

First, she had to say goodbye.

Coffee arrived, but still no Tristan. *He's late*, she realized. Her cell phone had no missed calls, not even a polite text message to show he cared. For two years Tristan Kennedy had kept her waiting.

No more. Toying with the three-caret diamond engagement ring on her left hand, the shiny weight of it used to feel hopeful.

Today it just felt awkward.

While she waited, Solaris sipped her caramel macchiato latte. The sugary warmth rolled down her throat and eased the tension. She would miss this civilized treat when she was camping in the grasslands. Envisioning it felt surreal, but life had opened a door of opportunity, one she intended to take.

Yesterday, National Geographic hired her.

She felt lucky. Thirty talented photojournalists had interviewed, many boasting professional portfolios with impressive work. They chose only one: Solaris Anne Sullivan. She was young, eager to work, and ready to travel. Goodbye San Diego. Hello world!

Happiness filled her whole heart and brought a wide happy smile. Next week she would be on safari in Kenya photographing exotic wildlife most people only saw at the zoo. It made her life in San Diego seem incredibly tame. Smiling felt good. She intended to smile much more in her new life.

The cheerful brass bell on the entrance door jangled a happy tune, announcing another escapee from the rain. Suddenly an odd hush blanketed the room, as if everyone turned to look at the doorway. Solaris didn't have to look, she heard women at nearby tables take a collective gasp.

Tristan had finally arrived.

He always had that magnetic effect on people.

Wherever he went women noticed the tall captivating man with perfect blond hair and piercing cerulean blue eyes. His gaze was the color of tropical seas. The man himself was equally exotic. One glance and most women were hooked. Tristan had real charisma, character, and charm.

He was also the smartest man she knew.

In comparison, Solaris felt ordinary.

Tawny hair waved past her shoulders, not an interesting shade, just basic warm caramel. She had light golden-brown eyes, a mouth that liked to smile more than frown, and an efficient lean figure capable of hiking up mountains and camping under the stars. There was nothing special about her.

No one gasped and had fantasies when she walked into the room.

But being noticed was Tristan's life.

They lived on opposite sides of the camera. He worked as entertainment reporter for the local news station. He had fifteen minutes on the air, five days a week. People tuned in to watch whenever Tristan Kennedy flashed his pearly smile and his deep trustworthy voice told exciting stories of glamorous events occurring in Southern California. He covered exciting rooftop nightclub openings, went to posh theater and art gallery premiers, and ate for free at five-star restaurants where the owners and chefs hoped for a positive review.

Tristan loved the spotlight.

"Hey Solaris," he jauntily greeted. Raindrops had turned his pale gold hair a slightly darker shade. Even that was attractive. "Can you believe this storm? This morning it was sunny. Now the sky is falling."

"I like rain," she argued, "it cleans the air."

"But I like sunshine. It's warm and friendly."

"Most tourists would probably agree."

Pleased that he won their silly debate he grinned, chuckling at his small victory. Then in one smooth move he leaned down, cupped her chin in his palm and captured her lips in a showy kiss. Tristan always greeted her this way. When their love was wild and new that hot possessive kiss used to curl her toes.

Today the affectionate display felt hollow.

In being honest with herself, Solaris knew the showy kiss wasn't for her emotional benefit. The dramatic entrance was meant to entertain his current audience, the coffee shop crowd. It had certainly captured attention. As she glanced around some female faces looked envious, others looked away, and most men seemed embarrassed for witnessing the scene.

"Been waiting long?" He asked, sitting down in the other chair.

"Only a few minutes," she lied and inside Solaris cringed, hating that she always avoided conflict by politely excusing his rude behavior. They both knew that he was half an hour late. Tristan should apologize. He didn't, of course. He never apologized. If she was unhappy with something, too bad. That was her problem.

Sorry was not in his vocabulary.

He leaned forward, noticing the caramel macchiato she was enjoying. "How can you drink that much sugar and stay healthy? It's like candy in a cup. Those things are bad for you."

"It's a skinny latte. It has all the caffeine and very little guilt. Besides, my coffee is healthier than all those beers you drank last weekend at that microbrewery grand opening downtown."

"True," he agreed with a laugh of remembrance of the boisterous party, "but I'm healthy enough. I go to the gym every morning. Your idea of working out is walking the beach taking pretty pictures of the sunset."

Offended, she started to object, but his response was faster.

"But I do admit that you look amazing in a red bikini," he smoothly added, using that charming voice to its full abilities. "I love seeing those sexy long legs."

Solaris didn't want to bicker about healthy lifestyles and didn't care for the compliment. Sexy didn't suit her mood. "I got the job," she abruptly announced.

His expression went empty and uncomprehending.

Now she was irritated. "You don't remember, do you?"

That famous winning smile instantly lit his face as if that bright friendly curve could solve all of life's problems. In his world, it probably did. But Solaris had become immune.

"Of course, I do. You interviewed with the LA Times."

"That was two weeks ago, Tristan. Yesterday I flew to Washington DC. You didn't even notice I was gone." It was impossible to keep frustration out of her voice.

His brow arched at the surly snap, and seemed genuinely surprised. The waitress saved him from replying by appearing at their table, sweetly trying to earn the handsome reporter's approval. Tristan complimented her hair, making the younger girl blush. He ordered iced tea and a fruit plate.

"I got the LA Times job, also." Solaris coolly informed after the flirty waitress left them alone again. "But I turned it down."

That snagged his attention. "The Times is prestigious. Why did you refuse it?"

"I told you why. You didn't listen."

His head shook. "That's not true."

"Really? When did we discuss my career choices?"

Obviously, he remembered nothing at all because his expression became the careful mask of innocence and Boy Scout honor. "Hmm, I think it was Saturday."

"No. It was a week ago Friday. I told you over dinner at your bayside apartment. I baked cilantro-lime chicken and we drank a Napa Valley Chardonnay. You even had an opinion," she curtly added. "You said photography talent like mine is rare, that I should have the courage to chase my dreams. Then you asked me to spend the night and we fooled around for a while. Do you at least remember that part?"

He seemed honestly hurt by the accusation. "I'd never forget time with you."

"Sure." Breaking up with him wasn't going well. Discouraged by the unsuccessful attempt to tell him how her life was changing, Solaris decided to leave. Discussing Kenya could wait. They could talk tonight. Shifting in her chair, she started to stand but the waitress brought his order. Tristan thanked her with gushing words and a debonair smile that made the girl giggle and blush as she walked away.

"Guess what?"

He cheerfully ignored the fact that Solaris was half out of her seat, her smile had disappeared, and he was in trouble. Amazing. "Let's not play the guessing game. Just tell me."

"I had an audition for Appraisal Studios."

"Studios?" She abruptly sat down. "Now you want to be an actor?"

"It's still the news. They are starting an investigative report program airing Thursday nights, prime time on a major network. It's called 'Just the Facts' and features the unvarnished truth about products, corporations, and politics. It's dramatic and controversial, guaranteed to change opinions, influence how American's spend their money. The audition was for host." He paused dramatically, then leaned forward and gushed, "Sweetheart, they loved me. I get my own show!"

The air inside the noisy coffee shop suddenly felt too thin, burning her lungs with the next breath. She couldn't leave. Solaris felt riveted in her seat. "You'll be working in LA?"

"We record on location. Wherever news is happening, that's where I will be. The crew travels everywhere, snagging up stories that aren't just headlines news, but issues that affect the public. They wanted someone in front of the camera who people can trust. That's me!"

She felt euphoric, for pure selfish reasons.

"Wow. That's great." She almost laughed and silently scolded herself.

The purpose of this was to say goodbye. Breaking up with Tristan was supposed to be an emotionally draining moment filled with apologies and tears, some anger on his part. Not happy smiles or congratulations.

Goodbye should not feel like a celebration.

"And us?" She calmly inquired.

"You'll come with me, of course."

She immediately knew including her in his new life was an afterthought, a polite gesture. He never actually considered how she might fit into this new dream. Tristan just knew what he wanted: an hour on Thursday nights smiling for the camera, shining for America like a heroic honest-Abe star.

"I refuse to be your tag-along girl."

"That's harsh. Damn. Why not?"

"Because I did accept a job: a very good job." Shoulders squared with pride. "I got a photojournalist assignment with National Geographic. I leave for Kenya next week."

Blue eyes went wide. His suntanned skin paled.

He was definitely listening now. "Kenya, in Africa? Seriously?"

"Yes. My initial contract is for a year, all expenses paid. I have a crew, a camp coordinator, an armed guard, and a personal assistant. Kenya is our first stop, then we safari in Tanzania. This can jumpstart my career. If I work hard and write great stories to go with the pictures, important people will see my work. It's a huge first step toward my dreams."

"This is what you want?"

"Absolutely." Excitement filled her. "Someday, I want to work freelance and go wherever I choose."

He thought for a moment. "Where would you go?"

"Everywhere," she smiled, "absolutely everywhere." Solaris finally let the happiness show. It felt good to say the dream aloud. "I want to see the entire world. If it's on a map, if it's beautiful or interesting, I want to see it."

That brought serious disapproval to his handsome face.

"But you'll probably see the world before I will," she praised, quickly reverting attention back to Tristan. "News is everywhere, always changing. I'll be stuck on safari for months at a time," she wisely downplayed her own adventure. "At least you get hotel rooms. I'll live in a tent."

It worked. He grinned. "Poor you."

"See, you get the better job. Probably more money, too." Smiling wider, not caring about the money, Solaris tipped her coffee mug at him in salute. "Hosting a television show is a big deal. You'll be famous, Tristan."

"Damn, I really hope so."

Since the worst seemed over, nerves settled and her appetite returned. She hadn't eaten anything today. Solaris stole some cantaloupe off his fruit plate to munch on. Tristan watched her hand move. The diamond ring conspicuously caught the light.

"What about getting married?"

"Big important doors have opened in both of our lives. Marriage can wait." Now was the time. Solaris removed the engagement ring and gently placed in his hand.

He studied the diamond and looked a little sad. It was his gift their first Christmas together, two years ago. The proposal was dramatic and flamboyant, performed before his entire family. She had eagerly accepted.

But Tristan never could pick a date. Their wedding was always set for that illusive Someday. He never even asked her to move in together. She continued living with her older brother, Wyatt. Occasionally they enjoyed a romantic sleepover weekend at Tristan's bayside apartment, but mostly they lived very separate lives.

"Is this goodbye, forever?" He asked.

Envisioning her new life without Tristan's blond brilliance to fill the void, Solaris experienced that first awkward pang of being alone. But it was okay. Alone was acceptable. Her life would not be lonely. Photography and writing and exploring the world would consume every waking moment.

But she wished to keep his friendship. "Are you mad about this?"

"No, not at all. I want the very best for you," he sincerely allowed, "and I hope all your dreams come true. I know mine are. You are right, big doors have opened for both of us. We are parting ways because of our new jobs, not because we are breaking each other's hearts."

She felt relieved he saw it so positively. "I'm glad we will stay friends."

Decisively, he handed the diamond back. "Then I want you to keep it."

She tried to refuse, but he was adamant.

"I bought that ring for you, Solaris. Maybe we'll never get married, but our friendship is important. I know in my heart we will always be friends. No amount of time or distance will change that." He slid the diamond onto her unadorned right hand instead of the matrimonial left.

"There. I love you. Simple. No more promises."

It was sweet. For now, she left it on. Later when she returned to Wyatt's house, she planned to take it off. But she liked the reminder of the good memories they shared. Solaris knew she would return to its original red velvet jewel case that she had kept for two years simply because she loved the color red.

"You'll find someone else to love, Tristan."

"I doubt it." He said it flat, factual, not bitter at all. "I'm not looking for love. I found love with you. Now, I'm looking for the dangerous truth," he used a dramatic television host voice, "and I'm determined to find it."

His exuberant grin made the girl at the next table blink.

Would he dazzle women everywhere? Yes, he would. Did she really want to free Tristan from their promises? Yes, she did. By allowing him freedom to shine in the spotlight she became free to discover the woman Solaris Sullivan was destined to become.

"When do you start your job?"

"I fly to New York City tomorrow morning to meet my east coast production crew. I already met the LA guys. Then who knows? The producer said to pack my bags, prepare to leave my apartment behind for months at a time, and be ready to go anywhere."

"Wow. That's fast."

"I'm ready. I can hit the ground running."

He was leaving now. Goodbye was clear in his cerulean blue eyes. Tristan stood and all heads swiveled his way. He was too preoccupied to notice. Even his thoughts had left the café. The man had suitcases to pack, clothes to iron, and a trustworthy television persona to rehearse. His tea was untouched and the fruit platter only missed the cantaloupe she ate. Tossing money on the table to pay for their bill, he leaned down to plant a chaste kiss upon her forehead.

"Stay safe, my beautiful friend. Don't let the tigers bite."

"You stay safe too," they shared an affectionate smile, "If you ever want to talk, call Wyatt. My brother will always know where I am."

"I will."

"See you on the show, Tristan. Good luck."

"Thanks." That award-winning smile gleamed. "I'll always love you, Solaris."

"I love you too." Did she mean it? She cared about him deeply and wished Tristan great success.

That was love, right?

They were very special friends. She trusted Tristan completely. He was her truest friend. The only one she wanted to keep. That had to be love because their friendship was the only love her heart knew. If there were stronger kinds of love, Solaris had not tasted it yet.

"Today was a big day for us," he softly realized, "a life-changing day. Yesterday we were on the road to getting married, settling here in San Diego for the rest of our lives. Now we are both off for big adventures. Whatever happens next, I will always be grateful for our time together."

"Me too."

He gave her a jaunty salute. And one last charming smile.

Then Tristan walked away.

She watched him step into the pouring rain and out of her life. He never looked back. Keeping his blond head ducked down against the storm, he ran toward his white Mercedes and got inside.

Solaris sat alone in the crowded coffee shop, watching his red taillights disappear in a trail of mist and wondered if they would ever meet again.

Odds were against it.

The world was a giant place to explore.

Their door had officially closed.

Looking for Trouble

If you keep looking for trouble, eventually trouble will find you.

~~ Tristan Thomas Kennedy

Springtime in Peru was no Paris vacation, that's for sure. Why a civilized American woman born to appreciate life's finer comforts like air conditioning and sanitized community water would choose to spend months at a time camped out in a South American country was beyond him.

But Solaris was here, somewhere.

Tonight, Tristan was determined to see her.

That rainy afternoon in San Diego where they parted ways was six years ago. That day decisively launched both their careers. Tristan had dug deep, uncovering secrets both terrible and shocking. Then stood before the camera giving his best honest-Abe smile and spoke the unvarnished truth to an eager world, unaware of the potential enemies he might unearth.

Solaris spread her wings and soared like an eagle.

His source claimed she recently finished a freelance project in the green mountains of New Zealand for another pictorial travel book. After that, she flew to the capital city of Lima. She spent one night at her rented apartment in Miraflores. Then the photographer had traveled northeast up the Pan American highway to the Huascarán National Park and hiked the lower Andes foothills. Her regular base camp there was situated beside the great blue Llanganuco lagoon. It was a beautiful lake at the base of the mighty Huascarán Mountain. The pool held runoff glacial waters so pure the turquoise surface mirrored the snowy peaks high above. What would firelight look like reflected off that crystal-clear water?

He bet Solaris knew. Her photographs were always phenomenal.

The exhibition photo gallery she now owned in San Diego proved it. Tristan had walked those pristine display rooms at Christmastime, tempted to buy many of her limited-edition framed photographs. She also specialized in glossy photography travel books filled with personal observations of the places she had visited.

Life: as seen by Solaris Anne Sullivan.

Since he had no real home anymore and no walls to decorate with art, he bought the books instead. All of them. Tristan studied the pages so much, he memorized her words. He was awestruck by her talent for capturing incredible moments. He knew from working at his end of the camera, getting the right angle and exposure was hard, capturing the perfect timing of the moment was even harder. Solaris made it look easy.

His favorites were a four-shot series featuring two courting lions roaring at one another across an impassable jungle chasm in Africa. The canyon was deep with rugged rock walls plunging into a river, keeping the love-struck lion and lioness apart. In the first picture, tails whipped in frustration as they paced the edge. The male roared, exposing dangerous teeth toward the afternoon sky, letting the world hear his anger.

In the next shot, both wild creatures turned curious golden eyes straight toward the camera, as if sensing the woman hidden in the grass. It was eerie, yet beautiful. The third photo was famous. He'd seen it reproduced in numerous magazines. The moment Solaris captured was a million-dollar shot. The determined male decided to leap across the canyon. His powerful golden body arched against the wild blue African sky. His hearty muscles were dangerously strained. Thick paws and sharp black claws reached earnestly for the other side. The lioness waited, wide-eyed.

In the final photo, he safely landed. The couple affectionately rubbed heads. The lioness licked his tawny mane and face, welcoming her courageous mate.

Solaris named the series: *The Leap of Love.*

It was beautiful and sweet. Just like the photographer.

Tristan had hoped for a chance reunion at Christmas, but was told Solaris spent the holidays in Hawaii photographing volcanoes with her loyal assistant, Kianna Manakoa. The pretty Hawaiian native was like a sister to Solaris. They had traveled the world together since that first big safari in Kenya. Other travel companions came and went. Kianna never left her friend's side.

He considered flying to Hawaii, but learned Solaris was scheduled next in Switzerland and Greece, had an extended contract in Fiji, and then Australia would host the famous photojournalist. Her dream had come true. She was all over the globe. Everything beautiful and breathtaking in life, Solaris saw it. Through her photos and written stories, she shared her experiences with the world.

Last December he was merely curious, idly sifting through old memories. Now it was April and she rarely left his mind.

Tristan's life had not gone as expected. He was all alone on a one-man crusade for truth, had successfully alienated himself from higher society through his tell-all show, and saw no end to his loneliness. He missed the days when he had one true friend he trusted and loved, a woman who cared about him too.

Regret tasted bitter, difficult to dismiss. He had to see her.

Tristan's one true gift was gathering information. He had kept track of Solaris. Her early work in Africa was huge. Another expedition deep into the Congo solidified her career. Then her older brother Wyatt protectively stepped forward, legally becoming her business manager.

The gallery opened. Hometown sales soared. Her professional website brought global attention. Location themed display travel books featuring full color pictures and exciting stories were sold by the thousands, around the world. Today Solaris Sullivan's photographic art was available on everything from poster prints, framed limited edition canvas, calendars, to even ordinary coffee mugs. Thanks to Wyatt's overprotective nature and keen business savvy, she reaped the benefits of a financial harvest.

Her dreams were reality. Solaris could afford to travel the world, working freelance. She chose her own projects now, going wherever she pleased. But in between those grand adventures, she always returned to Peru. Year round, she kept an apartment in the upscale Miraflores district of Lima. This city was home. Why, Tristan didn't know. But something about the friendly South American country nestled between dangerous Columbia and wild Bolivia had captured her heart.

Tonight, it was Tristan's turn to do some capturing. Waiting at the bar of the popular dance club near her apartment, he felt impatient. Half swiveled in his barstool to watch the entrance, he slugged down another shot of tequila. The fiery liquid had become his friend too often in recent months.

Tristan needed a better friend.

He had a good friend once. Most people were lucky if life gave them one, true, trustworthy friend. Like an arrogant fool, he walked away from his.

This was his second chance. Solaris Sullivan had just arrived.

His breath caught and held. Seeing the woman who could have been his wife made the center of his chest burn, a sensation Tristan hadn't experienced in years. Why did his heart still do that? They weren't lovers anymore. He wasn't even sure they were friends.

Six years is a long time. Stupid heart. Damn, she was beautiful.

Her traditional Peruvian sundress looked velvety, woven from the softest royal alpaca. The crimson red skirt caressed shapely tanned legs. Belted at the waist, her figure was lean and mature, yet curvier than he remembered. The narrow straps skimmed over slim shoulders then scooped into a low reverse curve that left her upper back bare. She turned slightly. Beneath her uplifted hair, he noticed a colorful sun tattoo between her shoulder blades. That was new. The sun smiled. It was a happy sun. It was very Solaris.

Tristan loved her smile. Just like the sun tattoo, her lips naturally curved upward at the corners. The sweet feature made her whole face seem friendlier.

Her tawny caramel-brown hair had acquired lovely blonde sun streaks from life spent outdoors. The natural waves were secured with a red clip, twisted into a stylish knot and upswept to expose her slim neck. Long side-swept wisps framed her face and brushed against one cheek. Pretty. As she entered the club her amber-brown eyes scanned the crowded bar and across the patio dance floor. The place was filled with locals and tourists celebrating their Saturday night.

She found no one of interest.

Amazing. Solaris looked right at him.

His ex-fiancé didn't recognize him.

Of course, she expected a business meeting about a photojournalist contract, not a surprise visit from a shaggy blonde ex-television host who spent months digging up trouble, all in the name of truth.

His quest ended here, with her. Tristan piloted his private jet into the Lima airport this morning, praying as his wheels touched down on the black tarmac he successfully left trouble behind. Time would tell.

A familiar American classic rock tune played on the jukebox. As Solaris listened, her lips curved to hear the English words. Even in Peru you could count on hearing Angus Young's guitar snarl while Brian claimed they were all on the Highway to Hell. Amen to that.

Scanning the crowd again, Solaris clearly decided her dinner date must be late. Moving through the couples mingling near the dance floor, she parted the sea of people in a way he found irresistibly poised and confident. At the bar, she chose a seat alone. She was ten feet away. Still, not even a cursory glance.

Tristan was invisible.

Half-perched on her barstool, one hip was tipped in an impatient gesture that was naturally sexy, without trying to be. He liked the red skirt. Her legs were long and lean from walking the beautiful places of the world. The faint tan line at her ankles revealed she habitually wore hiking boots and socks while she worked, not sandals. It was cute. Ordering a beer in fluent Spanish, she politely thanked the bartender for the bottle of Cristal, a favorite in Lima.

Would she like it added to her tab, he asked?

"Sí, muchas gracias Míguel," she thanked him by name, proving she came here regularly. "Estoy esperando a un invitado para cenar. ¿Nadie ha pedido para mí?"

"I am expecting a guest for dinner," Tristan silently translated, *"Has anyone asked for me?"*

The bartender shook his head. Solaris sipped her beer and relaxed. Seeing an opportunity to chat, Miguel leaned both forearms comfortably against his side of the bar to visit. She inquired about his family and was told a funny story of his daughter learning to play the flute. Oh, the noise, the bartender complained.

Solaris sweetly assured him that someday the little girl would fill their home with beautiful music and he would be proud. The bartender grinned. Her kind thought pleased him. He asked about her trip north to the Andes Mountains.

It was stunning when her face brightened with enthusiasm. Jabbering in Spanish too fast for Tristan to translate everything, he did understand Solaris had tracked a big jaguar for miles into the lower Amazon, but never got a clean shot of the illusive wild cat. She wanted to return soon. The cat was beautiful.

Miguel asked if the weather had been kind to her.

Solaris said the weather in Peru could be an ever-changing adventure, but the people were always kind. The bartender beamed.

A waitress hustled over, shouting drink orders to Miguel. Catching the bartender visiting, she scolded him with a shaking finger and rapid-fire Spanish to leave la *Señora Luz de Sol* alone and get to work. Then the waitress graciously smiled at the American lady, apologizing profusely for letting the bartender intrude upon her evening.

The locals called her *The Sunlight Lady.*

Solaris was respected here in Miraflores. Interesting.

After that, the chatty bartender stayed busy and she sat alone enjoying her beer. Whenever someone new appeared at the doorway, she craned her neck to look and sighed with disappointment.

She had changed.

Harder around the edges, confident and courageous now, the years photographing the world were good for Solaris. She left safe San Diego far behind her and fearlessly grabbed life by both hands. Tristan felt proud of her. The sweet innocence he remembered in her face had matured into a determined profile of inner strength that required no apology.

Nor would she make one. This woman was a winner, on top of her game. Solaris had walked the wild fringes of life and was worthy of respect. The youthful sweetheart who wore his diamond ring had grown into a beautiful successful woman that any man would be privileged to love.

"Hello, Solaris."

She jumped and spun around. Her next breath stung. That dramatic deep voice from the past felt ethereal, like a ghostly touch from a life that was long forgotten. Solaris blinked with astonishment as she gazed into those familiar cerulean blue eyes.

She knew those eyes.

Tropical seas always made her think of him. Especially on calm sunny days when sunlight upon the water created that pure shade of aqua blue. But the man's face had become sculpted with sharper angles that spoke of life lived rough, a face that desperately needed a razor.

"Tristan?"

"Yes. How are you?"

"¡Dios mío! You scared me," she exclaimed, holding her pounding heart. Laughing from shock, she stood and quickly hugged him. The contours of

his body were solid, denser than she remembered. Even his voice seemed deeper than the one from her memories. Six years had brought a distinct edge to Tristan. But looking at him again, those trustworthy blue eyes remained the same.

"I can't believe it's really you."

"Were you expecting someone else?"

"Actually, I'm here for a business meeting."

"Lucky I managed to catch you."

"It really is lucky. Wow, the great Tristan Kennedy, live and in person, on location in South America," Solaris gushed, still recovering from the surprise. "I can't imagine what news story brought you to Miraflores. Nothing exciting ever happens in Peru, nothing Truth-TV worthy, at least."

"I'm not working."

"No?" That made her wonder. "What are you doing?"

"Right now, Sweetheart, I'm looking at you." Without asking permission, he cupped her chin in his hand, gently tilting her face up toward his. Solaris almost expected this grand welcoming gesture. But a breath away from the kiss, he paused. Blue eyes gazed into hers.

"My beautiful sweet friend," his husky voice was low and private, meant for her ears only, "You still hold a special place in my heart."

In that tender affectionate greeting Solaris saw regret in his eyes, regret that went clear down to the shadowy depths of Tristan's troubled soul. It was a moment that became seared into her mind, a moment that would later haunt, leaving questions.

The moment two busy lives stood perfectly still.

Then he kissed her. Her toes curled.

A funny awestruck whimper escaped her lips. He chuckled in agreement and strong arms claimed her waist. Tristan drew them together. His body was solid and warm. The years spent apart melted away.

That kiss became more than hello. It felt more like welcome back.

The familiar slant of his mouth expertly reuniting with hers was bewitching, like a dreamy taste of yesterday. But his touch wasn't like anything she remembered. This kiss didn't stop the world around them and make people stare.

It only stopped her world.

He tasted like tequila and a hint of lime. But his lips were tender and his embrace felt strangely protective, from a man who seemed familiar with danger. As they drew apart, his smile was grateful.

"Surprise Sweetheart, I'm your date tonight."

"My appointment is with you?"

"Yes. I called your gallery in San Diego. They said you were on expedition and sent a message to Kianna, setting up a dinner meeting for whenever you returned to Miraflores. Tonight, I got lucky. You came home."

Disappointment was difficult to hide. She swallowed hard. "There isn't anyone coming here offering an exciting new photojournalist contract?"

"Not tonight. Sorry."

He tricked her. It wasn't funny.

Solaris had hoped for another big project, maybe a film documentary narrated by someone famous. Those were popular now. Freelance work in New Zealand had revved her engine. Another book was ready for print, thanks to Wyatt's business savvy. But creative energy needed a direction, a topic to research and visually pursue: like exploring the virgin tributaries of the Amazon or the ancient Inca ruins at Machu Pico. She had hoped for something amazing with corporate backing and a fat guaranteed paycheck.

"Are you mad?"

"No," she fibbed, "I'm happy to see you."

Solaris took a good look at him. Dark stubble veiled his cheeks and chin. His beard was always darker than his head. Overgrown blond hair skimmed his shoulders and grazed blue eyes. A black t-shirt stretched across a taut chest that she didn't recall being so broad.

He looked masterful and intimidating.

Faded jeans had seen better days. She felt pretty sure, despite Lima's strict weapons laws, hidden inside the shank of his right boot was a bowie knife big enough to do some serious damage. This roughneck jungle warrior look was so uncharacteristic for Tristan that she did a double-take.

"You look like hell."

A laugh burst out. "Aw, that bad?" His head tipped in disbelief that she wasn't thrilled by his sudden appearance or swooning from that stolen kiss.

Solaris was not the same submissive woman who sat alone in a café watching him confidently stride away. Alone was all she had now. She had no room in her life for charming men or heart-racing romance.

"I think you look like heaven." That sultry voice used to feel exciting. Tonight, it only made her suspicious.

"Why are you in Peru?"

"I came to see you."

One hand went to her hip. "It's been six years, Tristan. You never called. You never wrote. My brother has my international satellite phone number. Wyatt always knows where I am. Not once did you contact me. Suddenly while I'm working in South America you decide to appear. Why?"

"I missed you," he evaded. "How is Wyatt?"

"My brother lives on Coronado Island now."

Tristan nodded as if he already knew. "I always liked that side of the bay." His expression grew thoughtful with memories of their hometown. "It's quieter on Coronado, friendlier than that mansion in La Jolla where you grew up or his glass penthouse the two of you shared. How are your parents? I heard Regina's designer clothing line is selling well."

Solaris cringed. She hated talking about her parents or the pampered luxury lifestyle she left behind. She wasn't that woman anymore. Never had been, not really. "Mother is fashionably superior and perfect, as always," she curtly informed. "Regina hates that I love Peru. It's so uncivilized."

"That's too bad. And Malcolm? I bet he'd enjoy seeing the ancient architecture in Peru. I'm surprised he isn't down here exploring the Aztec ruins with you."

That one hit another sore spot.

"My father is a busy man. His architectural firm won prestigious design awards for renovating older houses with improved environmental impact features and for building new luxury communities with beautiful parks for the children. He works seven days a week. Malcolm has no time for me."

"I'm sure he misses you."

"I doubt Dad even realizes I'm gone. I am beyond improving. We haven't spoken since I left. Do you really want to waste tonight discussing my screwed-up family?"

Lips charmingly curved. "Not really."

His attention wandered. Blue eyes devoured her hair as if he wanted to touch it. His gaze slowly toured her face. Then lower. He reclaimed old times with every heated glance. Yet his hands stayed contritely placed at her waist where they had been since they kissed.

Their bodies stood still. It was only her mind that reacted.

"You've become a beautiful woman, Solaris."

"Thank you." The compliment felt genuine. It was nice to hear. His expression still revealed private thoughts of physical approval. It had been years since a man looked at her with bedroom thoughts on his mind. And that man just happened to be the handsomest man in all South America.

"Are we still friends, Tristan?"

"I sincerely hope so."

"Then tell me the truth. Why are you here?"

He swallowed. "I wanted to say hello."

His attention swiveled as two men in collared shirts and dress slacks walked through the door. For an instant, fear flashed across his face. The men were joined by two women in flashy dresses. They were tourists on parade. His stance eased. Catching her watching, Tristan smiled down at her again.

"Dance with me?" He suddenly requested.

The fun rocking American tunes that played earlier had mellowed into tender Spanish love ballads. The club atmosphere had shifted. The romantic music moved dancing couples into graceful embraces, some more private than others. Hands touched, bodies warmed, smiles were shared.

The idea of swaying like that in Tristan's arms made her nervous. Despite claiming he looked like hell, Solaris was intrigued by the dangerous edge he had acquired. It was sexy.

Tonight, a sexy dangerous man kissed her.

Over the past six years, her social life was nonexistent. Work encompassed everything. She photographed beautiful moments in exotic places, wrote articles for travel magazines, produced her glossy picture books, and explored the world until she knew it by heart. Then she packed up her limited belongings and moved on, chasing the next grand adventure.

No one ever touched her or flirted. No one managed to warm her heart by his unexpected appearance. And certainly, no man kissed her or looked at her with real approval. No one ever said she was a beautiful woman.

Tristan did.

But feeling beautiful and enjoying clever flirtations belonged to the past. Her reality was hiking boots, campfire smoke, and braided hair. Not hot kisses, charming smiles, and dancing with handsome men.

"I don't want to dance."

"Please," he begged, "I came a long way to see you."

Solaris sighed. "One song, that's all."

Grinning because he won, Tristan grabbed her hand. But he didn't stop at the edge of the swaying crowd. He continued weaving through the sea of people, taking her out into the dusky night shadows of the traditional Latin open-air dance floor.

She loved these, but had never indulged. Enclosed by a high stone wall for privacy, out here people could sweat and dance and breathe. They stopped in a private corner where flowering ivy grew along the wall, starlight brushed his cheekbones, giving his blond hair a pale silky caress. Here the music wasn't as loud. The stars hung low in the night sky and the balmy sea breeze whispered of romance.

Here, they were completely alone. "Wait. I changed my mind."

"You promised me one song." Decisive hands gripped both hips as strong arms tucked her body snug against his. It felt familiar. But Solaris was determined to feel indifferent, to stay immune. As her arms laced around his neck, male warmth enveloped her. Dangerous heat created by a dangerous man. Heat that proved she was not immune.

"We should go back inside." But her voice wavered.

"Later," he murmured against her ear, "Right now, I want to dance with my friend." Persuading, one hand stroked down her back. "We were good together once, weren't we?"

"Sometimes we were."

He drew back, looking down at her. Regret shadowed those blue eyes. "I could have been better to you."

"Yes. You could have been."

"Honesty," he lightly chuckled, "That's a new one for us."

"We were honest."

"No. We were polite friends," he firmly decreed. "We pretended love was the magic answer and worked hard to avoid conflict or say difficult things. Smiling was easier than harsh honesty. No one's feelings got hurt. That isn't truth. It's going through the motions."

"Wow. You've really thought about this."

"Too much." Tristan gathered her close again. It felt like old times. He was a pattern of life she easily recognized, an easy step to fall back into. Solaris had to admit, this dance in the dark was nice. As they moved to the music his lips brushed against her temple, leaving a small repentant kiss.

"I was self-centered and stupid," he quietly judged, "I was too focused on myself to treat you right. I made you carry the weight of our relationship. Whenever I screwed things up, which was pretty damn often, I never made it right. Never apologized. But you were sweet, always making excuses for me. The way I acted was wrong. I hope you can forgive me. I really am sorry."

The night air felt weightless, too wispy with tangled emotions. His quiet words stung her eyes and did painful aching things to her heart. Here beneath the stars on an exotic Peruvian night, Tristan actually apologized.

Sincere words Solaris never thought she'd hear.

"You've changed, Tristan."

"Maybe I just grew up."

"We both have."

"I like the woman you've become. You are strong and independent, in charge of your life. You are so talented. You photograph Life's most beautiful moments. The stories of your adventures make people want to see rare animals in the rainforest, to walk beside erupting volcanoes, and camp in the Serengeti savanna where the night comes so swift it swallows everything except the stars, and you fall asleep by a circle of firelight while listening to lions roar in the dark."

He had read her travel books. She was shocked he could accurately quote words she had written. "You followed my career?"

"Naturally. You were my fiancé."

"So? Lots of people get engaged, but never marry."

"We are special. Maybe I never called, but I never forgot my truest friend," he tenderly confessed.

It took her a minute to process that. They swayed, but her heart raced.

"I still have your ring."

He looked happily surprised. "You kept it." Tristan breathed, smiling like he'd won the lottery. But his next thought was sobering. His face held shadowy regret again. "You deserve a better man than me, Solaris. I've always known it. That fact still has not changed."

"Yet, you flew here to see me tonight."

"Yes. I am here tonight. With you."

The music sang of love. Solaris closed her eyes and slowly danced in Tristan's arms. Over the years, she wondered where he was. Occasionally she caught his show on television and felt in awe. The man had powerful impact. His research was infallible. People paid attention when trustworthy Tristan Thomas Kennedy exposed the truth. He singlehandedly changed American shopping trends, closed illegal businesses, forced pharmaceutical companies to create better medicines.

Nights when Solaris slept alone in a tent listening to wild things creep in the night, comforted only by her own courage, she imagined his posh life in the spotlight and felt certain Tristan never slept with danger at the door and he rarely went to bed with his arms empty.

It felt unfair.

"Did you find a woman to love, Tristan?"

19

"No. I never looked. Did you find love?"

"I was too busy."

His smile flashed. "Lucky for me."

Dancing to the romantic Spanish music, his embrace tightened. He was here tonight. He came to Peru to see her. It was forever since a man held her like he really meant it. The few times she tried dating never worked out. No one fit into her life. Work took her away before casual acquaintances could become anything more. In the end, they always said goodbye.

Tristan had returned to say hello.

The song stopped. Solaris suffered a pang of disappointment. The troubling sensation was strange and unexpected. Tristan must have felt something too. He tucked his head against her cheek, made a small growl of regret and didn't let go.

Suddenly, she didn't mind dancing in the dark. Solaris wanted to reclaim the good of yesterday. As if reading her mind, his cheek moved. Unshaven bristles rubbed against tender skin. Whispering her name, his mouth brushed with slow sweet remembrance along her jawline. But he didn't kiss her. His cheek lay beside hers. Melting together as one, she listened to Tristan breathe and wondered what he might be thinking.

"Are you okay?"

He sighed, "I'm just really grateful we're still friends."

"Me too." Then another Spanish song played. But this one drummed a hip shaking rhythm. Forgetting the sentimental moment, Tristan gave a short cheerful laugh and stepped in a slow-quick-quick box pattern, bringing her with him. Their feet moved into the cozy intimate steps of a Latin rumba.

It was sexy, fun, and made her smile.

He was skilled, easy to keep up with. His hand cupped the small of her back, guiding her body to mirror his. Their hips naturally shifted and tipped together in playful movements. The seductive dance brought images of other things Solaris had not enjoyed in forever.

They used to dance like this in San Diego, but with flashy exaggerated steps that made everyone stare. In the past, his public displays were meant to entertain others and make life exciting.

Tonight no one saw them dance in the dark.

Tonight, his affection seemed sincere.

Be rational. No man flies halfway across the world just to dance beneath the stars with an old lover.

Tristan Kennedy was handsome, successful, and famous. He could have any woman, anywhere—rich, beautiful, exotic women. Instincts shouted that her friend was in trouble. He looked rough and edgy, as if his life of fame and prestige had unexpectedly hissed and revealed sharp fangs.

Apparently, he hissed back.

Defiance seared those taut shoulders. Willpower etched his face. His hands were calloused. She'd never known Tristan to have working man's hands. The mature male body pressed against hers was solidly built and that finely-honed form wasn't earned from lifting weights inside an air-conditioned gym. Even his clothes spoke of days lived dangerously.

He wasn't here for romance. He said he was not working. Yes, there were deeper reasons Tristan had flown to Peru. But why did his personal agenda include her?

The sexy song ended and he automatically gathered her close, laughing aloud. "God, I have missed you."

His declaration sent an involuntary quiver up her spine. Her body might be willing to play along, but her heart was wiser. "How can you say that? We have become strangers."

"You were my best friend once."

Solaris stepped back, needing to be strong. "You walked away. My life moved on."

"I meant to keep in touch, but my job took over my life. I was everywhere, digging into everything. Soon the months became years. I was too busy chasing the next story to notice." His honesty was still so shocking. "But things are different now. I've realized what matters."

"Which is?"

"My friend matters. More than you know." Those trustworthy blue eyes gazed into hers. She felt silly for doubting his sincerity. He always had a flare for the dramatic. Maybe Tristan Kennedy actually was the kind of man who would fly to Peru in search of the woman he missed.

Solaris hoped his affections were real. "This date originally promised a nice dinner."

His expression was suddenly equally hurt and surprised. He looked down at the ground, swallowed hard, then lifted his chin to meet her eyes. "Is that an invitation... or are you saying goodbye?"

"An invitation, of course." Her smile reassured. "The restaurant down the street has fantastic steak and spicy shrimp. Besides," she teased, "big strong men should not live on tequila alone."

His mouth tilted in a boyish smirk. It was cute. "I only had a few courage shots."

"A few? You taste like agave and lime."

"Do I?" His laugh was thick with guilt, the hands claiming her again warm, and the observation earned her another lingering taste of Tristan. This kiss was familiar. It was easy on her heart.

"Let's enjoy your visit," she held his hand.

Smiling, he seemed satisfied now. "I'd like that."

Tristan felt happy. Solaris was still his friend. Time and distance had not erased their special bond. Leaving the dance club, they wove between people enjoying their Saturday night. He lost her hand when someone cut between them, but heard a female cry of annoyance and immediately felt her fingers snag the back pocket of his jeans. Glancing over his shoulder his heart tripped to see her naughty grin.

"Got you," Solaris laughed.

"Don't get lost."

"This place is a jungle."

Now he grinned too, "You would know."

They still held hands as they walked down the street. It felt natural, like old times. Tristan wondered if he should have married Solaris. "This is nice," she suddenly said and he agreed. Yes, he should have married her.

But life cannot step backward. It can only move forward.

In the upscale Peruvian themed restaurant with red tablecloths and bright painted walls, they ordered margaritas and toasted to friendship. Relaxed and smiling, they told stories about their career adventures. Laughing was easy. Solaris made him forget trouble. But when dinner arrived the conversation lagged. They suffered through awkward silences neither could fill. Idle chit-chat felt weighted by her unspoken questions of why he was here and what did he want?

Questions Tristan would not answer.

But the food was the best he had eaten in weeks and looking at her pretty face, how the light captured the amber-gold shades in her light brown eyes, and seeing the upward curve of her sweet lips made everything wrong in his life feel almost bearable.

He was tired of being alone. For such a famous man, he sure was lonely.

Dancing in the moonlight was a terrible idea. Hints of her floral scented skin still lingered on his. The same soft rose, jasmine fragrance she wore in San Diego. Light, feminine and alluring. She was so familiar, yet wonderfully different. Tristan wanted to rake his hands through her tawny warm-blonde hair. The underneath was darker, almost brown, but the top layer was golden from capturing sunlight. If he reached across the table for the red clip, making her thick hair tumble down, would she slap him?

Probably. Solaris was not easily seduced.

She was a rational woman, in control of her heart. Always had been, never really falling head-over-heels. But she had been kind, going with the flow, letting him think he won.

"It's early. Let's go to my place." She innocently invited after their empty plates were taken away. He had already paid for their meal, leaving a generous tip for the hardworking Spanish waitress and his compliments to the chef. "My apartment has a big terrace that overlooks the ocean. We could sit up there and talk for a while."

It took him a second. "I think... that's a very bad idea."

"Well. That was honest."

Slowly, she folded her cloth napkin into her lap, as if each fold were a carefully protected emotion. Solaris stared down at her hands, hiding her thoughts. But her sweet face betrayed the truth. When she met his gaze again Tristan knew his words had stung. "I suppose you decided coming to Peru for a stroll down memory lane was a very bad idea, too."

"Not at all," he quickly revised. "Coming here was the smartest thing I've done in years. I feel honored that you were once mine. The minute you walked into the club tonight, I knew I still cared."

Listening, she leaned closer.

"But I am the past," he conceded, "I see it in your face. Dancing with you was sexy and fun. I miss our good times. You're a beautiful woman. I love making you smile."

"We aren't lovers anymore." She quickly reminded.

"Exactly," he firmly agreed. "Our friendship has new boundaries. I respect that. But I know the things you like," he hinted, leaning closer so his words became more private. "I know what makes you smile. Touching you is familiar, so natural. Breaking those boundary rules is very tempting. So you see, Sweetheart, being alone with you anywhere near a bedroom is a very bad idea, Solaris."

She thought about that and seemed to like knowing he wanted her. Then suddenly, she wasn't happy at all. Elbows resting upon the table, she quietly demanded, "Then I deserve the truth. Who are you running from?"

"I'm not in trouble," he automatically lied.

"Did you quit your job or get fired?"

Wow, she wasn't holding back anymore. "I took an indefinite leave of absence." He immediately saw that explanation wasn't good enough. "Something else became more important than my career," Tristan evaded and downed the last swallow of his margarita, wishing for something stronger. "I spent Christmas in San Diego," he volunteered.

"Oh? How was it?"

"Educational. I did some research."

"What story were you chasing?"

Chasing, indeed: more like being chased, shot at, and then he was sent running again. Weeks ago, he wondered if the woman across the table from him were involved. Looking at the truest friend he had ever been privileged to love, he sincerely hoped Solaris was innocent.

Carefully, he wove his tale. "I found evidence of twin girls, separated at birth. One girl enjoyed a life of privilege in San Diego, never realizing she had a sister. The other was a difficult child. No one wanted that girl. They even lived on opposite coasts. Foster home records from Florida state that twin was hard and rebellious, yet incredibly smart, with a narcissistic cruel personality."

"How long ago was this?"

"Years ago. Before we were even born."

"Then why are you interested?"

Now was his chance. He watched her face for signs. "Because I think as an adult the troubled twin found her successful sister. That's where everything gets hazy and strange. She went to San Diego. Then the woman simply dropped of the planet."

Solaris drew back, brow pinched. "What happened to her?"

"That's my big question. It's an unsolved mystery." Hesitating, because he could simply end the story there, he decided to plow forward. "But some powerful corrupt people have devoted their lives to burying the past. They will silence anyone who threatens to expose the truth."

Amber-brown eyes widened. Three heartbeats. "Are you in danger?"

He wondered how honest he could be, but seeing the fortitude in her amber-bronze eyes, Tristan knew his only hope with Solaris was to tell the truth.

"My life expectancy is improving."

She sucked in a deep startled breath. Conflicted emotions played across her face, proving she still cared. "Are you safe here, with me?"

He nodded. "Yes. No one knows I'm here."

"Good." But she still looked worried.

"If we had stayed together and been married," he smoothly shifted to something less treacherous, "if I had supported your career instead of pursuing my own, would we have children by now?"

A shocked laugh burst out. "I don't know. Sheesh, Tristan. I never thought about it."

He had. "Would you have liked a family?"

"Maybe. Eventually," she thoughtfully acknowledged, taking the question serious now. "But photography has become my life. I have no room for anything else."

"You love your work."

"Yes, I do." And her beautiful smile proved it.

"Growing up, was your family happy?"

Suspicion narrowed her eyes. She didn't answer, but something painful shadowed her features. The clothe napkin in her hands was folded and refolded. "Why do you care about this?"

"Because in college, the first time you met my parents you said they were perfect because they loved with their hearts, not their bank statements. That haunts me, sometimes."

She seemed surprised he remembered, but said nothing.

"Were your parents ever in love?"

"Love is irrelevant to Regina and Malcolm," she defensively shot back. "Money and power mean everything. Wyatt was older and watched over me. But after he left to tour the world as a Naval Officer, I became a burden. So yes, I did envy your family. Without Wyatt, I had no one at all."

"He loves you."

"Yes, my brother loves me very much." Thinking deeper, tilting her chin to study him, her lips pressed together in a resentful line. "Did Wyatt send you? He can't still be mad because I skipped Christmas. Surely he can understand why I would rather melt inside a molten volcano in Hawaii than endure two weeks of Queen Regina's disappointed scrutiny."

Without knowing it, Solaris had answered all his questions. This was why she lived in Peru and felt driven to outshine all other photojournalists in her field. Malcolm and Regina. Unfortunately, the approval she worked to earn from her parents would never come.

"Wyatt doesn't know I'm here."

"Then Dad must have sent you."

Tristan couldn't stop the rebellious smirk.

"Why is that funny?"

"Sweetheart, if Malcolm knew I was sitting here, looking at his beautiful daughter tonight, he would march down from his ivory tower and personally have me crucified." Shocked by his harsh words, her jaw dropped. "He never believed I was good enough for you."

Her head shook. "That isn't true."

"When I asked his permission to get engaged, I followed his whole neurotic 'no shoes on the white carpet' routine and respectfully met with him to ask for his blessing. Malcolm refused and had me thrown out of his office building. I asked you anyway. You accepted. So, I won that battle."

Outraged at the news, Solaris tossed her white cloth napkin upon their red tablecloth. The cotton had deep creases where she had pinched folds with her hands as they talked. "Are you saying—nothing I have ever done has pleased my father?"

"Malcolm is a complicated man."

"But he was absolutely furious when we broke up. He praised you, said I was stupid. He told me touring the world was a mistake, that letting you slip away was a huge mistake and photography would ruin my life. That was the last time we spoke. Six years, I have lived with that terrible conversation. I thought you were the one thing he approved of."

"Sorry. I'm not your Prince Charming, Sweetheart."

Her face was suddenly taut with anger. "Now I see what this is."

"I don't understand."

"Great distraction tactic," she tightly congratulated. "We're only discussing my family so you can avoid telling me the truth about why you are here. That vague story meant nothing. Keep your secrets. I've heard enough for one night. Goodbye, Tristan. Have a nice life."

His heart clenched.

Standing quickly, Solaris hurried away.

Unprepared, it took him a minute to react.

Tristan caught her at the arched entryway of the restaurant. It was artfully decorated with a colorful mosaic of painted flowers and Inca symbols. The bright orange and red swirls matched the smiling sun tattoo on her upper back.

"Solaris? Wait." Feet kept going, taking her out of his life. "I'm sorry. Really, I am." Hearing the apology, she stopped walking. "I'll tell you everything. Please. Don't go."

Solaris turned around. They had an audience. The restaurant owner was striding their way. He looked professional and proper in his neatly pressed navy-blue business suit. He was not happy with Tristan. "Are you good, la Señora Luz de Sol?" he asked in heavily accented English. "Is this gentleman a problem?"

"No, Señor Sánchez," she sweetly reassured, "This is my friend from America." Smiling, she offered Tristan her hand in a show of good faith. "Gracias for dinner. The spicy shrimp was deliciosa, as always."

He smiled wide at the compliment and proudly smoothed his tie, "Muy bueno," the owner nodded with pleasure, "very good. Have a good evening. We see you again soon?"

"Sí, very soon. Buenas noches." Decisively, she led Tristan outside to the crowded sidewalk. She was still mad, but kept his hand laced with hers. Miraflores was in full Saturday night swing. The dance club where they had met thumped with energetic music. Laughing voices carried into the night.

Moving away from the crowds as they walked toward her apartment, they were finally alone.

"Why do they call you The Sunlight Lady?" he asked. She sighed, not speaking to him. "It's a nice name," he added. "They like you here."

Her gaze met his. "You think so?"

"Yes. It's very respectful."

Those pretty lips curved. "When I first visited Lima, I loved the Miraflores district. I wanted to learn Spanish so I talked to everyone I met, practicing until I became fluent. People smiled at me. I thought they were incredibly friendly," she lightly giggled. "Turns out, I was the friendly one. The locals gossiped about the happy American lady photographer who was always smiling. Somehow Solaris translated into Sunlight and The Sunlight Lady became my name here."

He liked the story. It was sweet. "Then you got the tattoo?"

"Yes. My smiling sun never frowns."

"It suits you."

Tristan realized it had been years since he felt the genuine happiness she described. Solaris lived life so fully that her inner sunlight touched everyone she met. She was special. Everyone saw it. Once, he sparkled inside like that. He wondered how he had let his life become such a dark tangled mess.

They silently walked on.

"I'm still mad at you," she finally huffed.

"I know. At least you're talking to me."

"Then trust me, Tristan," she begged. "I'm your friend."

He felt cornered. "The story about the twins?" She nodded, remembering. "I think someone was murdered," he honestly revealed, "And everyone involved covered it up. All I have is a hunch. No evidence. But I was reckless. People know I was digging into the past. Needless to say, certain people would love to see me silenced."

"What people?"

"A man from Columbia, for one."

Her bottom lip suddenly puckered as if she wanted to cry. "Oh Tristan, what have you done? No one messes with the Columbians. People like that don't go away. You do. The truth doesn't always have to be exposed. Can't you just leave it alone?"

"Not this time."

Her face blanched with sorrow and fear. They walked around the corner, beachside, no longer on the main streets. The merry sounds of Saturday night faded away, carried out to sea with the rolling waves. They reached the quiet entrance to her upscale apartment building. The plush modern lobby was brightly lit and safe. Tristan turned and lovingly kissed her forehead.

"Now, go upstairs. Goodbye, Solaris. Forget that you saw me."

"Like hell I will. Don't tell me what to do." Angry again, she gripped his hand, forcing him inside the lobby. "We said goodbye once. You will not walk away from me again."

"But, Laurie."

She glared at him. Only Wyatt called her Laurie, her brother's special name. Spoken from the one man who loved her more than anything.

"You—go inside. Right now." She gripped his hand tight. Keeping up appearances, she greeted the front desk security attendant by name and politely wished the man a good evening. Bypassing the elevator to the top floor, Solaris made him march up twenty flights of stairs. Not once did she slow down. The livid stair climbing workout took the edge off her temper and stole all the tequila courage he had left.

Of course, with his luck, she had to live on the top floor.

In the foyer entrance to her penthouse apartment, he refused to come in. "Okay, I walked you up. It isn't goodbye. I'll call. We'll keep in touch. Now go inside and lock the door. Please?"

Opening the heavy oak door with her key, Solaris reached inside and flicked on the interior lights revealing terracotta tile floors with brightly colored Peruvian furnishings. Red was the dominate color, splashed with yellow, blue, and orange.

Home looked like a happy place.

"You will go inside, right now," her tone was uncompromising, "We need to talk and apparently you need a safe place to stay."

His head shook, overgrown blond hair skimming his eyes. "This is a terrible idea."

Hands on her hips, she smartly asked, "Is it a terrible idea because bad people want to stop you from exposing their dirty little secrets," her eyes gleamed with anger. "Or because we're friends who used to be lovers, so getting naked together might be fun."

He swore. "That was blunt. Damn. Okay... both."

"Lucky for you I've dealt with guerrillas before. I can handle myself. This isn't my first trip to South America." She opened the door wider, "And this isn't my first merry-go-round ride with you, either." When he hesitated she added, "Don't make me yank that knife out of your boot and use it on you."

"It isn't a—," Tristan stopped himself from saying what was hidden inside his boot. "I can't win this battle with you, can I?"

"Not tonight."

Tristan gave her a surly huff. Standing in the hallway arguing with Solaris was not getting him anywhere and would only draw attention. "You've been warned."

"Duly noted. Now get your ass inside."

Closing the door behind them, he locked the deadbolt. Out of habit, he immediately took charge of their safety, prowling every room. He felt her angry eyes watch him check the large kitchen, inspect the comfortable living areas, both bathrooms, all the closets. He found the spare bedroom filled with expensive photography equipment. Then Tristan had an edgy evocative look through her bedroom. Gold cotton sheets and a red satin robe left his head full of dangerous thoughts of another kind.

"Are we good?" She finally asked.

"Sorry. Checking is a habit."

"Seems to me you've acquired some pretty unsavory habits, Tristan Kennedy," she griped, yanking the red clasp from her hair.

That tawny mane tumbled down. Twisted waves fell nearly to her waist, making him swallow hard. It was stunning. Her hair had never been this long. In San Diego, she always kept it trimmed. Six years of virgin growth was healthy and thick, the color of warm caramel candy.

Then as if she had a headache Solaris closed her eyes, bent over at the waist, and flipped her head upside-down. Both hands slowly massaged the back of her neck and scalp, rubbing away pain.

Her hair touched the floor.

His mouth watered.

Fingers kneaded. She swiveled her head in small circles, making small hmm sounds as if rubbing it felt wonderful. Tristan had to stop himself from plunging his hands into that silky hair to help.

"Stop it. Damn. That isn't fair."

Standing upright again, she quickly flipped her head over, ruffling the hair even more. Amber eyes opened, annoyed. "But I have to rub it. Pulling my hair up like that always makes my head hurt."

"Then please, save my sanity. Leave it loose."

Her funny little nervous laugh released the tension and made them both smile. "You like it long?"

"Sweetheart, I like everything about you," his voice felt rough. He had to swallow. "The woman you've become makes me feel extremely stupid for walking away."

Color flushed her cheeks. Her gaze warmed. "Is that the truth? We're alone. You don't have to be dramatic. Your current audience already approves."

"What is that supposed to mean?"

"You've always had two sides: the exciting dramatic man who turns a simple kiss into a grand moment that makes everyone stop and stare. You love to impress people. And then you can become the thinking-feeling compassionate man, who only appears when we are alone."

"I never knew you felt that way."

"Would it have mattered?"

"Yes. I did those things to impress you," it bothered Tristan that his intentions were so acutely misunderstood. "I thought you liked big dramatic moments. I don't care what other people think. I wanted to give you grand moments. I tried to make your life feel exciting."

She was speechless.

"I really am sorry," he apologized. "Maybe we should have talked more. You've always been so rational, always thinking out your emotions instead of just feeling and falling. To me, those big dramatic moments held us together. You smiled. It proved our love was real."

"Gee. That's one huge misunderstanding."

"I'd say so."

"We should have talked more," she repeated.

Tristan quickly disagreed, "I was pretty ego driven. I admit, I did enjoy showing off and letting people see how great we were together. Even if you objected, I probably wouldn't have listened."

"Wow. The truth is very eye-opening."

He shrugged, "Welcome to my world, Sweetheart."

"Maybe we didn't know one another very well. What do we have now? Are you a new kind of lion hunting me in the night," she coyly questioned. "Should I be afraid to let you into my life again?"

"Probably."

"I'm not." Silence hung heavy in the air.

Tristan wondered if he should leave.

With a tense huff, she raked one hand through her hair in a frustrated move. The waves tumbled back down and brushed soft against her cheek.

He had loved her once.

The funny feeling inside his chest whispered that he still loved her. But it was different now. Mature. Wiser. Respectful: something he lacked six years ago. Solaris was his truest friend. He'd love to spend hours making her smile. He knew exactly how. Tristan didn't say a word, but her golden-brown eyes were wide with awareness. The good they had shared was so real he could taste it.

"Yesterday is over, Tristan."

"I know."

Her tongue clicked. "Then stop thinking about sex."

"Sure. I'll get right to work mastering my dirty mind. Bad thoughts," he scolded himself, "bad thoughts. Don't picture Solaris naked. Oh wait," he quickly added with a dejected grunt, "I already know how beautiful you are naked. It's one of my favorite memories. I guess I'm doomed."

The corners of her lips quirked upward. "You've developed quite a knack for this whole honesty business. It's very likable."

"Everything about you is likable."

"Hmm. What should we do about that?"

"Nothing. We are adults. We can handle it."

She looked relieved. "Then I'm changing my clothes. Would you like to watch and remember our past, or will that make you crazy too?"

"Certifiable." Hands extended out to her like being handcuffed. "Lock me up and throw away the key. Please, oh please can I watch?" He dramatically begged.

She laughed. That sunny smile was sweet. "I'm changing alone."

"Good idea. I'll wait right here."

"Promise not to leave?"

"I promise."

She took a few steps and turned. "Are Columbian's really after you?"

"There is a certain influential gentleman in Bogotá who I'd rather avoid. Sorry I scared you. We are safe. No one knows I'm here. I own a private jet and flew here this morning, alone. I never travel commercial anymore. Getting a pilot's license was safer than being mobbed by fans at every airport terminal. And checking the room is a habit. Too many nights in strange hotels made me a little paranoid."

That seemed to satisfy her. "Then make yourself comfortable," Solaris offered. "I have beer, wine, and juice in the fridge, rum on the counter, and if you need another shot of courage I have tequila."

"Thanks. Want anything?"

"Surprise me."

Watching her walk away, he smiled when she discreetly closed her bedroom door. He heard the lock softly turn. Trust him? Not a bit. Tristan moved to inspect the drink situation in her kitchen. Seeing Solaris was hard. So many unexpected feelings had resurfaced.

But she didn't love him anymore. It was too late. Their chance was over.

Maybe trouble would go away. Then he could start over, win her heart again.

No, the dirt he had stirred up was mountainous. It would not go away. He needed more evidence. In time, he could bring justice to the innocent. Being in Peru would buy that time.

When Solaris returned wearing denim shorts and a simple red cotton tank top, Tristan was still contemplating the greater evils of life, staring blankly at the gold label on a bottle of Spanish wine. He couldn't recall anything that it said.

"That was fast."

"And your slow. I thought you'd be slamming down shots of courage already."

"My courage is good."

Tristan liked how natural she looked. Her feet were bare. Toenails were neatly painted wildfire red, her favorite color. The big toes had tiny white smiley faces. She looked so innocent walking across the Saltillo tiles toward him. It made him recall mornings in San Diego when she stayed the night at his bayside condo. Mornings he took for granted.

"Cute toes."

"Thanks. They are my happy feet." She stopped near him, both hands folded behind her back. "What are we drinking?"

"I hadn't decided yet."

"Ever try a Captain Courageous?"

"No. What's that?"

"Two parts pineapple juice, then equal parts light coconut rum and Captain Morgan black spiced rum, on the rocks. Pour me one in a tall glass. I feel like celebrating." Her courage drink sounded tastier than tequila. Following her recipe, he made two stout cocktails in tall hurricane glasses.

She even had straws. But when Tristan handed her one, he realized Solaris still had both hands hidden.

"What are you hiding?"

"I have made a very important decision."

Here it comes. She was asking him to leave. But in her eyes Tristan didn't see rejection. He saw something else entirely. He set down their drinks. The unspoken expectations in her face made him swallow hard and take a step back. His butt hit the counter and he was cornered.

"What did you decide?"

"You need to shave," she handed him a pink ladies razor and a canister of flowery smelling shaving gel.

He scowled. "I can't use these girly things."

"You can, and you will. Right now." She pointed to the guest bathroom. "It's a brand-new blade. It may be pink, but it will get the job done."

He scowled. "Why do I have to shave?"

"You haven't used a razor in weeks. Your face is rough. Those scratchy whiskers will not touch my skin, again. I am officially off-limits unless you shave."

"But we don't have to be like that." Suddenly reluctant to accept the invitation for intimacy, Tristan refused. He placed the razor and shaving gel on the counter beside their untouched drinks. "Sorry I kissed you, earlier."

"I'm not. Despite whatever trouble you are in, I enjoy your company. You make me feel beautiful."

"You are beautiful."

"See, I think that's funny. I feel like an extremely ordinary woman." She was rational again, thinking not falling, in total control of her heart.

His was thudding like thunder.

"But it's nice to hear that you like how I look. It's been years since anyone noticed. My work is my life. Adventure makes me happy. I don't have time for romance or feeling pretty. I spend my life alone. It's hard sometimes. But you are here tonight. Enjoying our friendship is better than feeling lonely."

"Do you need a friend?"

"Yes, Tristan, I do." Moving toward him, the distance narrowed. She tipped her chin, gazing up at him. "I don't know what tomorrow will bring and I won't make any promises. But you are staying with me tonight."

"I'll sleep on the couch."

Her head tipped. "Is that really what you want?"

"No. But it's smart."

"We're adults," she casually repeated his earlier affirmation, "We can handle whatever happens."

"We will see."

She took another purposeful step forward. His body tightened in response. Both hands gripped her waist. "Being with you is easy. You are the best part of my past, the only part I miss," her husky welcoming words teased. "We can deal with complications tomorrow."

"Sex isn't emotionless. You could get hurt."

"Whose heart are you protecting? Yours or mine?"

"Both."

"Can't friends comfort one another?"

Unable to resist anymore, Tristan closed his eyes and kissed her deep. Solaris made a soft mewling sound. It felt good to touch and taste and not be alone in the world anymore. After all this time, she still held a place in his heart. She was always the one person he instinctively thought about whenever something fantastic happened and he wanted to share it with someone special.

When they came up for air, she was smiling.

"I still love you, Solaris."

"And you are still my truest friend," she honestly allowed without giving emotional weight to anything untrue. "Is that acceptable?"

"I can live with that."

"Good. Now please shave. Your rough whiskers are making my face raw." It was true. Kissing her had left pink marks on her chin and cheeks.

First, he tasted his rum. "Mmm, it's really good."

"Captain Courageous is my favorite."

While he shaved Solaris watched from the bathroom doorway, leaning one hip casually against the frame. Curious eyes followed a routine that for him felt ordinary. She used to do that when they were engaged. It brought back odd nostalgic memories.

"Tell me about the Columbian."

"Right now?" He slid the razor across his face, removing white foam and two weeks of dusky growth. Like many natural blondes, his beard and eyebrows were darker than his head, nearly brown. Clearing the stubble made Tristan golden again. Watching her reflection in the big mirror covering the whole wall, he rinsed the pink razor in the sink. She looked serious and wanted answers.

"What do you know about black market diamonds being smuggled into America? Have you seen evidence of illegal activity down here?"

"No. Peru is a peaceful country. Crime is strictly monitored. Guerilla groups hassle people on the roadways sometimes, but they are rebels coming from Columbia, Ecuador, or Bolivia."

Tristan shaved another line down his cheek. "I went undercover in Columbia, working on a story. I wanted to stop American people from buying jewels that fund cartel groups. I broke into a mine owner's house in Bogotá. Among other things, I found sales records tracing to an anonymous connection in San Diego. So, I went there too."

"What did you find at home?"

"Trouble, lots of it. Someone knew I was poking around. One night three men broke into my condo, the one by Mission Bay. I kept it, as my home base. That night, I happened to be there. And I had a gun."

He watched her slowly absorb that news. "You shot them?"

"Two. The third one got away. The police identified them as members of a Columbian cartel. That's when I knew I'd stirred up something big and someone powerful wanted me silenced. But the cops called it self-defense and closed the case. They shot up the whole place and I only fired twice. They had bigger crimes to tackle than two dead illegal immigrants."

She gasped, "You killed them?" Watching her wide eyes in the mirror, he nodded. "But, I thought shot meant like, in the knee."

He chuckled because her face had paled. "Sweetheart, you've toured the world on dangerous adventures. Are you saying if a charging rhino was coming after you, you'd just scream and shoot him in the knee?"

"Well, no."

"Then pretend I shot two angry rhinos."

"Oh god, I need a drink."

While Solaris disappeared into the kitchen, Tristan continued shaving. The face he revealed looked far too civilized for the man beneath that skin. If Solaris paled because he killed two men, she'd faint over everything else he had done. She reappeared in the doorway. Half her tall drink was gone.

He chuckled, "Better?"

"Getting there," she drank another long sip through the straw, for good measure. "Tell me more."

He started shaving the other cheek. He had to admit, it did feel good to tell her, at least the glossed over version of what he had learned. "I don't know how the product gets into the States. But I discovered that independent jewelry store owners all over California are innocently purchasing black market diamonds that were faceted and graded with false laboratory certification. Mom and Pop places buy them, people who can't afford much so they buy wholesale, at the lowest price."

"Are the FBI aware of this?"

"Not yet. But they will be. I've been gathering evidence. At the jewelry stores I visited, I saw legitimate paperwork for New York lapidary specialists, but the official seals and serial numbers were forged."

"So... they're smart, too."

"Very. Sales are conducted online through registered accounts, gems are delivered by private courier. The money trail is laundered, impossible to trace. But somewhere in San Diego is an illegal gem cutting operation flooding the market with diamonds coming Columbia. The Cartel leader used to live in Florida, now he hides in Bogota to escape the law. He can't get legal gemstone certification since he's associated with guerrilla groups. The blood diamond trade caused severe regulations to global mining finances. So, he works outside the law. That's the story angle I'm working."

"How do the twin girls tie in?"

"It's all just theory and speculation."

"Then speculate for me."

"I believe the rebellious twin girl from Florida and the Columbian man were in love. They met there, before he fled to South America. Whatever happened in the past, it gave him power over people in San Diego, also making his gemstone business in America possible."

She was silent for a moment, thinking. "Is my father involved?"

Tristan's heart stumbled, but he told her the truth. "Malcolm is a powerful businessman in San Diego. There is a chance he may know something."

Solaris swore and drained her Courageous rum in one long slurp. That drink was too strong to drink that fast. Tristan knew it would make her sleepy, which might be a good thing. They couldn't do anything stupid if his beautiful temptation went to asleep.

"Show me."

He almost cut his chin. "Show you what?"

"The evidence," her words slurred a little.

He chuckled relieved she hadn't meant something else. She was, after all, a very smart woman. She already figured out the 'something' in his boot wasn't a knife.

"You should sit down."

Solaris sat on the long marble countertop beside him. "Something is driving you," she continued her thoughts. "You don't care about protecting my tyrant dad. What is so important about this story that you're willing to put your life on the line to expose the truth?"

"Can you keep a secret?"

Her empty glass was set down. "Yes. Absolutely."

"Forever? Do you promise to tell no one, not even a hint?"

"Cross my heart," and she did. "Forever."

"I believe you." Leaning over, he lifted the pant leg of his jeans to retrieve the odd bulge inside the upper part of his boot. He slid out a narrow gold cylinder. Tristan placed it in her hands.

Amber eyes were wide. "What's this?"

"A very special jewelry box. Open it."

The gold edges had a leaf shaped clasp. Laying it flat in her lap, she gingerly lifted the little leaf. Tristan heard a small gasp. He didn't have to look at the padded velvet interior. He had already memorized every detail of the ruby necklace Solaris held in her hand.

"Oh, Tristan," she gasped. "You stole this from the Columbian?"

Yes, she was quick. "Retrieved, not stolen. Someday, I'll return it to the rightful owner."

Holding up the large teardrop shaped ruby that was suspended by a sturdy gold chain, Solaris studied it. Twenty-three carets of blood red gemstone caught the bathroom lights, reflected in the mirror.

Tristan had to look at her. He waited for that moment, a flash of recognition, anything that might suggest she had seen this before.

Nothing. Not even a blink.

"I don't understand." She looked from the gemstone to him. "Why would the Columbia keep a necklace that he could sell for millions? Any sentimental value seems trivial compared to the money he could make."

Solaris really was innocent.

Tristan vowed to protect her, at any cost. "That necklace knows secrets. The Heart Stone has been hidden for many years. It's the key to the past. That ruby knows who did things and why. It has a story. When I have all the facts, I plan to tell it. That necklace may be beautiful, but the Heart Stone changed some good people's lives. They deserve to know the truth."

The red ruby gleamed. "The Heart Stone," she softly repeated. As the suspended gemstone turned on the chain, she watched the red facets reflect and flash. "But it's shaped like a teardrop."

"Love is the reason we cry," he told Solaris the legend. "Without love inside our hearts, no tears would ever be shed. You must care to cry. But love also brings tears of joy. To the woman who wore this, all tears were beautiful things, created by love so strong it overflows."

"Wow, that's deep. Someone must have really loved her. And she must have loved him, too."

"Yes. This was his wedding gift."

An odd shudder ran up her spine. "Love is the reason we cry," she murmured. "It feels sacred." Reverently, Solaris returned the ruby to the jewel box. "You should leave this story alone."

"I wish I could, I really do."

She looked at it nestled in the red velvet lining, then closed the lid and latched the gold leaf. As if holding the case made her uneasy, she suddenly handed it back to him. Tristan slid the gold cylinder back inside his boot. It wasn't a great hiding place, but it was all he had.

"Don't get hurt, Tristan. You'll break my heart."

Hearing it made him flash a defiant grin. "Nothing will happen to me." His face finally was clean of stubble, smoother than he'd seen in weeks. Rinsing the girly pink razor under the warm water one final time, he cleaned off his cheeks and chin too. Drying his face with a towel, Tristan turned to get her approval.

"Better?"

"Much better." She grinned. "You look like the old you."

"The old me, huh? Well damn. That's a shame."

"Why do you say that?"

"The old me was a selfish arrogant jerk who only cared about himself," glancing in the mirror again he remarked, "I hoped I'd look like someone who gave a damn now." Seeing his golden starlet reflection unchanged, he gave a disenchanted sigh, "I guess I'm stuck looking like--"

"Shut up and kiss me, Tristan." He did.

The sun rose far too early for Solaris to feel pleased. Eyes still closed, lying beneath the soft sheet, she smelled coffee brewing. It took several seconds to register who would have made it, and why that man had spent the night.

Eyes opened, "Tristan?"

"I'm right here." She turned toward that dusky morning-rough voice. He was across the bedroom, comfortably lounging in her favorite leather armchair. He wore only yesterday's jeans. His impressively etched chest and abs were bare.

Solaris sat up, clutching the gold colored sheet to her body, relieved to realize she wore a red satin nightgown. Last night they laughed and kissed and drank Captain Courageous. They sat on the terrace talking, watching the moonlit ocean. Then she must have fallen asleep. She only vaguely recalled Tristan helping her in here, didn't remember changing clothes at all, but felt fairly certain she slept curled up next to him all night.

"What are you doing over there?"

"I was watching you sleep."

"Why?"

"Because you let me, so I am."

He looked too serious. She didn't like it. "That doesn't make any sense," one hand raked through rumpled tawny waves. "I'm foggy. What happened last night?"

"We got drunk, sat on your terrace, talked about Life and Love, and then you fell asleep smiling. I stayed with you, just like you asked me to. It was the best night's sleep I've had in months. So, thank you."

"Are you leaving now?"

"Do you want me to go?"

"No. I most certainly do not."

"You should, you know," he dryly advised, taking a long sip of coffee, "I wouldn't blame you, if you asked me to leave."

"What happened to you? I don't like waking up to find you sitting across the room in deep thought, analyzing me like a news story you can't quite figure out, and looking like you have a heart full of regret."

"You think I have regrets?"

"It's written all over you."

Leaving his coffee mug on the side table, Tristan rose from the chair and joined her in bed. One strong hand pushed against her shoulder. Lying her down against the pillows, his body covered hers. Keeping the sheet between them, his kiss was soft.

"No regrets. Not where you are concerned."

"You regret other things?"

"Too many things. But never loving you."

Solaris couldn't return the sentiment. Saying it felt like a twist of words, a gray area where affection and caring might be confused with commitment and lifelong devotion. Did she love Tristan? She cared deeply for his safety and happiness, valued his friendship, and enjoyed his company. They were very special friends. Lovers from a time before the world became a giant realm to explore and conquer. They were together again, in a time when his world had become dangerously small.

But love? She felt certain real forever-type love was deeper, something her heart hadn't felt yet. Love should be an all-consuming emotion, not something to think about and analyze. Maybe someday she'd feel it.

"Is there someone you care about, Laurie?" He affectionately asked, again using the name that only her brother ever said. "Am I here with you this morning where another man has the right to be?"

"No. You belong here with me."

"For now," he carefully added.

"I'm sorry, Tristan. You say that you still love me, but things have changed. Yesterday you were my past. I had moved on. Now you're back, but love isn't a switch I can flick inside. I need time."

Cerulean blue eyes were shadowed with sadness.

"Does my honesty hurt you?"

His short laugh shook her belly where his chest lay upon her. "You can't hurt me. I'm stronger than that. I'm glad you stay true to yourself, no excuses. You used to forgive me too easily, say things just to be polite."

She knew it was true.

"But last night you demanded the truth. I gave it. You made me shave. I did. We fooled around a little, got toasty, and you let me sleep beside you all night. I am satisfied with that kind of love."

The inner workings of his mind were profound. This was the side of Tristan he never let show: the poet inside of the curious news reporter. Inside, he was a very good man. A caring man.

"This is nice," she smiled, hands sliding up the taut muscles of his bare back.

"What, all this honesty? Or touching me like that?"

"Both. And not being alone. Alone sucks."

He chuckled, "Yes, it does."

Tristan looked dangerously handsome this morning. Her fingers stroked through blond hair ruffled from sleep and Solaris wondered if he might let her cut it. No, she quickly decided she liked it. The overgrown hair fit the man he had become. "What happens now?"

"We take it one day at a time." Then he grinned, "But we should probably do something about buying some birth control, just in case we decide to improve our social life."

"Good idea." Last night they laughed to realized neither had any condoms and she stopped taking the pill years ago. Sex, obviously was not a priority in either of their lives. It made her feel better. He was as unprepared for anything serious to happen, as she was. Tristan told the truth. He came here to say hello.

"If we had slept together, would you regret it today?"

His head shook, "Only if you got pregnant. The timing is all wrong and your career would suffer. I'd never do anything to hurt your photography."

The thought of losing the freedom to see the world and explore made Solaris swallow hard. That freedom was precious. "Is that what you were thinking about so seriously, before I woke up?"

He half-grinned, "Actually, I was wondering why I didn't marry you."

"Oh god," she panicked. "Now you want to get married?"

"No. I have nothing to offer you. Maybe someday I will."

There it was again, that illusive *Someday*. "I deserve better."

"I agree. Believe me, I know you deserve better than me." He exhaled hard and rolled onto his side. Looking down at her, his head remained cradled in one hand. "Can I tell you something really important and will you seriously think about what I'm saying?"

"I guess so."

"Someday you will meet a man who is right for you." She started to object, but he forewarned, "We've been friends forever. I will always hold you inside my heart. But I'm not the right guy for you."

Hearing it made her sad. "Yes, you are."

"No. I never have been. And I never will be."

"How can you say that?"

"Because I don't make your heart stop," he candidly stated. "Your heart never forgets how to beat whenever I walk into a room."

Solaris clicked her tongue at him, "That isn't true. You can't possibly know what my heart does."

"I do. It's something you can't hide. Your face is too honest. If that magic fire happened inside you, I'd see it. You care, I see that much in your face. For me, it is enough."

"Tristan, this is nonsense." She started to squirm away from the awkward conversation, but his hand held her fast.

"No, listen to me." He urged, waiting for their eyes to meet.

"Okay. I'm listening."

"Someday, you will meet a man who makes your life come to a stop. Nothing will ever feel the same. I honestly hope you find him. I hope your heart kicks so hard that you can't ignore it."

His words stung her eyes and pierced her heart.

"That's the kind of love you deserve, Solaris, the kind of love that sparks a fire and makes everything good inside of you come alive."

Love like that was a dream, a fanciful romantic wish. It wasn't real. Love that strong only lived inside the imagination.

Eyes wet, she sniffed, "Love like that doesn't exist."

"It does. I've tasted it."

"Don't be dramatic. I don't stop your heart."

Cerulean blue eyes lit with humor, "That's my girl." He chuckled and looked pleased, "Always so realistic and level-headed, keeping your emotions under control," his hand gently dried her wet cheeks. "You stopped my heart the first day of Journalism class in college."

"I did?"

"Yes, but you dismissed me with a polite smile. It took a month to convince you to have dinner with me. Then I spent every moment of our two-year engagement making every effort to impress you, doing my very best to spark a fire, to help you find reasons to love me too."

"But I do love you, Tristan."

"Not like that. Our friendship is good. We have trust. Understanding. Respect," he named the elements binding them together. "But great love should change your life. It should kick your ass and shoot a hole right through your heart."

She panicked again. "You feel that, over me?"

His playful grin teased, "Not exactly. Your emotional kick is nicer, easier to take. My heart stays intact. But I do believe it does happen."

"What makes you so convinced?"

"Because good people deserve a happily-ever-after," he softly decreed. "And you, Solaris Sullivan, are the finest person I know. If you never find a love that changes your life, then happily-ever-after truly does not exist."

Tears fell. She couldn't stop them. "But you're the only one I've ever loved."

"Exactly. I am your first love. But I'd bet my bottom dollar, I won't be your last. When you do find a good man, someone who earns a place in your life," he sternly added, "I hope he realizes how lucky he is."

"It's you, Tristan. It has to be."

"We will see."

For months afterward, his words haunted. Solaris tried to forget. But memories of that quiet morning conversation were powerful. They were words spoken from his heart. He was her truest, most trusted friend: a friend who loved her. Remembering always brought tears to her eyes.

Solaris wished Tristan could stop her heart.

My Truest Friend

Your courage humbles me.

~~ Tristan

"Will you please come with me," she asked Tristan later that morning. Solaris was working on her laptop at the dining table, mapping the route she wanted to follow into the high sierra jungle of the Andes. There was a jaguar prowling the foothills along the Amazon tributaries.

He was a king of cats. Beautiful and majestic, his coat was gold with black rosettes, and he was bigger than any jaguar she had ever seen. She snapped his image from a distance, twice. This time out, she was determined to get some decent shots of the illusive hunter. He was going to be famous.

"When do you leave?"

"Tomorrow morning. My crew is getting supplies today. We'll camp in the rain forest. It's green and beautiful. There are exotic birds and animals everywhere. The jungle is paradise. You'll like it."

He stared out the living room windows at the sea, watching the waves roll into shore. He'd done that several times already today. She wondered what it meant.

"How long will you be out?"

"Only a few days."

"And then where will you go?"

She slid her seat back and turned to him. "I'm open for suggestions. But I'd like for us to stay together." Leaving the window to finally look at her, Tristan smiled at that thought but the easy optimism he tried to project didn't quite reach those honest cerulean blue eyes.

"Won't your crew think it's strange if I tag along?"

"Are you kidding?" She had to laugh, "The great American truth-seeker Tristan Kennedy comes to Peru for vacation and decides to join our photo shoot. Everyone knows we were engaged. They'll be thrilled."

That seemed to convince him.

"I checked into a hotel nearby yesterday," he conceded. "I need to get my things and make some phone calls. Then we'll see."

Alone in his own hotel room, Tristan felt a fist of tension inside again, a tight knot he endured for months. But with Solaris that doomed feeling disappeared. Now reality was back. He hated doing this. It was wrong. He knew it. But this was the only way trouble would stop. Dialing the number with his cell phone, it was answered quickly.

"It's Tristan Kennedy."

"Well, Mr. Truth Seeker," an arrogant male voice greeted. "I heard Navarro wants your head mounted on his trophy wall." The man chuckled, but it was cold and cruel. "What did you possibly do to anger that lunatic?"

"I stole his heart."

The man scoffed, "Always the smart mouth."

Literally, Tristan has stolen his heart, a blood red ruby. "Tell the Columbian to call off his hunt."

Course laughter came. "If Navarro wants to find you, son, consider yourself dead."

Tristan drew a courageous breath. "You won't help me?"

"The devil himself can't help you now."

Reluctantly, he challenged, "Then look where I spent last night. Open your email." With his phone camera, he sent a picture. It was Solaris, sleeping in the bed they had shared. Long tawny hair fanned across the gold pillow and a sweet smile curved her lips. Seeing it again clenched his gut in a twist of betrayal.

God, I'm a dog. Solaris trusts me. This has to work.

Tristan knew exactly when the picture was seen. The man bellowed like a bull. "You bastard! How dare you involve Solaris! You went to Peru? Damn you. If you hurt her..."

"Shut up," he ordered. "I'd never hurt her. I love her. Solaris should have been my wife. But if you don't stop Navarro, I'll tell her the truth," he threatened, "the whole ugly truth. Especially the parts about you."

The man sucked in a sharp breath. "You wouldn't dare."

"Try me. Stop Navarro, or I'll show her the evidence. All of it. And then I will tell your secrets to the whole world."

"Going to her was a dirty move. I hate you, Tristan. You'll pay for involving Solaris." Then the man hung up. The dead phone connection felt like a death sentence. Suddenly his knees gave out. Tristan had to sit down. Bravado gone, courage lacking, he sat hunched over in the bedside chair with his blonde head cradled in both hands.

Had that one phone call destroyed everything?

He half expected his hotel room door to be kicked in now, a bullet to silence him forever. The air felt tight. His heart ached. Solaris could never know he used her picture to buy his freedom. He'd rather die than see the disappointment in her beautiful face.

The phone rang. Tristan jumped. "Yes?"

"Fine. You win," the man angrily snapped, "I'll rescue your sorry ass. Now get the hell away from Solaris."

"I am staying."

"Does she want that?"

"She loves me. If you let Navarro hurt me, it will break her heart." It wasn't a complete lie, although the love part was a gray area.

"Then you are both extremely stupid." The man hung up again. But now Tristan could breathe. On his end, he calmly clicked off the recorder where his phone was wired through his laptop, protecting the signal from being traced. This was one more tool to use, one more piece of the puzzle to show Solaris, someday.

He prayed he never had to. That voice was unmistakable.

Hearing it really would break her heart.

He had been gone all day. Solaris packed up her photography gear, met with Kianna for lunch, pretended life was normal and prepared for the expedition anyway. Being a good little sister, she called Wyatt in San Diego. Her brother fussed after hearing her plan to hunt down the jaguar.

He worried too much. Nothing bad ever happened.

Wyatt made her promise to keep her satellite phone charged. She agreed and secretly liked that he watched over her from afar. But for some odd reason she failed to mention that Tristan had reappeared. It was just one night. She drank too much and fell asleep. Making the night newsworthy seemed foolish.

By evening Solaris gave up hoping for company. Tristan had walked out of her life again. But at ten-thirty she heard a knock upon the door. Cautious, she peered through the peephole, feeling relieved to see blond hair. She opened the door.

He held a single red rose. "I thought you skipped town."

"No. I'm still here." A black duffle lay beside his boots and a sturdy leather backpack was slung over one shoulder. He looked stressed, drawn too tight around the eyes and shoulders. He handed her the rose, "Sorry."

Solaris savored the fragrance flower. "What exactly are you sorry for?"

"Anything and everything: the past, the future. Whatever I might have done, or not done, that might make you stop being my friend."

"That will never happen." He looked relieved. Solaris let him come inside. His duffle bag landed on the Saltillo tile floor with a thump. The backpack followed. Hands free, they found their way around her waist. "You thought I might turn you away?"

"I knew it was a possibility." Lowering his head, the tender hello kiss quickly gained heat. "Mmm, you smell nice. I thought about you all day. It made me crazy."

"They have pills for that, you know."

His brows arched, "Crazy pills?"

"Sure. It's the opposite of Viagra. It's called *No-Lovin*. It makes you wear tons of ugly clothes and feel too cranky to get friendly."

"Oh god," he chuckled at her joke, letting out a rough sound of relief that proved how tense he had been, "then give me a double dose."

The solid male body pressed against her was tempting. "That's no fun."

"Maybe so, but it's safer."

"We're safe. I bought protection. At the store," she quickly clarified, "to improve our lonely social life."

His smile was warm, kind. "You thought about me too."

"I did. Friends can play, can't they?"

"Yes. We can."

"I'm tired of being alone, Tristan."

"Me too."

It took her two weeks to track down the jaguar. Tristan was accustomed to the comforts of five-star hotels and resorts, not sharing a tent in the jungle. He hated smoky camp food, animals prowling at night, and the endless dirt. He wanted a shower.

But he tried not to complain.

After their one fun reunion night together, he felt too guilty to sleep with Solaris again. Their relationship had changed. Being together was comfortable and easy, but sex wasn't love. It only complicated things.

Sex could wait. She seemed to agree.

Everyone in camp had responsibilities that kept life running smooth, except for him. Tristan felt out of place and in the way. Then Kianna put him in charge of guarding Solaris while she roamed the Amazon searching for the illusive jaguar.

"Can you shoot, Tristan," the lithe lady with an iron will and island charm asked early one morning. He liked her whispery soft accent and the unique way she always spoke using Hawaiian words mingled with English. It was oddly beautiful.

"Yes. I can shoot a gun."

"Good. Straight?" He nodded. "If my kaikauhine found trouble, could you be her kahu ali'i and bring my Ohana back to me safely? No harm?"

Tristan already knew that Ohana meant family. "First, what is *kaey-kou-hee-ne*, and could I be her what?"

Shaking her long black hair that wasn't braided yet, Kianna laughed at his mangled pronunciation. "It means sister. Solaris is my Sister, in my heart. And I asked you to be her royal guardian, special and strong. Like someone who truly loves her."

"Then yes. I can keep her safe."

"Ho'ohiki—*Promise?*" She defined the Hawaiian word.

"I promise. Ho'ohiki. And I do love her," he confided. Kianna earned his respect. She had loyally traveled with Solaris for six long years, sharing an adventurous life they both dearly loved. They were family. She even bragged that in Africa she was severely injured, hundreds of miles from a hospital. Solaris stitched the wound herself and gave a blood transfusion that saved her life. To Kianna, that gift bound them forever.

"I've always loved her. And I always will," he continued his confession. "The sweet Sunlight Lady is my special *Ohana* too."

Kianna grinned with real approval. "Very good." Then she told Hector, the gruff camp supervisor, to give Tristan two pistols and a loaded hunting rifle. The big man grunted and complied. Normally the stern bodyguard from Rio de Janeiro walked the hills with Solaris, keeping her safe. But yesterday he tripped over tangled vines. Hector never complained that he was hurt, but apparently Kianna noticed the slow gimp to his walk this morning.

"Don't let her stay out after dark. Not here in the Amazon." Hector sternly ordered in a thick Brazilian accent. "She forgets time, gets too focused. Jungle animals hunt at night. It's your job to bring her home safe."

"I promise to protect her. You can trust me, out there. Now go let Kianna wrap up your sprained ankle."

"Sí. Gracias," Hector grunted thanks, then added. "Kianna say you are her Ohana, almost got married. Maybe she still be your wife?"

"We both know that Solaris deserves a better man than me."

Hector actually smiled, "Eh, bad man, great woman. Pretty good match."

After that Tristan had a purpose. He spent from sunrise to sunset following Solaris through the Amazon. Hector became his friend. The others in camp warmed to his presence, telling stories of their adventures in foreign lands with the famous photographer. He felt grateful to Kianna for opening the door for him.

Finally, Solaris found the jaguar.

The beautiful black and gold king was lying in the warm sunlight near a clear pool of water. He was napping. They stepped into the clearing, shocked to see him. Solaris motioned to Tristan.

He'd seen this signal enough times that he immediately sat down, making himself perfectly still. He enjoyed watching her work. Crouched in the thick green underbrush, focusing the camera, she captured the jungle king with her high powered telephoto lens. The jaguar sat up, licked a front paw, unaware. Then as if the king suddenly knew he was a star in her personal spotlight, he swiveled his head in her direction.

From his view, Tristan could see Solaris clearly. The stare-down between woman and cat was stunning. He was armed and ready, if things went wrong.

Finally the jaguar casually stood, slowly stretched a long muscular body in sinuous languished movements that revealed every powerful muscle. Solaris captured it all. Finished showing off, he dug deadly claws into the ground in a show of force.

Click, click, click.

39

As he strolled away into the dense jungle, the jaguar glanced back at the talented lady hiding in the tall grass. She captured that smug kingly look too. It was a beautiful moment.

Then the jaguar was gone.

Solaris looked at Tristan and grinned. He knew what that meant. Her job in the Amazon jungle was finished. They could finally go home.

On their long drive back to Lima everyone was exhausted, ready for the comforts of civilization, but Solaris still rode the emotional high of capturing the jaguar. He was gorgeous. She was dedicating an entire book to him, to her search and how priceless those final moments with him were.

Yesterday, it was too late to leave camp. Driving winding dirt roads in the dark was dangerous. So, they spent one more night in the jungle. But early this morning their four Land Rovers loaded down with camping gear drove a rough mountain road in the Andes foothills. The air was humid. Clothes stuck to warm skin. Everyone wanted a shower.

Kianna sat in the front with Hector, who always drove them. Solaris sat in back with Tristan. Their Land Rover was the last in line of four vehicles that bumped and trudged along the narrow dirt road, one eventually taking them to the Pan American Highway. The road to home.

They would sleep in Lima tonight.

Looking through the passenger window, her side dropped into a steep canyon. She wondered how deep the ravine was. Pretty deep. She could not see the bottom. Out Tristan's window was a towering hillside. It looked rugged too. She'd be glad to see pavement again. A soft bed would be nice.

Was she losing her wild side? It was possible. Can't sleep in tents forever, especially with a man who clearly hated camping. Since leaving Miraflores, they hadn't done anything more than kiss. At night, Tristan simply stayed with her. Sex was on hold. But Solaris wanted him to stay in her life. They could work out the complications. But work was important too. She wasn't sure where she wanted to go next. Most of it depended on Tristan.

"If I went to Ireland to work, would you come with me?"

"Maybe." He yawned with disinterest and stretched out in his corner of the seat. "I was in Dublin once. Terrible food, great beer. Tiny hotel. Lumpy bed. It rained every damn day."

She mentally scratched that one off her list. "How about Switzerland?"

He made a face, "Too cold."

"I could take some time off." That made Kianna glance back with hope. "Not too long," she added. Her constant companion's disapproving pout made her feel selfish. "But I could take a few weeks." Now Kianna smiled.

But the blond man wasn't listening. Blue eyes had closed.

Solaris nudged him. "Hey. I asked you a question. If I took some time off, would you stay with me?"

"Sure."

But he was fading. "Tristan?"

"Hmm?"

"What exactly are we doing?"

One eye opened. Then he scowled to realize she was serious, opened both eyes, giving the conversation his full attention, "Right at this very moment in time, or with our lives in general?"

"Life. Our life."

"That depends on you," he declared. "How important are we, to you?"

"Well, pretty important."

"Prove it," he challenged, sitting up. "If I asked you to disappear with me, to stop your photography until I get my life straight again, would you do it?"

He had asked the impossible question. It put a lump in her throat and did strange awful things to the pit of her stomach.

"How long would I have to stop working?"

"I don't know. Maybe a year."

"A year!" Her voice squeaked. "I couldn't work?"

"Yes. And no one could know where we were."

The idea stole all the air out of her lungs.

"That's what I thought," he solemnly assessed as Solaris struggled to find air, fighting overwhelming panic that she might lose the one precious thing making her special. Photography was her entire world.

Without it Solaris would be lost.

Tristan leaned closer and cupped her face in his hand. "Breathe. Focus on me." Slowly, the panic attack eased. Her lungs found air again. Releasing her face, he leaned back in his seat.

"Sorry. Damn it. I hate whenever I do that."

"You panicked about losing your work?" She nodded, eyes stinging. "There's your answer Solaris," he dryly assessed. "Think about that. You know why I'm here. I told you the truth. I can't keep running, hoping for the best. If you really want a life with me, I need time to fix mine first."

She tried to argue, but he held up one palm.

"Let it go, Sweetheart. Your heart didn't lie. It told the truth. We are what we are. Friends. That is all we will ever be."

Closing his eyes again, Tristan folded both arms over his chest and slumped into his corner. Quickly, he was asleep. Solaris hated that he could close himself off like that, shut down and ignore the world. Men seemed talented at doing that. But she knew it hurt his feelings that she wasn't head over heels in love, that her work came first.

Friends. That is all they would ever be.

Deep inside her rational heart, she knew it was true.

After several somber silent miles Kianna turned in her seat, glanced at Tristan to be certain he was sleeping, and softly gave her opinion, "Rest would be good for you. The heart needs to a quiet place to grow stronger, now and then."

"I know," she whispered.

"Do you, my Ohana? Family isn't just those we are born with. Family is the ones you carry inside your heart. Kao nohea kane pilialoha, Mau Loa.
Your handsome man is bound by love, Forever.

"So am I, but different."

"No, the same. Friends, lovers, family: they all love. Hearts only have two doors, in or out. No halfway." Expressive fingers and hands emphasized the words in a graceful language of their own. "Standing in your heart's doorway refusing to choose helps no one, and hurts everyone. Especially you."

"I don't stand in my heart's doorway."

"Then embrace the good, don't resist."

"You just don't understand."

Kianna clucked her tongue, "I understand you better than you do. See the aloha. Do not be a lolo pa`akiki wahini, always wikiwiki around the world." Her hands imitated people running. "Instead of having a nani 'aha'aina male, you will noho ho'okahi."

See the love. Don't be a crazy stubborn woman, always rushing around the world. Instead of having a beautiful wedding feast, you will live all alone.

"I'm not a crazy stubborn woman!"

Tristan's blue eyes popped open. "Oh yes you are."

Solaris glared at him. "You were supposed to be sleeping."

He sat up, interested now. "Hey, you two are the wicked wahini whispering secrets. I can't help if I'm a curious man who knows when to shut up and listen." Kianna laughed that he called them wicked women. Hector grunted and grinned, proving he was listening too. "See? You women think we ignore what you say. But we do pay attention, right Hector?"

"Si, we men listen. Listen is smart."

"It was a private conversation," Solaris defended.

Tristan disagreed, "Not here. Not today. And thanks, Kianna. *Mahalo*," he corrected. "Whatever you said to her hit the mark. She looks royally pissed. Maybe being called stubborn was something Solaris needed to hear."

"Indeed, she did."

Angry at everyone for ganging up on her, Solaris shut her mouth, folding both arms over her chest.

"*Lolo* means crazy?" Tristan inquired to Kianna.

"Yes. 'Ae," she nodded.

"But in camp, you always call me a *lolo Nene*." He recalled her words, "That makes me a crazy what?"

Kianna giggled. It was cute. "You are a crazy wild goose."

Hector grunted again and let out a real chuckle. "Good one. Tristan the golden goose." Again, he laughed, but it was good-natured. "A gold goose with a gun."

"Gee, I sound so heroic." But he grinned.

"Hey, you earned it, tough guy." Kianna wisely contended, "You were the *lolo Nene* always griping about dirt and campfire smoke, complaining instead of smiling, praying the jungle gods would send Solaris a jaguar king so we could go home and shower."

"I never complained." But Kianna scoffed. "Okay, maybe I did."

"At least you admit it. Your good stuff, Tristan." Kianna reached back and patted his knee. "Just a crappy camper," she amicably teased. "Your prayers were answered. Solaris captured her pretty cat, Wyatt will sell the pictures so we can all get paid, and you can sleep in a soft bed tonight."

"I can't wait." Then realizing Solaris was still mad and might not be the best company in that soft bed, he asked Kianna, "What is *wikiwiki*?"

"In a hurry, fast, rushing—like a train."

That made him chuckle. "I like that one."

"Ae, Tristan. Very good word." Kianna giggled. "Don't live your life all *lolo wikiwiki*. Stop and smell the roses."

"But life is a crazy train."

"Ae, sometimes."

Suddenly the first Land Rover on the dirt road ahead exploded. A ball of fire leapt from beneath it as the gas tank burst. The violent explosion pushed the whole truck straight up into the air. Time stood still. When it came down again, flying metal and burning fragments were all that was left.

Solaris screamed. Hector slammed on the brakes.

Bullets rained upon the two remaining trucks in front of them. The big man swore and threw their Rover in reverse, going backward fast, making tires bounce precariously close to the edge.

"The cliff, Hector!" Solaris yelled.

"I see it. Shhh. Be still."

Kianna grabbed the pistols stored in leather holsters beside her seat and handed one to Tristan. Hector had his rifle that was always between the front seats. "Lay down, Solaris," she yelled, pushing her head down with one hand. Obeying, she unbuckled her seatbelt and crouched low in the floor between the front and back seats. "Stay down there. Be safe. I love you, Sister!"

"Kianna, what's happening?" She cried.

"Bandits: road rebels. We are under attack."

Hector had backed their truck up nearly fifty yards. Fast. Suddenly he stopped on a rough sliding skid of tires churning against dirt and rocks. Amidst the dust cloud to use as cover, Tristan immediately opened his door and stepped out. Hidden behind the steel frame of the truck, he fired once.

Solaris watched in horror as a man holding a rocket launcher tumbled off the hillside above the other trucks. Tristan fired again and another bloodied man slid out from behind a tree. In response, bullets rained down. They were just out of range.

"Oh my god, we're going to die!"

Hector fired his rifle. A man clutched his chest and crumpled. Then Kianna shot someone. His fall created a landslide of rocks as the bandit tumbled off the hill. The bloody lifeless body landed on the road with a sickening thud.

Solaris screamed again.

"Put your head down! And be quiet!" After he yelled at her, Tristan grabbed a loose tarp from the storage area and tossed it over her. "Hide!" One hand shoved her body deeper into the floorboard crack. Now she lay flat upon her stomach. Then he slammed the truck door. She was alone. Kianna and Hector had left too.

Shots were fired and returned. People were running, shouting.

Solaris couldn't see anything, but heard another explosion rock the ground, shaking the Land Rover. She didn't know when she started crying, but when her hands covered her mouth to keep from screaming, she discovered her face was wet. Closing her eyes tight, she tried to listen for familiar voices, proof the people she loved were still alive.

Kianna shouting. Tristan answering. Hector swearing in Spanish. Boom, boom, boom went the guns. The bandits were getting closer. Return fire peppered the hood of the Land Rover. Terrified a bullet would find her, Solaris flattened her body even more, trying to stay small and hidden beneath the tarp. She was defenseless.

Opening her eyes again, beneath the driver seat Solaris glimpsed silver metal. Reaching for it, fumbling to grab the object, she was disappointed to find it was only a screwdriver. Clenched in her fist, it brought little comfort. The world outside had become a war zone. She couldn't hear Tristan or Kianna anymore. They were busy fighting for their lives. She still heard the sharp retort of a pistol, now and then.

Suddenly the door at her feet was violently flung open. A man's voice shouted. Someone flung off the tarp. Rough hands grabbed her legs, tugging her out. Kicking hard with her boots, Solaris almost escaped. Then the large man caught her hair in one fist, another around her waist, hauling her outside. Dark eyes, corrupt face, cruel intentions.

The man took one look at her and grinned. "Yo la encontré. Aquí está. Vamos," he shouted to the others. *I found her. Here she is. Let's go!*

The man recognized her. This wasn't highway robbery.

This was a kidnapping!

Suddenly her vision blurred. As if seeing a waking-dream of buried memories, Solaris recalled another man with dark eyes and cruel intentions. It was long ago. She was small and he was big. She fought and got lucky. But someone else... it was a memory purposely forgotten.

"No!" Solaris reacted. Drawing back her arm, the screwdriver clenched in her fist was shoved deep into the man's neck. He snarled in pain. Dark eyes rolled white. Hands gripping her tensed, clinging to her body. Blood squirted as she drew the screwdriver out of his flesh, preparing to drive it in again.

Half the man's face exploded. She screamed.

Tristan stood there, pistol aimed. The end of the barrel still smoked.

"Oh god," shoving at the bloodied corpse, his lifeless arms and legs were tangled with hers in a death lock. Frantic to be free, Solaris stepped away from the open door of the Land Rover. Fighting and panicked, crying and still screaming, above the sounds of her own terrified voice she heard Tristan yell to stop. It was too late.

Her feet slipped over the edge. As the ground beneath her weight disappeared, the dead man was flung free, falling a hundred feet. His body bounced off a small ledge about halfway down, then plummeted, disappearing into the shadowy ravine.

Solaris was falling too, belly pressed against the hillside in a screaming kicking fight for her life. Hands and feet dug into the cliff. Grass blades sliced. Rocks ground against tender flesh. Nothing she did stopped the fall. Sliding, her fingers finally wrapped around a slender tree trunk. Latched on hard, she hung there. Looking up, she saw Tristan peering over the edge.

"Hold on!"

But her hands were raw. Bloody fingers slipped.

"*TRISTAN*," she screamed as she fell.

Clinging to the steep slope, Solaris fought gravity ruthlessly pulling her downward. Legs struck big black boulders. The rocks didn't yield. Her bones did. She heard the sickening crack and felt her left ankle bend. Then she bounced off, careened around the boulder, sliding further.

She fell on the ledge, hard. Lying flat on her back, everything hurt. It knocked all the air out of her lungs. Opening her eyes, a hundred feet above the dust cloud she had created in her fight to stay alive, the face of her truest friend looked down. Maybe she imagined it, but those blue eyes looked wet.

Then unconscious curtains closed out the sunlight.

Solaris knew no more.

She was too still. Lying on her back, Solaris lay deadly still. It created ice in Tristan's heart. The path of tumbled rocks and dirt she tore down the mountainside was enough to make his eyes burn. She had fought so hard. It wasn't her time to die.

"Is she alright," Kianna ran to his side, still holding a pistol. The fighting was over. They had shot every rebel. But some very good people had died too.

"I don't know. Where's Hector?"

"Checking on the others. It's bad."

Looking around the road, bodies were everywhere. Some of them Tristan knew. Others he wished he could shoot all over again just to make them pay. Two trucks were only twisted metal and flames. The other two were pocked by bullet holes.

"We have to get Solaris."

"She has rock climbing gear in back. I'll get it."

Quickly, they put the harness on Kianna, who was lighter and more agile, also the most experienced climber. Hector secured the ropes to the hitch of the Land Rover. Not only would they need to help Kianna down, the men must pull Solaris up. Tristan held the slack in the rope secure, playing it out slowly.

Kianna dropped over the edge and belayed in small skilled hops down the hillside. In her backpack was the rescue harness, a medical kit, and water. Feet nimbly touched down on the ledge. Tristan watched her kneel down, taking Solaris' pulse. Time ticked painfully slow.

Finally, she looked up. "She lives," she called out.

Tristan released tight breath. Kianna tried to wake her. Eyes were slow to open. When Solaris finally sat up and coughed, crying out from pain, Tristan felt everything inside him change.

This was his fault.

The call he made hadn't insured safety. It brought danger to Peru. These were Navarro Altreaz' men, come to kidnap Solaris to get her away from him.

Only one man could have ordered that.

Tristan was meant to die here today. Not Solaris. Yet she was, battered and torn. It wasn't until he and Hector pulled both women up to the top of the cliff and Tristan held his truest friend in his arms again that his heart remembered how to beat right.

But it stayed cold. Regret chilled deep.

"My leg is busted," she told him.

"We'll fix it."

He used his knife to slice up the left leg of her jeans to inspect the damage. The ankle was purple and swollen, but no bones had pierced the skin. "Good thing you were wearing long pants," he congratulated, "if you'd been wearing shorts, the hillside would have ripped off your skin."

Holding up both bloody hands, she grimaced, "It kinda did." From elbows to fingertips her flesh was raw and dirty. Her shirt was shredded along her stomach.

"Damn. I'm so sorry." From the well-equipped medicine kit the crew always carried, he found antibiotics. He shot some into her arm.

"Oww!"

"Seriously? Your leg is broken and your skin is torn to pieces because you fought the mountain and won, but you wimp out over a little needle in your arm?" Her eyes watered. All her courage was gone. It was lost on a ledge halfway down a steep canyon in the Peruvian wilderness. Courage she might never find again.

Next, Solaris received a shot of morphine. This time she didn't complain. While he gently cleaned her dirty wounds, the pain killer kicked in. Mellowing quickly, Solaris finally noticed Hector angrily inspecting the bodies of the rebels looking for identification. The good people they had lost, Kianna respectfully wrapped in blankets.

Her face puckered. "I want to go home."

"Peru isn't home anymore."

"I meant San Diego." Big frightened tears slid down her dirty cheeks. They left muddy wet tracks. The morphine made physical pain fade, but her emotions were high and tight. "We need to go home, Tristan. Together."

"Let's get back to civilization first. You need a doctor." Then he called the airlift helicopter in Lima from her satellite phone.

In the Lima hospital, they X-rayed the fractured ankle and declared she needed immediate surgery. No way, not the knife. Not here in Peru, not like this. Solaris refused.

"Call Wyatt," she begged to Tristan.

"Okay, but you talk to him. Your brother wouldn't appreciate hearing this from me."

The emotional phone call to San Diego resulted in her immediate release from the Lima hospital. Wyatt chartered a private jet. Her brother wasn't a man anyone argued with, especially when it came to his baby sister. Overprotective was too mild a word. The Peruvian doctor blanched upon taking the phone from Solaris to listen to the worried man's tirade. The leg was immediately wrapped in a temporary cast to stabilize the bones. Her torn skin was disinfected and bandaged. The hospital pain meds were increased, soothing the pain.

Wyatt had impact on people. Solaris would be on American soil by morning.

"This sucks," she griped late that evening from her wounded warrior position on the couch in her apartment, "I have the worst luck."

"You'll heal. Overall, I'd say you're pretty damn lucky."

Unable to help, she watched Tristan pack all her belongings for the flight home. It was depressing. She felt groggy from the pain meds. The temporary cast was bulky, her arms and palms bandaged in white gauze, and her ribs were tightly taped because she cracked two bones when she fell on the ledge.

"I look like a mummy."

He paused in packing her camera equipment inside padded travel bags. "Sweetheart, you look beautiful to me. I'm just grateful you are alive."

Her mind couldn't stop reliving the attack. "They knew me. Did you hear that man?" He nodded and wore a scared straight expression that was not reassuring. Something about Tristan had changed. He had hardened inside, as if he couldn't feel anything but revenge. It scared her. "Why would someone try to kidnap me?"

"To get you away from me," he flatly stated. "Once they had you, they would have killed me. I guess they didn't count on us fighting back." Now Solaris was officially terrified. "I have to finish this. I never should have involved you," he fumed, mostly to himself, "they can't hurt you and get away with it. I have to end this."

"This was the Columbian?"

"Yes. But I doubt he would have acted without orders. I have a hunch this involves someone else. Orders to kidnap you go all the way to the top."

Solaris shuddered. All these years she had traveled the world without incident, had never lived in fear. Today that innocence felt naïve. Suddenly men with money, power, and cruel hearts wanted to destroy everything. "What are you going to do?"

"Just trust me. Everything will be okay. Your flight leaves tonight. Wyatt will be there when you land. My jet is fueling. By the time you land in San Diego, I will already be working to end the trouble, once and for all."

"Then do you promise to come home?"

"Yes, I promise," he nodded curtly, all business now. He finished loading everything she owned in a delivery truck. Men took her belongings away to the airport. The jet would be loaded and ready when she arrived. Her apartment was empty, except for furniture. It looked lonely. "Ready to go?"

"I guess so. Will I ever see this place again?"

He didn't lie. "No, Solaris. You are not safe in Peru, anymore."

It made her cry. The drive to the airstrip was tense and silent. Hector had caught a commercial flight to Brazil to be with his family, but Kianna was coming to San Diego. She was already there, wide-eyed and shaky. As Tristan got out of their car to help Solaris onto the jet, Kianna ran hugged him.

"You did good today."

"I could have done better."

"You kept your promise and saved our girl. You truly are her royal guardian. Mahalo, Tristan," the sweet lady thanked, "You have manawale'a: a generous heart. Life will bless you." Eyes glistening, she gave him another grateful hug. Then Kianna ran hard toward the jet as if she could not leave Peru fast enough.

"She's scared," Solaris told him.

"She should be. You almost died today." Leaning on Tristan, she balanced on one foot. Those blue eyes were determined and not the least bit afraid. Anger had turned inward, becoming strength.

"Come with us. Right now, please?"

"Just go home and be safe. I brought trouble into your life. Now, I will fix that. I owe you that much. Soon, today will seem like a bad dream."

"You saved my life today."

"No, I didn't. If I hadn't shot that man, you wouldn't have fallen. He was already dying. You stabbed him in the jugular. I saw it. With a screwdriver, of all things," he scoffed.

"It was all I had."

"We left you defenseless. That was stupid. Then I interfered and things got worse." Overgrown blond hair tumbled across blue eyes as he looked down at her bandaged body. "This is my fault. But I didn't even think. I saw his hands on you and I wanted him dead."

"I love you, Tristan."

His expression was relieved and a little sad, "Today you do. Today you are scared and hurting. You will be strong again."

"But I mean it."

For a long moment, he looked into her eyes. "Remember what I said about real love?" She nodded and started to cry. "Our love is special, but I am no good for you. Today proved it. You deserve a good man, someone who'd never hurt you," he gruffly condemned his own actions.

"You'd never hurt me."

"But I did, Solaris, don't you see? All your pain is because of me. Love should make your life better, not tear it apart. When the right one comes along, I want you to grab hold of love with both hands and never let go. Remember that," he begged. "Promise me. Please?"

Solaris couldn't understand why in a moment when her thoughts were muddled with medication and her heart was broken by the horror they witnessed today, Tristan would tell her to love someone else. "But I have you."

"Yes. You will always have me. You are my beautiful Ohana." He called her family. It felt true and right. But his smile was filled with regret and sorrow.

"Stay safe, Solaris. I love you."

"I love you too, really I do."

He kindly kissed her forehead. Then he scooped her up, carried her to the jet, and helped her get inside. When she was secured into a seat, he knelt beside her. Then he softly kissed her goodbye. "You're a better friend than I deserve, my friend for a lifetime," he tenderly declared. "I'm lucky to have you. You will always be in my heart. Remember that too, okay?"

"I will." Then he walked down the aisle and stepped out of the jet. The pilot closed the door. Looking through her porthole window, the last thing Solaris saw before they took off was Tristan's broad back and his blond hair catching the airport lights as he walked away.

Landing in San Diego, stressed from the long overnight flight, her leg ached. She had slept, but suffered nightmares that she was falling and people were dying.

Beneath that dream was a kaleidoscope.

It was a vision of truth, like a secret confession from the past, one her conscious mind fiercely denied.

But when Solaris looked at the images cascading through her dream, it felt too real, too intense. The vivid tunnel of thoughts swirled with flashes of phantom faces and half-remembered moments, pictures taken by a much younger mind.

It was terrifying. Solaris couldn't look anymore. It hurt too much.

Then the kaleidoscope dream closed.

Memories were locked away again, a Pandora's box her mind could not handle. There was not enough courage in the whole world to make her look at the truth again. That place inside her heart became invisible. Solaris didn't remember it at all. Even the terrifying dream was gone.

She felt empty.

But that emptiness was so familiar, she didn't question the hole in her life the forgotten childish memories had left. Life moved on.

Looking out her window as the jet taxied to a stop beside a large aviation hanger, she could see her worried brother waiting beside a black limo. Kianna scrambled out first and Solaris was a little surprised when she stood on her toes and hugged Wyatt. Of course, they were friends.

For six years Kianna was the business connection, sending him the edited pictures, planning her books, keeping the financial gears turning. Wyatt hugged the pretty Hawaiian lady tight. He told Kianna something that made her laugh and cry.

Solaris wondered what he said.

Then the big man was inside the jet, taking charge.

"Laurie. You're home."

Her towering brother scooped her up as easily as Tristan had. Stooping because of his height, he carried her outside. The morning sky was gray. Thick marine layer fog hung over the San Diego Bay, draping a damp veil over the Coronado Bridge.

"The sky is sad," she murmured. "There is no sun."

Wyatt's brown eyes were misty. "It doesn't matter, Solaris. You're the only sunlight that I need." He hugged her wounded body to his chest. His devotion made her cry. "I'm going to take good care of you."

He did, too.

Within an hour her entire worldly belongings were delivered to his house on Coronado Island and she was comfortably situated in a hospital bed. The pain meds made the world softer.

Now they were waiting for her doctor to arrive. Xrays already revealed multiple fractures, but and MRI exam showed tendon damage to her ankle.

She could hear Wyatt outside in the hallway, talking to someone.

He sounded upset.

"Does she know?" He asked. Then he loudly swore.

Just then, a nurse came to check on her. She turned on the wall television and gave her a remote control.

Solaris couldn't hear Wyatt anymore. Commercials overpowered his voice. After the nurse left, she realized she was watching the news. She started to change the channel, but an image caught her eye.

The remote landed on the floor.

A familiar face had appeared, charming the world with that handsome smile and those trustworthy blue eyes.

"Oh my god."

But the news lady said things that made the air suddenly feel thick with something awful that Solaris could not swallow. A strangled outcry rose inside her throat, but the words were stuck. Lungs burned, choking her in protest.

Her gaze was fixed upon the screen.

"We are deeply saddened to report Tristan Kennedy; the host of the popular investigative report program, *Just the Facts* was piloting a private jet that crashed in the mountains near Bogotá, Columbia last night. His family in San Diego has been officially notified. We are told Tristan was on a hiatus from the show, visiting friends in Peru. There are no survivors."

The lady said his plane was demolished, exploding on impact in hostile terrain so inaccessible, it would be impossible to retrieve his body.

Then a slideshow began of his dramatic life.

The music was tender and poignant. The tribute ended with another picture of his handsome face. That charismatic smile beamed right into her heart. Those trustworthy cerulean blue eyes.

She would never see them again. "No, no, NO!"

The strangled whisper finally broke free from her constricted lungs. As she gasped, air filled them completely, flinging an anguished heartbroken scream throughout the hospital.

It stopped everyone. And everything.

Wyatt stood in the open doorway.

"Good Lord, Solaris," he swore, but saw the television screen still showing Tristan and realized why she had screamed. "Oh, Laurie. We just found out too. His mom called me. I was coming in here to tell you."

"We were together in Peru."

"I know. Kianna told me."

"Tristan saved my life. He really loved me."

"Damn. I'm so sorry."

She sobbed, shaking. "He can't be gone. He promised to come home."

In three strides her brother was there, comforting as only Wyatt could. Bandaged arms clung to his strong neck.

But over his broad shoulder, she couldn't stop watching the TV screen.

There he was.

So close, yet gone forever.

While Tristan smiled at her from a place where the special friendship they shared would be written in the stars and carried forever inside her broken heart, Solaris curled up in that hospital bed and cried.

I am a Guardian

When I dream, I see the future.
My dreams hold the power to change your Fate.

~~ Joshua Solomon Archer

He woke in a cold sweat. Vivid images and critical words ran through his mind like frantic messengers on a mission. Joshua flicked on his bedside lamp, grabbing the notepad and pen on the oak nightstand. Without thinking, he wrote the orders.

Save the son. Protect the son.

Without any conscious thought of his own, Joshua quickly sketched a shoreline with two sets of footprints embedded in the sand. Finished, his pen hung over the paper.

Then a name came to him: *W. Thornbriar.*

His hand twitched and Joshua rapidly drew a tribal sun tattoo. Although his pen was black, he knew it should be bright orange, red, and yellow. The sun was artistic and feminine with slender sunbeams that curled outward in a playful way. The sun smiled.

He wondered how the tattoo would look on a woman's back and suddenly knew that is exactly where he'd find the happy sun, centered between slim shoulder blades.

Was W. Thornbriar a woman?

No, he felt sure it was a man. The sun belonged to someone new.

Closing his eyes, Joshua envisioned the man. Thirtyish with sandy brown hair styled in an overgrown, rouge-warrior way that Hollywood heroes had made fashionable. Light brown eyes. He was a big man, in control and living large. Attitude seeped off his broad shoulders. W. Thornbriar was the image of a perfect formidable alpha male, with one distinct exception.

He wore an obnoxious bright red tie.

Joshua's green eyes popped opened again. Interesting.

Pondering the clues, he outlined the rays of the sun, over and again. Suddenly words came, loud and clear in his mind:

La Sin you're a Lose the Soul.

What? He wrote it down anyway. What the hell did that mean? Why did he capitalize certain worlds? It felt all wrong.

Joshua read it aloud and upon hearing his own voice he realized he was translating it phonetically.

This wasn't English. It was Spanish.

La Señora Luz de Sol.

Better. The Spanish phrase felt true now.

The Sunlight Lady.

Joshua was glad he paid attention in college foreign language classes. It was an unusual name, a title maybe? It felt respectful, special and lovely in ways that made him unconsciously smile.

A beautiful name—for a beautiful woman.

The smiling sun tattoo belonged to the Sunlight Lady.

Were the two people a couple? Joshua got the impression they were close, the man loved the woman. Their bond felt like a ribbon of love, woven year after year until that bond was stronger than steel.

Married? Maybe. Definitely family.

The intuitive feelings faded. He would receive nothing more. But if Joshua ignored this, bad things could happen to good people. It wasn't normal. He knew it.

He lost normal years ago.

Swinging out of bed, he pulled on jeans lying in an oak rocking chair handcrafted by his grandfather. Raking one hand through sleep mussed woodsy-brown hair he let out a resolute sigh and flicked on the overhead lights. The antique brass fixture hummed a little, then silenced as a soft white glow lit the bedroom.

Walking barefoot across aging oak floors polished smooth by decades of Archer feet, the thick slats comfortably creaked with sounds of history and a life well lived. Green eyes focused upon his goal: the leather-bound World Atlas on the table.

The dreams were his call to action, bringing valuable clues. The book of maps would show him where to go.

Some people had jobs. Joshua Archer had missions.

Born to a heritage far more revolutionary than anything his colonial forefathers envisioned when they boldly sailed from England to American, the modern Archer family had evolved from simple Bostonian settlers and shopkeepers into Guardians of the innocent. A powerful heritage passed down for generations.

The precognitive dreams foretold of impending danger. By following the summons, sometimes just by being at the right time and the right place, Joshua could change a person's fate.

There used to be seven of them.

Last year, a difficult mission stole their father.

But Leland and Elizabeth Archer trained their children well. No secrets were kept from Lincoln, Theodore, Victoria, Joshua, and Madison. Each knew their sacred duties and the selfless sacrifice being born an Archer required. And each longed for the day when the intuitive dreams no longer came. Linc and Theo were older and seemed immune to the dreams now. Both had families of their own with the women they loved.

Their mother's dreams died with their father.

Only Joshua and his younger sisters still dreamed.

In college when his gift surfaced, overnight he changed from a brilliant business management student attending MIT Boston, to being a shaken visionary who received knowledge from nowhere logical at all.

Now the dreams of danger were as normal as his favorite morning coffee.

At the table, Joshua purposely cleared his mind. Focusing, he held the leather-bound book against his bare chest, breathing slow and deep.

Tonight's message was serious.

He had never felt a summons this powerful. Intuitive energy flowed through his towering body, having a life of its own. It was in the night air, on his breath, a weight carried upon his shoulders.

It was a heartbeat.

Strong, so strong the call to duty was this time. As if his own life might depend upon it.

Nonsense. I choose my fate. Taking control, Joshua lifted the leather book high over his head. Then he drew a breath and dropped the heavy Atlas on the table. It landed with a noisy thud. The pages fluttered back and forth with an odd shuffling of mental energy that used to disturb him, but now he accepted the strangeness.

It popped open to California.

He felt relieved. Last time he dreamed of danger he was sent to Duluth, Minnesota and froze his ass off all winter. A summer in California sounded nice. Joshua had been cooped up inside this antiquated Boston colonial mansion for months, tending family affairs that in truth, were not his affair at all. Suits and ties and boardroom meetings were a noose around his neck he would happily leave.

Thanks Dad; some inheritance. I would rather still have you.

Eyes closed again.

Letting the energy flow, his open palm hovered over the map.

Suddenly his index finger jumped toward the page. Eyes opened. Joshua grimaced. It landed in the Pacific.

But tilting his finger, he realized his fingertip touched an area just outside of San Diego, on the long narrow slice of sand called Coronado Island.

He knew of it, but had never been.

A seaside tourist town, elite and expensive, the island was made famous by the historic Hotel Del Coronado with its elegant white walls, Victorian structure, and red roof turrets. On the south end was a Naval base where SEALS and jet pilots trained. Coronado Island was a peninsula. The slender beach called Silver Strand connected the southern end to mainland near the border of Mexico.

Tipping his head, a dark aura covered that area.

Silver Strand Beach.

He committed the name to memory. Someone was going to die there.

Unless I prevent it.

Staring at the map, Joshua already heard the rhythmic rush and tug of the ocean roll through his subconscious, energy coming from forces pulling him toward Coronado.

Was this urgent? Should he leave tonight?

No, trouble had not arrived yet. The warnings came early. Danger was on the horizon. Soon he would be needed.

That firm conviction settled inside. Being there might change the future. His mere presence would alter events already set in motion, moving danger in another direction, maybe diffusing it entirely. Joshua got the feeling he should pack everything.

This one might take a while.

A knock on the bedroom door snatched his attention. "Come in."

"I heard you drop the book," Victoria declared upon entering. Her curious Archer green eyes saw the Atlas lying open to reveal California. But her face remained smooth of emotion, giving away nothing.

Another Archer family gift.

"West coast," she observed, meeting him at the table. Attention focused upon the map, one slim finger thoughtfully stroked across the page. It came to rest, ironically, in the exact spot his had touched.

Coronado Island.

"I didn't mean to wake you."

Lifting her hand from the map in a ladylike gesture, fingers modestly smoothed the blue sash on her velveteen robe. The gaze that met his was guilty, but amused.

"Your dream woke me. I felt it, too. By the time the Atlas hit the table, I was already standing in the hallway with my ear pressed against your door."

"You're too sensitive. And too curious."

She smiled. "Madison says that too."

"Is she still sleeping?"

One shoulder lifted to suggest anything was possible tonight. "Baby sister is restless. Twenty-four and three-fourths is a very rough age."

"Especially for an Archer."

If they made it to twenty-five the dreams of danger never came. It was their one hope for a normal life.

Madison's birthday was coming in July.

She still had a chance at freedom.

Victoria was born gifted with gentle intuition, never knowing normal at all and his Guardian instincts were stronger than any Archer had experienced in generations.

For Madison, the only thing uncanny in her princess-perfect Bostonian life was her impeccable sense of fashion.

"I hope the dreams will skip Madie," he wished. "It only seems fair that one of us gets to enjoy a normal life."

Victoria disagreed. "Even if she never dreams, normal won't happen. Madie would be the first to agree that she's different from her friends. I think all Archer's are born destined to walk in the world, but never fit in. It's our family curse."

Joshua gruffly scoffed. "That old curse story is bunk."

"It's our history," his sister upheld. "We're the twelfth generation since Liam Archer loved Amaryllis Caldwell. His bad choices changed our future. When she was arrested for healing people with herbal cures, he should have defended the woman he loved. She was burned as a witch in Salem. He did nothing. Fear overpowered his love. An innocent woman died for helping people. Life cursed our family. Now all Archer's are duty bound to help the innocent. Our only hope for freedom is to find a love that is stronger than fear."

"That's just a legend."

Victoria defended her beliefs, "And yet tonight you dreamed of good people in danger, innocents who need protection from harm. You are a man who does not fear, who cares enough to step forward and quietly change their fate. Why is that, brother?"

He didn't know why. "I think we're gifted, not cursed."

"Gifted is a nicer way to see it."

Once again Victoria's fingertip stroked across Coronado Island on the map. "This one feels serious for you, Joshua. Not a quick fix. You can't just walk in and discreetly stop a stalker before he attacks, or keep a drunk driver from accidently killing an innocent family, like you have done before. This requires much more. You should pack well. Don't fly. Take your Jeep. You will need it."

"My thoughts exactly," he gave a short laugh, "I had just decided to buy new tires and get the oil changed. Can you read minds now, Victoria?"

"No, I'm simply sensing your energy," her discreet smile curved. "You feel like a man whose heart is already halfway out the door."

"Not yet. I still need to prepare."

"The dream was different tonight."

He nodded. "I've never felt anything this strong."

Looking at his concerned sister, Joshua saw a woman with inner grace that would make their forefathers proud.

"Let's call the board of directors today to change the Archer-Greenfield corporate charter. I'm putting you in control."

Feminine hands fluttered. "Don't do that. I am happy to oversee things while you are gone. When you come home, you can be acting CEO again."

"No, you deserve respect and full authority. The company needs a strong figurehead. Linc and Theo sold their company options years ago. You, Madison, and I own equal shares. She isn't ready for management, but you already run Boston's hospitality training headquarters and oversee New York. Handling the rest of the country shouldn't be too hard."

"I'll do it on one condition. If you ever want it again, the job is yours."

"Never. I hate the suit and tie."

Victoria smiled, full this time. Her elegant face looked even prettier. "Dad always hated it too. He called the tie a noose." Recalling the headstrong man their father was made them both a little sad. "If you need help in California, do you promise to call?"

"I do promise. I'm not Dad. Pride is not an issue. Everything will be fine. I can handle a little trouble. Now, go back to bed and sleep. Tomorrow will be a busy day."

"Alright, love you."

"Love you too."

But turning from the table they saw another woman standing in his bedroom doorway. Chiseled aristocratic features and high cheekbones accented her pretty face. Archer green eyes were round and angled at the corners, almost like a cat. Brunette hair fell in soft curls to mid-back. In sharp contrast to Joshua and Victoria's classic appearance, this woman was strikingly beautiful.

Already dressed in skinny blue jeans and a fashionable teal sweater, she casually leaned one hip against the doorframe and seemed only mildly interested in anything she might have overheard. Her expression was unreadable; a gift of inner composure that all Archer's were taught to perfection. But an odd emotion glistened in those exotic green eyes.

"Madison. Sorry if I woke you."

"I was awake. And I agree. Victoria should run the hotel management company," the youngest sister loyally stated. "You're a natural leader, Sis. You have my vote." Then one arm quickly raked over her face, drying wet eyes with her sweater sleeve.

"Hey, are you crying? What's wrong?"

Madison sniffed. "I want to come with you, Joshua."

He refused. "No. I work alone."

"But you need help this time."

"You are not ready."

"You underestimate me, brother." Her stance became defiant. "I shoot as well as you can. My instincts are strong. Dad always said I could be anything that I want to be. I want to be your Guardian."

Joshua was not negotiating.

"I understand why you're worried. Losing Dad shook us all. If I need help, I'll call. Dad was too proud to reach out when he was in trouble. I am not Dad," he firmly added. "I'm not proud. I know my limits."

Her expression remained adamant.

"I am a Guardian too. You will need me." She drew a ragged breath. "Like it or not, I am assigned to you."

"You can't be." He denied, "You haven't had the dreams yet."

"Tonight," she sighed, "I did."

Those three words snatched hope right out of his chest.

If the dreams had come, then Madison's future was set. Her cognitive gifts would grow now. They would dictate her life. The doorway had opened. No longer was she free to choose her own destiny.

She had crossed the Archer Guardian threshold.

"What did you dream?"

"I dreamed of you, Joshua." Those green eyes glistened again. "And the things I saw tonight, I won't let happen. I can change it. I am an Archer. That means something."

"Tell me what you saw."

Her head shook. "Take me with you," she urged, "and I will."

"You warned me. That will change it."

"Even the strongest Archer can need a Guardian. I know it has never happened, but now it has. I am yours. Sometimes just by being at the right place at the right time, you can change someone's fate." The rebellious youngest sister quoted wisdom their family lived and died by. "I can change yours. Do what is right, brother. Take me with you to Coronado Island."

Madison knew his destination.

Neither he nor Victoria had said it aloud. "We leave soon," he bluntly informed. "Pack well. Say goodbye to your friends. We may not see Boston for many months."

"Longer," her bottom lip quivered. "Much, much longer."

"You think we're going to California to stay?"

With a curt nod, Madison abruptly turned away from the open doorway. They heard the heels of her boots briskly click-click on oak floors.

He was stunned. "Is she right, Victoria?"

"Yes, I believe she is. I feel it now, too. Whatever waits for you two in California is huge." Giving his arm a reassuring squeeze, she hustled out the door, chasing down their headstrong sister.

Joshua stood alone. A new door just opened in his life. And Madison was coming with him. He wasn't sure if he liked it.

California was a tourist haven of sun, fun, and beautiful people. It took two months to step away from responsibilities in Boston and another ten days to drive across the country with Madison, who liked to sightsee. They had stopped at every point of interest between Massachusetts and California. But the long haul west and the legal proceedings Joshua endured in handing over his position with the company were worth it.

He had rented a beach house, right on Coronado Island. The two story had lots of windows and a white railed balcony on the upper lever with a fantastic view of the Pacific.

Plus, Joshua was no longer CEO of Archer-Greenfield Metropolitan Developments. Victoria now wore those polished shoes. The hotel management company was their family legacy. It began with a quaint Boston inn owned by William Archer and hosted by sweet innkeeper Claire Greenfield. Many generations later, Archer-Greenfield Metro successfully managed first class hotels and restaurants nationwide.

But Joshua was no hospitality host. He didn't care if the napkin should be folded into a swan, felt sheet thread count was a glorified number just to make manufactures more money, and thought hotel spa personnel and gourmet chefs were snobby.

After their father died, he tried to care. Let Victoria care. She was amazing at the helm of that dignified world, an elegant lady born to lead with a kind word and genteel smile.

No more suits and ties. Joshua couldn't be happier.

He liked living by the ocean. The color of the water was different here, friendly blue, more inviting than his familiar chilly gray Atlantic. The Archer family home was on the outskirts of Boston, surrounded by thick forests that silenced sounds down to mere ghostly whispers.

Now he enjoyed wide open spaces and sunshine. For the past week, he fell asleep listening to the ocean gush and roll.

Yesterday, Madison deserted him.

Apparently, he didn't need a Guardian. Yet. Secretly, Joshua hoped her story about having the dream was a big fat fib. Driving across country she chatted and laughed, unconcerned by trouble. His sister loved to talk. She was good company, his favorite person. Victoria was too serious, with too many rules. But Madie had a quirky sense of humor and a rebellious attitude that made rules seem silly.

Maybe she just wanted playtime in California. Yesterday she bought a black Porsche 911, a racy turbo with sleek Carrera red leather interior. Then she hugged him goodbye, claimed she had work to do with the San Diego hotels affiliated with their company and roared away.

Madison had a unique job with Archer-Greenfield. She was their hotel spy. Wearing wigs and character clothes, using false identities she stayed as a normal guest. Then she discreetly inspected everything from kitchen cleanliness to the pool chlorine levels.

It was a game, but it did keep the hospitality industry on their toes. No one knew what Madison Archer really looked like.

She was the queen of disguises.

He had a flair for camouflaging himself, too. Today the heir to a multi-million-dollar hospitality legacy wore ordinary navy cargo shorts and a stonewashed blue t-shirt with a giant shark logo across the chest.

His toothy shark warned, "I Bite!!!"

The shirt was touristy, but he liked it. Joshua didn't care that his casual appearance would have given his stuffy forefathers fashion convulsions. It fit the situation. He blended into the crowd.

Most people wanted to leave an impression. People liked to be remembered, to feel special. Because of his abilities, Joshua tried to be totally forgettable.

Most days he succeeded.

He had casually walked the streets of Coronado for a week, virtually invisible. He mingled so well, not a single person tried to strike up a conversation. Joshua strolled sidewalks, glanced at people, and went into gift shops searching for Mr. W. Thornbriar. Today he decided to circle town in his Jeep, driving seaside neighborhoods hoping for an intuitive sign. Nothing. Not even a hint of danger. If anything, life here was too sublime. Maybe it isn't the right time yet.

Waiting at a stoplight on Orange Avenue, Joshua felt tempted to park somewhere and walk the main street one more time. Somehow, he had to pinpoint the one person who drew him to Coronado Island. It never took this long to find his target.

W. Thornbriar was an elusive man.

A flash of red behind him in traffic caught the sunlight and drew his attention. Joshua glanced into the rearview mirror. The woman next in line at the intersection drove a cherry red four-door Jeep.

Hers was a Sport edition, recently waxed, reflecting every ray of the June sun. The black Rubicon he drove from Boston was two years older, with mud caked inside the wheel wells, and a layer of dust on the hood. He wondered if her shiny toy ever drove off-road. His beast certainly did.

The woman glared at the red stoplight as if mentally willing it to turn green. "Come on, come on," she impatiently mouthed.

Curious now, he adjusted the mirror to see her better.

She must be late for something. Her lips were drawn into a tense line and both hands clutched the steering wheel with an agitated impatient grip.

She was pretty.

Tawny hair fell in soft waves, fashionably parted on the side. He couldn't see the ends. It must be long. She had a pleasant face. She wasn't a striking beauty who made men stop and stare, but Joshua liked what he saw. Her look was natural. Real.

She was the kind of woman a man could talk to all day, kiss to sleep at night, and happily wake up beside the next morning, a woman any man would be proud to call his lover and friend.

Darker eyes, maybe brown. The corners of her lips naturally curved upward at the corners.

That feature made her lovely, more approachable.

She was beautiful in a warm summertime way that made the clairvoyant Guardian envision bare feet walking the beach and long afternoons spent by the sea. Laughter in the dark, watching the stars. Kisses, lots of summery sweet kisses. Damn, he needed to find his target soon. Joshua was so bored he just mentally pulled character imprints off a total stranger at a stoplight.

Focus, Archer. Whoever she might kiss, it won't be you.

Looking forward again, the light was still red and traffic continued through on the busy cross street. Waiting, his gaze was drawn back to the intriguing woman reflected in the mirror. Consciously obtaining information this time, he closed his eyes and purposely focused.

Impressions came fast and vivid.

Joshua saw her hiking breathtaking mountains, sailing down exotic jungle rivers, and exploring ancient ruins of civilizations built by people long gone from this world. But she wasn't conquering the land, she wasn't a fearless adventurer. She was a watcher. Like a tiger in the grass, the woman spent life crouched and hidden, never disturbing what she saw, only observing. She quietly waited, patiently hoping for that perfect moment when the sun would shine just right and Life would offer up a beautiful moment to capture and save forever.

Green eyes opened. Wow. Who the hell was she?

Suddenly his Jeep lurched forward, shoved hard from behind.

The stoplight had turned green. Shit. Instead of waiting until he saw it too, she had expected him to drive forward and slammed on the gas anyway.

Joshua shook his head at her in the mirror. She defensively held up both hands as if claiming it was his fault, not hers. Cars behind them honked. Turning on his blinker, he turned the corner, driving to a small public parking area. She followed, but parked a full car length behind him. Finding his insurance card, he tucked it into his back pocket, shut off the Jeep engine and got out.

The woman didn't move. But her lips were moving. It looked like she was having a whole conversation with herself, scolding and then answering. Her windows were up. Joshua couldn't hear her voice, but those lovely curved lips were not happy. Hands occasionally flapped around, emphasizing whatever was on her mind.

Great, he got hit by a raving lunatic.

An attractive lunatic, but still, this wasn't good. But it was mildly amusing. Folding both arms over his broad chest, Joshua leaned his backside comfortably against the side of his Jeep to watch. She caught him looking and made an offended annoyed face. He wiggled one finger in a "come here" gesture. Her head shook in refusal. Then she said something that made those brown eyes watery and sad. That cute bottom lip puckered. Fists scrubbed over wet cheeks. Then she gave up. Her forehead lowered, leaning on the steering wheel in defeat.

"Hey lady," he called out loud enough she could hear; "do you need a doctor?" Her head didn't move, but one hand waved him away in a dismissive gesture that meant she wished he would disappear. Or maybe that she could disappear.

"Are you hurt?" The hand waved again. "You aren't armed and dangerous, are you?" No response this time. She sat there crying, forehead resting upon the top of her steering wheel.

What a rude crazy emotionally unstable woman. Joshua couldn't figure out why she refused to get her ass out of the Jeep and talk to him. Maybe she had no insurance. California was strict on that. If he called the cops, they would slap her with a big fat fee and a ticket.

Maybe a few driving classes.

But she drove a Jeep that was easily worth thirty-grand. It looked new. Not a scratch on that shiny red paint. No, the woman's problem wasn't insurance or money.

Leaning over to inspect her front bumper, he didn't see any damage.

Maybe this wasn't worth pursuing. He should wave goodbye and continue his search. If his Jeep had a dent, oh well. He needed to find Mr. Thornbriar, not console a lady who was obviously having a bad morning before she ever bumped into him.

Standing upright again, Joshua saw the woman was still upset, but her tears had become anger. Her head subtly moved as if she were still having that internal argument, one that no one was winning. Palms suddenly pounded against everything in reach. She accidently hit the horn. The abrupt toot made her jump.

It almost made him laugh.

Finally, she looked up at him.

Yeah, crazy lady, I'm still here.

Giving up, she leaned back in the seat and unbuckled her seatbelt. Reluctantly, she opened the truck door. The left leg that swung out and met the pavement was covered in a thick white walking cast from her red painted toenails to the knee. No wonder she ran into him.

She had no business driving with a busted leg.

"Oh god! Laurie, are you alright?" A tall businessman shouted, running out of an office building across the street.

His red tie flapped and the cream-colored dress shirt looked ready to bust buttons across his burly chest. Mr. Business was muscular and fit, not a man anyone would dare shout back at. Proving it, Laurie's eyes stayed focused upon her foot.

The man frantically waved and shouted louder as if somehow, she didn't hear the worried spectacle he was creating. Without hesitating or looking at cars, he charged right across the busy street.

Traffic in both directions noisily skid to a halt.

He ignored the honks and angry voices. A lady driving a convertible lost her sunhat in the street and two crying kids in another car were now wearing their ice cream cones on their shirts.

Nice mess.

"Are you hurt?" Mr. Worried rushed to Laurie.

"I'm fine. It was just a dumb accident." Her voice was smooth yet sweet, like sipping warm cocoa on a cold winter morning.

She closed the red Jeep door, providing Joshua with a better view of his intriguing morning distraction. The unbroken leg was long, tan, and lean. The body above it was nicely curved and promising. Caramel warm-blonde hair fell nearly to her waist.

Damn. Beautiful.

Seeing the whole woman brought fast impressions of climbing towering mountains while breathing air so thin it made your thoughts take flight, of swimming in lakes of crystal-clear blue water, and camping beneath a humid green jungle canopy while listening to wild things prowl in the night. Would she do that? Maybe.

His impression of a tiger felt stronger. Not a tiger—a jaguar.

Sun-kissed skin looked healthy against her red Bermuda shorts and white cotton tank top. The narrow straps of her shirt left graceful shoulders mostly bare. A white canvas sneaker was laced onto her right foot. Someone had drawn smiley faces on it in red marker, apparently praising that foot for not breaking too. It was cute.

The clothes and smiley shoe were too civilized for the adventurous lifestyle he envisioned, but Joshua had to admit the whole package was extremely appealing.

"I'm fine. Go back to your office."

"But Laurie," the man objected in an anxious whine not befitting his impressive size, "you had an accident."

"It was no big deal."

"I should call an ambulance, anyway."

Now she was angry. Her eyes met his. "Wyatt Thornbriar, you will not!"

Joshua felt dumb.

The man was W. Thornbriar, the exact name that brought him here to Coronado Island.

Wake up, Archer.

He was too preoccupied with Laurie to notice Wyatt had stylishly overgrown sandy brown hair and wore a bright red tie, exactly how he dreamed that night in Boston. He realized they were parked across the street from an office building that proudly proclaimed: Wyatt S. Thornbriar, Executive Investment Management, Inc.

But he walked this area just yesterday. How did he miss seeing that?

It wasn't time yet. Today I am needed.

Joshua didn't know who Laurie was, but Wyatt obviously loved her. They looked several years apart in age. The hardy tenacious business man and the slim youthful lady seemed like an odd pair to be married, but who knew these days.

It was California, after all.

"If you call an ambulance," she defiantly told Wyatt, "I swear I'll officially have you committed for being the world's biggest fussy mother hen."

"I'm not a hen," he smirked, "I am a rooster."

"Then stop clucking at me like the sky is falling."

All teasing was instantly wiped off his face. Serious was a scary look for Wyatt. "But Laurie, you could have whiplash."

"I have survived far worse."

Arms crossed over his broad chest. "Exactly. I should take you to the doctor."

"Absolutely not. Now, please go back to your office," she begged, shoving at his shoulder. "I will handle this. I am not hurt. I promise that I would tell you, if I was. And please, Wyatt, stop fussing over me. The world still turns, the sun still rises each morning, and life is moving forward again. I didn't shatter. Okay?"

Wyatt resembled a devoted puppy she had spanked on the nose. "I just love you, that's why I worry."

His sincere sentiment stole the fire from her attitude.

"I know. And I'm grateful." Emotions made her eyes misty again, "I love you too. I don't know what I would do without you."

Arms opened, giving Wyatt a generous hug. She patted him affectionately on the back. Her hand made a solid thunk sound. The man looked capable of wrestling a dinosaur into submission. He needed a clairvoyant Guardian's protection? Right.

"See you at dinner tonight?" Wyatt asked after they hugged.

"Sure." She half-smiled. "It's your turn to cook."

He chuckled, low and playful. "Then I'm ordering pizza."

"Cheater. I cook you real food."

"If I could make Swordfish a'la Siciliana as delicious as you made last night, I would cook for you. But I can't. Everything I touch burns. So, I will serve you Pizza a'la Box," that earned Wyatt a small amused smile, "Just two easy steps: order and pay. Even I can't mess that up."

"Okay." Her head shook, amused. "Pizza a'la Box is fine."

"Cool. See you at seven?"

"It's a date."

Laurie watched Wyatt confidently stride back across the busy street. Shoulders squared in a posture of official authority, the big man held out one hand to stop traffic. Cars screeched and honked at him anyway. He didn't care. Shaking her head, she sighed, long and loud.

Resigned to her fate, she finally hobbled toward Joshua. "I'm really sorry that I hit you," she muttered.

Then her gaze met his.

Her eyes weren't ordinary brown. They were softer with more captured sunlight, a golden amber color. As she looked at him, those lovely curved lips parted on a surprised gasp.

Their first up-close encounter made his mouth go dry.

Joshua was in trouble.

He had one rule: never get involved. Unfortunately, if the legends his sisters believed were true, that meant he doomed himself to always dream of danger. Without finding a love that overpowered fear, Life would continue to give him people to protect until the day he died. If the Archer family gift was a curse, at least Fate gave them one doorway out.

Love could release them.

But he was no fool.

Maybe Linc and Theo found freedom through love, but their father dreamed his entire life. Love had not released him. So, he let Madison and Victoria cling to their hope.

Joshua had no aspirations for romance, no illusions to shatter, and no wish to find his happily ever after.

He only wished to touch her.

To taste those sweet curved lips, just once. A simple wish, but it held infinite complications.

Something happened to her too. Catching a sharp intake breath, she made a funny confused noise and stopped walking. She stared at him. Eyes were wide. Her expression a mixture of awe and shock. Fingers rubbed across her heart as if it wasn't beating right.

The wish to touch her grew stronger.

Determined to stay focused on his mission, Joshua pushed those feelings aside. He refused to let a beautiful woman distract him. He was here to protect Wyatt. End of story. Years of practice at hiding his emotions helped him recover quickly.

"You shouldn't be driving."

"The cast comes off next week."

"And that makes it right?"

She was instantly offended. "Bumping into you has nothing to do with my leg. It's healed." The foot stomped to demonstrate. "See, solid." But the bones felt tender because she flinched. "The accident was just bad luck."

"We make our own luck."

"Excuse me?" Eyes narrowed in displeasure. "That seems awfully judgmental coming from a man who couldn't pay attention enough to notice that the stoplight had turned green."

"You hit me. The accident is your fault."

"So, sue me."

"Maybe I will."

"Wonderful." Both arms flapped skyward in a manic motion, "That would just make my delightful charmed life just absolutely super-perfect," she declared with such sarcasm, he felt bad for her.

"I was kidding."

"It wasn't funny."

"Sorry."

"Whatever." Leaning her foot out sideways since it couldn't bend at the ankle, Laurie knelt over and inspected the damage. Their Jeeps were almost the same height. Steel bumper had met the rubber edge of his spare tire. There was only a small red paint transfer. She rubbed it with her thumb and the red mark disappeared.

"There." She stood, dusting her hands. "All fixed."

"You still should not be driving."

"Thanks for the advice, but I'm late for an important meeting." She swung around to leave with a movement so abrupt, tawny hair flipped over one shoulder. That's when he saw it. On her upper back was a bright orange smiling sun tattoo. The exact same tattoo he drew in Boston. Vividly, he recalled the message.

Protect the Sun. La Señora Luz de Sol: The Sunlight Lady.

"Wait ... Laurie?"

Turning again, posture tense, her mouth was a suspicious taut line. "I don't recall giving you my name."

"Your very big, very worried friend said it."

"Oh, I guess he did." Her wary stance eased, "That's my brother Wyatt, who worries enough for ten people, especially lately. I swear if life doesn't improve soon, he'll give himself a heart attack over me."

She glanced across the street. The man in question stood outside his office, arms folded over his chest. She gave him a little finger wave. Wyatt tipped his chin, questioning why she was talking to Joshua. Biting her bottom lip, she shrugged.

"He's all I have in this world," the quiet introspective statement wasn't spoken for his benefit, "The only one who matters, anyway."

"It's good that your family cares."

"Cares? Sure. They care." Her cynical tone was bitter," That's why Wyatt and Kianna are the only people I've seen or spoken to since," focusing on his face again, remembering she wasn't alone, she blinked back wet glistening in her eyes before misery could spill over and embarrassed them both.

"Sorry. I'm venting."

"I get it. Hitting me sucks and I wasn't very nice about it," he sympathized, regretting he let his unexpected attraction to this beautiful woman make him seemed calloused to her problems. Obviously, she had more going on today than a simple traffic accident.

"I'm sorry, too. Really, I am. Want to start over?"

"Gee, wouldn't that be nice? Start over. I'd love to rewind life." She glanced down at her cast, "Unfortunately it's impossible." Issuing a huff of distaste, one hand raked through long side swept bangs that tumbled back down against her cheek and framed her face at an attractive angle. Her beauty was authentic and unpretentious, very likable.

Touchable.

That impulse resonated heat all the way through his core. The wish Joshua felt to touch her clashed just beneath his heart and fought against his code of honor, creating anarchy inside. Nothing had ever felt this potent, demanding his attention.

"I don't mean to be so emotional," she apologized, "but life has not been a cupcake party lately. I'm not coping very well."

"No harm done. We're fine, Laurie."

She looked at him funny. "My name is Solaris, actually. And you are?"

"Joshua Archer."

"Solaris Sullivan," she formally introduced, offering her hand to shake. Taking it, the fingers in his grip felt soft nestled against his large palm. "Wyatt is the only person who ever calls me Laurie. He's older and thought Solaris was too adult sounding, plus he's a tiny bit overprotective, so I was always his '*Little Laurie*' to take care of. But now we're grown. I don't know why he still says it."

"Maybe he likes watching over you."

"Hmm, good call." One side of her lips curved up. "I guess he does."

Glancing at the overprotective man who looked ready to charge across the street again to defend his sister, Joshua wisely released her hand. He needed to get his act together. Fate sent him here for Solaris, too. How Wyatt fit in, he didn't know, but this woman was important.

Protect the Sun.

He would.

Even her name, Solaris, was Latin for *of the sun.*

"Why is his last name Thornbriar, but you are Sullivan? Are you married to someone?"

"No. It's a long silly teenage rebellion story."

"I'm an excellent listener."

Amber eyes cast him a sidelong glance. Clearly, she wasn't convinced of that yet. But she asked, "Have you ever wished that you had no family baggage to drag around?"

"All the time, actually."

That seemed to give them common ground.

"Our father is Malcolm Thornbriar, the award winning real estate developer. Our mother Regina has made a name in designer clothing. Wyatt was a high ranked Naval Officer, and then became a successful investment broker. As a teenager, I rebelled against our parents."

"Most kids do."

"I was extreme. When I turned eighteen, I legally changed my last name. But I wasn't very creative about it," he liked her nervous little laugh, "I stole Wyatt's middle name. I thought he'd be furious, but he loved it. He hated the name Wyatt Sullivan for himself, but thought Solaris Sullivan was a strong name. Now I stand apart. I share my brother's name, but no one associates me with the Thornbriar family. Everything I became in life, I did on my own. It's better this way."

"That's actually a very cool rebellion story." That pleased her. Friendliness warmed the air. "Solaris is a unique name."

"My middle name is Anne, very ordinary. And you? Joshua what?"

"Solomon."

"Whoa," eyes widened. "That one carries some weight."

"It could be worse," he shrugged. "My brothers are Lincoln Abraham Archer and Theodore Franklin Archer. But we just call them Linc and Theo, for short."

"Why the presidential names?"

"The Archer family have been New England patriots since colonial times in Boston, some of the original settlers. Honoring history is tradition. In addition to Lincoln and Theodore, my sisters are Victoria Hope and Madison Liberty, so I'm grateful for Joshua Solomon, a more biblical name. At least my name isn't Truman or Ulysses."

Her bright smile was pretty. "You have a big family."

"Too big sometimes," he agreed. "Someone is always being too bossy. Someone is always mad. Someone has to keep the peace. Thanksgiving is insane and Christmas breaks the bank."

She chuckled. "Sounds like fun, actually."

"Let's trade."

"Hah," the quick laugh bursting from her lips was adorable. "You actually want Wyatt?"

Together, they looked across the street at the formidable overprotective man still watching them with disapproval.

"Well, maybe not."

"I thought so."

Relaxing as they talked, she lost that guarded edge. Solaris was naturally friendly, a smiley happy person. Special, like no woman he'd ever met. That special light came from the inside, as if life approved when she smiled.

"What happened to your leg?"

She looked at the cast, choosing her words. "I fell down a cliff."

That one stunned him. "What were you doing on a cliff?"

"Two months ago, in April, I was on location in Peru, near the Amazon basin. I fell and cracked two ribs. I tore up my hands too," she held up both palms to reveal faint pink scars, "but they healed already. I broke several bones and tore some tendons in the ankle, so they did orthoscopic surgery. It's taking forever to heal."

Someone wanted her dead. Joshua felt it now.

Glancing down at the white cast on her leg, he realized he was looking at evidence from the first failed attempt on her life. She had survived. But she was still in danger. When he viewed Solaris out of the corner of his eye, a dark ominous aura completely enveloped her body.

"Why were you in the Amazon jungle?"

"I'm a nature photojournalist. I was tracking down a wild jaguar." There was obviously more to the story, but she didn't offer further details. But it explained why he sensed tents and stars and jungles, had envisioned her hiding in the grass waiting to capture the perfect shot.

A camera shot, not a gun. And a jaguar, not a tiger.

She wasn't dangerous. Why would anyone want to hurt a woman who saw beauty in the world and shared it with others?

"South America sounds exotic."

One shoulder modestly shrugged. "I work that area regularly."

"You travel alone?"

"No, we always have a crew. My bodyguard Hector and my assistant Kianna have traveled the world with me. She coordinates everything we do with Wyatt. He's my financial manager," she added, glancing at her worried brother again. "I swear, those two talk on the phone eighteen times a day."

He vowed to research her travel companions.

"Kianna lives here?"

"Yes. She went to Hawaii to visit her family for a week, but she quickly returned. She stayed with me at Wyatt's place until she found a house of her own. Now she manages our online sales and my display gallery in downtown San Diego."

"She must be a good friend."

"Very good. Like family. Kianna says our wild vagabond days are behind us, that strong women need roots and our roots are here."

"You live an interesting life, Laurie."

Her mouth opened to correct the casual name that he liked because as a Guardian, he watched over people too, but her impulse faded as she remembered something else, something painful that made amber eyes water. "You have no idea."

It was sad and lost sounding, as if she had been spinning on top of the world, but her life suddenly went sliding sideways into the unknown. Judging by her leg, maybe that is exactly what happened.

"I'm really late for a meeting." She abruptly remembered and turned, but his hand quickly caught her upper arm, turning her back. It put them face to face, inches apart.

"Let me drive you," he gently offered.

"That isn't necessary."

"Humor me."

"But I don't know you."

He released her arm. "My name is Joshua Solomon Archer-Greenfield. I just drove cross country from Boston. I lived there in a big house that belonged to my father and to eight generations before him. Old colonial thing with too many rooms and white pillars," he described. "I carved my name into the oak banister when I was six. Dad loved that."

Listening, she made an amused snicker.

"I attended MIT for a business management degree to please the family, but took a few psychology classes and quickly realized that I am not my father. I am not ruled by the past. I make my own future. So, I majored in Life instead. I like to travel, hate cauliflower, and wore braces in eighth grade. There," he smiled wide and friendly, showing off the pearly straight teeth, "Now you know me."

That earned him some approval. "Impressive resume." Curious, she asked, "Does your colonial Bostonian pedigree come with letters of recommendation?"

"Nope, you'll just have to trust me."

Her chin tipped, "Are you trustworthy?"

"As trustworthy as any man, I suppose. I'm no boy scout," he conceded. "But I'm no chainsaw killer, either."

"Good. That's such a relief," she let out a dramatic sigh. "I was worried about being chopped into tiny bits today." A light laugh curved her lips. "In fact, when I woke up this morning, avoiding chainsaw killers was the very first thing on my mind."

He liked her sense of humor. It was quick.

"I think you're safe. I'm fairly harmless, most days. Well," he quickly added, "except for Tuesdays."

"Oh? What happens on Tuesdays?"

"As long as I always get my morning coffee, you'll never find out."

Her laugh lightly percolated, as satisfying as the robust breakfast blend he habitually enjoyed. Joshua felt lucky they had met. He wouldn't mind hanging out with Solaris, letting his presence change the danger in her life.

He could happily look at her all day.

He didn't have to touch. He could keep those adult urges under control. No problem.

"Now, about your meeting, where can I drive you?"

She was a stubborn woman.

"Don't you have better things to do?"

"I had no plans," he fibbed. "Besides, I feel it's my civic duty to protect the innocent citizens of San Diego from your cast-inhibited driving."

"It comes off next week."

"Yes, you said that."

Apprehension tightened her face. Solaris was nervous and wanted to go, but he needed to stay with her. Beautiful or not, he still had a mission. The dark aura of danger around her was very real.

Just by being there, he might change her fate.

"Today you need a safe reliable driver." He hooked one thumb toward Wyatt. "Plus, it would make your brother worry less."

She looked at the scowling man, did a funny face-palm action, made a rude childish noise, and then peered at Joshua between splayed fingers. "Impossible."

"Why don't you ask him?"

Her hand lowered. That stubborn tilt of her chin gave Joshua the wild urge to kiss her.

Damn, Archer. Get that under control.

But he was quickly learning everyone had a weakness. Apparently, his personal temptation had amber eyes and long tawny hair, a smiling sun tattoo on her shoulders, and lips that curved upward in the sweetest way.

"I don't need Wyatt's permission."

"Good. Let's get moving."

Striding toward her Jeep, he opened the passenger door. His assumption was right. A photographer is never without her tools. He grabbed the hefty black leather briefcase embossed with Canon emblems.

"What else do you need?"

"I'll get the rest," Reluctantly, Solaris hobbled over, grabbed her red Coach purse from the front seat, pocketed a red smart phone, and locked her shiny red Unlimited.

The woman liked red.

Immediately, her cell phone rang. "Yes?"

Across the street, Wyatt was loudly questioning her sanity. He didn't need the phone. Half of Coronado Island could hear.

It took a moment for Solaris to convince her overprotective brother that Joshua wasn't a dangerous criminal. Wyatt was a hard sell, but finally gave in. Climbing into the passenger side of his black Jeep, she licked nervous lips.

"Are you sure about this?"

"Positive. Trust me, it will be fun."

Turn My Life Around

More than words can say, I have wished for you.

~~ Solaris

"There is a Navy base on Coronado Island. You look like a SEAL or a high-ranking officer. Is that why you are here?" Solaris nervously chatted as they drove, feeling the need to do something more polite than openly stare at Joshua.

"No."

The way she felt near this man was startling and exhilarating. Joshua was handsome in a rugged, athletic, slightly imposing way that commanded her attention. His woodsy brown hair reminded her of the polished heart of dark European oak. He was tall and strong, deeply appealing to a woman who enjoyed a hearty encounter with nature.

She liked his Boston accent.

From his lips, she wasn't Laurie with the long EE sound at the end how Wyatt said. For Joshua, she became Laaw-RAY and it was beautiful. Others pronounced her sunny full name like SOlawress. But he rolled it into something far more exotic sounding.

Everything he said felt old world and wonderfully historic, like he had stepped out of a land with cobblestone streets, timeless red brick buildings, and proud sailing ships. She wondered what his father said when young Joshua carved his name into the banister of the Archer ancestral family home.

It felt surreal that he grew up in a city where Paul Revere forged silver for the wealthy, where Samuel Adams drank ale in taverns and rallied men to action, and Benjamin Franklin wrote speeches that had built the foundations of freedom. Her American history was cowboys and Indians. His was the Mayflower.

They came from opposite coasts and opposite worlds.

He was an attractive man, built to excel at both business and pleasure. There was a solemn gentleness in his eyes. Green eyes, she noted. A pure grassy color, like tender leaves in springtime.

Joshua Archer wasn't a man who stood out in a crowd, who stopped women in their tracks, making them lustfully sigh. He was not a man who did dramatic things to make the world take notice.

He blended. Almost as if he meant to blend.

But something about him made wild feelings zing around inside her like lightening bugs trapped in a glass jar. Everything silent inside was suddenly bursting with life.

It made her think of Tristan.

Solaris sighed. She actually went an entire hour without thinking of him. Every moment of every sad day for two long months he had occupied her mind and heart. If it wasn't so terribly tragic, the small reprieve might have felt like an accomplishment.

"What brings you to San Diego?" She asked.

"Work."

"How long are you staying in California?"

Green eyes immediately glanced her way, "Indefinitely."

Joshua didn't volunteer more but that scalding glance felt weighted. Her body reacted. She blushed. A fine sweat bathed her brow. She felt too warm. Turning toward the air conditioning vent, the breeze was cool. Solaris hoped the movement was casual enough he wouldn't notice.

He noticed.

"Wow," he breathed. Reaching across the small space between them his fingers stroked her hair flying in the air current. Eyes met. Her heart did a funny stutter-step. Joshua's hand slowly brushed down her arm.

As they touched she suddenly envisioned a room with white rumpled sheets and white lace curtains. Antique brass ceiling lights emit a soft glow. An old oak table dominated one corner.

On it was a leather-bound book, a book of maps. It lay open to California.

As if he knew, a tiny sly smile curved his lips.

Something about that page made him happy. Or maybe, it was what he found here. Then retreating from the touch, his wandering hand joined the other holding the steering wheel. Green eyes focused upon the road again.

The strange intuitive sensation was gone.

Solaris felt certain she had seen glimpses of his home in Boston. "Where the hell did you learn to do that?"

His head tipped, "What?"

"When you touched me," she faltered, saying it aloud felt crazy. "Do you have a big brown leather book of maps at home?" He nodded, eyes widening. "Well, when you touched me, I saw it lying on a table. It showed California."

"Cool." He glanced at her, arching a brow because she was so befuddled. Joshua, however seemed extremely pleased

"No, that felt weird. Don't you think so?"

He chuckled, "Nope."

Solaris wished he would just talk to her. This one-word thing was killing her. Earlier he talked. Now he just answered quickly and drove. Conversation eased tension, kept her from feeling sad. But Solaris suddenly realized in his presence her mind felt invigorated, clear of the despondent morose weight she endured for two long months.

Who was this man?

And why oh why couldn't Tristan have made her feel this way? If he had, she never would have hesitated when he reappeared in her world. She would have loved him with all her heart. But she hesitated. She held back her love. Now he was gone.

Life was cruel.

"What is Boston like this time of year?"

"Green."

"Like California?"

"Greener."

The next long silence made her fidget. In the back seat of his Jeep, Solaris noticed a traditional rosewood longbow and a modern steel crossbow, arrows, archery shooting gloves, and a leather backpack. "Do you hunt or just target practice?"

"Both."

"Okay. That's it." Both hands suddenly flew in the air. "I can't ride with you. Turn around. Right now."

His expression was totally confused by her outburst. "Why?"

"Geez, Joshua. You're killing me. You talked earlier. But now I feel dumb trying to get to know someone who won't answer my questions. Can you drive us and speak more than one word at a time?"

"Sometimes."

One corner of his mouth quirked upward when she made an exasperated noise.

"Sorry."

"You aren't. You think the crazy woman is funny."

"No, Laurie. I think it's extremely interesting that you want to get to know me." Green eyes grazed over her, then back to traffic on the road. "I've been in Coronado a whole week and this is the most anyone has said to me."

She found that odd. People always talked to her. "Why not, aren't you friendly?"

"I can be. Do you always ask so many questions?"

"No. Sorry." One hand rubbed the back of her neck, tight with tension. "I don't know what's wrong with me. Maybe it's you. I think you make me nervous."

"Babe." Joshua shot her a heated look. Those intense green eyes said everything. Attraction warmed the air. That hot gaze brought unexpected thoughts of walking sandy shores holding hands and waking up feeling grateful to be alive.

No one had ever called her Babe.

Tristan always used Sweetheart, but it always had a condescending tone, like talking to a little girl not a woman. From Joshua, that one affectionate word felt like a profound compliment. It sounded deliciously sexy in his deep bedroom voice.

"I make you nervous?" he asked.

"Your crossbow makes me nervous."

"Then we're even because cameras make me nervous," and he smiled.

It was a real full-blown friendly smile, not the sly amused tug at his lips she observed earlier. That simple warm curve transformed everything about his face. Seriousness suddenly became clever, magnetic, and impressive.

The man trying to blend into the world certainly didn't blend right now.

He captivated.

It was the finest perfect moment she had experienced in years and Solaris wished for her camera. "What would happen if I took your picture?"

It only took him a second to decide. "Your camera would explode," he made a graphic explosion noise and one hand made a bursting movement, "just like a vampire in the sun. Not the 'sparkle and look pretty' vamp, either. Your expensive Canon would hiss and scream like Dracula, cursing you as it burst into flames."

Solaris laughed and decided she really liked when Joshua Archer smiled at her. "I think I'll keep my camera to myself."

"I would appreciate that."

He didn't say anything more, but the smile stayed. The way his handsome face looked in the warm June sunlight was worth keeping silent. Solaris loved watching beautiful moments. This was a great one.

As he drove, he automatically followed the right street going across Coronado Island toward the long, curved, blue bridge. "You seem to know your way around."

"I've explored the island."

"Technically, it isn't an island. They just call it that."

"Yes, it's a peninsula. Silver Strand Beach on the southern end connects to Imperial Beach near the Mexico border. Coronado is a slender strip of land that forms the natural harbor of the San Diego bay. It's like Cape Cod," he compared. "But with warmer water."

"Is the Cape a pretty place?"

He nodded. "Imagine a forest so thick you could get lost in five minutes, with a deep bay of water on the inner curve. The outer curve is the edge of the known American world. The only thing separating you from England is the cold Atlantic sea."

"It sounds amazing." It felt wonderful to talk. She craved conversation. For two months Solaris had locked herself inside Wyatt's house, mourning Tristan. Today was the very first day since attending his funeral services that she had been anywhere.

And she met Joshua.

Today she met a man who made her heart dance when he smiled.

Why did she have to feel this way about a total stranger? Why couldn't her heart have gone wild over her most trusted friend, a man who loved her right up until the day he died?

Or was killed.

She had not told that secret to anyone. Her solemn promise to Tristan stood firm. She kept all his secrets. She never even hinted to anyone that he came to Peru to escape trouble. But Solaris often wondered about that ruby necklace. He was so adamant, so determined to solve the mystery. Holding the Heart Stone that one time, the necklace felt precious. Unfortunately, since April she had personally proven that love truly brought many tears. The nights she cried over Tristan were countless.

"Joshua, can I ask you something personal?"

"If you want," he casually allowed, but his serious mask was firmly into place again, "but if your question is too personal, I might not answer."

"I can respect that," she licked lips that went dry every time their eyes met. "Do you have someone special in your life who might really hate the fact that you decided to drive me around today?"

"No. I'm a loner. And you?"

"Photography has been my life. I guess I'm a loner too."

"Maybe we can remedy that."

Solaris wondered why Joshua would offer to remedy their aloneness. She didn't need company. She was perfectly fine spending every day since Peru missing an adventurous career she dearly loved, mourning Tristan, and wondering why those two things were gone.

She was fine, perfectly fine. That's what she told Wyatt every day.

Please. Who am I fooling? Even Wyatt knows I'm a mess. Until this morning at a stoplight when she slammed on the gas instead of waiting for his Jeep to move, Solaris felt lost.

Joshua changed that. Hitting him saved her.

"I think I'm glad we met." Looking at him those green eyes held warm approval. The slight curve of his lips was reassuring.

"Good. Me too."

They had reached the two-mile-long sweeping arch of the Coronado Bridge. As they drove across the towering blue steel highway, the view of San Diego from so high above the water always seemed special. As a little girl, she always plastered her face against the car windows, straining to see more of the world. Solaris refrained from doing that now.

She had seen the world. It kicked her ass.

"I can't believe you ran out of questions," Joshua motivated kindly, giving her permission to indulge curiosity.

"Okay. How old are you?" That one felt silly to ask.

"Twenty-eight, born December third on a snowy Boston morning," he amiably offered, "Your turn," he added with a teasing glance."

"Wow, we're almost the same age. I'm December eighteenth. Born right here on Coronado Island. Pretty sure the sun was shining. It usually is." The small talk made Solaris relax. Joshua seemed more at ease too. His expression was approachable now, no longer guarded.

"I'm fifteen days older," he bragged.

"Older isn't wiser, you know."

His easy laugh was nice. "It's true," he agreed. "But we're a good match. Sagittarius' are thinking people, naturally creative, intuitive, and independent. They are optimistic and love living life to the fullest. As a rule, they choose jobs that make a difference in the world."

"How do you know that?"

"My sister Madie likes personality profiling. We drove across the country together." He gave a short chuckle, "She talks a lot."

His sister sounded interesting. "Where is she now?"

"Exploring Southern California, I guess. Madison is a loner too," he shared, trust in his voice, "She is a Leo, a self-assured independent Lioness. Needs no one, takes care of herself, and loves big drama and excitement. I pity the man who dares try to tame her."

Solaris considered her family for a moment. "Wyatt is May second. What's that?"

"Taurus, the Bull."

A laugh burst out. "Well, that explains everything."

It felt good to smile.

Once they crossed the bridge Solaris gave Joshua the address to her father's architectural firm in the downtown business district. Following her directions, upon arrival Joshua parked outside the stoic white thirty-story building that had been Malcolm Thornbriar's official headquarters her entire life. His name was displayed on every door in gold.

She dreaded this meeting. Six years is a long time for silence. Their last conversation was ugly. Her father was not a forgiving man. "This won't take long," she told Joshua as he found a place in front to park and turned off the Jeep engine.

He looked at the building, reading the name. "Your meeting is with your Dad?"

"Yes, and I'm very late. He'll yell at me, tell me whatever he wanted to say, and dismiss me again. That's how quick this will be."

"I'll walk with you." Joshua immediately got out and walked around the Jeep. He opened her door. Solaris had not unfastened her seat belt. Both hands stayed clutched together in her lap. Her body simply refused to move.

"Are you scared of him?"

"Just procrastinating. Wyatt told me what Dad wants. It's a photography job. The client is horrid, a real egotistical monster. Naturally, I'll refuse the job. Then he'll yell at me and we will fight. I really hate conflict," she tried to explain, feeling no more courageous than a moment ago. "I lived halfway around the world just to avoid these power-play games."

Joshua looked at the shiny glass doors where her father's name shouted his omnipotent presence, and then back at her again. "You're a good person, Solaris," he kindly assessed, but with a tone of authority. "If someone wants to yell at you, they can yell at me first."

"No, you don't have to—"

Reaching around her waist, Joshua bent forward into the Jeep, unclipping the seatbelt at her left hip. His chest was inches from hers. All business now, his attention was focused upon helping her out of the seat and inside to her meeting.

Solaris held perfectly still. Leaning inside how he was, his recently shaven face was so close she could smell Downy fabric softener on his shirt and fresh citrus-woodsy aftershave on his smooth skin.

He smelled wonderful.

A funny whimper-sigh escaped. She couldn't help it. Life had been so rotten and gloomy lately, everything about this man felt like a glimmer of hope in a sad world. Hope she desperately needed.

Joshua looked at her. It took a second for him to realize why she made that sound. Then his green eyes dilated, making them dark and alluring.

Awareness warmed the air. "Laurie?"

"Joshua, you are too close to me."

That gorgeous sly smile flashed, "Am I?"

"Yes. Please step back."

He didn't. "Hmm. Maybe I like being close to you."

"Then we have a big problem."

Nodding, he agreed, shifting a little so their faces were even closer. He drew a solemn breath, choosing his words. "Yes, it seems we do have a problem. I thought it was just me. But you're going to be major challenge for me, aren't you?"

It was a question she couldn't answer.

"Coming here, I was prepared for anything. Not this. Not meeting you." Noticing her ragged breaths, he softly added, "Damn. This is bad. Do you have any idea how many rules we could break together?"

"Too many," she whispered. "I can't breathe."

That amused him. "You are breathing."

"Not right. The air feels thin. You really should move."

Joshua made another dusky chuckle. He didn't move away. Instead, the hand that released her seatbelt came to rest comfortably along her hip. Now his chest faced hers. That position didn't nothing at all to relieve the irrational attraction that came from his close proximity to her rapid prancing heart.

"I can't do this," she warned.

"We haven't done anything ... yet."

"I know. I'm sorry. You must think I'm crazy. I don't know why I'm acting so ridiculous. This morning I felt fine." Listening to her nervous chatter, he simply arched one dark brow to question that statement.

"Okay, I'm not fine. I busted my leg in Peru, lost all my courage forever, and put a career that I love on hold, indefinitely. In one horrific day, I lost all sense of who I am. I didn't just fall down a cliff. I fell into an emotional abyss. Before this morning, I spent the past two months locking myself away inside Wyatt's house, refusing to come out."

"Why would you do that?"

"Because life kicked my ass, so I refused to participate anymore. It felt like the right thing to do. I thought if I could control life, then nothing else terrible could happen. It was a good plan. It might have worked. Every day was exactly the same. Every day was safe. But then I saw you and—"

Her gaze met his and held.

"I thought you looked beautiful," he softly confessed.

"Don't tease the crazy lady."

"You aren't crazy. When we met, I envisioned you hiding in tall grass, waiting for the perfect shot. I had no idea you were a photographer, but I imagined you climbing high mountains and sleeping beneath the stars. Who's crazy? Maybe I am. Things happen. So don't be so hard on yourself. I think we were meant to meet today."

Life whispered to pay attention. Solaris definitely was.

"We met by accident."

"There are no accidents. Not in my world."

"But I hit you."

"Life hit us," he gently revised in a way that felt true, "Life shoved us right together at a stoplight on Coronado."

Breathing felt easier. Her heartbeat slowed. She liked the intriguing gleam in his springtime green eyes, the solid weight of his arm along her side, and how Joshua Archer made her smile.

"Things like this don't happen."

"Why not," his voice was husky, deeper now. "Haven't you ever been insanely attracted to a complete stranger before?"

"No. Never."

"Me neither. Today it happened." His strong body shifted closer. Alarmed by the move, she inhaled deep. One hand shot out, reflexively resting upon his firm chest.

"What are you doing now?" She gasped.

That smile. It was naughty and playful, and oh so handsome. "I'm going to kiss you now," Joshua softly murmured, as if asking permission to break all the rules. "One kiss, that's all," he allowed. "Maybe it will cure us of this impulsive wish to touch. We won't wonder anymore. Then … we will know."

"You wish to touch me?"

"Babe," he breathed. The answer was obvious. Again, that one word felt like a sincere compliment. Solaris liked it. With her hand upon his chest, she noticed his breathing wasn't stable either.

"Say no, and I won't do it."

"One kiss," she approved. "Then we will know, right?"

Joshua smiled. Her eyes closed. Warm lips gently met hers. Just a tender taste, it felt nearly innocent. As her lips softened in acceptance, his mouth slid a little, tilting to achieve full contact.

Innocence melted. Wishes won.

Giving a manly rumble of amazement, the experimental kiss deepened as Joshua showed her what mere words could not express. The man had expert communication skills. She leaned into him, the strength of his body pressed against hers. It felt good. He kissed as if this moment was beautiful, something he wanted to savor. Long and slow.

It was a kiss to remember.

He didn't stop. And she didn't want him to. He tasted vital and alive, like hope. Their one kiss did plenty to satisfy their curiosity. Solaris didn't think, couldn't analyze her emotions and stay rational.

All she could do was feel and fall.

Touching Joshua was wonderful. Finally, he drew back. Opening her eyes, he looked oddly amused. "Laurie. Babe. Let go." He glanced down between them. Her hands were fisted tight into the front of his t-shirt, holding him close.

"Oh god, I'm so sorry." Quickly smoothing the cotton material in a frantic embarrassed motion, his threatening 'I Bite' shark now had finger pressed wrinkles on its cotton face. That didn't look very tough. But the chest beneath her hands felt taut, unyielding. Warm.

"You need to stop doing that."

"But I'm trying to fix it."

His short laugh was sexy, heated. "I don't think we're fixable. In fact, I'm fairly certain if you keep touching me like that, our hot little attraction problem will only get worse."

She stopped patting his chest. His eyes were honest with wishes.

This man would not lie. He would not charm or convince, find dramatic ways to work his way into her life.

He would ask.

Solaris wished Joshua would kiss her again. But he didn't. Shifting his body, he moved away at last, but the look in his face boldly revealed that one kiss didn't satisfy him, either.

"This feels spooky."

"Welcome to my world. Spooky happens," chuckling at his private joke he stood beside the Jeep door while she got out. Standing together, she liked how tall he was. Being near him felt safe: as if nothing bad could happen with Joshua Archer there. "Let's go meet Daddy," he declared. "Then I'm buying you the best bacon cheeseburger in California."

She grimaced. "Gah, calorie city."

"And pizza with Wyatt tonight is healthy?"

"I'll eat one slice and a small salad," she defended, "he has the rest. Plus, a giant salad drenched in blue cheese crumbles, croutons, and dressing."

He found that funny. "Your brother is built like a bull, apparently eats like a horse, and worries like a mother hen. How did a successful businessman become such an animal?"

"Maybe it's our shark, mother. Regina is successful," she patted the wrinkled Great White on his shirt, mostly just to cheat and touch the intriguing man beneath it, "she's a predator and Mother Regina definitely bites.

"Will I meet her?"

"For your sake, I hope not."

The offices of Malcolm Thornbriar were stark white inside. Joshua had never seen a building so glaring pristine. White marble floors were glossy clean. White walls held no artwork, remaining sterile of interest and purposely bare. Big windows surrounding the outer walls let in white light. Even the offices had white desks and furnishings.

The only color was the people.

"How long has he worked in this building," Joshua wondered as they cut through the busy front reception areas, followed a long hall past offices, and finally entered a private elevator so white it looked brand new, like it had never been touched. She pushed the button for the thirtieth floor.

"My entire life." Solaris looked tense. Joshua decided to hold her hand. She didn't seem to mind. He hoped she found his presence reassuring.

"But it's so clean."

"Dad has a few quirks. To him, this white on white world feels calming and beautiful, like an architectural temple or his personal sanctuary."

His brow creased. "Sounds like extreme OCD, to me."

"It is obsessive." One tanned shoulder shrugged. "I guess I'm used to it."

"No wonder your favorite color is red," he noted.

Solaris swiveled to face him, stunned. "How did you know that?"

"Easy: a red purse, red shorts, red phone, red jeep." His observation pleased her. She squeezed his hand and the corners of her lips made that cute uplifted curve. Joshua loved her smile. It made her seem so friendly. "How many people work here?"

"Sixty or seventy, but most never see my Dad. He has strict social standards. When he walks through to leave or come in, no one dares speak to him. Malcolm contacts people through his computer or the phone, if he wants something."

"It's strange for the boss to stay so isolated."

"He's a controlling man and thinks people should know their place. Each floor has a very distinct purpose, a hierarchy. Secretarial on the bottom, then construction managers going up, real estate development, property management, his attorneys are higher, and his architects next. Above everyone, isolated like some sort of king, is Dad."

They had reached the top. When the elevator opened on the thirtieth floor he expected to see a formal foyer where a secretary would greet them. Instead, the entire floor was open, without walls, with ceiling to floor windows on every side, like a gigantic glass crown jewel atop an ivory tower.

Far across the room Malcolm stood with his back to them. He was staring out the windows at the blue San Diego Bay and sunny Coronado. An imposing man, he was solidly built, like an older version of Wyatt but with neatly trimmed silver gray hair. Even his hair was a shade of white. His dress shirt was white and his neatly pressed slacks were white.

Bare feet sunk into plush white carpet.

"Oh yeah," Solaris whispered, "take off your shoes."

Joshua followed her example, removed his loafers and set their shoes on a white shelf by the elevator.

"Now wait right here, okay?"

Then Joshua watched Solaris slowly walk the entire length of Malcolm's cathedral style sanctuary, all alone. Each step on the thick carpet was silent. Even sound seemed offensive here. No air moved. Even the sounds of the city were too far away to hear. The silence was stifling. When she reached his side, standing at the sunlit windows, Solaris was the only color in a sterilized world, a beautiful butterfly surrounded by cold snow.

"You are late!" Malcolm snarled as she drew near.

"Yes, Father. I do apologize. I had car problems."

"There is no excuse for tardiness," his hateful words bit. He still had not looked at his daughter. "Have you no manners, child?"

Her stance turned rigid.

"I am not a child. I am a grown woman," she spoke with civilized diplomacy, words of a lady not bending to fear. "Six years, we have not spoken. That day, you said leaving was a mistake, that I was stupid and would fail. But I have traveled the world, explored every beautiful corner, and met with great success. I didn't fail, Father. I thrived. I believe I have proven myself worthy of your respect."

Now Joshua understood her reluctance to see Malcolm. Six years was a long time for bitter silence between daughter and father.

"You wanted this meeting." Solaris continued, her voice calm and controlled. "Here I am. I apologized for being late, politely. You preach good manners. Then you should accept my apology, graciously. Do not speak to me with that superior tone, expecting me to grovel and bend to your iron will. I am not one of your employees. I am your daughter."

Malcolm finally looked at her.

His mouth didn't turn upward at the corners like his beautiful daughter. Instead Joshua saw long hard lines carved into a face that could never be pleased. Hands were clasped behind his rod straight back. The only sign of emotion were tightly clenched knuckles. The man was furious.

"You still dare to defy me, Solaris?"

"I do not fear you. There is a difference."

"You think standing up to me makes you strong?"

"I do what I must to survive."

"Is that what the world taught you?"

"No, Father. You taught me." Her chin tilted, refusing weakness or submission. She looked him square, never flinching. "I learned to survive your vicious attacks long before I had to deal with the true wild animals of the world."

The Thornbriar overlord drew a sharp breath that hissed. In that heartbeat Joshua knew Malcolm wanted to strike Solaris, to hurt his valiant daughter for daring to be the one person he could not control. His right shoulder flinched.

Joshua was already striding across the room.

"Touch her and you will pay."

Malcolm whirled around, finding him standing there. It's said the heart and soul can be seen in a person's eyes. His light brown eyes were nothing like his daughter's.

They held no inner light.

"How dare you! Who are you, her bodyguard?"

"Today I am." Looking at Solaris, he gauged her reaction. Her pretty face had blanched, but in those lovely amber eyes Joshua saw a sweet gleam of gratitude. She gave a tiny nod. "Apparently, she needs one."

"Are you threatening me?"

"You threatened Solaris. I protect her. Hostility will not be tolerated."

Malcolm scoffed, "I'm calling the police."

"What will you say happened?" Joshua solemnly asked, "Truth is, you nearly slapped your daughter for speaking her mind. But I stopped you. I doubt the authorities will appreciate hearing what I witnessed. Or... maybe," Joshua gambled on a hunch, "I should just call Wyatt."

Malcolm steamed. Fists clenched at his sides.

His instincts were right. Wyatt was her official protector in the family. No one, not even the tyrant father would be allowed to mistreat Solaris. Why one man would hate her so deep, and the other would cherish her so extremely was baffling.

"My son is a busy man."

"Then treat your daughter with respect."

Malcolm curtly nodded to agree, but his lips were tight.

"I'm going right over there," Joshua pointed beside the elevator door. "Finish your meeting. Politely. Do not provoke me again." Then he turned and left them alone, but stood with his back against the wall prepared to snatch her away from here, if necessary.

For a while their tones were subdued and mannerly. Malcolm asked about her broken leg, then about her photography, and inquired how long she would be staying with Wyatt.

Indefinitely, she said.

Travel plans?

Traveling the world was over. Her answers were quick and factual, nothing like how a family normally shares their lives. Solaris did calmly volunteer that she was angry he never came to the hospital, never called or visited her at Wyatt's house.

Malcolm simply stated he knew she was resting and recuperating, that she was well cared for with her brother. Then he asked her to take a photography job and she flat refused.

"I will not help that egotistical monster."

"You will, if I ask nicely."

She paused, "Are you asking me nicely, Father?"

He took a crestfallen breath. Shoulders slumped. The tyrant looked apologetic and a little ashamed. "Yes, Solaris, I am asking you nice. As nicely as I know how."

She hadn't spoken since they left Malcolm's office. Solaris sat in the passenger seat, arms folded, jaw set in tight suppressed anger. Eyes glared out the window, but she saw nothing. Joshua had driven for fifteen minutes in the opposite direction from Coronado Island and she never noticed. Finally, he parked the Jeep and rolled down the windows. A warm seaside breeze brought the scent of salty water mingled with a flavored overtone of grilled hamburgers and French fries. Leaning his forearm across the top of the steering wheel, he turned toward her. Solaris was lost in thought.

"Talk to me."

"I don't want to."

He shut off the engine. "Well, we aren't moving until you do."

That met with a stubborn glare, but she quickly realized he was equally resistant. She sighed, "I hate that you saw that. Hate that you had to help me." Eyes glistened not from sorrow, but from rage. "And I hate that I couldn't refuse to do that stupid job. Why did he have to ask me nicely? Damn it. This photoshoot will be a nightmare."

"I'll go with you."

"No, I appreciate that, but I can manage Queen-zilla alone."

Glancing around, Solaris finally saw dozens of people walking, running, and riding bikes on the seaside boardwalk. It was Southern California at its finest, complete with roller-skating bikini clad women, sunbaked surfers riding the ocean waves, and vacationing families building sand castles on the beach.

"Why are we at Pacific Beach?"

"I like it here."

"Please, just take me home."

"But I promised you a cheeseburger," he pointed to the boardwalk restaurant they parked beside. The second-floor windows faced the ocean, giving a great view of the beach. "We're going up there first. Then I promise to take you home."

She became sulky. "I'm not hungry."

Joshua took another approach. She was retreating from life again, refusing to participate. He couldn't let her. He had seen the courageous intelligent woman Solaris was, had glimpsed the woman who explored the world and found beauty in every wild corner.

"I'm proud of you. Malcolm was rude, but he didn't make you cry."

She made a noisy scoff. "I've wasted enough tears on that man."

"Why does he talk to you like that?"

She blew out an angry breath. "I wish I knew. He wasn't always like that. When I was little, he used to have a heart." Memories stirred in her face. "He was different back then. Everyone was, I guess."

Toying with her seatbelt, she frowned.

"One day, I suddenly stopped being his precious little girl. Wyatt was away serving our country as an Attorney in the Navy and I was all alone. Overnight, everything changed. But that was so long ago, it hardly matters anymore. Now, Dad is heartless and cold with everyone, except with Wyatt."

"What makes your brother special?"

She hesitated, licking her bottom lip. "Can I trust you?"

"My sisters would tell you definitely, yes, I keep secrets very well."

That seemed to satisfy. "Wyatt secretly owns Dad's architectural firm."

Joshua was shocked. "How is that possible?"

"Wyatt has always been good with money. Years ago, after he stopped being a Naval Attorney Officer, he made some wise investment decisions and his global stock options paid huge profits. But here, the real estate market floundered. Dad was bankrupt. Wyatt bailed him out and restructured the corporate assets. To do that legally, he had to assume ownership. On paper, Dad became the acting CEO. Now, Wyatt never interferes, but Dad has him formally assigned as the corporate investment advisor."

What a tangled web. The son was the boss.

"What about his own investment firm?"

She made a funny scoff. "That office just gives Wyatt something to do. His income is substantial. He's a self-made multi-millionaire playing at business because he's bored. He likes to socialize, using the investment firm to establish himself in the community. He gets invited everywhere. But sometimes he just drives away for a while. He has a storage facility full of expensive cars and motorcycles. His Coronado house is paid for and he owns a dozen more around San Diego. Most he rents out, but I think he lives in a few. He's very private. I know he dates, but I never meet those women. Wyatt is an extremely smart, very wealthy man."

"And he handles your photography business too?"

"Yes, but he never takes a penny."

One thing was obvious, "He really loves you."

"Yes. I love him too. I'd be lost without Wyatt." She sniffed and looked heartbroken again.

It was time to bring her tender heart back to something good. Joshua needed to make Solaris smile. Leaning closer, narrowing the space between them, he softly asked, "Remember what we did right there in your seat, just before we went inside to your meeting?" Amber brown eyes widened as she nodded. "It was our first kiss."

She swallowed hard. "You say that as if there might be more."

"There could be. Did you enjoy our first kiss?"

"Well... I did try to rip off your shirt."

Joshua grinned, "That was fun."

"I'm embarrassed."

"Don't be. We did nothing wrong."

"It was reckless. We barely know one another. Have you done that before?"

"Never." She wasn't convinced, still looked wary. "Would it make you happier to know that I don't flirt, don't date, and I have not had a girlfriend in years. Women rarely notice me. Usually, I prefer it that way."

"Why?"

"My life has strict rules, a code of honor that all Archer's live by." It was more information than he normally shared, but Solaris was becoming his personal exception. "Today I met a woman who I couldn't resist. Maybe it was impulsive and felt a little reckless, maybe I should have waited, but kissing you really was fun."

He loved when her beautiful lips curved. "Yes, it was."

"Fun moments matter," he softly advised, watching Solaris calm as she listened to his voice. "Today, you kissed a stranger. We both liked it. A first kiss, but not our last. Now, let's take a few hours to become friends. Maybe later, if things go well, I might let you try to rip off my shirt again." That earned him a laugh. And a very nice grateful kiss.

It had been years since Solaris had visited Pacific Beach. Comfortably positioned between popular Mission Beach to the south and plush La Jolla on the northern coastal curve, it was a great place to spend the day. Life here was easy, carefree. Trouble seemed a world away. Summer was in full swing. Solaris enjoyed watching people walking the boardwalk, others lying on towels on the wide creamy beach, and playing in the sea. The waves were good sized today, bringing out surfers and water lovers of all ages to enjoy the warm California sun. It was a beautiful June day.

Joshua was great company. Upstairs, they found a table beside the open windows, letting in fresh air and sounds from the beach. They both ordered iced tea. A tiny part inside smiled when he didn't order a beer. Somehow, tea seemed more appropriate. They sat side by side on the bench seat facing the ocean. But he didn't touch or push her to talk. She liked that Joshua gave her time to come to terms with his presence in her life.

Finally, she looked at him. "Thank you."

"For what, exactly?"

"Thank you for rescuing me today."

"Did you need rescuing?" That sexy grin made her heart trip and fall. He was being playful again. When Joshua wasn't being serious, busy blending into the world, real friendliness lit his pale green eyes.

"I definitely did. Just by being there, you changed everything. Without you helping me today, I would have told off my father, said mean things I'd regret, and stormed out. Our riff would have become permanent. Then I would have locked myself inside Wyatt's house again and thrown myself the pity party of the millennium."

That last bit seemed to worry him. "Will you still?"

"No. I like what I found today, and who I found." Honesty paid off. Pleasure warmed his handsome face. "Will I see you again, after this?"

"Yes. You will." Factual, not even a maybe to consider, "Will you go to dinner and a movie with me on Saturday night?"

"But today is only Monday."

Joshua watched her for a second. "But you hoped to see me before then?" He accurately guessed and she nodded. "You will. But don't you think after the crazy way we met today, we deserve an official date?"

"I do. Saturday would be nice. And thanks for asking. A real date makes me feel better about wrinkling your shark shirt."

She liked his laugh. It was natural and sincere.

The waitress brought their iced tea. Solaris ordered a salad. But when Joshua ordered a bacon jalapeño cheeseburger and fries, she changed her mind and ordered the same. It earned her another sexy approving grin.

"Good choice. The burgers here kick ass. Madie and I found it the first day we arrived. We had driven three thousand miles cross-country together, living on coffee and too much conversation. We found a place with warm sun, great food, and a beautiful view," he nodded at the seaside world beyond their open window. "We thought we were in heaven."

"Welcome to Southern California."

"Thank you."

When their burgers arrived, Solaris was surprised how hungry she was. Along with a prancing heart and sparked curiosity, a healthy appetite had returned. She ate the whole thing and half her fries. Joshua didn't say a word, but those green eyes held gentle compassion that she liked. He was a very nice man.

"Tell me about traveling the world," he asked, opening the one door in her life that she was happy to share. Solaris spent the rest of lunch telling stories of places she had photographed, detailing the finest of her life's grand adventures. Except for Peru.

If he noticed that omission, he let it slide.

After they ate, they kept sipping tea and visiting. Solaris felt reluctant to let this end. Talking to Joshua was nice. Suddenly a busty blonde in a sparkly gold bikini stopped on the boardwalk below the restaurant and looked upstairs at them. Right at Joshua. People everywhere nearby noticed the sleek woman, almost as if she meant to capture attention.

She was beautiful. Eyes were hidden by oversized black sunglasses and her long straight hair had thick bangs that hid part of her face in a mysterious alluring way. Wearing gold heels that accented those long legs, her stance was all sassy attitude.

The woman pointed up at Joshua and shook her head as he had done something bad.

"Do you know her?"

"Unfortunately," he grumbled.

Her heart faltered in a weird stutter-step. When Solaris looked back down at the boardwalk, the woman was gone. But a commotion at the restaurant entrance proved the sexy blonde was climbing the stairs. The California bombshell had wrapped a gauzy gold sarong around her waist. The flashy material drifted around those shapely ankles.

"Let the games begin," Joshua muttered.

"What does that mean?"

"You'll see."

Ignoring everyone else, caring nothing for the attention she received, the woman sashayed across the room, aiming right for their table by the open windows. Solaris tensed.

"Hi'ya gorgeous," the stunning blonde cheerfully greeted, leaning over to give Joshua a red-lipstick kiss on the cheek as she swept by.

He barely glanced at her. "What are you doing here?"

Not answering, the uninvited guest sat beside Solaris. She moved with the ease of a woman in total control of life, who answered to no one, and broke all the rules. Glancing down at the white cast on her leg, red lips made a slight frown. "Wow. Bummer," the voice was pure Hollywood vanity, low purring and sexy. "Bet that busted leg really pisses you off. Breaking it was a real life-changer, huh?"

Solaris fumbled for words. "The cast comes off next week."

The woman tipped her chin, wondering, "And then what?"

"Life hasn't told me yet."

The blonde approved, offering her hand to shake. "Well then—I'm Madie," she announced with an impish smirk, "I don't bite," she teased about Joshua's shark t-shirt. "But apparently, that Archer does. Nice shirt, big brother. I want one."

"You need one. Don't lie to Solaris. You do bite."

Madison had a surprisingly good-natured laugh. The sex-kitten overtones were gone, replaced by a friendly Boston brogue. "Hey, top of the food chain, baby. That's me. Only the strong survive and I'm a survivor." Reaching over, she stole a leftover French fry from Joshua's plate. "Mmm. See? Chomp, chomp." Then she growled like a monster and ate it.

He scoffed, "Yeah, you're one scary shark. With lipstick and high heels. And what the hell is that outfit?" He scanned her, clicking his tongue. "I pity the men of San Diego."

"They can look, but no one can touch."

"Good rule, little sister. You should stick with that."

"You should too, brother Romeo." She gave him a naughty knowing grin. "Besides, all people see is an arrogant blonde with flash and dazzle. Blonde, curvy, and conceited. I could commit the crime of the century and later, no one could honestly say what I really looked like."

"Stick to crimes of the heart," he teased, and then quickly added, "I'd laugh my ass off if you ever got tossed into jail."

"Victoria would bail me out."

"Don't bet on it."

"Touché." Madie turned her focus toward Solaris again. "Rule number one in my world: first impressions can be deceiving. Never judge by what you see. Judge people by the truth inside your heart."

"I don't understand."

Her head coyly tipped, "Do you really think I'm just a flirty beach babe who waltzed in here to make goo-goo eyes at Joshua and ruin your day?"

"Well, I—hmm. Maybe?"

She laughed and removed the dark sunglasses. Her eyes were gold-green. Archer eyes. Like Joshua's, but with pale golden tones like her eye were shot with light. Without the oversized black lenses, her face was exotic. Eyes tilted up at the corners, like a cat. Watching her audience's stunned reaction, she removed the blonde wig. Madison's real hair was deep sable brown, twisted into a bun at the nape of her neck.

"Wow. It looked real."

"Nope, just a good wig. Here is the real me." Letting Solaris watch, Madie unpinned the thick hair and ruffled it with her fingers, letting it fall in long cocoa curls to mid-back. The dark hair changed her entire appearance.

Grinning like a sly cat with a secret, Madison found a makeup wipe in her black purse and removed the dramatic red lipstick. Fake bronzer came off next. Her real skin was porcelain smooth. The makeup had altered her face, changing tone, jawline, and cheekbones. Now that took talent. Then she stuffed the blonde wig into her handbag and pulled out a modest black cover-up dress that she slid on over the flashy gold bikini.

"Hi. I'm Madison Liberty." She grinned so friendly that Solaris smiled too. The Boston accent was thick with east coast heritage. "And it's true, I occasionally bite."

"Solaris Sullivan. I am in awe."

"It's a pleasure to meet you." They shared a small laugh. "I feel bad. You look so stunned. Didn't Joshua tell you what I do for our company?"

"No. We never got that far."

"Archer-Greenfield is a hotel management, training center, and hospitality supply firm. We own it," she pointed from her chest to Joshua's. "Our sister Victoria runs it. I stay at hotels we manage and spy on things, making certain the facilities maintain our high standards and the staff we trained follow protocol. Thus, the disguise. I can pretend to be anyone. I just can't look like myself."

"You were working today?"

Letting out an unladylike snort, green cat-eyes rolled. "If you call lying by the pool testing cocktails, working. It's a mindless job, most days. But it has some nice perks."

"I'd say so."

Clearing his throat, Joshua handed several twenties to their waitress for their bill plus a generous tip, swung long legs off the bench they had shared and stood. "Now that the show is over, I'll be right back." Panicked that he would walk away and leave her like that, Solaris looked up at him questioning, "You want your camera from my Jeep, right?"

She swallowed. "How did you know that?"

His smile was compassionate and held unspoken understanding, a real connection between hearts, warming her more than the afternoon sun.

"I just knew." Then Joshua put a firm hand upon his sister's shoulder. "Play nice, Madison Liberty. No more games."

"Of course not," she crossed her heart. Then Madison softly laughed when Solaris achingly watched Joshua walk away. "Does big brother realize he totally rocked your world today?"

Her head swung back around. "Oh Lord, I hope not. How embarrassing." The unexpected attraction seemed foolish and impulsive, but there was no judgment in Madison's eyes, only kindness. She was a striking beauty, softer now, non-threatening. Something about her smile made uneasiness disappear. She seemed trustworthy.

Solaris felt like she had found another friend.

"I won't tell him."

"Thank you."

"No problem. Girl talk stays between us. My older sister Victoria and I used to share secrets. Men don't need to know our private thoughts," she wisely declared. "Let them watch us and wonder."

"I agree."

"So, how did he find you?"

It was an oddly phrased question. "Actually, I found him. I hit your brother this morning with my Jeep, so Joshua decided I need a safe driver."

"Superman righted the wrongs in your world."

"He sure did. I'm grateful, too." Then she realized, "but tomorrow I'm on my own."

Madison leaned closer, speaking privately of secrets that only women can share, "Bet you anything that today with him isn't a one-shot deal."

"Well ... Joshua did ask me out for dinner on Saturday night."

"You said yes?" Solaris nodded. "Okay, so you two have a nice steak dinner and go see that latest comedy movie," she plotted out their future, almost as if she could see it. "You laugh and talk and have a lovely time.

Then what if Joshua wants to stick around for a while, see you again? Will you send him away?"

Solaris hadn't thought that far. "I don't have summer flings."

"Neither does he."

That made her pause. "Then maybe we shouldn't date."

Madison looked past her for a moment. It was weird. Like she saw something in the air. When she finally focused on Solaris again, she smiled with genuine approval.

"No, I think you two should date. It will be good. But be warned, Archer's don't date casually or fool around. Especially Joshua. He's the strongest of our family, a dedicated loner, not inclined to need others." Her expression turned vague again, wistful as she decided, "But you've changed that. Wow. I didn't see that coming."

"I didn't mean to."

"Don't feel bad. Alone isn't good. Having someone special to spend time with is better that being alone. Besides," she added, "it's too late to stop it now. He's falling and you're falling." Madie sagely advised, far wiser than her youthful years. "You two should be smart and fall together. Most people dabble at emotions, like treading water," she smiled, proving she liked to talk. "But treading water emotionally takes a ton of effort, barely keeps you from drowning, and never gets you to shore."

"You know, I never thought of it that way, but it's true."

, "Be smart. Fall, Solaris. Don't tread water. Your safe shore is closer than you think."

Those were deep thoughts to process. "But we only met this morning."

"It doesn't matter." Madison gave her a sisterly smile like Kianna did when giving profound advice. "One moment at the right place, in the right time, and with the right person can change everything in life. Personally, I think this change was a fantastic one."

"Gee, you make us seem so serious."

"Meeting the right person is always serious. Joshua would never admit it, but all Archer's believe in happily ever after. We must believe. Love is our only hope. If love that is stronger than fear can't save us, nothing can." It was said with unvarnished conviction.

Solaris shivered at the warning. Most of it made no sense whatsoever and left her feeling like Joshua had a strange price on his head.

"I'm not looking for love."

"Neither is he. But I see the potential. You're just shocked by today, not ready to accept the good you've found together, in such a short time." It felt right that Madison voiced her own feelings aloud. "Relax. He's shocked too."

"That makes me feel better."

"You're safe with Joshua."

"That's funny." She snickered, "I do feel safe with him."

Madie smiled wide. "Then I say if destiny hands you a cup of sunlight, you'd best be a smart woman and savor every precious drop."

Those perceptive words felt like a gift, things she needed to hear. "I haven't had much sunlight in my life, lately."

"See? You're due for some happiness." Standing, Madie shouldered her hefty black handbag full of tricks. "Sorry to shock and run," her light laugh made their meeting seem so normal, "but Life calls. It really was a pleasure to meet you. We'll see more of each other this summer," she predicted. "I hope we become very good friends."

"That would be really nice. I could use a friend."

"Then it's settled. We are friends."

Smiling, the confident woman walked away.

"Hey Madison," she paused after Solaris called out and glanced back over one shoulder. "Thanks for being honest."

"You're very welcome, Sunlight Lady. I'm glad he found you. Please, give my brother a chance. He's a very good man." Leaving questions hanging in the air, the feisty Archer sister trotted down the stairs, her long brown curls bouncing. Then Madison strode around the corner wearing her modest black sun dress, just an ordinary woman disappearing from view.

Joshua waited exactly where Madison knew he would be, leaning against the brick wall of the beachside restaurant, his eyes focused upon the black Porsche 911 Turbo parked beside his Jeep. He even wore that distrustful expression she expected to see.

"Care to explain what the hell just happened?"

"First, tell me why you kissed Solaris."

Drawing a long breath, his jaw tightened. "She told you."

Brown curls shook in denial. "Solaris would never kiss and tell. She's a lady. Life told me."

He swore and looked like Madison punched him in the gut.

"You're on my radar. Big time. The moment you met her this morning, I knew. My senses went haywire. I've been tracking you in my head ever since. Did you know, if I concentrate hard enough, I can hear your voice? Boy, that one is a serious kick in the pants."

Joshua shoved away from the wall and let out a tense huff, "Your gifts are growing stronger."

"Exponentially, even as we speak."

"Damn, Madie. I thought you lied about having the dream." Looking at her with sorrowful eyes, Joshua said it with such family love that his unreserved kindness melted her tough armor. Her own eyes burned. "I hoped you would be skipped."

"Ta-da." Arms flung in the air. "I'm cursed too."

"It isn't a curse. We are chosen."

"I don't feel chosen. I feel globally unhinged."

He sighed heavily again. "What can I do to help?"

"Teach me," she begged. Fiercely independent, asking for help was hard for Madison. Just saying it made a stifled sob catch in her throat. "I can't function like this. I need to learn to be strong like you."

"It's that bad?"

"Yes. And getting worse, day by day." It was official. She was going to cry. Before the tears could fall, Joshua tugged his sister against his chest and gave the hug that she so desperately needed. Apparently, the strongest Archer was going to rescue everyone today.

"You'll be strong. I promise to help you. We're a team now, Madie." Holding her shoulders, he gazed at her puckered face. "But you should have told me. We drove across the entire country together. You never even hinted anything was wrong. Why did you keep this a secret?"

"I hoped it was a glitch."

He scoffed and looked incredulous. "A glitch?"

"It seemed logical to hope. Compared to you and Victoria, I'm a late bloomer. You were in college when it hit. Victoria was born with it. So, I hoped my craziness would change its mind and just stop."

"It doesn't. Conquer this, or it can conquer you."

Stepping away before she broke down and cried right here on the sidewalk, Madison wiped wet eyes. "I'm okay. Go back to Solaris. Call me later, or something. Not that you need to actually call me," she dryly added as an afterthought, "because if you think about me, I will know. If you kiss her again, I will know."

"So, I have no privacy anymore, right?"

"None. Sorry."

Unexpectedly, Joshua grinned. "That's okay. Now that I know, I can block you."

"Dang, you really are strong. Teach me?"

"I will," he reassured. "It's all a matter of focus. Go to Coronado tonight. Stay with me. We'll talk there. Got your key?"

Madison felt relieved he offered. "I do. And thank you. Sorry I barged in on you like that, but I had to meet her. Solaris is very special," she looked past him, seeing things she would not share, "She is meant to become a part of our lives."

"You feel it too?"

"Of course. She is *la Señora Luz de Sol*, the Sunlight Lady." When his jaw dropped she added, "It was in my dream. Plus, I saw her tattoo. But I sense danger. Who wants to kill her?"

"That's exactly what I intend to find out."

"We can stop it."

"Yes, Madison. We will. Together."

Watching Madison drive away Joshua knew without turning Solaris had left the restaurant, saw them talking, and politely left them alone. Striding around the corner, he found her down the busy boardwalk. She sat on the wide concrete seawall watching surfers ride the rolling waves.

Long tawny hair was now loosely braided to hang over one shoulder, taming it from the light breeze. The sun on her back smiled. The white cast hung over the wall, suspended above creamy beach sand she could not touch. She looked lonely.

"I brought your camera," he stated, sitting beside her.

"Thanks." But after she removed it from the case and made a few adjustments, she didn't take any pictures. Solaris put the strap around her neck and sat with it nestled in her lap, disinterested and lost in thought.

"You saw us talking," he established.

"I did. You looked mad, like maybe you were arguing. So, I left."

He chose his explanation carefully, "Madison just said some things that I didn't like, but they were things I definitely needed to hear."

"You were discussing me."

For the first time in his life Joshua wished he could tell an outsider their family truth. "We did, then we talked about us, about being a better team. Little sister is staying at my place on Coronado tonight."

Amber eyes immediately met his, "Is she alright?"

"Let's just say that Ms. Scary Shark might have bitten off more of Life than she could chew," Joshua simplified. "She asked her big brother for help. Everything will be fine. She'll be back in charge and telling the world to kiss her ass again in no time." Everything inside his chest simmered when Solaris smiled.

"I'm glad. When I saw her crying, I felt bad."

"You liked Madie."

"She definitely earned my respect."

"In twenty minutes?"

Studying the ocean for a long moment, considering her own delicate answer to a tough question, a flicker of sadness shadowed her pretty face. "I guess I'm drawn to honest people."

"Madie can be brutally honest, to a fault."

Solaris quickly disagreed. "Brutal honesty is mean. Madison is tough, but she has heart. She isn't mean. Most people pretend to be honest about tough things. But they aren't, not really. It's just a polite varnish of words, polishing your feelings so the truth doesn't sting so much," she thoughtfully explained.

"That's deep, but I get it."

"Madison has no varnish," she decreed. "She says absolute truth. No polish, no apologies. But she says it with compassion. When you listen with an open mind, you feel like those words are a gift. You actually feel grateful for hearing the truth."

Joshua realized that Solaris had just defined exactly how he felt, too. Whenever Madison told you the truth, you did feel grateful. Knowing she trusted him to teach her to be strong, that they really were a Guardian team, he felt armed with something making him stronger.

"Exactly, what happened while I was gone?"

"Girl talk."

"About me?"

Reaching over, she found his hand. Fingers laced into his. "I can't share girl talk. You are a man. Girl talk is sacred. You and I should stick with polite polish, for now. It's safer."

Joshua agreed.

Suddenly Solaris made a funny startled-aware sound as if Life had whispered a secret. She leaned back, looking down the boardwalk behind them. "Oh, I see," she murmured to herself. Taking the lens cap off the professional Canon camera, she aimed.

Making expert adjustments to the focus, framing, and light exposure, she took a picture of a man carrying a little girl who wore a pretty white sundress. The lacy skirt draped over his arm. Adjusting again as they walked closer, she watched the pair through her telephoto lens. When the girl pointed at the sea, Solaris captured it. The man laughed and hugged her to his chest like a proud daddy.

She captured that moment too. Lowering the camera again, the photographer grinned. "That was a good one."

"Can I see?"

Locking the lens, replacing the cap to keep the glass clean, she held the hefty camera so he could view the digital screen on back.

"See, it's just a daddy and daughter taking a walk."

The little girl was only two or three, with soft baby features and bright blonde curls that looked like, a halo of gold in the sunlight. Her white dress gleamed against her father's tanned skin. The next picture showed the girl pointing at the ocean and the man looked too, both smiling. The girl's cheeks were pink with excitement. Blonde hair ruffled in the breeze. His was darker, but had caught the sunlight too.

In the last one, the father hugged her tight, his head tucked against hers. Eyes were closed as if he wanted to save this moment forever in his heart. Small arms had reached around his neck, her innocent face nestled beside his cheek. It was a moment of pure parental love.

"That's beautiful. What will you do with it?"

"Give it to them," she declared, swinging both legs over the wall to stand on the boardwalk. The man and girl were only a few feet away now.

Calling out, Solaris introduced herself, shook his hand and gave a business card from her camera case. Showing him the photographs she captured, the man's eyes grew misty as he explained that he rarely saw his daughter. He was forced to move here for work, but his daughter still lived in Oklahoma with her mom. Today was the first time they had been together since Christmas. They were on their way to meet Mom for lunch, who had gone shopping. The pair had flown in late last night and this stroll on the boardwalk was the first time the girl had ever seen the ocean.

"How much do you want for those?"

"Nothing. I wasn't working." Taking the memory card out of her Canon, she placed it into his palm. "This belongs to you."

He refused, offering payment.

"My gift is free. I haven't worked in a while. Guess I lost my motivation," she glanced down at her white cast and the man sympathetically frowned too. "Seeing you today helped me. That's payment enough."

Decisively, Solaris gently closed his fingers around the small memory square that held precious moments of his life that had been forever captured by a kindhearted stranger who saw beauty in the world. "Keep it. Please. Today is your special day with your daughter. One you will want her to remember. I just happened to be here to witness. No charge. Honest."

The man's jaw tightened with emotions that strong men try not to show. He swallowed hard. Then he slung his free arm around Solaris, gave a grateful barking laugh that released the awkward emotion, and planted a kiss on the top of her head. She was a little surprised by the hug, but laughed too. As the pair walked away, the man's step had an optimistic spring. The girl looked back and waved. "Bye!"

Solaris waved, gave a light chuckle, kneeling by the black briefcase to put her camera away. Photography time was over. Joshua watched, feeling certain she was gifted with intuition, too. She just didn't recognize it.

"You made his day."

"He deserved a good day."

"What made you look down the boardwalk?"

"I don't know," she shrugged. "It just happened."

"But you made a funny sound."

"Did I?" Finished packing away her gear, she stood close to him, no longer wary. "Sometimes I get a feeling," she touched her stomach, "like butterflies, only better. I've learned to get ready whenever that happens. When the man got closer, the feeling got stronger. I turned and there it was: a beautiful moment. So, I captured it. That's why I wanted my camera, earlier. I felt it coming. How did you know?"

He didn't lie. "I sensed it." Their gazes locked. He ached to touch this extraordinary woman. Solaris was integrity, excellence, and beauty: the finest parts of Life, inside and out.

"Like I sensed your book of maps?"

"Something like that."

"We seem uniquely connected," she approved.

Joshua knew he was hooked. "I think it's nice."

"Yes, it is," she softly agreed. "I never told anyone about my butterfly feelings. When I pay attention to it, good things happen. Do you ever get strange little nudges like that?"

"All the time," he honestly acknowledged, then chuckled. "But Life never politely nudges at me. It shoves."

Lips sweetly curved. "Like it shoved us together?"

"Exactly."

As if drawn by his will, she stepped right into his arms. But they didn't kiss. His hands wandered no further than her waist. For several grateful moments, he simply held her, cradling Solaris against his heart.

"I had a really good day, Joshua."

"Me too. Ready to go home?"

"Sure."

Coronado Island

To have a friend, you must be a friend.

~~ Madison Liberty Archer

Waiting for Joshua to come home was boring. Madison ate some roasted chicken she found in the refrigerator. Then took a quick shower to rinse the sunscreen off her skin, let her brown curls air dry, and enjoyed being ordinary. No makeup, casual denim shorts, and a plain yellow tank top. Being a chameleon was fun, but she had bigger challenges to tackle. With Joshua on her side, she could conquer this mental monster.

Hopefully.

Trying to stay busy, she watered the flowers growing in the back yard. She talked to the stray orange and white calico cat that eyed her with suspicion from his safe perch on the branch of the cypress tree.

"Go home, buddy." She told him. The cat made a forlorn mewling sound. "Don't you have a home?" The cat blinked. The calico had a funny black patch circling one yellowy-green eye. The base color was white, but his body was mottled with odd orange splotches that looked like a pirate coat and his legs had four black boots.

He wasn't wearing a collar.

She named him Captain Henry Morgan.

Cleaning the house for a while kept her busy. Later, she emptied the house garbage into the steel dumpster in the back alley and locked the back gate. Talking to the King of Pirates again, he purred and licked black paws. Madison wiped down the kitchen and all three bathrooms, although everything was already relatively clean.

Joshua was a tidy man.

Even his laundry was neatly folded.

The sun was setting and cat still sat in the tree, looking at the house. Madison decided that Captain Morgan must be hungry. Since they had no cat food, she took him pieces of the roasted chicken. As soon as he smelled food, the big cat jumped down from the tree and marched across the yard like he owned it. He ate quick and then gave her a rough mournful, "Rraaow," asking for more.

"Okay, but don't tell Joshua."

The Captain ate another fistful of chicken, sat back on his rump and licked his front paws. Then he purred to say thank you and rubbed against her bare legs.

Madison was smitten.

"Come here, buddy." Scooping him up, she felt ribs. Yellowy-green eyes were grateful but disheartened. The big tomcat was homeless.

"Joshua will shoot me."

But Captain purred.

An hour later, Madison and the happily fed calico sat in a cushioned deck chair on the white railed second story balcony that faced the ocean. Captain Morgan was pretending to sleep. She watched Navy fighter jets roar and scream skyward as they left the airstrip. Pilots were practicing touch and go flights from the Naval Air Station North Island, executing training exercises over the Coronado skies. On the distant horizon where the sun was beginning to set and turn the sky pink, she could see the outline of an aircraft carrier.

It was reassuring to see evidence that she and Joshua were not the only people determined to keep innocent lives free from harm.

As it grew dark and stars mselves in the night, she closed her eyes and instantly saw her brother. Joshua had been blocking her, quite effectively, too. But he was distracted now, focused on someone else.

Madison saw him with clarity.

He was telling Solaris goodbye. They were at her red Jeep, here on the island. He wanted to kiss her. The attraction between them was intense. Joshua wanted to touch Solaris, but strict Archer rules clamored in his mind. The internal war created emotional chaos inside her brother. But he didn't give in. Instead he opened his arms and pulled her close, hugged her against his heart. They stood that way for a while. A sense of acceptance surrounded the pair.

Then static. Joshua blocked her again.

Madison opened her eyes. "Tricky brother," she told Captain Morgan. "I hope she doesn't break his heart."

Captain mewed to agree.

She waited, thinking about the things she knew but could not tell him, doubting she would ever become as strong inside as Joshua. Right now, controlling this beast seemed impossible. Everything she saw made Madie want to fight or cry.

Below the balcony, a black Jeep finally rumbled into the driveway. He tried to park inside the garage that he opened with a remote, but her Porsche was already there. It was parked slightly sideways, hogging more than half the space. The garage door growled closed.

"Sorry!" she called down over the balcony railing.

"Who taught you to drive, Madison?" He barked, getting out of his black beast.

"You did."

Joshua looked up. "What the hell are you holding?"

"Oh. This is Captain Henry Morgan, the King of Pirates." She hugged the calico, making him wave one black booted paw. The Captain didn't mind. He was thrilled about his impending adoption.

"Is that the cat from the back yard?"

"Yes. He was hungry." Giving them a nasty scowl, Joshua slammed his Jeep door a little harder than necessary and marched inside the beach house. "Oh shit."

Madison dropped the cat in the deck chair and ran barefoot through the upstairs rooms. She liked the new oak floors of this house, prettier than the worn smooth centennial flooring from home, but her bare feet skid a little on the slick surface. She nearly wiped out as she ran. Scrambling, she met Joshua at the base of the stairs in the living room.

"Sorry. I should have asked." He didn't look happy. Madie tried another approach. "We can take him to the humane society in the morning," she offered.

Captain Henry Morgan had followed her. She heard his thick paws thump-thump in a funny rabbit hop down the oak staircase. She didn't look. A whiskery face rubbed against her bare ankle. Captain yowled for attention and she ignored it. Joshua grumbled something about taking responsibility and knelt down. Snapping his fingers, the big cat lazily sauntered over to him.

"You fed him the roasted chicken?"

"Yes. I felt sorry for him sitting out there in the tree."

His fingers rubbed furry ears and stroked down his multi-colored back. Captain purred. "That's okay. I bought it to feed him."

"Oh. Really? Well. I ate some too."

Joshua chuckled, "Good job, Madie. You ate the cat food." She childishly stuck out her tongue. "He's been out there in the tree all week. I thought he'd get tired of glaring at the house and go home."

"Maybe this is his real home," she judged. "The beach house is rental property. Maybe the people who use to live here jumped ship and left poor Henry outside, all alone."

"That's what I suspect, too."

Seeing his expression soften, she felt better. Joshua hated animal cruelty. Deserting a domesticated animal was heartless and her brother had a big heart. Proving it, he rubbed the cat with both hands. Captain purred loud, then the badly painted calico flopped over on the oak floor to show how friendly he was.

Joshua rubbed him more.

When he finished, the big cat seemed to smile.

"Captain Henry Morgan," he repeated as he stood, brushing white and orange hair off his hands. "Did you check? Maybe this is Miss Pretty Kitty."

"Nope. Boy. Neutered. He's even declawed. At one time, somebody cared enough to take care of business. Now, he's all alone."

Sensing a sympathetic heart, the tom wandered her way again. Yellowy-green eyes looked up at her, hopeful. He meowed, sad and raspy. That's when Madison noticed Captain had a small black goatee streaked under his white chin and a tiny black squiggle above his upper lip. The tips of his ears were orange. So was the tip of his tail. Suddenly that neglected oddball cat represented all the cruel injustice in the world. He was a misfit. So was she.

Madison scooped him up again.

Captain was in heaven.

"He sure is funny looking," Joshua declared.

"I think he has character."

"No, honey. You have character," he chuckled. "Henry looks like he stole a box of finger paints and did a drunken Picasso painting on himself."

Madison liked that. "Aaarrgh, Capt'n Archer," she snarled like a gruff old pirate, holding Henry up to face Joshua. Her hands around his ribs, his long body stretched out, looking like a furry puppet. With a flicking tail.

"We pirate's don't take no sass from you land-lovin' pilgrims." She wiggled Henry as she gave him a voice. "I likes me rum and I likes me roast chicken. Now give us yer' loot Matey, before I kick yer' royal booty down to Davey Jones locker!"

Joshua busted out laughing. The man was too serious most of the time. Madison loved making her brother smile. "Oh god, Madi. You're too funny."

"We misfit pirates aim to please," she curtseyed, hugged the rogue tom for a moment and set Captain Morgan down. The cat mewed up at Joshua, who was still snickering.

She knew she had won.

"Can we keep him?"

"Sure."

It made her whole summer.

"Tomorrow, buy him real cat food. I bought a cat box and litter, yesterday. It's in the garage. It he's staying inside tonight, get everything set up so he can use it. I suspect he's already housebroken."

She grinned. "You already planned to keep him."

"Don't tell anyone, but I felt bad for Captain Morgan too. It's a cool name. It suits him. Welcome to your new family, Henry. Trust me, this family sticks together. You're stuck on this Archer ship now. Let's get some meat on your skinny bones." The pirate purred and followed them into the kitchen. Joshua found a bowl and gave him the rest of the chicken.

"Now, about you," his expression grew serious again as they made their own dinner of spaghetti and meatballs, "how are you? Inside here," he tapped his own chest.

"It's better whenever I'm near you. That's why riding out here didn't bother me. We stayed close the whole time. But then I left you and it got bad. When we are apart my senses go nuts. You haunt me. I hear your voice, I know what you are doing and who you are with, and if you are in danger or not. I swear I could track you down blindfolded."

"You really are assigned to me."

"Looks like it."

"No Archer Guardian has ever been assigned to watch over another family member before." His stern expression implied this was monumental. "Whatever life is bringing our way, I'm grateful you're my Guardian, Madie."

It warmed her inside. "Thanks. I'll do my best."

"You said Solaris was in your dream. Did you see Wyatt too?"

"Who is that?"

"Her brother: big guy, solid as a rock, sandy brown hair."

"No. I saw Solaris running. I saw you fighting dark shadows, like people I couldn't see. There were guns and," she refused to tell him the rest. "I woke up and knew we were coming to Coronado Island. It's good that you found her. What time are you meeting her tomorrow?"

Joshua dropped a meatball on the floor. "How'd you know that?"

"You let your guard down for a minute."

His brow arched. "See anything interesting?"

"Not really. Just two people who wanted to kiss, but hugged instead. Nice move, brother. You'll win her trust, earn her friendship, but those silly puritan rules waging war inside your head seriously need modernizing."

Joshua grinned. "You think?"

"Hell. I know."

That amused him. "Solaris promised to meet me on the sun deck at the Hotel Del Coronado at nine. We're having breakfast. Want to come?"

"I'd be a third wheel."

"No, she likes you. After you shocked her speechless with your blonde goddess routine, you made a very positive impression." While Joshua poured two glasses of iced tea, he told her what Solaris said about speaking the truth, polite polish, and sacred girl talk. Then told the story of how she gave those beautiful pictures to that man.

"She sounds incredible. I knew she had a good heart." Secretly, Madison was thrilled she had encouraged Solaris to give Joshua a chance. "Maybe I'll go with you tomorrow morning. It's weird not knowing anyone. In Boston, I know tons of people. I'd love to have a real friend."

"That's a good idea. You two becoming close would help all of us. Solaris has shades of death and danger surrounding her. I need to figure out why."

"You see auras?"

"Sure, so does Victoria. Don't you?"

"No. I see," one hand stirred circles by her temple in a crazy sign. "I'm not sure what to do with the epic visions of apocalypse and destruction that I see."

"You see pictures?"

She nodded. "With feelings. It's like I'm there."

"Wow. Okay. That really is epic. But don't worry. We'll figure it out."

But Madison recalled those insights and felt anxious. "Can I stay here with you, for now? Being off on my own wasn't a good idea. It's easier when we are close."

"My house is your house. Come and go as you please. Just promise to tell me if you decide to stay in a hotel. I know you get bored. That's fine. Have fun. Work, explore California. But unlike you, I don't have a built-in tracking system. My gifts are different. Don't make me worry about you, Madison."

"I'll let you know where I am."

"Thank you."

"But you must promise to tell me if you ever need privacy. Don't let me walk in here late one night and see naked people. I'll go blind."

He almost choked on his iced tea. "Naked people? Damn, Madie."

"It could happen."

Joshua adamantly disagreed. "Have some faith in me. I won't sleep with Solaris. She is my assignment. I'm here to protect her. I am her Guardian. That is all." Madison was not buying his arguments. She laughed aloud. "One kiss does not make her my girlfriend."

"Oh brother, you lie to yourself."

"We'll see."

Joshua crept into her bedroom at dawn. Madison's lessons started today. As he reached for her shoulder, he almost laughed aloud. His sister's cotton sleep shorts and purple tank top were covered in fuzzy white fur. Captain Henry Morgan slept along her side. Except, he lay upside down in the bed, head down, tail toward the pillows, and his legs dangled straight up in the air. Madie's hand lay on his furry spotted belly.

Yellow-green eyes opened, saw Joshua leaning over them and blinked. Then the happy tom yawned wide and leisurely stretched like he was in heaven.

"Crazy cat."

At his whisper, Madison's body jerked like she'd received an electric shock. Eyes flew open as she sat up and immediately took a swing at him. Joshua blocked it with a forearm. Another quick jab connected with his chest. Springing up with ninja finesse, his sister pivoted and kicked out hard.

The Captain yowled and ran for cover.

Joshua caught her foot by the ankle, grabbed her hip and flipped her over in the bed, tucking the leg behind his knee. Then he leaned over Madison in a body lock just tight enough she could not move.

"Nice reflexes."

Hearing his voice, she drew a deep breath. Consciousness set it.

"I see your kickboxing classes were effective." He released her.

She rolled to face him and blinked. "Oh, it's you."

"You weren't even awake and you fought like that?"

Fully aware now, she apologized, "Sorry." She sat on the edge of the rumbled bed and raked both hands through her wild brown curls. "You shouldn't creep up on me," she huffed, breathing through the adrenaline still charging through her veins. "Don't do that again."

"Next time I'll react faster."

"Did I hurt you?"

"No. But you scared the holy hell out of Henry," he hooked one thumb toward the laundry basket where wide yellowy eyes glared at them from the shadows. "Brave pirate," he chuckled as Madison rushed to him, scooped up the big cat and cuddled him like a cherished baby. "And that's why your purple night shirt is covered in white hair."

"He hates being alone."

"Don't we all," he dryly commented, turning to leave. "Get ready. We're running the beach to get warmed up. Guardians must stay strong. Then you can show me what else you know."

"You're training me?"

"Learning to use your gift happens on the inside. You will train yourself. I can show you the way, give advice, but only you can learn to harness your full potential." Closing the bedroom door, he left her with that thought.

When Madison met him on Coronado beach, Joshua stood watching the ocean. The waves were big today, thundering into shore.

Curls tamed in a ponytail, she was ready for action in sleek black shorts and a strappy hot pink sports top that hugged her curvy body. Madison ran at him full blast. In a sideswipe motion, at the last instant she spun and kicked, but he easily outmaneuvered her long legs.

She was all energy, no focus.

Joshua caught her knee with his, hooking her leg.

They both went down.

Laughing at the game, she sprang to her feet like a cat and charged down the wet sand without him. It didn't take long for Joshua to catch up. His legs were longer and she was burning out fast. After she sprinted full out for a while, she broke stride and turned around, walking with one hand on her aching side.

"Life isn't a race, Madison," he advised, walking beside her. "It's a marathon. The finish line isn't the only goal to achieve. To really win at life, you have to conquer all the small tough moments along the way."

She grinned, "Okay, I must learn self-control. I can do that." She squinted at him in the morning sun. "Are you conquering your tough moments, brother?"

"Most days."

"Did you have self-control yesterday?"

"Not especially," he snickered and took off running again. Just thinking about Solaris put a strange twist inside. He felt conflicted, torn between duty and desire. Even his dreams last night were a lusty tangle of wishes that had no place inside his Archer Guardian heart.

When Madison caught up to him at their starting place near their house, he took off his running shoes, pulled off his t-shirt because he was warm, and from his shorts pocket he handed her a black blindfold.

"Put it on. Take off your shoes. If you can track me anywhere, prove it."

Nodding curtly, she obeyed. With sounds being muffled by the large waves, he stepped away. Slowly, he put distance between them. Bare feet were nearly silent. Then he ran. Hard. She tipped her head and followed. Running right, then to the left, he looped in a big circle around her. She turned, always facing him.

Madison loved games.

Fun-loving and playful, normally chasing her brother on the beach would have made her laugh. Not this time. Her face was smooth of emotion, betraying nothing.

A true Archer Guardian. He was impressed.

Taking another approach, Joshua charged in fast and swung his foot out at her ankles. She blocked it, catching him hard in a tangle of legs. He went down and rolled in the sand.

She smirked, just a little.

Jumping up, they ran together at an all-out sprint. Madison didn't hold her arms out like an unsighted person might. She didn't stumble. Her steps were sure. She chased him as he wove and dodged. She never faltered.

Madison chased him right into the ocean. When they hit the cold sea, she didn't panic or remove the blindfold. When Joshua went into deeper water, testing her abilities, his sister dove through a big wave that crashed over her head. She swam with long sure strokes straight up to his chest. Deep in the waves now, the undercurrent was strong. It pulled at their bodies and felt dangerous, much stronger than he had anticipated.

"Swim, Joshua!"

Another wave tried to take them out to sea. He clasped her hand. "Don't let go. Stay together, no matter what." Using all his strength against the water, he tried to tow them both toward shore. She swam hard too, kicking those strong lean legs against the riptide. It took a while, fighting the flow of the ocean, being pummeled by thundering waves crashing over their heads, bouncing them around. But they stayed together. When their feet finally reached sand again, she seemed relieved. Together, they trudged out of the sea to the safe shore.

Madison still wore the blindfold.

Worn out from fighting the current, she plopped down in the dry sand. Water dribbled off her body and hair. Drenched and drained too, Joshua decided sitting down was a great idea. First, he knelt in front of her and removed the blindfold.

"You amaze me."

"I did?"

"Yes. Good job."

"Thanks."

Pulling on his tee shirt again, wishing he had thought to bring towels, Joshua raked both hands through wet hair and sat down beside her.

"How did you know where I was?"

"I see it," she simply stated.

"In your mind, you can see me moving?"

"No. I see pictures of where you will be."

Joshua felt stunned. "You see the future?"

"At first, I do. But the instant that I get involved in that future it becomes something else. It's like the future is a room with open doors. I have to choose one. Blocking your kick was easy. Running after you was easy too. When we dove into the ocean, I suddenly envisioned you lying on the shore, half drowned, spitting up seawater. But you gripped my hand and immediately I knew the undertow wouldn't get us. Together we could make it back to shore. And we did."

He felt so proud of her. "Now you know what your gift is."

"I don't understand."

"When you participate in life, you have the power to change it. Those forewarnings are the choices you have: the doors are the possible endings. Knowledge is your power, Madison. Choosing the right door changes things. If you learn to harness that and use it to do good for others, you could become even stronger than me."

She finally smiled. "I love you, Joshua."

"Love you too. We make a good team."

"We will be, eventually. I have to master my crazy Mind Monster first." Squinting a little, she looked down the beach and swallowed hard, "Want to know what I see in your future?"

"Is it bad?"

She thought for a moment, then Madison hid whatever she really saw, met his gaze and laughed, "I see a nice hot shower. Then a hot date with a hot lady photographer."

"Breakfast at the resort is not a date."

Standing, he offered his hand and pulled her up too. Their feet were too wet and sandy for shoes. They carried them. Feeling proud of Madie, glad they were together, he slung one arm around her shoulders as they trudged through the thicker sand toward their house. The slope inland was gradual but the beige sand was soft around their feet, making walking slow. Doing this daily would definitely build muscles.

"You are coming to breakfast with me today, right?"

Madison sighed, "Solaris won't want me there."

"Maybe you should ask her."

Joshua pointed toward the concrete stairway where the neighborhood sidewalk along Ocean Boulevard dropped down to allow people onto the sand. A woman stood on the steps, her white cast keeping her from walking on the beach. She looked embarrassed to get caught watching. A thick black professional camera hung by the strap looped over her shoulder, but he knew a minute ago that lens was aimed at them.

"You knew!"

"I felt her there," Joshua waved. Solaris hesitated. Then she waved back. "She's been watching us for a while."

"I totally missed that. She isn't in my circle of focus. How'd she find us?"

"Maybe she's lucky."

Madie scoffed. "You don't believe in luck."

"No, but I do believe Life brings people together when they need it. She needs a friend. You do too. There your friend is, Madison," he gently advised. "She's standing right there feeling nervous, thinking about leaving. She'll walk away now. Then Solaris will avoid us because she's embarrassed we caught her taking pictures. Are you going to let that future happen?"

"Absolutely not!"

Madison took off at a run, charging through the last forty yards of thick sand. Walking at a casual pace, Joshua gave them time to talk. Plus, he needed a moment to look at Solaris, to think about self-control, and to vow he would not kiss or touch her.

Today she wore navy blue dress shorts with little gold sailor accents, a lacy white blouse with a camisole underneath to keep the sheer material from being see-through, and the white smile sneaker. A thick French braid lay over one shoulder. It was tied with a red ribbon.

She looked so pretty.

The women were laughing. He could hear their happy voices and saw budding friendship on their faces. Solaris was showing Madison the pictures she took of them. She pointed to one. Both ladies looked at him and gave a secret smile.

Oh boy. That looked like trouble.

Maybe he didn't want them being friends. It was probably too late. They already spoke that secret female language of arched glances and low giggles that held mysterious meaning, a language no man could ever accurately translate.

As he approached, Solaris asked Madison to join them for breakfast at the Hotel Del Coronado. "I haven't worked in a while. Since I'm living here now, Wyatt says I should photograph people instead of wildlife and nature. I need practice. Would you like to be my model today? Whatever I shoot, you get to keep."

His sister was thrilled, bouncing on her heels. "I'd love to. Since it's a historical place can I pretend to be someone classic and vintage, but elegant? I'm envisioning auburn hair and dark chocolate brown eyes, pale skin with red lips. A little cleavage," she tugged at the well-endowed neckline of her sports bra. "What do you think?"

"You can be anyone you want."

"Ooh, this will be fun!" Excusing herself, Madison announced she was taking a shower and ran across Ocean Boulevard toward their beach house, leaving them alone.

"You just made a friend for life," he praised.

"Not for life. Just for today."

"Trust me, little sister is extremely loyal." Joshua stopped walking a step below her, which put them face to face. "You're awake early. Did you get another case of the butterflies?"

93

"Yes. But I had no idea my fluttery feeling would be you." She looked happy that he remembered her photography instinct and would talk about it with such casual acceptance.

"Did you drive?"

"Wyatt's house is only a few blocks away. I walked." She pointed up Ocean Boulevard, closer to the Hotel Del and further inland.

"We're almost neighbors." He noted, making her lips sweetly curve. Joshua thought about his stupid vow not to kiss or touch.

"I took your picture," she anxiously blurted. "Sorry."

He grinned. "Your camera didn't explode?"

"No, but you might."

"I'm not mad. I was kidding yesterday."

"Yes, but today is Tuesday," she flirted, offering a red travel thermos she brought from home, "Want some coffee? I'd hate to see what you become without your morning caffeine."

He lifted the lid and took a sip. The coffee was flavored with caramel creamer. "It's good. Thanks for sharing."

"No problem," while Joshua sipped again and decided he liked the sweetened brew, Solaris nervously chatted to fill the silence, "I figure, you kissed me—well, I kissed you, too. You seem like a well-mannered man. Since we kissed already, I guess sharing a little morning coffee isn't too terribly uncivilized."

He grinned as his mind went south.

"If you do it right," he huskily told her, "good morning coffee should never be civilized."

Solaris blushed. "I meant sharing a mug. You know, drinking after each other. Wow. Your mind is corrupt."

"My thoughts are totally innocent."

"Is that why my face feels hot and you're smiling like the Cheshire cat? No, I think somehow sharing a simple cup of morning coffee translated into ideas of a sexy good morning breakfast in bed."

"Sex isn't innocent?"

"Joshua!"

He chuckled and asked, "Can I see the pictures?"

On the digital view screen on the back of her professional DSLR camera, he saw Madison blindfolded, tracking him and her smirk when she tripped him. Then he saw their leap through the big waves. Then numerous shots as they swam ashore together, fighting the current. In the next one he had knelt down, removing her blindfold. Madison's wet back was toward the camera, but Solaris had captured his proud big brother expression.

It was a nice moment.

Then they sat together on the sand, heads leaning together as they talked, backs to the photographer. Blue waves spread out before them like the endlessly changing future. In the final shot brother and sister were walking toward her through the creamy sand.

He had looked up at Solaris and smiled.

"That one is my favorite," she softly confessed.

"I was happy to see you."

The honesty made her swallow hard. "I almost left. Then you smiled at me and I decided to stay. I was worried you might think the crazy lady with the camera was a weird paparazzi stalker. I really was shocked to find you out here this morning."

Joshua covered the coffee and set it on the step by her feet. When he stood upright again, they had somehow moved closer. "But you listened to those butterfly feelings," he prompted, hoping she might recognize her intuitive gift, "and something good happened, didn't it?"

"Yes. I got to see your fun, playful side."

"You didn't see that yesterday?"

"Not too much. You were very serious."

Taking that as an invitation to play, his hands found her waist. His vow not to touch her had lasted ten whole minutes.

Her breathing became unstable.

Amber eyes were wide and questioning.

Today she smelled like peach vanilla perfume. Unlike he and Madison, Solaris had taken time to get ready this morning. He still looked rough, had sand on his skin, and needed to shave. But he saw approval in her eyes.

It made his vow seem silly.

"You look really pretty today."

"Thank you," she glanced down at the cute nautical themed shorts that were neatly ironed. Then her gaze met his again. "I have to be honest. Last night, I managed to convince myself that our spooky attraction wasn't real. Then I got up this morning and dressed knowing I'd see you, hoping today you would smile at me. I came to the beach expecting to see dolphins riding the surf. Instead, I found you and Madison chasing each other around. When you smiled at me, it was almost as if I had wished it."

"Maybe you did."

They were a breath away from kissing. "Let's not complicate things yet," she whispered, drawing back. "It's early. Complicated things can come later."

"We still feel spooky?"

"Very. You're in my head, Joshua. Right here too," fingers touched her upper chest. "No one has ever accomplished that."

"I feel the same way."

"But you aren't shocked. Why is that?"

"Maybe I adjust faster. Come inside with me. I need to shower and change before I spend another day trying real hard not to touch you, not to complicate life, and not to kiss you until we both forget all the rules."

He watched her lips slowly curve. Solaris seemed to breathe easier now.

"Then I'll drive us to breakfast," he continued. "Pancakes aren't complicated, are they?"

"Not usually." Taking her hand, Joshua led them across the palm tree lined street. Traffic was light. The town was stirring.

Down the next block to the north, he noticed a man wearing all black, sitting astride an expensive Ducati Streetfighter motorcycle. The sleek racing bike was dark stealth black. His helmet was on, the sunshade visor lowered to hide his face. Parked beside the road, the rider leaned forward on the handlebars, watching them intently.

How long had he been there?

The motor idled in a low rumble, but the kickstand was down. Even more threatening than the black clothes, a dark ominous shadow clung to the rider. The danger surrounding him was so strong Joshua saw the warning aura without even trying.

"Laurie. Babe. Go inside the house!"

But she was frozen, wide-eyed, staring at the Ducati rider.

The rider shook his head at her.

It was a subtle move, but Joshua saw.

Apparently having seen enough, the rider roughly flipped the kickstand up with the heel of his boot, gunned the engine to obnoxious loud levels, and peeled out in a slow smoky circle that took him in the opposite direction and left the air smelling like burnt rubber.

They watched him roar away.

"Friend of yours?" He asked Solaris.

"No friend of mine would act like that."

Considering the athletic size and apparent height of the rider, Joshua had a suspicious thought, "What is Wyatt doing today?"

"I don't know. After dinner last night, he got a phone call and took off. I assumed it was to see a woman because he dressed nice. Wherever he went, he must have had a good time, because he didn't come home."

"Is that normal for him?"

Solaris nodded. "Wyatt is a sworn bachelor who enjoys living larger than life and is extremely secretive about his affairs. I don't question his lifestyle. Usually," she swallowed, "he does not question mine."

"He had issues with me."

She didn't look happy. "My brother wants to meet you. Wyatt didn't say where or indicate when. It doesn't matter, if he wants to talk, he'll find us."

"That sounds like fun. Not."

"Wyatt isn't the enemy. He's family."

"Right. I'll keep that in mind."

Glancing down the street where the black racing bike had sat before it noisily roared away, he recalled the broad tense shoulders and attitude of anger surrounding the rider.

Joshua knew he'd just met enemy number one.

Inside, the two-story beach house wasn't as large and opulent as Wyatt's mansion, but it had friendly charm that fit the Archer's personality. Oak flooring had a new luster and seashell cream walls were nicely decorated in a nautical theme. It had lots of windows to view the sea.

In the living room, a big calico cat mewled a raspy greeting.

"Hi, Henry. Good boy." Joshua bent to rub his head. The tom purred and looked at him with a happy gleam in his yellow-green eyes. "Solaris, meet Captain Henry Morgan. This was his home before we moved in. He's a nice pirate. As long as he gets fed and gets to sleep with Madie, we're allowed to stay aboard his ship."

She found the idea cute. "You must like cats."

"I like animals. But Captain claimed Madie as his damsel in distress."

Upstairs, they heard a door open. Madison appeared at the top of the stairs wearing a thick white robe. Her dark curls were wet, but clean, hanging to mid-back. "I heard voices. Are you showering now, Joshua?"

"Got to. I'm all sandy."

"Then come upstairs with me, Solaris," she offered. "We can chat while I get ready. It will be fun." Then she noted the white cast on her left leg. "Help her upstairs, brother."

"I can do it," Solaris independently assured, proving her ability by climbing a few. "Wyatt's house has stairs."

Both Archers watched her, that focus felt protective.

"Does it still hurt?" Madison asked as she climbed.

"No. After two months, its healed. Now it's just awkward." When she safely reached the top, Joshua walking behind her in case she fell, they looked relieved. Solaris found their concern silly, considering the dangers she had survived in the past. But then, she did live with mother-hen Wyatt now. Worry was his constant state of mind.

Madison guided her into a bedroom on the left end of the hall.

"Don't take all day getting beautiful," Joshua warned. "I'm hungry." At his own bedroom door he turned and smiled at her. So handsome. Fluttery heat knotted inside her chest.

"That smile sure looks complicated, to me."

"It might be." Smiling wider, he closed the door.

Being with Madison was fun. Solaris got comfortable in a plush burgundy armchair while her model for today tried on several dresses. It was nice to have a friend who had style. Kianna was like a sister, but they never discussed beauty. Their everyday look was a braid or ponytail, hiking boots, sunscreen, and a hat. Functional, not fashionable.

Together they settled on a white sundress reminiscent of the fifties, with a flared skirt and slender fitted bodice that accented her slim waist and feminine curves. It was perfect for the historic hotel. Solaris tried to convince her to wear her own hair, but Madie thought her brown curls were boring and chose an elegant auburn wig that tumbled in fiery waves past her shoulders and had bangs that covered her own dark brows.

"I bleached my hair once, years ago in high school," Madison revealed as she adjusted the wig in the wide bathroom mirror.

"Did you like it?"

"Hated it. It was horrible." Happy and sociable today, the Boston accent was thick as she chatted. "I didn't choose a nice blonde shade, it was platinum white. Awful, a truly awful color. I looked like some futuristic anemic alien." That made Solaris laugh. "Victoria took me to the salon so they could color it back, but the chemicals dried it out. Huge hair mistake. It took forever to get it healthy again. I had to get it trimmed regularly. Have you ever cut yours?"

"Not in years."

"Color?"

"Never. This is all me."

"It's really pretty. I like the sun streaks. You have natural beauty. Victoria is like you, very classic and ladylike. It's a quality I envy."

"Thanks. But I think your beauty is exotic."

"Nah," Madison laughed with self-depreciating modesty that made her extremely likeable. "I'm just a chameleon. But it's hollow play-acting. I've never done anything important that makes a difference in someone's life. I have too much imagination, not enough moxy."

"What does 'moxy' mean?"

She turned from working on the auburn lady in the mirror. "Guts. Inner strength. Courage."

"Then I think you have tons of moxy," Solaris disagreed. "It takes courage to move across the country and start a new life. It takes guts to make new friends. You made friends with me in twenty minutes yesterday. You said all the right things, showed me who you really are and proved yourself trustworthy. That isn't easy. So, you must have inner strength, or I wouldn't have liked you."

Madison was pleased. "Thanks. I'm glad you see inside the heart."

Applying mascara and eye shadow with skill, the effect made her pale gold-green eyes look bright hazel. Then she put in dark brown contacts. They weren't like ordinary lenses. No green showed through. Her eyes became deep chocolate brown. The eye makeup looked sultry, her eyes very large and seductive. It complimented the auburn hair.

"Can I ask you something, between us," Madison inquired as she worked. "Do you promise to tell me the truth?"

"Only if I get to ask a question too."

"Ooh, a game." Madison giggled. "It's a deal."

"You go first," Solaris prompted.

"Okay. Who was the man on the black racing motorcycle? I saw him when I came inside. He seemed really mad that you were with Joshua."

Her first instinct was impossible. The very idea made her heart clench in a painful broken ache. "The only man who might care who I'm with," Solaris swallowed rising sadness, "is gone. I've haven't lived in San Diego for years. I honestly don't know who it was."

"Your brother cares. Is he a problem?"

"Wyatt is overprotective, but I think he means well." Unfortunately, with Tristan gone, her worried brother topped the list of mysterious men who might have been hidden behind that black helmet and dark clothes.

No one else would watch her.

No one else loved her enough to care.

Madison suddenly swiveled around, now a glamourous stranger. Her smooth skin was luminous with blush swept over high cheekbones. Ruby red lips. Auburn waves, the sultry doe-eyes, and white sundress lent mystery and innocence. Her colors complimented the historic white walls and red roof of the Victorian hotel. She would be amazing to photograph.

"Now ask me your question," Madison amiably allowed, coming into the bedroom. "I know you have a good one." She sat on the bed. "Whatever you ask, I promise to give the truth."

"Yesterday, you called me Lady Sunlight. Where did you hear that name?"

Madison took a deep breath, choosing her response. "Would you believe I heard it in a dream?" She finally burst out. "In that dream, I saw your face and the smiling sun tattoo on your back. Then yesterday, there you were." She gave a shoulder shrug to lighten the shocking confession. "Sometimes I just know things like that."

Solaris could only make a tense sound.

"Are you mad?"

"No, not at all. I believe you about the dream. And somehow," she realized, "that's okay. In fact, everything we talk about feels okay. Yesterday your brother walked into my life and we just," she wiggled agitated fingers in his general direction of the house, at a loss for words. "I swear the spookiest things keep happening to me. Why is that?"

"Joshua says that life brings people together when they need it the most. You need a woman friend to trust. I need a friend too. Voilà, here we are."

"And Joshua? I don't need—that."

"Every woman needs *that*," his witty sister laughed.

Solaris giggled at the naughty joke. "Sheesh, I can't even think about sex. And him," she breathed the word. "Just being near Joshua makes my heart race."

"See? What you share is strong."

"But it's so complicated. And scary."

"Maybe you just need more moxy."

Solaris agreed. "Yes, I definitely lack courage. I used to have it. Tons of it. Somewhere in the past few months, all my courage disappeared."

"We'll find it again."

A knock rapped on the closed bedroom door. When Madison opened it, the handsome man standing there looked nothing like the casual tourist from yesterday and even less like the surf soaked athlete from this morning. He looked like a well-bred gentleman.

"Whoa, where's Joshua," his sister teased, leaning out the doorway to peer dramatically down the hall. Then she gave up searching and scanned his neatly pressed smoke grey summer slacks and matching collared polo. "Whoever you are, you look very civilized, Mister. What happened to my super-cool brother who bites?"

"Grrrr," he growled, curling his lip.

Madison laughed. Solaris decided she liked both Archers.

They knew how to make her smile.

It was cumbersome moving around with the cast, but Solaris enjoyed working again. For the first time in two horrible heartbroken months, she felt happy. First, they toured the hotel. She held Joshua's hand and told the Archer's stories of historic people who had loved and played at the grand Hotel del Coronado.

Now breakfast was over and they were in the center garden patio. Joshua watched from the sidelines, letting the women have their time. A crowd was gathering, curious. Madison's white dress looked pristine against the green plants and historical structures. The morning sun accented her complexion, making that auburn hair gleam. Soft piano music was being rehearsed in the ballroom where someone's wedding preparations were going on.

It created a beautiful atmosphere. People liked to watch.

Madison was nervous and stiff at first, giving only staged smiles. But Solaris helped her feel comfortable in front of the camera. "Let your emotions show in your face. Let it be real. Natural," she captured shots as Madison's expression softened.

"Now tip your head away from me, just a little," the photographer instructed, capturing more images. "Close your eyes. Think about seeing white doves in a blue sky. Now open your eyes and see them flying above the red turrets on the roof." Rapidly, she captured several images of that moment. "Perfect. You let the idea show, that time. Your eyes were softer and you looked like you had seen something beautiful."

"Cool. This is fun."

"Now walk away from me, slowly. Like you are thinking." Madison did, creating images of a lone woman walking through the beautiful garden. "Now stop. Turn your shoulders as if someone just called your name. Look beyond me." Solaris captured every changing movement. "Sweet. Now turn a tiny bit more. Good. Now just your shoulders. Yes. Look at the doorway to the garden. Serious face. Yes, very good. You look classic, truly a lady."

That pleased Madison. The small smile softened her face.

"Now, lift one hand lightly over your heart. It aches. You love someone, miss that person. Think about that." Solaris caught the wistful moment as she zoomed in on Madison's face, then out again, getting various angles of the shot. "See a handsome man standing in the doorway." The idea created incredibly romantic pictures. "You know him. He's the one you've missed. Do you see him?"

"I do."

"Tell me what he looks like," Solaris asked.

"He's tall, dark, and dangerous, of course." She laughed at the idea, then grinned like she had a naughty secret.

"Beautiful. You look amazing. Now slowly say the words, 'I adore you,' and say it like you are giving that man your whole heart." Madison did. The words and imagined emotions made her look breathless and expectant, then lips pursed on 'you" with a sweet air kiss. People applauded.

She laughed aloud, remembering they were not alone. Solaris captured that moment too. It was natural and beautifully real. They had gathered a crowd of curious observers. The photographer and her exotic model were more interesting to watch than anything else happening on an ordinary Tuesday.

"Are you having fun?"

"I am. You're great at this. I feel like a star."

Then Madison tipped her head back, auburn hair shining in the sun, closed her eyes and slowly twirled to the romantic piano notes, letting the flared dress gradually catch air. When she stopped twirling, the ruffled skirt stayed aloft for a few seconds longer.

It made a fantastic photo.

The crowd cheered. Solaris smiled and put the lens cap on her camera. "I think we have enough shots. I took about fifty. They're really good. I'll crop and edit them later." Then she showed Madison the rough images from the digital view screen on the back of her DSLR. Their heads bent together, blonde and red.

"Those are incredible. Did you get some of your moxy back?"

They shared a secret friendly grin.

"You know... I think I did. Thanks. It felt really good to work again."

"Cool. Glad to help. I'm changing my clothes now."

Madison enjoyed being a model, but she knew Joshua wanted private time with the talented photographer. Meeting her yesterday sparked intrigue, but seeing her in action today only fueled that fire. He was captivated. Those pale green eyes were riveted to her every move. Joshua saw nothing else, only Solaris. She was a beautiful woman, inside and out.

He deserved someone special.

Someone in the crowd gave Madison directions to the public restroom on the lower level of the hotel. As she passed through their observers, she received numerous compliments. She gave all the credit to Solaris. The locals knew the famous photographer.

Many people smiled.

Shouldering her reliable bag of tricks and the garment bag she had packed from home, she made her way downstairs and changed into dressy pink shorts, a rose print summer blouse, and cute strappy sandals. Looking in the mirror, Madison decided to leave on the auburn hair and brown eyes.

Today she was a classic lady. It was a pleasant role to play.

Suddenly, her heart kicked as Madison felt a strong urge to check on Joshua. She closed her eyes for a second, seeing him in her mind. They had relocated to the beachside of the hotel and stood on the red brick sidewalk encircling the Windsor lawn.

Hurrying in that direction, the intuitive feelings grew stronger.

Yesterday the guardian gift made her feel unhinged. Their morning running, chasing, and fighting the sea together helped. She was stronger now. Today the insight felt acceptable. Joshua had shown her how to choose a future, to change the bad she saw.

That knowledge was empowering.

Striding through the hallway skirting the lower level gift shops, she saw a man alone in the shadows. His back leaned against the white wall.

Walking closer, Madison got a good look.

Sandy brown hair was overgrown, but still looked sexy. His stance was determined. The resilient angles of broad shoulders were unforgiving. He wore a black t-shirt and black jeans. Now that was tall, dark, and handsome. She couldn't see his face. He was looking at someone on the Winsor lawn. Solaris and Joshua.

They stood together in the sunlight, innocently absorbed in one another. Joshua's hands rested at her waist and Solaris looked up at him in an expression of rapt expectation. He said something that made her look happy. Then he leaned down and kissed her.

"Hey. Romeo. Get a real job."

The man's head whipped around.

He glared at her with whiskey brown eyes.

Suddenly her senses went crazy. It was like being stabbed through her mind with white hot truth. It hurt like nothing she had ever known. But as she blinked through the pain, the man shoved away from the wall and took long strides in the opposite direction.

"Wait," she whispered. Madison was stunned by sensations, flooded with knowledge. He was already several yards away before she regained the ability to speak or move.

She ran after him. "Stop!" The man kept walking. "Solaris deserves to be happy." His boots stopped dead, his spine taut, as if her words shot him in the back. Slowly, he turned around. The smoldering dark gaze narrowed upon her was lethal, but his unshaven face was both shocked and furious.

"What did you say?"

His voice was deeper than she expected. Another shock.

"You heard me. Stay away from Solaris."

No one told this man what to do. Madison knew that fact in a heartbeat. The firm set to his bristly jaw became defiant. "Who the hell are you?"

"A friend. Someone who cares about keeping her safe."

He gave a harsh sarcastic scoff and swore, "And I don't care? Lady, you have no idea."

Madison did have ideas, too many. "You think lurking in the shadows watching her with Joshua will change anything? It won't. It will only push them together faster. Now get a real job and leave Solaris alone."

"Kiss my ass, Princess."

Then he turned and loped away toward the hotel parking lot. Madison sprinted after him, but she was loaded down by her heavy purse and garment bag. The silly strappy sandals slid on the red brick sidewalk.

He had purposely upset people as he ran past.

Everyone got in her way.

By the time she saw him again, he was sitting astride the black Ducati racing bike. He saw her and gave an arrogant sly grin. Then the black helmet slid over his head. He started the engine, leaned low over the body of the bike, and roared south toward Silver Strand Beach.

"Damn! Damn, damn."

Madison wanted to follow him, but her black Porsche was in valet parking. She had to wait for it to be retrieved. She had driven separately, expecting Joshua and Solaris would want time alone after the photo shoot. She was right about that. But this twist she hadn't seen coming. Impatient to leave, after she gave the valet her ticket, she realized something.

She didn't need to hurry.

She could feel the Ducati rider. In her mind, Madison saw him flying down the highway past Silver Strand Beach. "Oh, my god." She even knew his intentions. He would take the peninsula road through the border town of Imperial Beach and loop around to the main freeway again, turning north toward San Diego. He didn't care if the drive took him away from Coronado. He was burning off steam.

Everything about him was dangerous. She wasn't secure enough in her abilities yet to trust everything her mind said about the man, but the intuitive link to the Ducati rider was strong.

"I can track you, Lone Ranger," she muttered.

With that decided, Madison composed herself, patiently waited for her car to be retrieved, gave the valet a gracious tip, and politely left the parking lot without causing a scene. Instead of following the rider south toward Silver Strand, she calmly drove north on Orange Avenue through town.

"I can do this. I know I can."

At a long stoplight, she sent Joshua a text message, telling him to have a great day and she would see him tonight.

He sent a smiley face.

Then the hunt was on.

Expect the Unexpected

Around and round we go.
Where Life stops nobody knows.

~~ Wyatt Sullivan Thornbriar

Wyatt was beginning to doubt his sister's sanity. What the hell was Solaris doing, holding hands with Joshua Archer, strolling past gift shops on Orange Avenue and smiling as if Life was magical.

It wasn't magic.

Life was a mess.

One phone call, one simple hello proved it.

The words that voice said had lanced shards of cold fear inside his heart. Afterward, he spent the whole morning fuming, piecing together answers to things he should have been told years ago.

Everything he learned only brought more questions.

Now it was past noon and Wyatt was hungry, running out of patience, and out of options.

He had to see Solaris.

Striding down the sidewalk scattered with summer tourists casually enjoying the Coronado Island ambiance, Wyatt worked his way toward the couple. They lazily sauntered along, holding hands, window shopping for things neither had any interest in buying.

They were more interested in one another.

As he got close enough and drew a breath to call out her name, the man suddenly turned around.

It was eerie.

Green eyes glared with suspicion and the man's stance became extremely protective of his sister.

"Hey there," Wyatt greeted, striding forward, covering his surprise with friendliness. "You must be Joshua Archer. I'm Laurie's brother."

"Yes. We met yesterday, from across the street." Joshua looked distrustful, but formally offered his hand to shake. "How are you, Wyatt? Have you done anything interesting today?"

It seemed peculiar the man would ask that question, especially after the past few hours Wyatt had charged through.

Naturally, he lied.

"Not really. I had a boring morning, actually."

The other man's chin gave a curt nod.

Wyatt knew he wasn't winning any points there.

"Hey Laurie," he leaned down and gave his sister a quick hug. Then held her at arms-length and scanned her outfit.

"You look pretty today."

"Thank you."

"Word on the street says a famous photographer was taking pictures at the Hotel Del this morning," he teased, implying that small-town gossip had already reached his ears. Another lie. "How'd it go?"

"Fantastic." And she blessed him with that sunny smile. Wyatt released her and sighed. Maybe life still held a little magic, after all. "You were right. I needed to work with people."

Of course, he was right. Solaris had become a mourning hermit, refusing to leave his house. Seeing her stepping up to the plate and taking another swing at life, being with people and smiling would heal some of the broken parts inside.

He just didn't like seeing her so obviously attracted to this Archer guy.

No, he didn't like that at all.

"How's the leg feel?"

"A little tender, but I'm going slow."

"Talk to the doc about it, okay?"

"I will. Next week."

Needing more time with her, Wyatt realized they stood across the street from his favorite Mexican food restaurant. Seeing it, his empty stomach complained, grumbling that man could not live on coffee and stress alone.

"Did you guys have lunch?"

"Not yet. Want to join us?"

"Sure!" It was said with enthusiasm he might have felt, if not for Laurie's mysterious new friend and that alarming morning phone call. "I could use a cold beer and some hot salsa. Do you drink, Archer?"

"Sometimes. I like dark rum."

"Laurie does too. It's her favorite."

"In moderation," she quickly justified. "Too much rum makes me sleep like a baby and wake up feeling like a bear."

The men chuckled, having experienced that before.

As they waited at the crosswalk for the light to change, Solaris told Joshua her recipe for a Captain Courageous.

"Those things are dangerous," he commented to prove he was listening. But something caught Wyatt's attention.

A woman.

A big floppy sun hat covered her hair. It was the round woven kind with a wide brim sold in all Coronado gift shops. Thick black sunglasses hid most of her face. Both looked touristy, but this woman was no tourist.

Her stance was all attitude.

She wore pink shorts, a cute summer blouse, and strappy sandals. She had a slim waist, very nice curves, and long legs. Great legs, actually.

Interesting attitude.

She stood beneath a shady tree, halfway down the block.

But she couldn't hide. She was beautiful.

And she was watching them.

That night while Joshua waited for Madison to come home, he broke out his laptop and did his homework. They had spent half the afternoon visiting at the restaurant with Wyatt. He seemed friendly, laughing and telling stories about Solaris, but it felt like he tried too hard.

He was hiding something.

Joshua didn't like it.

Online, he discovered Wyatt Sullivan Thornbriar had been a Naval Attorney Officer who honorably served ten years and came home to San Diego. The man was wealthy by his money of own making and owned global stock investments in everything from commodities to computer firms. His real estate rental properties spanned the entire California coast, even north beyond San Francisco. He collected exotic cars like they were mere toys.

Joshua searched hard, but found no ownership papers on a black Ducati Streetfighter. That didn't mean Wyatt wasn't the rider.

It only proved he was smart.

His name was on Malcolm's employee list as investment advisor, Solaris had said, but he showed no income from the architectural firm beyond a monthly salary that was modest and drew no suspicion.

The only thing of interest between he and Malcolm was a single vaguely described stock investment several years ago for over five million dollars: money that had apparently kept the corporation out of bankruptcy.

Next, Joshua researched Kianna Manakoa.

Older than Solaris by three years, the assistant had traveled the world handling the business aspect of their photography adventures.

Kianna was the direct tie to Wyatt.

She was a pretty woman, courageous, and strong. Trustworthy, she was like family to Solaris. In candid pictures, the two were always smiling. The Hawaiian lady now lived somewhere in San Diego, managing the downtown photo gallery and online sales, promoting re-prints on six years of pictures from around the world.

The business thrived.

Joshua learned that one photograph could be worth thousands, re-printed as limited-edition canvas art. More if sold to a travel agency or other corporate advertiser. Solaris may not be currently working, but the beautiful moments she had captured would stand as an artistic legacy for many years to come.

It was interesting research work, but Joshua felt distracted by thoughts of someone with amber eyes and a smiling sun tattoo. He read travel articles Solaris had written and gazed at her beautiful pictures, discovering the brave woman she had been before she broke her leg.

It was nearly midnight when Madie arrived.

"You're up late," she greeted.

"Everyone is." A happy calico pirate lay beside him on the couch. Yellowy eyes blinked and the Captain yawned.

"We're his shipmates now."

"Looks like it," closing the laptop, he noticed Madie looked drained. "Where did you go after the photo shoot? You didn't have to leave. We spent all afternoon at a Mexican restaurant with Wyatt. I kept wishing that you would appear, but you never did."

"I know. I felt you. But I had stuff to do."

Offering nothing more, she pulled off the auburn wig. Sighing heavily, she flopped down in an armchair and kicked off her strappy gold sandals. Her own dark hair was tamed in a tight brown twist at the nape of her neck.

He never got used to seeing Madison in wigs and disguises. Her role play characters always felt like talking to total strangers.

That was why she was so good at it, he realized.

Madison did become someone else. It wasn't just an identity façade, she adopted the personality too. She'd make a fortune as an actress.

"Damn I have a headache," she complained. "All this mental interference happening inside my head is exhausting. There are just too many possibilities to choose from. Too many doors to peer through. I think today fried my last brain cell."

He waited for more explanation.

None came.

"Are you going to share your mentally exhausting day," he finally prodded, "or do I have to guess?"

Madie perked up, "Guess."

Now they had a game. "You went shopping."

"Eeegh," she made a buzzer sound, "wrong."

"Aliens abducted you, made you teach them proper Boston English, and let you fly their spaceship."

She laughed and shook her head, so he guessed again.

"You followed the Ducati rider."

Her smile disappeared. "Joshua?"

"No, I can't read minds," he assured when she blanched. "We saw him parked on our street this morning. I suspected he had reappeared when I heard a bike roar away from the Hotel Del Coronado after the photo shoot. You disappeared too, so I did the math."

She looked guilty.

"Next time tell me the truth," he sternly scolded. "Don't send me a 'have a nice day' text and spend your day alone, tracking down trouble."

"Okay. Sorry. But I did want you to have a nice day."

"We did. Thanks. Why did you go off alone?"

"I figure it's important for you to be near Solaris." She explained, "With him watching her like he is, having someone protect her is important. But we need to learn what he wants and how dangerous he is. You can't be everywhere, so I did my part. That's what partners do."

"I appreciate the help." He was starting to like having a partner. "What did you find?"

"Not much. More questions, dead-ends that made no sense. No real answers. But I know one thing for sure, the Ducati rider is furious at you for being with Solaris."

"Yes, I noticed. I think its Wyatt."

"Her brother?" Madie's head tipped, questioning, but that could mean anything. "What does he look like?"

"Big guy, light brown hair, tons of attitude."

"It sounds like him. Especially the attitude. I lost Mr. Attitude around noon, but I found him again around sunset." That would fit the same timeframe of when Wyatt had spent time with them. "But when I found him again, he wasn't doing anything very interesting, mostly just watching other people."

"Who?"

"Malcolm Thornbriar and his wife."

That gave Joshua an uneasy feeling.

But Madison casually yawned, "Are you seeing Solaris tomorrow?"

"I hope so."

"Good. Keep her close. When you are near her, it changes everything bad that I see. You keep her safe. I'll play detective."

"Promise to tell me if you need help."

"I promise. I know my limits."

Madison yawned again and stretched like a cat. "I'm beat. Right now, I need sleep." Scooping up Captain Morgan in one arm, her giant purse weighed down the other shoulder. It looked heavier.

He got the odd impression that she carried a gun.

"Are you armed?"

"Clever brother," she grinned. "I applied for the California handgun permit when we were in Boston. I passed the test here, last week. I'm licensed to carry concealed now," she proudly revealed. "I got them today."

"Them?"

"Sure. One shiny boomstick for each hand."

"Do you really think guns are necessary?"

"I think that you always carried a handgun in Massachusetts, but forgot to get licensed in California. So, I handled the legalities for both of us." Then she sweetly leaned down and kissed his cheek. "Good night, Joshua. Sleep well."

"You too."

"Love you, big brother."

"I love you too, smart sister."

As she carried happy Henry upstairs for the night, Joshua saw the colors in her aura brighten. He knew his sister had accepted her abilities. She was back in control. But the visions gave her a headache. He could see the red streaks of pain radiating around her crown. Being a stubborn Archer, she wouldn't tell him what she saw, wouldn't share secrets, no matter how bad.

Madison was determined to change it.

Mornings were the worst time for Solaris. It always began with that awful heartbeat of awareness between waking and sleep when her heart knew that she would never see Tristan again, except in her dreams.

Today she woke up crying.

It wasn't the first time, and probably would not be the last. But her dreams last night were not about the courageous friend she lost.

They were of Joshua. Beautiful dreams, filled with hope.

Dreams wishing for love.

And on that waking breath when she left those happy dreams behind, her conscious mind opened, and the wishes of her heart faced reality, Solaris thought about Tristan and felt incredibly guilty.

"No," she sobbed all alone, "I'm a horrible friend."

The logical mind shouted that she had done nothing wrong, but her conscience argued that her attraction to Joshua was a disloyalty to Tristan. She didn't mean to. She still loved him.

But Joshua was different. More.

With him she felt alive, like a better person.

Solaris rolled out of bed. That heartsick feeling stayed as she bathed, carefully keeping the cast dry. She was tired of that constant physical reminder of Peru. The awful guilt didn't leave as she dressed for the day in a tank top and denim shorts.

Sadness only increased when she gimped downstairs to an empty house.

She really was all alone.

Wyatt had not come home last night. Again.

They had no formal agreement to keep in touch, but she checked her cell phone anyway. Nothing. Texting or calling him at this point would just prove how needy she was.

She refused to do it.

Looking to make certain she was alone, hoping by some chance she was wrong, his white Mercedes and red Dodge Viper were parked inside the five-car garage beside her red Jeep, but his silver Chevy Silverado truck was missing.

In her current emotional state, it made her angry. Why did she live with a man who obsessed about her wellbeing, but didn't have the courtesy to reassure her at night that he was somewhere safe?

Joshua wouldn't do that.

He was a gentleman. He even asked before he kissed her. Every time. He wasn't a man to steal affection with passion-sparked kisses that made everyone look. His kisses were sweet and were always laced with a beautiful promise of real fire.

Someday. When the time was right.

The wish for love returned. It ached so deep that tears fell.

Wandering back through the massive mansion, Solaris had never felt more alone in her life.

But she had spent two months here, alone every day.

What had changed?

Her thoughts returned to the man who changed her.

What would Tristan think about the hot, confused, excited way Joshua made her feel? Or say? In her heart, Solaris knew exactly what he would do. Her friend would swallow his pride and tell her to give love a chance.

Remembering their days in Peru together, she could still see that last memory of his face, still hear his deep voice:

"Our love is special, but I am no good for you. Today proved it. You deserve a good man, someone who'd never hurt you," he gruffly condemned his own actions.

"You'd never hurt me."

"But I did, Solaris, don't you see? All your pain is because of me. Love should make your life better, not tear it apart. When the right one comes along, I want you to grab hold of love with both hands and never let go. Remember that," he begged. *"Promise me. Please?"*

Like a fool, she had blindly promised Tristan.

Now that promise felt like betrayal.

Heartbroken, Solaris slumped down to the pale blue marble floor and cried. By the time Wyatt found her that way, she had decided to never leave the safe confines of his house again. It was the only place where her life stood perfectly still. Nothing bad could happen here.

"Laurie! Are you hurt?"

"Go away," she sobbed.

But he didn't. Her brother scooped her up, carried her to the granite breakfast bar in the kitchen and firmly sat her upon the solid stone slab. Then Wyatt quickly inspected her legs and body with a flurry of hands, searching for the place that must be bleeding or broken. Only something painfully damaged could produce so many hysterical tears.

"Stop! What are you doing?"

Solaris batted at his worried hands until he stopped. Wiping her eyes, she sniffed. "Put me down, Wyatt."

"Where are you hurt? Did you fall?"

Taking in his sleep-deprived face, his overgrown sandy brown hair a little wild as if he'd had a rough night, her bottom lip puckered.

"You look awful."

"Solaris. Dammit. Are. You. Hurt?"

"Only on the inside. Guess it's just a bad day."

He let out a huff. They had endured bad days, too many to count; days where all she did was sleep and cry. Wyatt had counseled her through every one. He was her rock, the safe harbor from life's storms.

"But yesterday you were happy."

"I know. I'm so selfish. It was wrong."

His expression went blank with shock.

Then he drew back and scowled as if she were crazy. "Are you saying you are having a major meltdown because you actually had a GOOD day? Are we throwing a pity party for a man who lived his life on the edge and enjoyed more than his fair share of good days?"

"Well... yes."

It sounded so stupid when he said it like that.

"Seriously?" Wyatt growled, shaking his head.

"I just feel so guilty, because of Joshua."

"Then do us both a huge favor. Don't."

"But Wyatt—"

"No. Stop. Not now." He held up one big hand. "I can't even think about this." As if his brain refused to process one more thing, Wyatt groaned, pulled up the nearest barstool and lay his head on the granite countertop.

"Are you drunk?"

"Hell no. I'm a happy drunk."

True. And Wyatt definitely didn't look happy. He decided the cool granite against his unshaven cheek wasn't soft enough and folded thick arms as a pillow instead. Then he closed tired brown eyes and sighed in relief.

His resilient body looked exhausted. Solaris realized he was wearing a black dress shirt and dark jeans. "Where were you last night?"

"Out."

"I see that. Were you with a woman?"

"Lord, I wish."

She continued to scan his appearance. "There's mud on your boots. What were you doing in the mud, Wyatt?" One brown eye opened, questioning. "Where did you find mud on Coronado? Were you even on the island?"

Realizing she wasn't going to let him rest, he lifted his head, which apparently ached by the way he still cradled it with one hand.

"Do you own a motorcycle?"

"Why are we playing twenty questions?"

Solaris didn't like his surly uncooperative attitude.

"Because yesterday a man who wore dark clothes and rode a black racing bike watched me with Joshua. I couldn't see his face. He wore a black helmet. But I knew he was mad. Everyone who saw him did. Then he spun out and drove away. It felt like a warning." Her voice had rose to a hysterical pitch. "It was you, wasn't it? Were you trying to scare me?"

Wyatt looked at her, head in hand.

If he was thinking, the mental sparks were firing slow.

"Answer me, damn it."

"It wasn't me. I swear." But Wyatt didn't seem surprised, didn't vow to find the mystery man and beat him senseless. His blasé reaction felt off.

Way off.

"Do you have a problem with me seeing Joshua?"

He didn't lie. "I don't like it."

"Because of Tristan?"

He let out a pained frustrated groan that started deep in his chest, "Laurie, this is insane. Tristan was no saint. Far from it. You didn't marry him, with very good reasons. He wasn't right for you. Don't immortalize the man."

"That seems harsh."

"The truth usually is."

Wyatt was sleepy. Brown eyes looked bloodshot and he was blinking slower. As if he felt too exhausted to even sit up straight, he still had one elbow propped on the counter and cradled his head in one hand.

"But you liked Tristan."

"Wrong."

"What?"

"I didn't like anyone you've dated. Truth is: I would have a major problem with any man you decided to let into your life, especially someone who might break your heart."

That made her pause. "You think Joshua will hurt me?"

"I don't know. He seems decent enough. He was good company yesterday. He's intelligent and educated. He clearly comes from old traditions, old money. Joshua makes you smile, so that earns major points." The protective tone she expected to hear from Wyatt had returned, "But no one hurts my sister. In case you haven't noticed, I'm a little obsessed with keeping you safe."

At least the big man saw it.

"Believe me, I noticed. No one else made me call them twice a day on a satellite phone when I was in the Sahara. No one else shipped me snake anti-venom and leather clothes guaranteed to keep bugs from biting whenever I worked in the Outback. Only you cared enough to interview and hire a permanent traveling assistant for me. You couldn't be there. But you made sure Kianna kept me straight."

He looked guilty. "I just love you."

"I know. I love you too."

"You're special."

She scoffed, "I'm nobody. Dad hates me and Mom just finds fault. You're the only one who sees anything good in me."

"You are a good person."

"No, I'm a terrible person. I shouldn't see Joshua again."

Wyatt scowled. "Don't be stupid."

"Now you suddenly approve?"

He groaned again. "Damn it. I'm too tired to talk right now." Proving it, her brother scooted closer and placed his tired rough cheek upon her lower thigh. Eyes drifted closed again. But his well-developed arms loosely draped around her hips, as if she was his personal responsibility to protect.

"Better?"

He nodded. "Thanks." Her red cotton Bermuda shorts where smooth against his bristly unshaven cheek and her thigh was probably softer than his hard forearms. He visibly relaxed when Solaris affectionately smoothed his rumpled sandy brown hair. It used to look stylish, like a darker Thor, but now it needed a trim. He hadn't shaved in a week or more, but her brother probably didn't care.

"You are special," he sleepily murmured with eyes still closed. His resilient body slumped deeper into the chair. "It was great once. Everything was." He murmured wandering thoughts. "They had so much love. Then one day," he drew a weary sad breath. "You got lucky. You just don't remember."

And then he began to snore.

"Wyatt?"

He didn't move. "What don't I remember?"

Solaris had to sit on the granite countertop for almost an hour. Wyatt slept deep. Normally he didn't snore. Today was a major exception. It was funny sounding, but she felt sorry for him.

No one should become this tired.

Finally, he stirred enough she convinced him to sleep elsewhere. Apologizing, Wyatt helped her down from the countertop. Then he hugged her tight and stumbled upstairs to bed.

Solaris never learned where her brother was last night, why he had mud on his boots, and didn't believe him about not being the Ducati rider.

Everything conflicted inside. He was friendly to Joshua yesterday. Was their chatty social lunch just for show? Who knew: men could be so complicated. But one thing was certain. Wyatt remembered something important that she had clearly forgotten.

It was great once. Everything was.

What could that possibly mean? Wyatt sounded heartbroken over it.

They had so much love. Then one day—what?

Something terrible, obviously. But the love part was the most confusing. Wyatt couldn't mean their coldhearted parents. Perfect Queen Regina and obsessive Ivory Tower Malcolm were never in love. Why those two self-absorbed people ever decided to have children was one of the saddest mysteries of her life.

But she had Wyatt.

He was her family. She loved him, deeply. But he worried too much. Especially if his obsession to keep her safe had gone so far, he chose to follow her around on a black Ducati.

If it was him, which instincts said it was, they had a major problem.

Solaris knew it would be hours before she could question her brother again. She washed her face, put on a little makeup and pulled her air-dried hair into a side ponytail. Puttering around the house was boring.

She decided to get groceries. The pantry and fridge were bare. They were eating restaurant food too often. Even if Wyatt could afford it, eating out wasn't healthy.

On impulse, she almost called Joshua for a ride.

Then she stubbornly changed her mind.

Maybe Wyatt thought her morning guilt trip was ridiculous, but he was wrong. Everything with Joshua was too intense, too fast. It made her feel too much. Her attraction to him was not rational.

She wasn't falling in love with him.

Would not, could not, fall in love.

Joshua sent her two text messages. By mid-morning he decided to call. Solaris didn't answer. But he was tuned in to her now. She saw the messages, but had a serious case of cold feet. He hoped that situation was fixable, but regardless of the outcome, he still had a job to do. Romance was secondary to protecting her.

He was a Guardian. They must stay friends.

But for the first time in his life, he wanted more.

"Hey, imagine finding you here."

Solaris looked shocked to see him pushing a grocery cart he had quickly filled with essentials he and Madison needed. There was only one major grocery store on Coronado Island. Meeting there should not have surprised her that much.

Avoiding his gaze, she inspected the contents of his cart. "Will Captain Morgan actually eat all that cat food?"

"Probably. He's a big guy."

"You'll turn him into a giant."

"He was abandoned, Laurie." He gently explained, wishing she would look at him. "Henry was left outside, all alone. He's a house cat. He can't defend himself and doesn't know how to hunt. So, he sat in a tree in the backyard, hoping someone might rescue him. Madie did and he's grateful. I just think the poor Captain deserves a good family now."

She bit her bottom lip. "Wow. You're a really nice man."

Inside, he wished for romance. Wished hard.

Then Solaris finally looked up. Those lovely amber eyes stared at him. Unconsciously, one hand rubbed over her heart. He wondered what it meant. Damn, she's a beautiful woman. Tawny hair hung in a loose side ponytail, lying over her left shoulder. The long ends curled in soft spirals, as if she let it air dry.

"Is your hair naturally curly?"

"Huh? Oh, some. Sea air makes it more."

"It's really pretty."

Solaris looked thrilled at the compliment. The corners of her lips even curved upward. Then a dark thought seemed to cross her mind. The smile disappeared.

"I think we need to talk."

"We should finish shopping first." Joshua pointed to the frozen fish in her basket. "I'd hate for those mahi and shrimps to get warm and be ruined."

"I'm done."

But she wasn't finished shopping. There were no salad greens in her cart. Besides the fish, he only saw food for Wyatt. She had picked out beer, steaks, cheeses, and breads.

No Solaris healthy food.

He decided to play along.

"Well, I still need lettuce and carrots." Joshua waited for her to agree she needed them too. She just stared at him, looking lost. "Then I have to take everything home, put it away. Feed Henry." Another strange silence followed. "Would you like to meet me someplace later?"

Her behavior was rattled and confused. "Why?"

"You said we needed to talk."

"Oh. I did."

She looked ready to sit on the floor and cry. He caught an image of Solaris doing exactly that, curled up sobbing on a pale blue marble floor inside a house too big for one person. She was alone, surrounded by original artwork on the walls and expensive dolphin statues.

Wyatt's house, it had to be.

"Alright, we can play this thing one of two ways," he took charge of their strange public encounter. "I can pretend I don't see that you're upset about something. We can smile and walk away. That's the socially acceptable thing to do. Polite polish, you called it. Then no one's feelings get hurt. We don't have to say anything real."

A flicker of emotions clenched her jaw, but softened her gaze.

"Or we can be honest," he gently encouraged, "and you can trust me to understand why you've been crying."

"Does it show?"

"You cried all morning, didn't you?"

Solaris sighed and shoulders slumped, apparently giving up whatever internal fight she was battling. She looked at the floor. Hands gripping the cart trembled. Joshua felt certain her next words would be to get the hell out of her life.

"I did."

"Why?"

"Because I had a really good day, yesterday," she quietly confessed, honestly meeting his eyes. "I always do, with you. But I'm scared. It's all happening so fast, it's so unexpected. I'm trying really hard *not* to find a place for you in my life."

"How is that battle going?" He patiently asked.

"Not too well."

It was enough to make him smile. Watching him, Solaris seemed in awe, as if somehow that smile opened all the closed doors between them. Her fists on the cart relaxed. The tension melted from her body.

There was a wish for romance in the air.

"I like you, Joshua."

"Enough to let me into your life?"

Her eyes were damp again, "I think you're already there."

"Then let's finish shopping, take care of the food we both need. Then we can go somewhere quiet, just us. Maybe we really should talk."

Solaris agreed.

Taking a chance, knowing she might refuse, Joshua slowly walked toward her. Then he opened his arms. She came to him in a rush. Her body hit his hard and Solaris hung on as if touching him might save her.

It felt so right, it scared him too.

"We're going slow, slow, slow," he chanted against her ear.

She was holding her breath, trying not to cry.

"Breathe, Laurie. It's alright. I'd never do anything to hurt you." As she softened against him and her arms tightened, he added, "I promise, Babe. Promise with all my heart."

Solaris wasn't sure why Joshua was at the grocery store, but instincts whispered he was there on purpose. He was so calm and patient with her crazy emotional instability. Even when she tried a polite polish of words, he spoke the truth instead.

After she hugged him in the canned foods aisle until people were looking at them strange and they were laughing, Joshua helped her get salad greens she would have wished for later. He was observant, seeing things other people would have overlooked.

Driving home, Solaris wasn't sad anymore, felt no guilt. She felt hopeful. She had invited him over. He promised to meet her at Wyatt's house, later. She gave him the address. He was there in record time.

"That was fast," she greeted, opening the door.

He had brought her a big red hibiscus flower. They grew everywhere in Coronado and she loved them. Saying nothing, Joshua slid the flower behind her left ear, the slender stem held secure by her side pony.

"In Hawaii, when the women wear their hair on the left side, it means they belong to someone."

Solaris laughed at his mistake. "No, the rule is how if flower is worn on the left side, not how they wear their hair. Wearing a flower on the right ear means she is available and looking. Hawaiians are big on symbolism. Giving a flower to someone is a sign of aloha, of good wishes for that person."

"Does yours belong on the left?"

She looked at his handsome face. "Yes. I think it does."

Moving close enough to touch, he breathed, "Aloha, Solaris. I wish you much happiness and joy in life." Then Joshua placed both hands on her shoulders and tenderly kissed her forehead, right at the spot where she thought too much, the place that always hurt when she cried. "May all your beautiful wishes come true."

It touched her deep. "You've been to Hawaii."

"My family owns a place on north shore Kauai, near Princeville."

She grinned. "Then you probably knew about the flowers."

His playful smile flirted, "Yes, Babe. I did."

She loved the endearment, but had to ask. "Do you call all women that?"

"No. Never," Joshua looked surprised to realize he had been saying it. "That is your name. Babe. As in: *My Babe*. I knew it the day we met." Solaris sighed at his sweet thoughts and lightly kissed him, "Do you like it?"

"From you, I definitely do."

She welcomed him inside. Joshua helped her finish putting away groceries. He seemed comfortable with everyday smallness. She made glasses of sweet iced tea and he peeled potatoes for their pot roast dinner they put in the crockpot. Then she gave him a mini-tour, excluding upstairs, since Wyatt was still sleeping.

The house was ultramodern with soaring ceilings and lots of tinted glass. Nooks and corners were filled with an eclectic collection of ocean themed bronze statues, mostly mermaids and dolphins. The walls boasted dozens of Wyatt's favorite photos from her career. It was something she was accustomed to seeing. But Joshua walked from picture to picture, fascinated and in awe, asking her to tell him what she was feeling in the moment she took each one.

"No one ever asks me what I felt. They only care about where I was and what big adventure I had."

"But none of them know about your special butterfly feelings," he discreetly reminded, "do they?"

"No. That was between us."

"Thanks for sharing," he took her hand as they walked. "I like hearing what prompted you to be at the perfect place and the perfect time, and how living that perfect moment felt."

"You don't think it's weird?"

"Not at all. When life whispers something important, wise people listen. Your intuition makes you very special."

Solaris wondered why people kept saying she was special. She was ordinary, out of work, scared to move forward in life, and generally messed up inside. Poor Joshua didn't have a clue.

My Babe. I knew it the day we met.

In her heart, she carried that same instant possessive feeling for Joshua. It happened the first moment they spoke and was growing stronger, every day. She wanted more tomorrows with this man. Wanted to remember how to smile. Solaris decided it was time to tell him why she was such a wreck. He deserved to know she wasn't always so broken.

Finished with the tour, they sat outside on cushioned chaise loungers by the pool. Wyatt's back yard was landscaped with tropical flowers, surrounded by a high privacy wall draped with blooming ivy. It was quiet and green, a nice place to talk.

"Sorry about the grocery store," she apologized.

"We're fine. I'm adjusting too. It takes time to wrap your heart and head around having someone new and important in your life."

He was such a good man.

Solaris summoned courage, "You should know that I wasn't always like this. Peru seriously changed me."

Then she told him about the guerrilla ambush, the trucks exploding and people shooting. She described hiding inside the truck, flat under the tarp, and how the man tried to kidnap her.

Joshua heard about the screwdriver she stabbed into his neck, how they fought and she fell down the cliff to the ledge. She summarized Kianna's rescue climb down to get her, the flight home, and how she stayed locked inside Wyatt's house for two long months.

But somehow her story didn't include Tristan.

She wanted to share everything, but wasn't sure how to begin. Saying anything at all about Tristan would mean having to explain his secrets, why her ex-fiancé came to Peru running from trouble and about the story he was chasing.

It meant talking about that beautiful ruby necklace.

No one knew his truth. Kianna didn't see Tristan shoot the rebel, his fierce anger, or know the reasons why he refused to come home with them, or why he blamed himself.

Solaris had told no one.

She promised to keep his secrets. That was one promise she would not break.

"Damn, you've been through hell." Joshua sympathized when she was done. "Why were those men trying to take you?"

"Who knows," she lied, telling the same story she gave Wyatt. "Kidnappings happen in South America all the time. People knew me there, maybe assumed we had some money. Guerrilla rebels probably thought I would be a quick paycheck."

"Wyatt would have paid."

"Yeah, your right," she dryly decreed. "But now he's stuck babysitting me. I used to tour the world, fearless and free. Now I'm scared to leave his house or live any sort of life because my courage is gone. I lost my career, have no idea what to do with myself anymore, and I wake up crying so hard some days that Wyatt comes home to find me curled up on the floor."

She hadn't meant to say that part.

"Is that how he found you today?"

"Yes. It wasn't pretty." Admitting it was hard. "And this wasn't my first bad day. We had two months of very bad days. So you see, my emotional meltdown with you in the grocery store was crumb cake compared to the deep fried gooey mess I keep dishing out to Wyatt."

"If I minded helping you," a dusky voice behind them announced, "I'd tell you, wouldn't I?"

Wyatt stood in the patio doorway.

Wearing black swim trunks and dark sunglasses, his brawny chest was bare. His hair was slicked back, wet from a shower. He carried a pitcher of iced tea in one hand and a bucket of cold beer in the other.

"Yes. You would tell me."

Solaris didn't care that he heard. Let Wyatt see that she trusted Joshua. Walking outside to join them beside the pool, her brother nodded his unshaven chin at Joshua how cool men do in greeting, refilled their glasses with tea, and then opened his beer and flopped down in the chaise lounge next to hers.

"Did you get enough sleep?"

"I'll live. Did you tell him everything?"

Solaris knew he meant Tristan and fibbed. There was a time and place for that truth. It wasn't today. "Yes. I even included the screwdriver."

Wyatt grimaced and pretended to gag. "God, I hate that part. My sweet baby sister kills a South American guerrilla rebel with nothing but a Phillips screwdriver. Guh."

"I think it was a flathead, actually."

Her brother grinned wide, laughed. "Go Rambo."

"Imagine if I had found a bowie knife under that seat."

"Better yet: imagine if I'd been there."

"You would have blown Peru right off the map."

"Hell yes." No longer friendly, Wyatt turned stern attention toward Joshua. "Looks like she's hoping you'll stick around, Archer," he challenged, none too lightly. "Laurie hasn't told that story to anyone except me. Kianna knows, but she was there and hates to talk about the good people they lost. It was the worst day of her entire life."

Solaris wondered how Wyatt could understand Kianna's feelings. His comment felt strange. "How do you know it was the worst day of her life?"

"We talk."

"Like friends?"

"Yes, Solaris," he sighed, "Kianna and I are friends."

"Oh. Really? Since when?"

"Since always. I did hire her and I did spend six busy years constantly talking to her on the phone handing business while you two toured the world. She also did live in this house with us for a few weeks after you came home from Peru. So, I believe I'm entitled to call Kianna my friend."

"Okay."

Wyatt turned his attention back to his original question, "Well, Archer? Are you going to stick around?"

Joshua wasn't deterred by the challenge.

"I'm here for the duration."

"Good to know," Wyatt deadpanned, which voiced neither his approval nor dissatisfaction, only a vague acceptance of the facts.

Men. And they gripe that women are complex. Please.

"Hey, by the way," he added to Joshua in a slightly nicer tone, "could you do me a huge favor and help Laurie with that stupid photo shoot downtown that Dad is making her do tomorrow?"

"I already planned on it."

"Cool." That seemed to earn some respect from Wyatt. "If I go along to help her, I'd be tempted to wring Queen-zilla's skinny bitch neck and burn all her fancy dresses. It would get ugly, fast. So, thanks for going."

"No problem."

Business taken care of, her brother tipped back his beer and took a big swig. His easy smile and casual attitude returned.

"Damn the sun feels nice. I love summer." Before them, the pool was beautiful turquoise in the June afternoon sun. "Hurry up and get that cast off, Laurie, so we can play in the pool and hit the beach."

"I'm trying. Monday morning: just five more days."

"Unless Doc says you need more surgery."

Solaris refused, "It will be just fine."

Her ankle would be fine, she vowed. Everything would.

Life had to be.

Pure Vanity

Beauty is only skin deep,
but ugly darkens the soul.

~~ Joshua

The photo session Joshua drove Solaris to was set at a glamorous rooftop nightclub in downtown San Diego that her client rented for the day. They arrived on the top floor to find it empty of tables and furnishings, but filled with people. Towering professional lights illuminated a shiny runway, stages were set in strategic locations, and along every interior wall were mirrors and tables where models prepared hair and make-up.

"Wow, this looks like a Hollywood set."

"Queen-zilla thinks this will sell more clothes," Solaris drying commented. "It's dumb and extravagant."

As he carried her camera bag, they wove through crowds of beautiful women preparing for the event. Solaris had more gear in his Jeep, but they had decided to wait to bring it up until she saw what the situation required. She followed, letting him guide her through the people.

Behind him Joshua heard a loud smack. He turned to discover Solaris had slapped the outstretched hand of a man who was reaching toward him.

"Yancey, stop!"

The hand retracted. "It's a free country."

"Not where Joshua is concerned. Find your own man, he's taken."

"Why do you always get the good ones?"

"Being female definitely helps."

Yancey looked indignant. His flashy silver-lilac business suit was tailored somewhere between a bad Peewee Herman skinny pants design and a spandex superhero outfit. "You didn't have to slap me," he whined at Solaris, inspecting the stinging pink fingers. "I was only looking."

"By grabbing his ass?"

Yancey grinned. It was defiant.

"That's it," Solaris declared. "You're in big trouble. Mother!" The entire room of beautiful models silenced. Everyone turned around to look. But the shocked silence only lasted a moment as speculative whispering insured. "Mother," she hollered again, letting her demand echo. No one answered.

"Regina Thornbriar, come here!"

From amid the crowd of lean bodies gossiping and speculating, a sleek blonde goddess immerged. She wore a gold evening gown with a neckline cut down to her navel and the straight skirt flashed skin from the slit high up the side.

"Good god, Solaris, stop yelling."

The woman practically exhaled sex. But Joshua immediately knew she wasn't about pleasure or for love. Everything about her was meant to entice and lure, to inspire deep insatiable need in men. Sex was her power.

But it was cold, as cold as ice.

Joshua was not impressed.

High heels clicked on the floor, the staccato noise punctuating the sexual overtures in a well-practiced walk, each step calling attention to those swaying hips and breasts too large and perky to be natural.

"What are you screeching about? And don't call me Mother," she hissed as she drew nearer, "it's embarrassing."

"Then keep your pet on a leash. Mother."

"Yancey? My talented designer isn't a pet."

"He tried to maul Joshua."

Like an indignant spoiled child, Yancey met the accusations with wide-eyed innocence, "Regina, darling. Your daughter is being extreme. This is just a silly misunderstanding."

Solaris interjected, "Your dirty little hand was this close," she held two fingers an inch apart to demonstrate, "to earning you a fat black eye."

Uttering a terrified squawk the garishly clad man indignantly marched away. Yancey scolded models lounging around in chairs, for wrinkling the designer dresses, verbally asserting his presence and stirring up a frenzy of activity again.

"You offended my designer," Regina reprimanded, frowning without making wrinkles, which struck Joshua as odd. She was older than her skin and body portrayed. Much older. He did the math. If Wyatt was thirty-four, that made his mother at least mid-fifties. Yet she looked as young as Solaris.

"Your designer is a jerk."

"He is the reason you have a job today."

"I don't need the money. I could leave."

"Oh yes, run away," Regina icily taunted. "Isn't that what you've been doing for years? Run away to the jungle. Go hide in some third world country to escape marriage and family responsibility."

"Don't make this about me."

"I wouldn't dream of it," she purred in a nasty condescending tone, "Today, you are simply an employee. Dear."

"I could care less about promoting your flaky designer," Solaris boldly declared. "I am only here because I promised Dad."

"Did Malcolm arrange this photo shoot?"

"He asked me, yes."

Her tongue clicked. "That is so typical. Malcolm can't please me himself, so he gets you to step in. Daddy's precious little girl intervenes. Do you enjoy being a buffer, Solaris? The little people pleaser never really grew up, did she? You just escaped reality for a while."

"I am fully aware of our reality."

"Are you? Truly? I sincerely doubt it." Regina's spiteful gaze lowered to the white cast still encasing her leg, "It seems your little adventure in Peru turned out poorly. Ahh, too bad. The world traveler has returned home to lick her wounds."

"Don't push me today, Mother."

Anger lit those contact enhanced crayon blue eyes.

"Just do your damn job." Regina spun and sashayed through the crowded rooms in search of the temperamental man. Finding Yancey, she coddled and cooed as if he were a delicate spoiled child. It was a pathetic display of attention.

Joshua felt sorry for the beautiful daughter. She deserved a warm heart, not a cruel cold shoulder.

Solaris let out a long-suffering sigh. "Sorry about that. We can leave now. I honestly don't care if I piss her off."

"Wait, let me get this straight." Joshua found the entire shocking scene hilarious. "I was nearly groped by a gay fashion designer, you agreed to take promotional pictures of Yancey's clothing line because Malcolm actually asked nicely, and that plastic Barbie doll is your mother?"

"Bingo. Sorry. Again."

Joshua laughed. "No wonder you and Wyatt call her Queen-zilla."

"Don't say that too loud. She'd have a fit."

"Impossible. Her face is frozen by chemicals."

The corner of her mouth smirked. "You caught that, huh?"

"I'm amazed she can even talk."

Amber eyes glint with mischief. "Ouch. Good one."

"You two don't look anything alike."

"We used to. But she hates me. Money can buy a new body, a new face, and erase time. She's spent plenty rolling back the clock. She has an amazing plastic surgeon. Everything about Queen Regina has been altered, adjusted, or rearranged."

"Lips?"

"Collagen injections, regularly."

"Nose?"

"Copied from some actress she reveres."

"Eyes, what color are they naturally?"

"Light brown, just like mine. She hates them."

"And those?" He cupped his hands by his chest in an oversized gesture, making her naughty smile appear.

"Definitely enhanced, beauty is bought, not born."

"That's sad and self-destructive." He made a wide-eyed face, impersonating Regina, "I wonder if she has to sleep with her eyes open," he chuckled at the idea, "I bet she does, her skin is pulled so tight. Damn. No wonder your Dad is a tyrant. Sleeping beside that must be scary. I wonder if her head turns all the way around, since she's really just a toy."

Solaris gave in to laughter, giggling away tension she had carried all morning. The whole ride from Coronado had been silent, filled with dread. Now she laughed so hard she held her side and pink cheeks were wet.

"Oh god, I pictured that." She giggled, "Toy Regina. Poor Dad."

Without thinking about the consequences, Joshua kindly wiped away glistening laughter tears that had spilled over.

"You laughed so hard you're crying. Your tears are beautiful, Solaris."

At those words she stopped laughing. Lips parted on a sharp inhaled breath. The lighthearted sound silenced.

"What did you say?" The moment turned serious.

"Your tears are beautiful. Some are, you know. Not all tears are tragic or sad."

She swallowed hard. "Tears from the heart."

"Exactly."

They stood close, too close for two people who vowed to take things slow. But Joshua could not step away. Surrounded by professional beauty mongers wearing designer clothing meant to charm and entice, Solaris Sullivan was the most beautiful woman in the room.

"Babe."

It was too husky, too possessive. Every heartfelt wish was in that single revered word. He felt relieved when her hand became nestled in his. The small trusting connection felt huge. Unconsciously moving closer by degrees, the separation between their bodies narrowed. The noisy people around them faded away.

They suddenly felt completely alone.

He'd never experienced anything this intense.

Yesterday he kept his promise and kept things between them casual. When they cautiously said goodnight after enjoying a pleasant dinner at Wyatt's house, Joshua only gave her a warm hug.

This moment demanded more. He couldn't look away from her, could not let go. Life became amber eyes, tawny caramel hair.

Her face was lifted toward his, eyes focused upon the goal. His other hand was on her waist, possessively pulling them tight together.

"Say no, Solaris. Make me stop."

"I don't want to."

"Damn."

The kiss was restrained, a comforting caress that acknowledged their merging worlds. But where their bodies met was warm and thrilling. As he tilted his mouth to taste her better, Solaris made funny murmured sounds that sounded suspiciously like, 'oh my god, mmm, more.'

Joshua smiled and deepened the embrace.

His touch lingered.

Kissing Solaris was delicious, like savoring a dessert so decadent, Joshua knew by the jubilant heat tightening his core that this one taste of her today would not satisfy his appetite.

Today he needed much more.

"Joshua," she murmured his name as they drew apart. Staring up at him, lips parted as if contemplating more kisses and perhaps a runaway ride to a place more private, Solaris took an awestruck breath.

Then she decisively stepped out of his arms. "Let's get to work."

"Let's admit we are amazing together," he offered.

Her head quickly shook, "We're just so terribly complicated."

"We could uncomplicated things real quick."

"I don't see how."

"Just be my girlfriend," he faithfully committed, "officially. No more casual hot encounters that experiment with our potential while we talk about what it means. We've tested it. We're beyond our trial run. Let's get serious and agree that what we have found together really matters."

Silence. She was barely breathing.

Actually, she was breathing, but all wrong. Staring down at the floor now, her hand lay over her chest, fist clenched, and her tiny frantic gasps seemed like the air had become too thin.

Joshua knew what they had found mattered.

In fact, they mattered to her very much. He had learned Solaris had a habit of hyperventilating when something tore at her heart. It happened the first time he got close. Right before their very first kiss.

"Answer me, Solaris."

Breath drew in sharp. She met his gaze. Swallowing hard, she fought for it and gained control. "You promised we would go slow."

"We will. But can you really say our attraction doesn't mean anything?"

"I have people to photograph."

After that she focused upon the posing models, giving instructions that made the women not only beautiful and sexy, but likable. Yancey's designer gowns were shown in the most positive light.

She was truly gifted.

As Solaris encouraged, telling the ladies to tip their head or turn their shoulder just right, to envision things that changed their facial expressions, even Regina ended up looking ladylike as she posed for the camera.

The photo session took all day.

Solaris worked through lunch break, occasionally snacking on a veggie plate Joshua made for her from the buffet of super healthy foods provided for the models. She thanked him, but they were polite, talking very little, the new barriers between them unmistakable.

It was evening before they were truly alone.

Packing up her photography gear, Solaris refused to look at him. Tension around her was intense. They were the last to leave.

Joshua had packed her tripod, professional lighting equipment and stands, and three large camera cases onto a rolling luggage cart. It was too much to carry in one trip and right now, he was not leaving Solaris alone to hide behind her walls. When they entered the elevator, he pushed the heavy cart to one side.

They shared the other half.

Quickly glancing in his direction, one hand nervously raked through her long tawny side-swept bangs. With her back against the mirrored wall of the nightclub elevator, she watched the floor numbers tick by on the digital counter. On the fifteenth floor, he hit the stop button.

Alarms sounded. Joshua turned that off too.

"What are you doing?"

"Getting your attention," he turned. Leaning both arms upon the wall above her shoulders, that position put them face to face. "Do I have it?"

"Stop this, Joshua."

Instead, he kissed Solaris.

He didn't ask. He just moved in fast and quick.

Expecting resistance, Joshua was shocked when her lips slid against his, achieving better contact. Eagerly, Solaris pulled him in. The stolen kiss succeeded. It gained an extremely warm reception.

Although his hands remained stationary upon the mirrored elevator walls, her hands were moving freely, exploring the contours of his body as if Solaris had ached to touch him all day.

Joshua let her.

When the heat between them became a little too intimate for an elevator, he grabbed those busy hands and held them up on the wall with his. Then he leaned in, pinning their bodies together from hips to chest.

She felt soft and hot.

Her round breasts yielded to his hard contours.

God, he wanted more.

"That was extremely honest," he breathed. "Now we can talk. The truth is, you like kissing me. And I like kissing you. Touching feels right. We should behave like adults and touch whenever we want, not wait until the tension gets so high it makes us crazy. Don't you agree?"

"Well. Yes."

"Do I belong in your life?"

"I said yesterday that you did."

"Then stop pretending that we're too complicated." He challenged.

"But... we are."

"This will work if we want it to. We can take things slowly, but we need to matter, Laurie. I am good with this, whatever THIS may be. Fast, slow, intense, casual—I'm all for it, as long as I know that what we are doing is real."

He half expected her to start hyperventilating again.

Instead, wide amber-brown eyes stared at him.

"Can you let go of fear, throw away all your ideas about how people are supposed to meet, how it should take months to fall in love, and have the courage to handle the shocking reality of us?"

"I have courage." Then her lips sweetly curved, "And how do you always know what to say? You read me too well. You're incredible."

He read her through his gifts. Someday, he'd tell her about the things that made all Archer's unique. "Babe, you have no idea. Yet."

"But I will?"

"Yes, Solaris. You will. I think we're meant to be together. And I am not afraid to open the door and see where it takes us. I won't live with regret. I will not hold back anymore and wonder what might have been."

Then Joshua kissed her again, proving he meant it. When they drew apart, a happiness illuminated her pretty face. She looked so alive, so vital. In his eyes with his abilities, he saw her aura. Solaris seemed to glow from the inside, a golden radiance of pure joy. He had never known a woman more naturally beautiful.

"Joshua, will you get serious with me," she asked with a smile, "and officially be my boyfriend? I'm tired of wondering what this means. I just want to be with you, to know our time together matters."

He almost laughed that she was turning it around, asking him instead of listening to him coax her into accepting their relationship.

"Yes, Laurie. I would love to."

Releasing her hands, he reached across the elevator to push buttons that would start them on a downward trek again. Bur before he could touch it, a fist snagged him by the shirt front.

"Not so fast." She demanded, yanking them together again. "One more thing. Are you going to stick around beyond summer?"

"I will, if you will."

"What does that mean?"

"Your photography means jungles and jaguars."

"Traveling is over. I saw everything that I wanted to see. It's time that I found a permanent home."

He liked hearing that. "I think I have, too."

"Why did you leave Boston?"

"Maybe I came here to find you."

"I'm serious."

"So am I." He sealed that honesty with another overheated elevator kiss that left her smiling the whole way home. Joshua didn't mind the introspective silence as he drove. He could see everything was just fine now.

After he helped unload her photography gear at Wyatt's house, she shared her thoughts. "Boyfriend doesn't automatically mean Lover," she clarified.

"Yes, I agree with that."

He waited, seeing what else was on her mind. Tomorrow Solaris would spend the day editing today's work. He probably wouldn't see her. She already gave Madison her Hotel Del Coronado photos. Joshua had looked at them. They were incredible. The next day was Saturday. Their promised first real date.

"Sex can wait until we're ready?"

"Boyfriend means that I want to spend time with you. I want to know you. Having dinner and going to a movie with me on Saturday does not automatically mean that we will sleep together."

She released a sigh of relief.

"Thank you. Now I can relax and enjoy our date without worrying it will turn into something that leaves me emotionally tangled."

"No tangles."

She grinned. "Good."

"But if I get too desperate to touch you," he flirted, "maybe I'll wear that shark shirt again. It brought me good luck."

She laughed and looked happy. "It wasn't the shirt. It was you."

He liked hearing that, too.

I Dare You

Rider be nimble, Rider be quick.
But never underestimate the power of
my black Stilettos and red Lipstick.

~~ Madison Liberty Archer

It was Saturday night. Joshua and Solaris were enjoying their steak dinner and an action movie for their first official date night. Madison felt restless. Following instincts that had become familiar now, she parked her black Porsche outside of the dance club in Pacific Beach. It was popular with locals and rocking loud tonight.

Madison could hear music from inside her car.

The restlessness increased, like a call to action. She considered putting on that auburn wig she had worn all week. But sitting there listening, sorting through all the possible futures in her mind, she focused upon one important end result.

Okay. No red hair. Tonight, she needed to be herself.

Letting chestnut curls tumble past her bare shoulders and down her back, she put on ravishing red lipstick and adjusted the slender straps of her black mini dress. It wasn't fancy. But it showed off her legs and flaunted some rounded cleavage while still allowing her to wear one of her favorite body enhancing bras.

A smart woman is never without her secret tools.

The stretchy black satin dress hugged every tempting curve.

Inside the dance club she found couples and noisy groups partying. Waitresses hustled to serve drinks. At the bar with neon pink and green lights Madison ordered a beer, then changed her mind and ordered two. Turning around to survey the busy room, she felt men watching, admiring long legs rising up from her black stiletto heels. Yep, the dress kicked ass. Men noticed her.

But not the right man. Where was he?

Then she saw him.

Alone in a far shadowy corner, he sat at a waist-high pub table for two. His back was against the wall. Overgrown sandy brown hair was ruffled like he'd just raked one hand through it. The beer in his hand was nearly empty. It was the same brand she just ordered.

Lucky me.

Why was he here? Then she knew. He was hiding tonight, but hated being alone. Madison had watched him all week. His movements were rarely predictable, always creating questions, but the Ducati rider was a constant hum in her head. Why they were connected, she didn't know.

Tonight, she intended to find out.

Across the room his brown eyes caught her gaze and held. It took a curious heartbeat, then recognition hit. As first he frowned and looked guarded. Then his unshaven chin tipped in a slight greeting.

Madison smiled.

By the time she casually strolled across the floor to his secluded corner, those whiskey brown eyes had noticed everything she wanted him to see.

Men. They liked to look.

And watching people was this man's specialty.

Without waiting for an invitation, Madison hopped on the other barstool, crossed her legs with artful etiquette, and offered the beer.

"What's this for?"

His deep voice was familiar now. Likable.

"You look thirsty."

"Do I?" If the Ducati rider felt rattled by her appearance, it didn't show. The man only let you see what he wanted you to. Two can play that game.

"Don't you like it?"

"I can buy my own drinks."

Flirting, Madison leaned forward over the small table, pushed the beer toward him with two fingers and gave him a sneak peek at cleavage.

"Well, Lover Boy—I bought you one anyway." He took it, giving a scowl for show. "Ooh, that's gratitude. You're welcome. Got a nasty attitude tonight?"

"Maybe. You look like trouble."

"Thank you very much for noticing," then she giggled when he glanced down the front of her dress. Such a man. So predictable. Satisfied his attention was sufficiently hooked, Madison leaned back in her seat, but his hand quickly reached out as curious fingers stroked a piece of her hair.

"I thought it was red."

"Nope. These curls are all me." He released her hair. Feigning disinterest again he grunted and took a long swig of his beer. "Maybe you prefer blondes?"

"Would it matter if I did?"

"Not really. Your taste in women will not change me, nor will they hurt my feelings." His brows shot up, surprised by her tart defiance. "I am, who I am. And I happen to like who I am, most days. Can you say the same?"

He smirked, "I am fully aware of my flaws."

"Is it a long list?"

"Most days."

Madison smiled wide and decided she liked him. The feeling was mutual. His stance had relaxed and eyes were memorizing her face, plus a few features below the neckline. Taking a drink from her own beer, she settled in for a chat.

"Got a name, tough guy?"

He hesitated a second too long. "Thomas."

"Thomas what: Thomas the hot racing motorcycle guy? Maybe it's *Doubting Thomas* who doesn't think he needs company tonight. I think its *Peeping Tom*, who likes to creep around the Coronado Hotel."

A smile curved his very kissable mouth. Damn, he was a gorgeous man. Chiseled cheekbones were sexy and fearless. It went well with his defiant chin that was covered with dark stubble. This was a face that could stop hearts. And probably broke them just as fast.

"Thomas Anderson. And you are?"

"Madison Liberty," she paused, wondering if her knew, "Archer."

He almost choked on his beer. "Shit. You're his sister? Ah hell. I thought you were just a photography model for Solaris." In one svelte move the man was on his feet. "That's it, I'm gone."

But as he knelt to snatch his black motorcycle helmet from beneath his barstool, Madison stood too. Then she stepped close. Inches away. Still kneeling, his eyes scanned up her legs. Rising slower than a man should who meant to run, when he stood again they were a breath apart.

"What are you doing?"

"Let's play a game," she softly suggested.

"I don't like games."

"Oh, but Hot Stuff, my game is fun."

"I sincerely doubt that."

Boldly placing both hands upon his taut abs hidden beneath that black shirt, as he reflexively pulled away from the unwanted touch she pushed, coaxing his very fine butt back onto the barstool. He sat again, back against the wall. The helmet in his hand clattered to the floor. Her lean thighs were centered between his muscular ones.

Madison had him cornered. "Truth or dare," she breathed.

"Dare. Truth sucks."

"I knew you'd say that."

"Why?"

"You look like a man with too many secrets."

"Princess, that's the understatement of my life." He flashed a smile, but it faded quick and held too much unspoken truth. His breath teased across her face, taunting her with an almost kiss.

"Whatever you have in mind for me, I'm not interested."

"Oh yes you are. Curiosity is killing you."

His hands had claimed her waist. "There are worse ways to die," he softly challenged, tugging her closer. Heat torched her in an unexpected rush as breasts pressed against his very solid chest. The man felt like red hot sin.

"Death by stiletto. Now that's something worth bragging about."

She smirked, "I'd break your bad boy rebel heart."

"I dare you to try."

"Don't underestimate me."

"Same here, Lady Long Legs."

The name made her smile. "You like what you see?"

"Maybe. But I still say you look like trouble."

Madison met his dare halfway, giving the Ducati rider a small taste of the trouble she could offer. Was it wrong to kiss him? Probably. But this kiss had a purpose. Everything she did tonight had a goal.

But damn oh damn, did he kiss good.

Strong arms drew her in. That small taste of trouble wasn't enough. He liked trouble and wanted more. She became plastered against him. It was a delicious stolen taste. He didn't just kiss. The man seduced her, slow and skillful, as if she were a new kind of candy he wanted to savor.

He won. Madison totally lost.

Her body betrayed her, hips instinctively swaying, tilting to fit better against him as his hands pushed against her backside, increasing their heat into an unbearable sensual ache. When she finally remembered her goal for tonight and drew back, she swore. "Holy hell."

Her breathless reaction made him chuckle. "I agree. Pretty damn good. Was that the game you wanted to play?"

"Sure," she calmly lied, "That's the one: *Kiss a Perfect Stranger*. It's my favorite game. Thanks for playing along." Then she quickly stepped out of his arms. "See you around, Mr. Anderson. It was lovely to officially meet. Now you know me. And I know you. We aren't strangers anymore."

Pivoting, Madison placed one foot in front of the other in a leisurely seductive walk she had perfected until the movement came naturally. Knowing he would watch, she let those patent leather stilettos carry her right out the door.

One. Two. Three.

At her car, she heard him behind her.

"Hey. Madison."

That dusky voice was exactly how she expected it would sound. But in her premonition, her heart had not jumped or felt too warm.

She coolly turned. "Yes?"

"Where are you going?"

"To find another perfect stranger to kiss, of course."

"Seriously?"

"Sure," she was thrilled he followed her outside. The kiss was a tasty lure. Now she needed to reel that bad boy in. Before tonight was over, Madison was determined to know everything about this secretive man.

"It was a great game. I smiled and you smiled. We were both a little bad, but no one got hurt," she amiably chatted. "Maybe I'll kiss every sexy eligible bachelor in San Diego tonight. Ooh, that will be fun. Do you think I'll get lucky and find my Prince Charming?"

Black helmet in hand, he glanced down at the sidewalk to hide a shocked laugh. His head shook as if he couldn't believe she said that. When he looked at her again, he grinned and didn't answer.

That smile was wicked.

"Are you an eligible bachelor, Mr. Anderson?"

"I might be."

"Are you Prince Charming?"

"Hell no."

Madison was amused by his vehemence. "I knew it. Good guys wear white." Her chin nodded toward the helmet and then his black Ducati Streetfighter parked curbside. "But bad boys wear black."

"You're wearing black, too."

"I'm not bad," she sexily purred, "I am Endlessly Intriguing."

"Yes, you sure are," he heartily agreed. "Come back inside with me."

"Why should I?"

"Because you want to. Then you won't have to kiss anyone else tonight," he persuaded, stepping close enough to latch one arm around her waist again, "we can play the 'getting to know you' game, and I won't be bored anymore."

"You think I can keep you entertained?"

He let out a barking laugh, "Yeah Princess, I do."

"Then you owe me a drink, Lover Boy."

He must be losing it. What was he doing talking to Joshua Archer's sister? Until tonight he thought the woman following him was harmless, a little nosy and unpredictable, but fairly harmless. The moment that long legged brunette beauty sat at his table and he looked into those pale green cat-eyes, he knew she was trouble. It was in the air.

But everything about Madison drew him in. Resistance was a waste of energy and time. Plus, she kissed like no one's business.

When they returned inside, their pub table was already filled. He bought drinks anyway. Now they stood on the upper deck, casually leaning against the brass railing. The music wasn't as loud up here. They talked for a while. It was friendly flirty banter. Madison was entertaining. She said clever things that were fun and made him smile.

"You must be the baby of the family," he told her.

"I am. What makes you say that?"

"Your sassy little 'It's My World' attitude."

She made a pouty squeak of protest. Hand upon one hip, Madison struck an offended pose that put a beautiful exclamation point on her wonderful sassiness. "It isn't my world."

"No?"

"Absolutely not. I am completely capable of sharing." Her pretty face gleamed with mischief. Trouble. She was trouble in a slinky black dress. Those sexy patent leather stilettos were killer.

"Did you follow me here tonight?"

"Ahh, Lover. If I say yes, it will feed your ego."

"If you say no, I'll call you a liar."

"Then let's agree on maybe."

Laughing, glad that he had someone interesting to talk to, he agreed when she offered to buy another beer. Just one more. What could it hurt?

Besides, he liked watching Madison walk away.

"Hey, how did we get here?" He asked as they parked, only vaguely recalling crawling inside her black Porsche. She gave him something. He felt sure of it. This went way beyond any drunk he had ever known. He felt euphoric, yet his body had become a wooden puppet with tangled strings.

Nothing worked right.

Madison had to help him out of the car.

"I know this place," he slurred in confusion, staring up at the seashell peach four-bedroom home neatly situated on a small hill on Diamond Street. It had beach charm. The front yard sloped up toward the house, keeping it above the street. On good days, it had a clear view of the ocean.

"I bought this place, oh man. Forever and ever ago. It was gonna be a surprise for—ahh, hmm," and then he completely forgot the name of that other woman, the one who had meant so much, but who went away.

"Yes, Mr. Anderson. This is your secret hideout."

He laughed. "How'd ya' know that?"

"I'm a very smart woman."

Suddenly, he felt happy. He liked smart women. They kept up, made life interesting, and sometimes even challenged him. And the woman beside him was the finest challenge he had ever met.

One arm slung around her shoulders, he leaned heavily on Madison as they stumbled to climb the flagstone steps going up the front walkway. Climbing the small hill, he looked at her and grinned.

"You're a wildcat, Madie Archer."

"That's nice. And you weigh a ton," she grunted. "Be a nice Lover Boy and help me get you inside the house before your lights go out."

"My lights are going—out?" He slowly blinked.

"Yes. Faster than I expected. Damn. Keys?"

He dug in his jeans pocket and found them. Leaning against the doorframe, he watched her open the lock.

He liked this beach house. There were other places he could stay, but the seaside getaway on Diamond Street in popular Pacific Beach was his favorite. It sat near the ocean on a landscaped knoll, but was miles away from anyone who might recognize him.

Being seen was not on his agenda.

"Couldn't sell the place, you know? Call me sentimental." He chuckled, half draped over Madison as she opened the door. They stumbled inside. Leaning him against the wall, she closed the door behind them.

"Kinda' glad I kept it."

"Oh? Why is that?"

"Cuz' now I got a place to escape."

She looked at him funny. "Escape from what exactly?"

That one took him a minute. "The whole evil lying world, I guess."

"Well, even Batman had a cave."

It made him laugh.

They made it into the living room. She tried unsuccessfully to guide him toward the red leather couch. Madison was talking about focusing and walking, two things he seemed incapable of doing anymore. Her voice was far away. Struggling to help him walk, they staggered, almost went down.

"I can do it," he said, righting himself.

But he lost the fight with gravity.

The whole house suddenly tipped sideways. Maybe it was an earthquake: a huge one. He was sliding. Through the drugged fog he heard Madison swear and felt arms try to catch him.

And then, nothing. And it felt good.

Almost like dying.

When he finally opened his eyes, he groaned. His head felt like a stuffed mushroom. He was lying cheek down on the floor. The slate tiles beneath his face felt cool, easing the vertigo swirling all rational thoughts together inside his brain. Maybe he should just lie still for a while.

Yeah. Lying here felt good.

Eyes closed. The world faded away.

When he found consciousness again it was with acute clarity. He had been out for a while. He knew by the ache in his body which was stiff from lying on the hard floor. Moving, he realized someone had handcuffed both hands behind his back.

"Goddamn sonofabitch!"

Fighting against the unwanted steel restraints, he heard a woman softly laugh. Then across the floor he saw a pair of patent leather stilettos waltz toward him. The black heels click-clicked on the stone tiles and the legs were long and sexy. A foot away, the woman bent over and flipped her head upside down. Curly brown hair tumbled too.

They were face to face. "Hello Lover Boy. Did you have a good nap?"

"Oh god, it's you."

"Mmm," she purred, "Mr. Anderson."

"Madison."

"Yes? Cool, you actually remembered my name."

"Yay for me," he complained.

"I didn't think that you would."

"What the hell did you give me?"

"Just a little Halcion."

"What's that?"

"A hypnotic sedative," she chuckled, far too perky for his sour attitude, "It's used to treat insomnia. Perfectly legal with a prescription, of course. Good thing *Dr. Illicit* runs a whole pharmaceutical company in the ladies' room at the nightclub. It's amazing what a hundred bucks gets you. We really should report that to the authorities, you know."

He groaned, "Evil woman."

"Now, now that isn't friendly."

"Do I look friendly?"

She giggled. "You must have been tired, Mr. Anderson. You slept a long time. It's almost dawn. You should feel much better now," she chatted. "Are your thoughts all nice and clear? You don't feel woozy, do you? If you feel bad, just close your eyes again. Don't worry. I'll keep you safe."

"Damn it, Madie. Let's not play this game."

"What game?"

"The one where I lose and you win."

"Ahh, Hot Stuff, you're no fun. I like winning." Madison grabbed his shoulder and shoved, rolling him onto his back. Then she promptly adjusted her black satin mini-dress and sat down on top of him, straddling his hips.

"Now what the hell are you doing?"

"Isn't that obvious?"

She was light enough he could probably toss her off. He was still handcuffed, wasn't sure if he could stand after being drugged, but his thoughts were clear. He shifted to dig his heels into the floor and fight, but Madison tsk-tsked, shaking one finger in his face like he were a very bad man. Then she casually leaned forward over his chest.

Prowling. Like a cat.

They were face to face again.

It made him pause. She smelled intoxicating, like an expensive floral cinnamon perfume. He'd been lured by that scent all night. As she moved he caught sight of curves and cleavage. He selfishly decided he liked how her body felt stretched over his.

Madison Archer was beautiful, stunningly unpredictable, and smarter than anyone he had ever known.

"Mmm, I like being in control, too."

"I can see that."

"Someone has to take charge of you."

He doubted that was possible. "You really think you're woman enough to tame me."

"Lover, you know that I am."

He didn't argue. "Are the handcuffs really necessary?"

"If I take them off, do you promise to play nice?"

He hadn't decided yet, but he quickly said, "Sure."

"Liar. But such a gorgeous liar," One soft finger affectionately stroked down his bristly cheek, "If you weren't so busy being bad all the time, I'd keep you company. Then you wouldn't have to sleep alone every night."

"Who says I sleep alone?"

"I do."

Then proving how unpredictable she was, that pouty mouth he had been fantasizing about all night suddenly molded over his. Despite his best intentions to remain angry at her, he groaned and wished for free hands.

He kissed her back.

Kissing her at the bar was mostly shock and awe.

This rocked.

He knew Madison liked it too because her body instinctively moved, sliding against his in a slow sensual dance. He doubted she even realized she was doing it. The movements felt too honest, to hot.

This was real fire.

He'd known heat before. But this was different.

She kissed like the wild nights might never end. "Madie, wait." He finally breathed, "This isn't right."

"No? Why not?"

"Because. We aren't, uh— we're not compatible."

She laughed aloud and playfully wiggled that lush body against his very aroused one, just to prove he was a complete liar. "Everything seems pretty damn compatible to me. Maybe you should shut up and kiss me again."

"I really shouldn't."

Suddenly, the playful flirty attitude disappeared.

Gone was that warm look of wanton invitation in her face. The hot pampered princess looking for a night of reckless sex quickly transformed into a mature confident woman with a mission.

"I ... see," her words were drawn out, like a judge giving a life sentence, "you are a guilty man. Have you anything to confess?"

He couldn't answer. This was the real Madison Archer.

This woman got her way in life not by the allure of attraction, but by calculated wit and wisdom. She had courage. A soul deep charisma shone in those pale green eyes. This woman took control of life, drew first blood, and never even flinched.

Seeing her truth made him swallow hard.

Even her voice had changed from the cutesy girlish tease to a mature smoky tone that meant business and would tolerate no bullshit.

"You think we aren't compatible," she said in a rich Boston brogue, "because you are pretending to be one man, when in reality, you are someone else entirely? Oh, Mr. Anderson. You disappoint me."

He swore. "My name is not Thomas Anderson."

"No shit. Your name isn't Neo either and judging by things I found on your laptop, you may know your way around computer systems, but this isn't the Matrix. And while I may be the nearest thing you will ever meet to a true Oracle, you my Liar-Lover Boy are definitely not The One."

Smart. Too Smart. Scary smart.

"It was a great alias. No one ever got it."

"I did. I got many of your secrets, actually." Her accent was thick now, rolling with wonderful ah's and long ooh sounds.

"You don't know jack."

That sweet tongue clicked. "You have seriously underestimated me, Sir. Most people do. It comes in handy sometimes. Tonight, it certainly did," she sternly judged, making him feel small. "I waltzed in there tonight and rocked your secret little world. You thought I was all slutty sex and no brain. Wrong, wrong, wrong. Maybe I should tell Solaris about our hot little adventure tonight. She might find our game quite interesting."

His insides turned to stone.

"Ahh, Lover Boy. Have you nothing to say?"

"I think you covered it."

"Did you underestimate me?"

"Severely." He swore, and meant it.

"Potty mouth."

"Devious bitch." But he immediately didn't mean to call her that, regretted saying the angry words. He felt bad. She wasn't an evil woman. Madison was smart enough to beat him at his own game. The woman was unorthodox and rebellious, but smart as hell and oh yes, she was endlessly intriguing.

"Sorry. Really. Pretend I didn't say that."

"Apology accepted. After all, I have provoked you."

"Teased, kissed, drugged, handcuffed—what's next?" He griped at her, "I can't wait for the tank of piranha's you have waiting for me behind door number five."

He liked her real laugh. It was spirited with just enough smile to make her beautiful. He really was in trouble.

"You're funny, when you want to be."

"Am I? Well you're my worst nightmare. Congratulations."

She found that extremely humorous. "I love honesty. It's such a game changer. Do you feel better for getting that off your chest?"

"Not really. You're still lying on my chest."

"Indeed I am. And here I shall stay, for now," she squirmed, getting comfortable on top of him. "Now you must answer one vital question."

"Maybe I will ... maybe I won't."

"You will," she solidly assured.

"What is your one vital question?"

"Well, I really like Solaris. She's a good woman with a very good heart. My brother really likes her too. I won't tell them about tonight or about you, only because I can see telling them your secrets will do more harm than good. And I guess I understand why you keep stalking her."

"Watching," he corrected.

"Sure, watching her. *Riiight*," she drawled in rolling Bostonian brogue. "Secretly following Solaris around on your super-hot racing Ducati, watching people, and hiding in the shadows hoping that no one will notice. Well, ta-da, Sherlock Holmes, I noticed."

"She's in danger."

"Yes, I agree. I also agree that we must keep her safe. I'm up for the job. Obviously, you signed on as her secret superhero."

"Is helping people a crime, in your book?"

She thought about it. "I guess you earn two points for trying."

"Just two?"

"Okay, three." Her head tipped to study him, those pretty cat eyes narrowing with pale gold-green disapproval.

"Although I have to say your personal motivations in life seem a bit dodgy for my taste. From where I sit, you look like a chronic member of Santa's naughty list. It's all you, you, you. What you want, what you need, and what you care about."

She tsked at him again. This time he did feel like a bad man.

"All in all, your life methodology seems radically askew, buddy."

He loved how she talked. No one had ever slammed him down mentally like this and no one dared challenged his life methodology, whatever the hell that was.

Santa's naughty list? Too true.

For reasons that defied logic, Madison had earned his respect. It felt like the things she said were a gift. Something he needed to hear.

"Personally, I think Solaris deserves to know the truth," she continued. "Not just about you, but about everything. But that's just my highly biased opinion, and what do I know anyway? I'm just a spoiled princess with nothing better to do than kiss perfect strangers in a bar. By the way," she frowned, "you are a dirty rotten toad. Not a Lover Boy and certainly not Prince Charming."

"Damn, Madie." He almost laughed at her endless chatter, except every analytical word she said was dead on, making him feel low. "Is there an actual question coming anytime soon? Or are you just digging my grave one insult at a time?"

"Oh. Well. Yes."

"I'd love to hear it."

"Are you going to stop them?"

"Maybe. If I can. I hope that I can." He wasn't sure how much she knew. It was possible she was bluffing. "Am I going to stop who, exactly?"

"Solaris and Joshua."

It kicked the bottom out of his heart.

"They belong together," she sternly enforced after he lay beneath her, silent for too long. "This is the real deal. Tonight, they are on their first real date. You know that. But you didn't follow them. Instead you went to the bar. Alone. Will give them a chance to find happiness, or will you cause trouble so big that it tears them apart?"

For long unforgiving moments of truth the beautiful interrogator hovered over him, watching his reaction to detect the answer.

Of course, he would leave them alone.

The whole thing just sucked. Solaris finding someone who honestly earned a place in her life was not something he expected to happen. But he had watched them together. Her heart was right there in every sunny smile. He knew her so well. Whatever she felt for Joshua, it was good.

She deserved something good.

Madison must have seen the raw truth in his face. Giving a heavy sigh, her head shook as if she felt genuinely sorry for him.

"Close your eyes, Mister."

"No. I don't trust you."

"Just do it. I'm getting up now. I may have kissed you and we both enjoyed that naughty game, but you aren't allowed to peek up my dress. And yes, I do wear panties," she chatted in a way he found charming. "No, I will not tell you what color they are."

He chuckled, "You're a riot."

"I am? Hmm. Well, I guess you're pretty okay, too."

"Thanks. And the panties are black," he added.

Her head tipped. "What makes you think that?"

"Black bra. You're a matching underwear kind of woman. Victoria's Secret probably loves your credit card bill."

The dusky laugh was superbly pleased. "You just admit that you checked out my D-cups."

"Hey, I'm a single man with a healthy sexual appetite and eyes," he defended. "You're the one who stuffed the ultimate temptation into a killer push-up bra."

"Ahh, very nice comeback."

And she smiled. That smile had promise.

Trusting, his eyes closed. He felt her lift, sitting on her heels over his hips. When her stilettos were steady, she grabbed his shoulders, pulling him up off the floor too. She was stronger than she looked. Sleek and sexy, but made of steel.

Staggering awkwardly to his feet, finding his legs held and wouldn't buckle again, the arms still handcuffed behind his back now tingled from the weight of two bodies lying upon them.

"Okay, you can look now."

Eyes opened. She stood in front of him. "Well gee, that was fun. Especially the part where you dope me and leave me passed out cold on the floor." he dryly congratulated. "Best date ever. Again, please."

Madison snickered. "You are one seriously screwed up man."

"Yeah? Tell me something new."

"Solaris deserves a chance at happiness."

"I know."

"Joshua wants to love her."

"Point taken. Can we discuss something else?"

"Like underwear?" She smirked.

"Please."

Instead Madison ducked around his bent elbows, slid behind him and unlocked the cuffs. They clinked together as she dropped the steel confinement into her giant black purse on the coffee table. What else did she hide inside that bag of tricks? He probably didn't want to know.

A gun? Maybe. That woman was armed and dangerous.

Rubbing his wrists where the metal handcuffs had dug into his skin, he looked at the floor where he had slept half the night. He waited for Madison to say something else.

He could take it, probably even deserved it.

But he felt surprised to hear her heels click-click, striding away. When he looked up, she was already at his front door.

"Hey, Madie?"

"What?" She swiveled, hips were all attitude, shoulders squared with resolve. Her expression was serious satin again.

The woman had the best poker face on the planet.

"Our kisses were really hot."

That pert mouth curved. "They had an interesting heat." Green eyes studied him, then her head tipped, questioning. "You should be furious at me. But you aren't. Why is that?"

"I've learned to respect smart beautiful women."

Her tsk-tsk wasn't very sincere, "Such a charmer. You're so bad."

"Takes one to know one," he accused. "Without charm and being bad, we'd still be strangers. You know, we could try this game again, sometime."

She gave a short sexy laugh, "Minus handcuffs?"

"Definitely. No drugs either."

"Sorry about that. You're a pretty big guy. I wasn't sure how much would take you out. Drugs really aren't my area of expertise. I probably gave you too much."

"I will live."

Glancing away from him to keep from laughing aloud, when those mischievous green eyes met his gaze again, a small snicker escaped anyway.

"That's good. All in all, I prefer my men alive and kicking. It makes the game more fun."

Damn, he liked her. "Will I see you again?"

Considering it, Madison vaguely looked past him. She had done that several times tonight. It was a peculiar quirk, but it fit her uniqueness.

"There is a distinct possibility our paths will cross."

It made him happy.

One thumb hooked toward his cell phone on the coffee table. His wallet lay there too. She must have taken them out of his pocket. "I got your super-secret number, Batman. If I get bored, I'll call. Play safe. And remember, the bad guys shoot to kill."

"You be safe too."

"Always. Thanks for caring." Then she remembered, "Your Ducati is parked inside the garage. Keys are on the kitchen table. I took a cab back to the nightclub and rode it here while you were take a little nap." Her wild-child grin curved. "That baby kicks ass."

"You rode my racing bike in heels and *that* dress?"

"Sure. It was awesome. Bet you wish you could have watched."

"Hell yes."

She blew him a kiss. Then she was gone.

Hearing metal lightly scrape as the door was locked from the outside, he grinned and wasn't the least bit mad. While he was knocked out cold on the floor and she spent the night rummaging through this house discovering every secret he kept: she had stolen a set of his keys.

He had not seen the last of Madison Archer.

Madison had a terrible headache. Pain pierced her brain and burned her eyes. It felt like the Civil War was being waged right between her temples. It was all his fault. Why couldn't the Ducati rider just spend a quiet Sunday with his very fine butt parked on the couch while he watched sports, like a nice boring man?

No, Thomas liked to stir up trouble and his actions echoed through her senses. Madison saw every alternate future for everything he did. The doorways and choices were endless. Some were good.

Most were very bad.

Feeling Joshua was easy. He was completely focused upon Solaris, letting his presence in her life deflect trouble and gently change the future. But the Ducati rider was focused upon fixing all the wrongs in the world, singlehandedly.

He was making her nuts.

Following him today wasn't an option. She pushed her luck last night by handcuffing the poor man. The fact that he wasn't livid was a small miracle. Thomas deserved some space. Too bad he was so stubborn. A confession would have simplified life. Madison knew his real name. Knew it the first moment they met. She understood why he worried about Solaris.

It would have been nice to hear the truth from him.

Last night after their naughty adventure, Madison returned to the hotel she had chosen for the night, since one future she had envisioned said that Joshua and Solaris might need some privacy. Normally she loved luxury accommodations. Last night the big room had felt lonely.

It was an odd feeling. Madison never felt lonely. She was one of those rare people who felt completely at peace with her own company. Damn Thomas. He messed up her happy solitude. Since Solaris was at Wyatt's, eliminating the chance she might walk into the house and see naked people, at dawn Madison packed her belongings and checked out of the hotel. Then as the sun was rising on a new day, she quietly slipped into Joshua's place on Coronado Island. The seaside house felt friendlier.

She slept until almost noon. And woke with a migraine headache that no amount of pain pills seemed to cure. If only Thomas would behave. Joshua was home today, too. His date last night had been tame and civilized, especially for two people on the verge of binding two lives into one.

Madie saw that future too. She hoped it happened.

"Hey, I cleaned this." Joshua complained when he saw their messy kitchen, "What are you doing?"

"I'm cooking dinner."

Surveying the countertops littered with pots and utensils Madison had no experience using, the potato peels splattered around the sink, and smelling the chicken roasting in the hot oven, he scowled.

But she felt proud. The chicken was almost done.

"You don't cook, Madie."

"I can. I just choose not to."

Joshua found the square hammer gadget that looked like a medieval torture device with spiked flat ends. She had left it lying on the counter by the cutting board. He held it up and didn't look happy.

"What were you doing with the meat tenderizer?"

"Is that what that's for?" She snatched the stainless-steel mallet out of his hand. "I thought it was a potato smasher."

The look Joshua sent was dumbfounded.

Her pride sunk.

"So, you boiled the potatoes until they were soft and planned to put them on the cutting board and just give them a good whack?"

"Sure. Isn't that how you make mashed potatoes?"

He pointed at the professional electric mixer. "I cut them into small pieces and stick them in that. Then I turn it on slowly and add milk and butter. Geez, Madie. You were going to destroy the kitchen. We would have had flying potatoes, everywhere."

She felt deeply offended by his superior tone. "Just because you, Mom, and Victoria always cooked at home doesn't give you the right to treat me like a child."

"Flying potatoes," he grimly repeated.

Madison still held the meat tenderizer in her fist. "Apologize."

"No. Put it down."

She refused. "You hurt my feelings. I worked hard to make dinner. I set the table with nice china and everything. It was supposed to be a celebration. We've become a team. I feel good about that. You should too. Now say you're sorry."

"For saving the potatoes from a horrific death?" he shook his head and laughed. "I don't think so."

The steel hammer flew at his chest.

Joshua was fast. His fist caught the handle, snatching it out of midair. He wasn't mad. Joshua rarely let life get under his skin. It would take more than a flying hammer to make her brother angry. He grinned, flipped it end over end, and caught it again.

"You're gonna pay for that."

"Why should I? I'm the one feeling unappreciated."

"Tell it to the poor potatoes."

Madison grabbed a plastic mixing bowl from the counter and flung it like a Frisbee. He used the hammer as a bat and hit a home run across the kitchen. The bowl clattered to the floor.

"Say you are sorry, Joshua."

Now they had a game. He grinned wider. "I will not."

He ducked as a big wooden spoon missed his head. Then paper towels sailed his way, unrolling in a thick white ribbon as it flew. As he watched the distraction, she moved quick across the kitchen.

Her glass of iced tea was emptied across his head and chest.

Joshua howled. "Madison!"

She squealed and ran out of the kitchen. But she didn't make it very far. In the dining room, a heavy saucepan flew from behind and connected hard with her butt, knocking her flat. "Uugh!"

She was sprawled out on the floor. Rolling over, Madison saw Joshua coming after her. She jumped up and sprinted through both arched doorways of connected dining room and back through the living room. Turning back to look for him, a plate he snatched off the dining table cracked off her forehead. The porcelain china shattered into several pieces.

"Joshua! That could have hurt."

"Did it?"

"Well, no."

"Then thank our Archer genetics for your hard head."

He ducked back into the kitchen, but quickly returned. Now he held an aluminum cookie sheet in one fist and a pitcher of water in the other. His shirt and hair were drenched. He looked serious about retaliation.

"I only used one glass of tea. That's a gallon of water."

"Yes, it is. You started this game. Now choose your weapon."

Madison grinned, dashed across the living room and snatched up the fireplace poker. Joshua had chased her. "Stop. Stop right there," she threatened, holding it before her like a sword.

"No. You soaked me."

"Because you hurt my wee tender feelings."

He snickered. "Ahh, poor little baby."

She lunged, trying to keep him away. He blocked the fireplace poker with the cookie sheet. "This means war."

"Bring it on, big brother."

Joshua chased her around the house, fighting and laughing. It was great fun. Finally, they bent the cookie sheet in half. He tossed it aside and grabbed a long red umbrella from the closet. Then they parried and blocked, skillfully fencing their way through the entire downstairs.

They met in a standoff when Madison trapped herself on top of the dining table. Round and round they fought, using the fireplace poker and red umbrella as swords.

Joshua wouldn't let her get down. And he still held the pitcher of water in one hand. "I should throw you in the ocean."

She banished the fireplace poker at his chest, keeping him at bay. "Your shirt and hair are dry again. And admit it, you're having fun. We haven't practiced like this in a long time."

"Your skills have definitely improved."

"Why, thank you kindly, Sir." She laughed, taking a bow. Suddenly Madison smelled smoke. "Oh no. My chicken!" She took a flying leap off the table. Game over, they both ran.

The oven door seeped with gray curls of smoke. As Joshua yanked it open, orange flames leapt out. The fire only danced more wildly as the pitcher of water soaked her burnt chicken. It didn't go out. He grabbed the kitchen fire extinguisher. The white foam suffocated the flames.

"Uugh." Madison complained. "That's a nasty god-awful mess."

"That was oil burning! Why the hell did it catch fire?"

"I don't know. Maybe it was the butter."

He scoffed. "You buttered a chicken?"

"Sure, like you do with the Thanksgiving turkey. I rubbed it all over the skin. Then I set the temperature super high and turned the oven to broil so it would roast up nice and brown. It shouldn't have burned. It only baked for," she glanced at the microwave clock to see the time, "well—three hours."

Joshua laughed so hard it made his eyes water.

"This isn't funny."

"Oh yes, it is," he snickered. "It's hilarious. Madie, a turkey cooks at a medium temperature and you cover it with foil to keep the oils inside. It's a big bird, so it cooks for a while. That chicken was small. Probably only needed an hour at 325. And the broil setting is for things like garlic toast, for only two minutes. That poor chicken was doomed the moment you bought it."

She felt silly. "Maybe I need some cooking lessons."

He was still chuckling. "Or a good cookbook."

"The fire alarm didn't go off," she noticed.

"It should have. Maybe it needs new batteries. Now that we know the alarms failed to call the whole city to our burning house, it's your job to replace them." She wasn't happy, but the fire department busting down their front door would have been embarrassing.

They opened all the windows to air out the house. The boiled potatoes had sat in the pot of hot water for so long they were disgusting mush. Those went in the garbage.

After Joshua removed the soggy chicken from the oven and threw the whole blackened pan in the sink, he couldn't stand the burnt smell anymore and decided to visit Solaris. Her cast was being removed tomorrow morning.

It would be another important day.

Madison saw their potential futures. She hoped they would choose the right one. "Will you tell her what dumb thing I did?"

"No. I don't gossip. Just clean it up."

"Cool. Thanks. You're my favorite person."

Joshua grinned wide, "Am I?"

"Naturally." She smiled. "Nobody else would play with me like that. People cling to their self-awareness and feel awkward instead of letting go and enjoying the moment. That voice inside would shout that adults don't play. So, even if they wanted to, they wouldn't laugh and have fun."

His head tipped, "Are we talking about Victoria?"

Madison snickered. "I guess I was. Our sister is too adult."

"And she'd say we were being reckless, that we might break something."

"We did. We broke the cookie sheet and a plate."

He laughed. "It sure was fun."

Madison agreed. Joshua hugged her and left.

While she was cleaning the kitchen mess, Captain Morgan appeared looking hopeful. But he sniffed the air, looked disgusted and walked away. Even the cat knew her cooking needed work.

"Fine, you snooty Pirate. I'll buy a cookbook."

Getting rid of the source of the smoky smell, Madison carried the chicken outside and dumped the charred remains into the big trash dumpster in the back alleyway. The pan went too. She gave it a final sassy salute.

"Rest in peace, Chicken Briquette."

Clunk, it hit the bottom of the steel container with a sad rock-hard thud. "Yuck. What a disaster. Now all because of you, Stupid Chicken, I get to buy a new roasting pan and clean the house too."

Feeling eyes upon her, she whirled around.

The Ducati rider casually leaned his back against the neighbor's tall wooden fence. Arms folded over his broad chest, he was eavesdropping on her eulogy for the cremated chicken. The grin curving his handsome face was deeply amused.

And sexy. Too damn dangerously sexy.

"Mr. Double-Life. What are you doing here?"

"I was in the neighborhood." Strolling forward as if finding Madison in the back alley talking to burnt dinner was not shocking at all, he stopped close and slowly ran his thumb across her forehead. It stung.

"He left a mark."

"What? Joshua did?" Her hand flew to touch the tender skin, discovering a lump that felt slightly bruised. "Well. That's just dandy. Hooray for me, I shattered a plate with my face."

Thomas softly chuckled. "With your hard head. Not your pretty face."

She realized that Joshua's beach house had many windows, front and back. He had obviously watched their fight.

"Stop spying on me."

"Make me stop."

"I could tell everyone all your secrets."

"You could," he calmly assessed, completely untroubled by her threat, "Which leaves the much larger question: why haven't you?"

He had her there.

Why hadn't she told Joshua? They were together all day. Madison could have hinted at the truth, but she had done nothing at all to betray this man's identity.

"What? No smart-ass comeback?"

"I'm working on one."

That earned her a cocky grin, "I bet."

Standing here in the dusky evening half-light with a man too handsome and smart for his own good, irresistible warmth stirred inside. Madison wondered how long she could remain cool and objective to their unique situation.

"How long do I have before you tell them about me?"

That offended her. "I'm no tattle-tell. I promised to keep your secrets and I will." Her firm objection clearly earned respect. "Besides, I get bored easily and you possess certain entertainment value."

"Sooo, I interest you." Judging by the sinful smolder in his voice, his mind had gone diving beneath the satin sheets. "Ditto, Lady Long Legs. I like sexy sassy women who dance on tables."

"I was not dancing on the table," she hotly shot back in her own defense, "Joshua needed to apologize."

"For?"

"Saying I can't cook."

Once again, another man heartily laughed at her lack of cooking skills. "Does that poor cremated chicken in the dumpster get a vote?"

Madison growled. "Don't make me hurt you."

His suggestive grin grew wicked. "Please?"

"You're terrible."

"Not I," he innocently denied, "You were the one causing Archer anarchy by declaring revolutionary kitchen war with the fireplace poker."

She refused to grin. "It was handy."

"Impressive fencing skills," he congratulated.

"Joshua used to be my sparring partner."

His chin tipped. He found that curious. "Who in modern America actually spends time learning to swordfight? It sounds a little old school, to me. Don't most women take martial arts classes for self-defense?"

"Kickboxing," she volunteered.

"So... those long legs really are your secret weapon." His brown eyes scanned down her body. She wore a pink summer tank top and denim shorts today. Nothing special, but he seemed to approve.

"You aren't allowed to look at me like that."

"It's a free country, Madison Liberty." She liked how his deep voice said her name. He must have remembered from last night. "I will look at you if I want to."

"I have guns," she warned.

"Very nice guns," he flirted.

"Lover, you must need a good ass kicking."

"You are very welcome to try." But he grinned.

She couldn't stop the smile. "Goodnight, Mr. Anderson. Go find someone else to watch. The show is over. I have a smoky house to clean and my bruised pride to nurse. After that, I'm calling it a night. You should too."

She bowed with flourish like a true performer.

"Goodnight, Madison."

Leaving him standing alone, she locked the tall yard gate behind her, making sure it rattled noisily into place. Not that a locked gate would slow him down if he really wanted inside, but just to make a point.

Do not enter.

At the back door she left standing open when she carried out the charbroiled chicken, Madison scooped up curious Captain Morgan. He'd waited with black boots standing on the threshold. The pirate loved his safe home too much to venture outside.

"Hey Henry. Want some canned cat food?"

The big calico mewed and purred, clearly preferring his Friskies to anything Madison might cook. As she turned to close the back door, down the block she heard the familiar roar of a Ducati.

Madison smiled.

She should have realized earlier that he was nearby. Her headache had disappeared. Now that he was driving away the throb in her temples returned. Maybe tomorrow she'd hunt him down. Tonight, she had a bigger headache to deal with: scrubbing out the oven.

Silver Strand

Life brought me to my knees,
Then the Winds of Change blew me away.

~~ Solaris

"No more surgery," Solaris told her surgeon on Monday morning. The doctor lectured. Her ankle was weak. More surgery might help. It was a waste of breath. She was adamant. "Absolutely not. Find another solution." The doctor sighed and looked at Joshua for help.

"Let's try physical therapy first," he suggested.

Solaris couldn't walk. The bones had healed, but the tendons were weak. Her ankle hurt to bear weight. "Two weeks, Laurie. If you haven't improved by then, I think you should listen to your doctor."

His solution appeased everyone. Agreeing, she received cortisone shots to strengthen the tendons and a stiff ankle brace for compression and support. She scheduled physical therapy sessions twice a week. Supported by sheer stubbornness and her deluxe new ACE ankle friend, she gimped to Joshua's black Jeep where she collapsed in the passenger seat.

She looked ready to cry. But Joshua didn't coddle or offer sympathy that might weaken her resolve. "We'll work to make it strong."

"What can we possibly do?"

"You'll see." He left the hospital and drove the main road through the island, passing both turns leading toward their houses. At the Hotel Del Coronado, he continued another four and a half miles south toward the narrow spit of land called Silver Strand.

Once, this place had seemed ominous.

Just by being near Solaris, he successfully changed that. Today it gleamed with sunlight. The long creamy beach was empty for more than two miles. Kite-riders and local surfers enjoyed the long rolling waves, but most venturing this far south stayed near the public parking areas where showers and bathrooms were conveniently close. The beach itself was nearly deserted.

"Physical therapy begins today," Joshua declared.

Looking at Silver Strand and the big rolling waves famous for bringing shells and sand dollars to shore, she asked, "We're walking in the sand?"

"It will strengthen your leg."

"My brace will get dirty and wet."

"We'll buy a clean one for at home," he pointed at her foot, "This one is your official beach buddy. I want you to walk the beach until you kick ACE's ass."

Seeing the logo on the black brace, she grinned. "You always know how to make me smile." Leaning over, he kissed that beautiful smile. "Thank you, Joshua."

"You're welcome."

He paid the parking permit and carried her camera bag, just in case. Holding hands, he helped her limp through the thick loose sand, heading toward the water.

When she reached the damp shoreline that was packed hard from rolling waves, Solaris carried her smiley sneaker and dug bare toes into the sand.

"That feels great. I've missed this."

"We're coming here every day."

She smiled wider now. "I look forward to it."

Solaris moved slow. Joshua matched her pace. He liked Silver Strand. The surf here was tall and began building over coral reefs a distance from shore. The sea rolled in lengthy white curls that sometimes spanned the entire length of the beach and rumbled with power as they broke. Salt spray moistened the air. After the waves broke, water slid toward them in shallow licks that kissed the beach, then pulled back again. The wet seaside glistened in the sunlight, like gold flakes were trapped in the sand. It was the most beautiful beach he'd ever seen.

"What makes the sand shine like that?"

"Mica flakes," she informed.

"It looks like gold dust."

Solaris gave his hand a small squeeze. She looked peaceful. Coming here was the right thing to do. "When I was little, I saved the sand in bottles. I had a whole collection in my bedroom window. But it never gleams quite the same way when you take Silver Strand away from its home. It only captures the sunlight right here on the beach, where it was born."

"You like this place."

"It's my favorite beach in the whole world."

They walked a mile.

Joshua watched the waves and held her hand. Seagulls waddled along the shore and circled overhead. Some sat on the dunes, warming themselves in the sunny sand. Pelicans skimmed the water, fishing. A flock of sandpipers ran down the waterline ahead of them, stopping occasionally to rapidly stick pointy beaks into the sand, munching on sand crabs. Then the whole group ran again. They were hyper little birds. Their spindly legs churning so fast they looked comical. As he and Solaris approached, the brown and white pipers didn't bother flying away, they simply ran further ahead.

"Hey, look." He pointed to movement in the water.

"Dolphins!"

Three raced through the large curling waves, riding the crests like nature's original surfers. They were joined by two more. It was a family, weaving through the water, playing in the summer sun.

"Wow, that's cool."

Automatically, Joshua slid the camera bag off his shoulder and held it while Solaris removed the professional Canon from the protective case.

"Thanks." She adjusted the focus and lighting to make the camera capture the action at a high-speed, with deep contrast to compensate for the bright sunlight and define the details. Then she watched the waves.

The dolphin family had turned, catching another big wave. They were riding it toward shore. As the water stood upright, inside the thick curl they clearly saw five bodies. Sunlight illuminated through the tall wave, making the ocean nearly sheer.

She captured a dozen rapid pictures.

Five faces came toward them now. It was surreal. Then playing a game of follow the leader, they zipped toward the south and followed one another right through the length of that long curl of seawater. She captured that, too.

The wave tumbled over and the magic was gone.

"Cool. That was a great moment!"

Solaris checked the digital screen. Her photographs showed incredible detail. The wave gleamed gold and blue, but inside it, the dolphins happily raced through the current, their sleek bodies sliding like surfers. Their entire profile was visible, from fins to intelligent faces. She even caught the instant they turned. Some were still looking right at the camera, but two had raced through the curl, bodies flying through the sheer water.

It looked like fun.

"Those will sell really well."

"Yes, they will. Thanks for bringing my camera."

"You're very welcome."

She put the camera away. On their return walk, they picked up sand dollars. Clam shells, scallops, and abalone shells littering the shore too, but Solaris liked the fragile white circles with their five-petal flower pattern.

"Here's a whole one," Joshua gave it to her.

"Ooh, it's perfect. Not a crack."

By the time they returned to the parking lot Solaris had a dozen perfect round sand dollars. Back in town they bought a clean ankle brace. But at Wyatt's house, no one was there. She confessed she hadn't seen her brother much lately, some days he never came home at all.

"Have you seen the Ducati rider again?"

"A few times, but he keeps his distance."

Joshua didn't like that she had seen the man in black. He had hoped the rider was gone. "I think it's your brother."

"Unfortunately, I do too." She told him about the morning he came home with mud on his boots. Since that day, Wyatt had not slept in his bed at night, but appeared sometimes looking worried and distracted.

"Want me to talk to him?" He offered.

"No. I will handle it."

Solaris washed and arranged the sand dollars in a blue glass dish. They looked nice with Wyatt's ocean themed sculptures. They made iced tea and went outside. Barefoot, she sat on the flagstone edge of the pool and soaked both feet in the lukewarm water. The left ankle was swollen and had pink marks where the brace held it tight as she walked.

Joshua sat too, but didn't put his feet in the pool.

"You'll be sore tonight."

"Probably," she agreed. "At least the cast is gone. I hated the constant reminder of everything bad." Eyes focused upon the offending foot. The afternoon sun reflected on the pool. Ripples from the small movements of her feet turned the bright reflective surface into rings of liquid gold. The circles expanded, slowly rolling all the way across the pool.

But Solaris wasn't happy anymore. Sad eyes watched the shiny circles drift and widen. Her thoughts went far away, too. Joshua waited and watched. Emotions played across her honest face. He didn't say anything. Her feelings seemed too personal to intrude. Even the aura around her body turned a strange shade of blue.

Like sea and sky and sorrow.

He'd never seen anything like it.

Finally, a tear ran down her cheek. "Trust me to understand," he simply offered. Realizing he had been watching, one hand quickly wiped her face. Solaris tried to pretend nothing had happened.

"I'm just tired."

Joshua didn't believe it. But he knew it was time to go. "Okay. Rest that leg. Will you be okay alone here tonight? I could send Madie over."

"I've spent years alone. I'm just fine." The answer was harsh. It stung. He stood and stepped away from the pool. Realizing he was leaving, Solaris pulled wet feet out of the water, dried them on a towel, then put on the clean brace. She walked him to the door.

"What time should I pick you up in the morning?"

"For what?"

"To walk the beach again."

"You aren't responsible for me."

Something had happened inside Solaris. Her aura was still that strange sad blue and her emotional walls were solid steel again.

"Caring about someone naturally carries responsibility."

"But I don't need a babysitter."

"Good. Do you need a friend?"

Her chin puckered. She looked so heartbroken. He didn't know why. But pushing for answers would meet with resistance. Whatever this was, she wasn't willing to talk. "I care about you, Laurie."

"I know. I'm fine."

"Call if you'd like company. Okay?"

She nodded.

Feeling hurt and confused, Joshua walked away.

Walking in the thick loose sand going down to the ocean on Silver Strand hurt like hell. Solaris was stubborn and kept going anyway. It would be easier once she reached the wave compressed shoreline. As dawn peeked through thick marine layer fog on the Pacific horizon, she trudged the beach all alone.

Yesterday, she hurt Joshua's feelings. She should explain about losing Tristan and apologize. Yes, she did need a good friend. She had one once. Now he was gone. Remembering was painful.

When she reached the hard-packed sand near the surf line, her sore ankle thanked her. It was tender today, but felt sturdier. Looking at the funny footprints the bandaged foot made, she saw the red polish on her toenails was chipped.

Tristan liked her toes. There were no smiley faces painted there anymore. She hadn't had happy feet since their time together in Miraflores.

Why did everything have to remind her of him?

She had felt so peaceful yesterday, walking the beach with Joshua. Trouble disappeared. But afterward at Wyatt's pool she watched golden rings of sunlight on the water and had thought about how small actions could create big ripples. It was a profound introspective moment.

One that hit her hard.

Tristan simply deciding to come see her in Peru had created a ripple through both of their lives that had devastating effects.

That one small decision changed everything, forever.

Mourning his shortened life had come crashing back through her heart. But more than losing him, Solaris also mourned her lost career. She missed the life of adventure and freedom she had loved. The dolphin pictures were great, but it was a chance moment. She couldn't spend her life sitting on the beach waiting for life to send her something amazing.

Her courage to chase down beautiful moments was gone.

Only sadness remained.

Sorrow had kept her company all night. Today she felt awful. Her heart ached, her stomach was in a knot, and her mind was a muddy mess.

She missed the good days.

Damn Tristan. Why did he have to come to Peru? Why did he become obsessed with that ruby necklace? The Heart Stone was gone now too. If the Columbian really was smuggling diamonds into the States, why had Tristan taken it upon himself to discover who his American partners were? The truth wasn't worth it, if knowing cost you everything.

He'd still be alive.

She'd still be touring the world, living wild and free. But she would not have met Joshua.

That sad thought made her heart ache too, for a different reason.

Solaris slowly walked for two hours. At times when her ankle hurt too much she took off the brace and stood in the cool salty waves until it felt better. Then she walked on. Reaching the breakwater near the Imperial Beach pier, she felt surprised to realize she had come so far south.

Her thoughts had been lost. She turned around. Coronado Village was a small blur on the horizon. Gazing down the long creamy curve of sand that she had walked, the parking lot where her red Jeep waited seemed an impossible eternity away. Two and a half miles.

Solaris knew she had walked too far. For a woman who knew the rules of nature, she sure was dumb today. She had no water, no cell phone, and no one knew where she was.

Wyatt hadn't come home last night.

Joshua deserved a sincere apology.

Who knew where in the world Madison might be.

She started walking. Halfway back to the parking lot the pain inside her tattered heart became unbearable. Trudging up the glistening golden slope to find dry sand, Solaris sat down. Folding her arms around bent knees, she lay her face upon them and cried.

"You look lost." Startled Joshua silently appeared, the woman sitting in the sand, head bent, arms wrapped around her knees, hastily wiped her face with the back of her arm. But he saw. Solaris had been crying for a while. Eyes that saw beauty in the world were pink and sad.

"What are you doing here," she asked.

"Direct orders from your brother. Wyatt came by my place looking for you. I told him what the doctor said about your ankle. He made me promise to keep you safe, saying he had important business in LA for a while. So, here I am."

"Wonderful."

"Isn't it, though," he glibly commented, ignoring how annoyed and moody Solaris might feel like being today. Whatever was going on, she needed to get past it. She squealed when he flopped down in the sand beside her.

"Joshua!"

Watching her fuss and fume, he smiled wide and happy, openly daring her to defy his cheerfulness. Her annoyed expression quickly melted. Joshua had learned Solaris liked when he smiled. Attraction warmed the air. Satisfied they were on the same page again, he gave her a cold bottle of water from the leather backpack he carried.

"Thanks."

He looked to the north where Coronado Village looked small in the distance. "You went too far today."

"I'm fine. I was only resting." After drinking some water, she made a resigned huff, "Wyatt put you in charge of me, then disappeared again?"

Joshua nodded. "Left like a man on a mission."

Her eyes narrowed. "What was he driving?"

"A pearl white Dodge Viper; loud and crazy fast."

"At least it wasn't a black Ducati motorcycle," Solaris solemnly judged and he silently agreed. "How did he look?"

"Rattled and worried." Joshua honestly informed. "Your friend Kianna was with him. She stayed in the car talking on the phone. She looked worried too. Whoever she was talking to was clearly upset."

"That's weird. How do you know it was her?"

He flashed a playful grin. "How many pretty Hawaiian ladies do you know?"

"Only one."

"Then it was Kianna."

Now Solaris was livid, but not at him. "Damn Wyatt, I called and left him messages several times yesterday. He couldn't bother calling me back. But he takes off to LA with Kianna. I can't imagine why they would be together, except for my gallery. If he's planning another photography job for me, I'll shoot him. I'm in no mood to be creative." Looking at him, she added, "And Wyatt should know you have better things to do than babysit me? The nerve. I can handle my own messy life."

"Everybody needs someone, now and then. In truth, even before he stopped by, I was coming to find you anyway."

"Why?"

Joshua held her gaze. "I felt drawn here."

"To the beach?"

"No, Babe. I am drawn to you, only you. Always you."

That simple soft statement hung between them. Solaris looked thrilled. Then other thoughts made her equally sullen. Whatever shadowed her heart, it was huge. Finally, she looked away, picked up a broken clam shell from the sand beside her hip and chucked it at the sea.

"I can't do this today, Joshua."

"I didn't ask you to."

"Yeah, well IT is still there anyway."

"And IT will still be there tomorrow."

"That's reassuring." They sat together in contemplative silence, both watching waves roll into shore. He liked counting the series. The ocean had a rhythm, a dance of blue water rolling against golden sand. It was a living entity, the strongest perpetual force on earth.

Waves came in long curls.

At the height of each powerful crest, sunlight gleamed through the upright walls. It was the instant that water fought gravity and won. Inside that thick wave was the place where their dolphins yesterday had raced through the curl, playing with such joy. He'd never forget seeing it.

The crests started out small and grew larger with each new surge, usually in a series of eight, sometimes ten. Troughs between crests deepened, waves stood taller. But as the water crashed more impressively and gained strength, the waves wore themselves out.

Riptides sucked, undertows pulled. Water smothered moving water. Then at the magical moment at the end of a series when the ocean had worn itself out, the surface would flatten and glisten in the sunlight, as if taking a deep breath. He liked that part.

It was the peaceful lull before the watery dance began again.

"Ooh, big one," she whispered.

"Babe?"

"The waves," she clarified. "They roll in a pattern, getting bigger and taller. Then they crash hard and go almost perfectly smooth. Then it begins all over again."

"I noticed that."

"It's peaceful."

"Yes, it is." Joshua knew if he wanted Solaris to trust him with her problems, he must open that difficult door for truth first. "When you saw the pattern of the sea, you read my mind."

"I did?"

"Yes. I was sitting here watching the crests get higher. When the biggest wave rolls, the undercurrents pull down, towing the water away from shore. Then the waves lay flat for a moment as the sunlight touches the sea."

"I love that part. It's like a blanket of liquid gold."

"My thoughts exactly."

A tiny smile curved. "I like our unique connection," she confessed.

"Me too." Joshua held her hand, lacing their fingers together. "But you need to stop crying all alone, pretending everything is okay when it isn't. You should share your worries with me."

She hesitated. "But it's mostly just dumb girl stuff."

Joshua chuckled, "Liar. Whatever is bothering you, making you sit on the beach and cry all alone definitely is NOT private girl stuff."

Her guilty grin was cute.

"It is, I swear. It is my private stuff to think about and I am a grown girl, so that officially makes it my private girl stuff."

Joshua leaned closer. "I like your private girl stuff."

A pink blush touched her cheeks.

"Damn, Archer. Whew," she blew out a tense breath. "Nice way to shift gears. I managed to go a whole hour without thinking about sex and you and me. Thanks for bringing that touchy topic to the front burner again."

"A whole hour: you and me?" Joshua chuckled, flirting, "Babe. I can do much better than that."

Solaris laughed. "All men say that. It's a nice theory," she teased. "But actions speak louder than those over-confident words."

"You want some action?"

Shifting forward, one hand reached around her other hip. Leaning so they were face to face, Joshua moved in slow, calculating her reaction with satisfaction. He liked watching her breath quickened by degrees. As he moved in for the kiss, the sad blue aura around her disappeared. In his eyes, Solaris glowed with happy sunlight.

He thoroughly enjoyed when she met him halfway.

The kiss sizzled.

"You like toying with me," she breathed in accusation when they finally stopped playing. They had rolled. Solaris had pushed him over. Now Joshua lay flat on his back in the warm sugary sand and a beautiful breathless smiling woman straddled his hips.

"I like playing with our heat."

"It is fun," she agreed, kissing him again, slower this time, savoring what they had together. Her face had a healthy glow and amber eyes held a wonderful welcoming light. Tawny hair was loose. Hanging over him, a long sheet slid past her shoulder, brushing his cheek. He pushed it back, letting the silky strands slide through his fingers.

"Sorry I've been so moody."

"Then talk to me."

"I'd like to. But I'm really afraid you'll judge me and get mad."

"I rarely get mad."

"But I've kept big secrets ... some bad ones."

"Everyone has secrets," he advised, thinking of his own life. "The trick is to find someone you trust enough to share them with."

Rolling away, Solaris sat in the sand again. Playtime had made her laugh and smile. Sharing secrets made her brow furrow.

"Do you have any secrets?"

Joshua sat up, too. "Sure. Big secrets, some bad ones," he repeated her words. "But I trust you. I'd like to share. Hopefully you won't judge me and get mad." Her eyes had widened, yet gleamed with unshed tears. "I'll go first, okay?" She looked relieved.

"For starters, I see auras," he simply began. "Since yesterday when we sat beside Wyatt's pool, yours has been a sad shade of blue. Those feelings were strong. I could see it. For me, it's like seeing the truth inside your heart. It makes me want to help you. I can, if you let me."

Solaris drew a deep breath. Then she giggled. "No wonder we have such an eerie connection. You have abilities!" Her laugh was happy. "You just try to hide it. But this is why you're so serious all the time."

"Life is serious."

She sobered in a heartbeat. "Bet my serious life beats yours."

"I doubt it. I see darkness too, the secret trouble that people try to hide. My gifts are strong. For generations, Archer's have used our abilities to protect others. We are trained since childhood to put others first, to protect innocent people with our own lives, if necessary."

"Wow," her breath whooshed, "Okay, you win. That really is serious."

"Madie is gifted too."

"That one I figured out already."

It surprised him. "Oh?"

"Madison said she dreamed of me. She knew things. Shocking things." The depth of his confession sank in. "I guess that means you dreamed of me too."

"Yes. I did."

"Madie knew my special name from Peru."

"La Señora Luz de Sol?" She nodded, smiling when he said it. "I heard it in my dream too. Madison and I are a Guardian team. No Archer has ever been assigned to protect another before. She is my personal Guardian. Which means: the job facing me in protecting you from harm, also puts me in danger."

He watched her swallow that news.

"Someone wants to hurt you, Solaris. I don't know why. Maybe you do. Regardless, I promise to do everything in my power to protect you."

His honor bound pledge made her eyes water again.

"I was engaged once."

Joshua was thunderstruck. "That's your secret?"

"Yes."

A knot tightened him inside. It was possessive, resentful of the man who might have claimed this beautiful woman as his wife. "Let's walk," he simply said. Helping Solaris stand, they brushed loose sand off their bodies, then Joshua held her hand as they slowly moved toward home.

"Okay. I'm listening."

Solaris told him everything about Tristan. She left nothing out. He became barely aware of the beautiful beach and rolling waves. The world focused, narrowing down to just two people. Her voice told a story, the good and bad, so clear he could see it. Even the feel of her fingers laced between his felt amplified, as if this moment mattered.

Life was taking a breath.

How Joshua reacted to this could change them.

"Tristan believed the Columbian sent those men to kidnap me and to kill him," she finally concluded. "His plane crash wasn't an accident. It was too sudden, too neatly done, crashing in the mountains where no one could investigate or question. I think he was murdered."

"Does Wyatt know this?"

"No. Tristan made me promise to keep his secrets," she softly divulged, "And I have, but trusting you is the right thing to do."

This is why he dreamed of Solaris. The danger was very real. If someone suspected she knew about the ruby necklace and the illegal gemstone operation Tristan had been researching, she was now a target.

"In Peru, you two were together again."

Solaris looked up at him. "Are you asking if I slept with Tristan?"

"I shouldn't," he sighed, "but I guess I am."

"We didn't, at first."

Joshua felt jealous. That unfamiliar feeling burned. But it was selfish. He was far from being an innocent man. At least Solaris had loved someone. He had never let anyone get into his heart. Until her.

"He appeared out of the blue. It took me by surprise. Work was my life. For the first time in years, I felt beautiful to someone. He made me feel special. We slept together one time. You can judge me, I understand. I'm not making excuses for my behavior. But I was extremely lonely and tired of being alone. Being with him was easy. It was familiar, even if it wasn't the right thing to do. Does that make sense?"

"It does." They started walking again.

"Afterward, we both knew our relationship needed to wait. On the Amazon trip, he simply stayed with me. I didn't love Tristan, not the right way. He said I was too rational, always thinking through my emotions instead of falling. Our friendship was important, and he accepted that. But when I met the right man, it would make my heart kick and everything good inside of me would come to life."

Solaris swallowed hard. Her foot flicked a clam shell. It skittered across the moist gold-dust sand.

"And then, I met you."

Joshua wondered if that funny gesture of grabbing at her heart she always made was significant. Did her heart kick? She nervously glanced his way. In her eyes he saw honesty, beautiful and true.

Life took on new meaning.

No, he could not judge. He had no need for jealousy. Solaris wasn't just telling him secrets, explaining the dangerous past that still haunted her today. There was something equally dangerous here, a risk she took with every truthful word.

Solaris had found the right man.

Her wish for love was right there on her face. Joshua saw the truth, the lifechanging truth. Her feelings for him were stronger than the fear of rejection. But she was nervous, hoping he wouldn't break her heart.

"This is why I needed us to go slow." She concluded on a wispy breath.

"I understand. Thank you for trusting me."

"Are you mad?" Her voice was tiny and scared.

"No. That would be dumb."

She gave his hand a grateful squeeze and seemed to breathe right again. He liked how she affectionately toyed with his fingers as they walked. It was sweet. "Thank you. I was so worried about this. Keeping this secret was tearing me apart."

"I will admit," he offered a truth, "when you first said you were engaged to someone, I felt really jealous."

"You were? Why?"

"Because you could have been Tristan's wife."

Her head shook. "No, he wasn't the right man."

"Am I?"

It was bold, but he had to hear it.

She didn't hesitate. "Yes, I believe you are."

"Then we should get serious about us," Joshua decided. "We're the real thing. We both knew it the moment we met. It's time we commit to this."

"Commit, like getting naked and making love, commit?"

Joshua's heart felt lighter. "Well, that's one very good way."

It was a day for surprises. "I'd like that."

"But I refuse to be someone you regret," he sternly warned. They had stopped walking. "Being with me won't happen just because it's easy and familiar, like sliding on an old comfortable shoe."

She scoffed and half-laughed, "Nothing about us is easy or familiar. It's all so foreign and spooky it makes my head spin. I can't imagine making love to you. Even with clothes on, you make my heart beat too fast."

"I do?" He grinned.

"Especially when you smile. Stop that." His happiness only widened, felt warm as the sunlight on his face. "Sheesh. I'm doomed."

"Then be mine, Solaris. Give me today together, the whole day. Be with me, let whatever happens come, and stay with me tonight."

Amber eyes widened. "Just like that, take the plunge? Jump right off the deep end: commitment, and sex, and breakfast in bed."

"Sure, the whole nine yards. We're ready."

Her giggle was cute. "You said it again."

"What?"

"Shooaah," she emphasized his Boston accent.

"Breakfast in bed," he leaned in, softly reminded.

"You're killing me."

"No, Babe. I promise to keep you safe. I'm your Guardian. But I also want to be your lover. Today, tomorrow. For as long as you will have me."

Solaris sighed in acceptance and looked around, noticing where they were. While they talked they had walked clear to the parking lot. They had stopped on the beach side of the brick half-wall that bordered the pavement. His black Jeep was parked beside her red one.

"I need clothes for tonight," she negotiated.

"Okay. We'll stop at Wyatt's."

"And waking up together tomorrow doesn't mean we are living together. I still live at Wyatt's house. When it's time for me to leave, there will be no arguments or guilt. We are committed to us, but a little space is still important."

"That's a good rule."

"And we can't say things we aren't ready for. Like love and forever."

"That's acceptable too."

"You should call Madison. We might need privacy tonight." He agreed. Solaris looked at their Jeeps. A satisfied smile curved her lips. Apparently, she ran out of rules. "I'm not on the pill. You get to buy protection."

"Babe. I already have." Joshua drew her into his arms.

The kiss was hot, sizzled with promise.

And his heart felt warm with wishes.

After a short stop at Wyatt's for Solaris to shower, put on the clean ankle brace, and pack for the highly anticipated overnight stay, they decided to enjoy brunch at the Hotel Del Coronado before going to the Archer beach house. The casual time settled her nerves, but expectations was building. Every glance, every sexy smile from Joshua made her heart dance. She wanted this to be right.

He leaned closer across their small table, green eyes bright, "Your glowing, Laurie," he softly divulged, looking not at her face, but around her head. "Your energy is pink."

New to the uncanny aspects of his world, she asked, "Is that good, or bad?"

"It's beautiful, the color of joy. It's very sensual. It suits you."

After that, letting happiness flow freely felt natural.

Solaris wasn't sure what she expected from Joshua when they arrived at his house, but she hadn't anticipated how extraordinary being him would be. Every emotion in her heart was exposed to his eyes. She knew because he told her. They had no more secrets. His gift was laid bare.

As was she. Her aura was bright red, fiery with passion, and orange like the sun, he said, lusty and pure. Then Joshua kissed her deep, hands claiming her body in ways she had longed for, but had feared.

She was stronger than fear.

All her fear was gone. Solaris was fully in the moment. Joshua left no room for thinking. She needed him, needed what they could be together. Their previous kisses had nothing compared to this heat. Clothes became obstacles in their way. His shirt tore as she tugged off.

Joshua laughed. "Hey. I liked that shirt."

"But I like the man wearing it."

That sexy playful grin approved, "My turn." With his help, everything she wore fell on the floor. Then strong arms gathered her to his chest. Touching him felt so right. The magnetic pull they felt since the day they met was given free rein. His body felt healthy beneath her hands. Athletic and strong, Solaris wasn't surprised when he finally growled something about soft sheets, scooped her up and carried her upstairs.

Then, Joshua laid her naked upon his bed.

Bright gold, he finally decided that her aura was colored, as he loved and caressed every exposed curve, making her smile with pleasure. He seemed to like doing things that engaged her body, erased her mind, and stole her heart. Solaris was falling.

She could no longer tread emotional water.

Her safe shore was right here with Joshua. This is love. Real love. With that thought, the emotional energy he saw radiating from her body made him stop for a moment and stare.

"Wow," he breathed. "It's like you're made of sunlight."

"Oh god. You look shocked. Is that bad?"

"It's amazing," he stroking his palm across her cheek. "I am in awe. Gold is the color of good magic and purest joy. You are so happy it's spilling over around you."

The truthful observation made Solaris feel incredibly beautiful: not with nice skin and hair and pretty eyes, but deep inside her heart. The places no one saw. But Joshua saw.

"It's you," she told him, "my joy belongs to you."

He smiled. So handsome. "Babe. Damn."

Solaris didn't say more. The next words waiting on her tongue felt heavy, laden with promise. Joshua hovered over her, watching her. He was breathing fast and still seemed in awe. Pale green eyes held keen awareness, a silent acceptance of why she glowed.

"We're important," he simply said.

"Absolutely important."

"Later, we'll talk."

"Yes, we will."

He was a patient lover. Attentive, savoring their first moments, he made a feast of her body. His mouth and hands worked slow seductive trails over her breasts, down her abs. She was his. Joshua held her captive by the look in his eyes and the unspoken wishes in his heart.

No man had ever loved her like this.

He liked to touch. His hands never left her skin. When his mouth lowered, tasting her most intimate places, Solaris nearly cried hot tears, desperately needing everything Joshua gave. The emotional high was overwhelming.

"Babe," he breathed as she quivered beneath his touch. "It's okay."

"I just," she shuddered as fingers stroked, "I'm falling apart..."

"Then let me catch you."

As first she writhed on the bed, unfamiliar with the deliberate feelings he invoked of lingering pleasure. The way he made love was addictive and playful. His touch was sometimes barely a brush across her most tender skin. Always murmuring tender encouragement, looking at her face to judge the emotional effect, Joshua made sure that first and foremost, his actions touched her heart.

Solaris knew real love, breathed love.

Tasted love upon his lips.

"More," she finally whispered. "Please."

As their bodies united, Solaris cried out with joy, needing that intimate connection with Joshua. Their combined heat made her burn for action. Still, he was patient. His tempo was slow, savoring every shift of their hips, letting her enjoy the weight of him, how his strong body fit with hers.

Today, she was in the right place. Doing the exact right thing.

With the only right man.

Her hands stroked up his chest, then around, gripping his firm backside as he moved. It was the dance of dreams, of wishes coming true.

The best dance of her life.

Joshua was her one true partner.

Watching his abs tense as the needs of his body demanded more, Solaris arched her hips, taking him deep. Pleasure sounded, low in his throat. As everything inside her core tightened and shivered, he met that moment perfectly. It was a beautiful moment. An honest life-changing moment.

Solaris knew that no other man would ever touch her.

For as long as they both lived.

She woke to see a late afternoon glow through his bedroom windows. Lace drapes hung over white nautical shutters. The slats were tilted slightly open, allowing her to see the summer sun had dipped low in the sky.

White sheets. An oak table sat in the corner. Similar to the room she saw in Boston. But the man who owned it was gone.

"Joshua?"

No answer. Solaris smelled warm food, like hot buttered potatoes and salty meat. Below in the kitchen, she heard noises. It made her smile. He must have an acquired an appetite of another kind. Heaven knows his hunger for touching her skin had worked off some calories.

He was true to his word.

They had made love all afternoon. Every time she thought they were through and it was time to sleep, he proved her wrong. For once, Solaris liked being wrong. Curling up, smelling him on the pillows, she dreamed.

Soft lovely happy dreams.

When her eyes opened again, she wasn't alone anymore. Joshua occupied one chair by the table. Wearing only denim summer shorts and a smile, he looked comfortably sexy. Two plates with hot ham slices and a loaded baked potato were on the table. His potato lacked a few bites. Hers also had a salad. Two glasses of iced tea waited.

Covered by only the white sheet, she sat up, clutching it over bare breasts. One hand raked through hair rumpled by a man's hands.

"Hey, Sleeping Beauty," he grinned. Once again, a handsome man had watched her sleep. But this man didn't look like he had studied her with a heart full of regret. Joshua looked happy.

"You can cook?"

His light laugh felt warm. "Yeah, I can feed us."

"I'm impressed."

"Are you?" Something hot sparked in his eyes, a gleam of mischief. She liked when he felt playful. He rose from the chair, stripped down to nothing but skin once again, proving he still wasn't done with her.

"Geez, you are a hungry man."

He grinned. "Then feed me, Babe." Leaning down on hands and knees, Joshua came to her. Watching her reaction, he leisurely crawled like a tiger right up the length of the bed they had just shared. They were slow sexy movements made by a man gifted with strength and courage, making him a trustworthy Guardian.

Her lover and protector. A man who saw truth. "You're glowing again."

"I didn't glow when I was asleep?"

"No. It only happens when you look at me."

It brought memories of warm bodies moving together in the afternoon sunlight, of looking into his pale green eyes as they made love and seeing a lifetime of wishes coming true. It was a private dance too precious to speak of aloud, a dance meant only for her memories.

He smiled, remembering too. "You're mine, Sunlight Lady."

Hands reached out, in motions that were protective and possessive, he flipped away the white sheet and covered her nakedness with his own strong body. The warmth of him pressed down, a promise of the playtime yet to come. Solaris stroked her fingers through his ruffled brown hair.

"I love you, Joshua."

A brow arched, he drew back a little. "Wow. Okay."

The easy joy tumbled, falling to her middle. "Was that wrong?"

"No, but I thought we weren't saying those words."

Solaris gathered her courage. She refused to be afraid anymore. "Well, you see it. There's no point hiding the truth."

He drew a breath. "You glow because you love me," he clarified.

"Yes, Joshua. I glow with joy because I love you."

His expression turned serious. Rolling to lay beside her, Joshua told her the legend his sisters believed, that a love stronger than fear could release them from being Guardians. The dreams of danger would end. He'd be free. But he had doubts. After all, their father dreamed until the day he died.

"Maybe his heart wasn't true."

"It's possible. Dad was good to Mom, but they lacked real passion and spark. Madie believes he loved someone else first, a woman he never forgot. But Mom became his partner in life. So, they made it work."

Here was the basis for her worry, she realized. Tristan. "I didn't feel real love, until you." Still, he looked doubtful. "You don't think my love can release you?"

"Time will tell. You'll have to forgive my caution. But being an Archer is hard. When we fall in love, we fall completely. Archer's love with all our hearts and hope it lasts forever."

Solaris grinned. "Most people do, actually."

His playful smile returned.

"You fell," she said for him. "I see it in your eyes and feel the love in your touch. The words will come, whenever you are ready."

He looked relieved. "You're in my heart, Solaris."

She knew it was true. That was enough.

Part Two: Shadows & Secrets

Thief in the Night

Bad boys rarely behave.

~~ Madison Liberty

Breaking into Malcolm Thornbriar's infamous ivory tower offices was easy. The basement door was an ageing steel contraption with a double deadbolt lock that hadn't been upgraded in twenty years. Bypassing the alarm and cameras was trickier, but he'd hijacked tougher systems. The password into the computer was simple. Anyone who knew him could guess that one.

But what he found turned his insides cold.

He had suspected. Now he knew for sure. Nothing was what it seemed.

And everything centered around Solaris.

He saved the stolen files onto a USB flash drive, erased all traces of his hack into the system, turned the computer off again, and made sure everything was exactly in place on the desk. The man was obsessive compulsive to a fault. If even the pen moved, Malcolm would know. Exiting the building the same way he entered, he was glad he wore gloves.

No prints.

Nothing could tie him to this place.

Loping toward the Ducati he left parked in the dark alley, he felt sure the information now hidden in his pocket was the one thing he needed. Rounding the corner, he stopped and flattened his back against the wall.

He had company.

Headlights flicked on.

"Get in," she ordered through the rolled down window of her black Porsche. The engine was turned off. She had parked beside his bike.

"How'd you find me?"

"I said, get in," she firmly repeated.

"Madison."

"Mr. Anderson," she drawled in a theatrical condescending brogue, "Must I teach you another lesson in manners? If a smart woman decides to save your very dumb ass from being arrested and making the morning news in a scandal guaranteed to blow your secret life to hell, you should say Thank You and take a ride in the smart woman's very fast car."

"Last time I rode in that car you drugged me."

"Handcuffed too, as I recall."

"There was that."

"Best date ever," she dryly echoed his previous statement.

Madison looked pale tonight, squinting like she had a headache. Glancing in her rear-view mirror, she seemed to be counting silently to herself.

"One minute."

"One minute until what?"

"You get arrested."

At that instant alarms rang out from down the block at Thornbriar headquarters. Noise screamed through the streets.

He swore. "What the hell?"

"You triggered it when you left. The lock clicked, but you forgot to slide the second deadbolt back into place. Being a good alarm system, it has done its job and notified the police that Mr. Thornbriar has a problem."

"Damn. Were you watching me?"

Madison ignored that. "Cops will be here in thirty seconds," she started the Porsche engine and revved it. "I'd love to chit-chat, Bad Boy, but I'm allergic to handcuffs."

"I'll follow you. Let's go."

Getting on the Ducati, he had no intention of following Madison or leaving his favorite toy to be impounded by the police. But as they discreetly drove through downtown San Diego and she managed to avoid every police car and every traffic camera, he decided following her was smart. But when she drove onto the interstate, he leaned low over the body of the bike and zoomed right past her.

Inside the car, he saw Madison laugh.

The game was on.

He spent the next ten miles weaving in and out of traffic, trying to shake the black Porsche.

It was impossible.

Madison drove as if she could predict his every move. Smarty pants woman. Damn, he liked her.

Finally, he raced down an exit ramp.

The black Porsche casually exited behind him. But whenever he reached the first stoplight, Madison rapidly turned right and roared around him as if something else was suddenly more important.

Out of curiosity, he followed her.

They went across the bridge to Coronado. Following at a casual distance, he watched her park the Porsche on a side street and run through the shadows toward the small boat harbor in Glorietta Bay.

He parked too.

Then he lost Madison in the dark.

When he reached the harbor, he saw a black Cadillac by the community docking pier. On the water was movement. Gliding toward the open sea was a mid-sized powerboat primarily used for ship to shore activities for luxury yachts. Striding away from the pier was a woman.

Blonde and busty.

It was Regina Thornbriar.

He could see her clearly in the streetlights.

She carried two large stainless steel briefcases. She was laughing, talking loudly to men who stood on the deck of the white cruiser trolling out to sea. Regina blew them a noisy kiss. Then she giggled like a happy teenager, threw the cases into her Cadillac, and quickly drove away.

Immediately, the cruiser gained speed. In minutes it was out of the harbor where speeds were limited. He heard the motor roar as it raced away toward the open ocean.

Then he saw Madison.

She stepped out from the darkness and walked along the illuminated waterfront through circles of yellowy streetlights. She looked at the spot where Regina had been parked. Then she stared out to sea. Somewhere out there was a much larger ship.

"Damn, damn, damn!" He heard her swear.

Leaving his hiding spot, Madison didn't seem the slightest bit surprised to see him emerge from the shadows.

"Looking for trouble tonight, Thomas?"

"Actually, I'm looking at Queen Trouble, right now."

She smirked. "Ha ha. Who played thief and almost got caught? I say you were almost the boiled lobster in the hot pot tonight."

"I got away with it."

"Yes, and you are very welcome." Squinting, she didn't look well. Hands rubbed the sides of her head. "No, I don't know who Queen Nasty met on that boat or why those steel briefcases made her so flippin' happy. I got here too late to learn anything."

"How'd you know I was going to ask that?"

Hands dropped to her sides. "I'm psychic."

"Smart ass."

He knew exactly what was inside those cases, who owned the luxury yacht he suspected was anchored offshore, and he now knew how illegal merchandise was being smuggled into the States. He should have guessed. Now he knew for sure. Regina Thornbriar was eyelash deep in secrets.

"Well, you're a royal pain in my ass," she retorted, "so there."

"That sounded very twelve years old."

"Shut up. I can't think. My head is trying to implode."

He felt bad for her. Stepping closer, he gently cupped her cheekbones in his palms, slowly stroking both thumbs across her tense forehead. Eyes fluttered closed as she allowed the unexpected kindness.

"Is that where it hurts?"

Madison groaned and looked ready to drop.

"Are you okay?" Blinking, the look she gave him was pained. A single tear slid down her cheek. "Damn. Now I know it's bad," he dried the tear and softly rubbed her beautiful face. "Can I help?"

Green eyes glistened. "You are helping."

"Is this your first migraine headache?"

"Maybe. Can migraines last two weeks?"

"I doubt it."

Madison sighed heavily and looked past him, seeing something else. Then those pale green eyes went wide. She yanked away.

"You have to stop."

"Why?"

"You can't like me. We aren't supposed to be together," then she focused on him again. Breathing fast, she looked panicked, guilty of something he didn't understand.

"I was only trying to help."

"You can't like me," she repeated.

"Why is me liking you a problem? Near as I can see, we're a perfect pair of Aces. If I didn't like you, there would be something seriously wrong with me. I can admit it. I met my match. And so have you."

"Dammit. Don't say that."

"I did. I meant it. Live with it."

"I have to go."

She pivoted away, but his hand caught her wrist.

"Then go home, Madie. You need to sleep."

"I can't sleep if you're out prowling around stirring up trouble," she adamantly accused, "Don't you get it? Everything you do," she hesitated and looked guarded.

"Everything I do gives you a headache?"

"Yes, it does. This killer migraine is all your fault."

He didn't understand why, but he believed her. "I'm sorry, Madie."

"If you want to help me, then please YOU go home. Stay inside your Bat Cave. Sleep. Behave yourself. Don't stir up trouble and don't leave."

It was a very strange request.

"For how long?"

154

"Give me peace until noon, tomorrow. Please?"

He had Malcolm's stolen files to read through anyway. It would take that long, maybe longer. "Let's make a deal. I'll behave myself for a whole day, but only if you promise to meet me tomorrow night."

"Where?"

"Pacific Beach, by Crystal Pier. Sunset."

"Why should I?"

"Just be there."

Madison nodded and her eyes glistened again. Then she turned and ran all the way to her car. Riding the Ducati, he followed. When she parked at Joshua's house he was relieved to see Solaris had finally gone home. Her Jeep was no longer parked in the driveway. It had been there since yesterday.

Not that it mattered. Solaris had made her choice. He could live with it. Joshua was the right man, the one who would never hurt her, would never leave her alone, and the man who would always keep her safe.

He had no room to judge. After all, it was her heart to give. If she finally chose someone to love, he wished her happiness. It would come.

Life liked it when Solaris smiled.

Joshua was a lucky man.

A funny looking orange and white calico cat sat inside the living room window, peering at the black Porsche in the driveway. Captain Morgan was on patrol. Seeing his favorite woman, the pirate jumped down from the window ledge, apparently to greet his damsel in distress. From the car, Madison grabbed her huge black purse, acknowledged his watchful presence with a grateful little wave and hurried inside. In the open doorway, he saw her scoop up the Captain.

Lucky pirate.

He waited. The lights went out downstairs. Then one came on upstairs in her bedroom. Five minutes later, that room went dark too.

Goodnight, Madison Liberty. Sleep well.

Then he drove home. And stayed there.

Exactly how he promised.

He had an hour before sunset, but felt too restless to wait anymore. It had rained today. Storm clouds still lay along the damp California coast. It was a nice break from the June summer heat.

He wondered if Madison had recovered from her migraine headache. He wondered if he would ever kiss her again. Then he wondered if she would show up tonight, at all.

He didn't have any exact plans. He just wanted to see her.

Putting on a gray sweatshirt with a thick hood that covered his hair and half his face, he decided to walk to Pacific Beach.

It was only a few blocks.

The horizon was colored misty gray. It was wet enough today the beach was empty except for a few local surfers riding the big storm driven waves. Finding a spot a little north of Crystal Pier that had a good view of the rest of the beach, he sat in the sand watching the ocean crest and roll.

To the south, he noticed a woman walking barefoot along the lapping wet edge of the waves. She moved slowly, as if deep in thought, her gaze focusing upon the sea. Dangling from her fingertips was a pair of gold sandals. A white scoop-neck top hung off one slim shoulder. Casual denim shorts. Her dark curly hair was tamed in a ponytail.

He liked watching Madison.

Hell, he liked Madison.

She was more than an Ace. She was the Queen of Hearts, at least the queen of his heart. That sassy sexy woman put a stiletto through it the very first night they played truth or dare.

He watched her walk along.

It was a very nice walk to watch.

Coming from the direction of Mission beach, she walked beneath the towering pier and looked small. Waves licked at bare ankles. She stopped for a moment, looking down the long line of pillars that stood tall and proud, holding up the pier and defying the angry sea.

What was she thinking? He'd love to know.

Then she walked on. Without ever actually searching the shoreline for her target, as she drew closer to him those bare feet automatically left the lapping waves and strolled up the dry sand. Somehow, she knew exactly where he sat.

"How are you tonight?" He asked.

"Better, thank you." She sat down beside him. "Did you find what you were looking for in Malcolm's stolen files?"

He didn't question how she knew that. "I did."

"What will you do with it?"

"I haven't decided."

"It could hurt people that you care about," she softly advised. "Don't expose Malcolm without telling Solaris first."

"I won't. She'll hear the truth, when I'm ready."

Arms wrapped around her bare knees, Madison remained silent while they watched the sun drop below dark storm clouds and slowly slide into rough seas. The sunset colors were muted. The sky was quickly growing darker with more oncoming rain. They could see the black line it created as the storm moved across the ocean toward shore.

"Thanks for behaving," she finally praised.

"Are you thanking me for behaving right at this moment, or all day," he teased. "I am on Santa's naughty list, you know. Behaving isn't easy and you look real damn tasty tonight. I was thinking about throwing you down in the sand and misbehaving, big time."

That earned him a cute girlish giggle. "You're a bad man."

"That's the rumor."

"No, it's the truth. Today sets an epic record for you," she flirted. "You haven't done anything bad all day."

"I'll make up for it tomorrow."

"No doubt."

It felt strange that Madison seemed to know his every move, but he had a theory about that, about her headaches that she claimed were his fault, and why when he had touched her face, she cried.

"Will you ever tell me the truth?"

She looked at him. It took a long tense moment. Understanding as only she could, her lips cleverly curved. "The truth about me?" He nodded. "I will, if you will," she challenged. "Do you really want to play truth or dare with me again?"

"Not really."

"Smart man. You know that I'd win." Standing, she brushed loose beach sand off the seat of her shorts. "Come on, Lover Boy," she urged, "Let's get out of here. It's going to rain again."

Getting up, he asked, "Where are we going?"

"To your secret Bat Cave, of course."

"I wasn't serious about misbehaving."

She laughed. "Yes, you were."

"Okay, the thought did cross my mind." Madison clicked her tongue at him. "I know," he sighed, "I'm bad."

"You're forgiven."

Leaning closer, she softly kissed his cheek. His hand claimed her lean waist. She didn't seem to mind. "It's a rainy night, the evil creatures are all inside, and my head still suffers from information overload. Tonight, let's pretend to be normal people. Let's get some Chinese takeout, relax on your couch, and watch television. No thinking required."

"Normal sounds great."

She smiled and held his hand as they strolled toward the boardwalk. It felt nice. Almost normal. Her Porsche was parked nearby. Pulling a set of keys from her shorts pocket, she deactivated the alarm. Then she did the one thing he had least expected. Madison let him drive.

"You trust me?"

"Don't push your luck, Lover. Trust has degrees and you're barely lukewarm. Just be a good Dark Knight and don't ask too many loaded questions. I'm here tonight. You're here. That should be answer enough. Besides," she softly added, "earning my trust would make you happy."

He knew she was absolutely right. "I'll earn it."

"You might." But she gave him a very promising smile.

The Porsche was wicked fast and purred like a tiger, much like the woman who owned it. He drove them to his favorite stir-fry restaurant, paid for their order, and parked her car inside the garage of his seaside getaway. Within an hour after eating her teriyaki chicken and watching sitcom reruns on television, Madison had curled up asleep on his leather sofa.

She looked vulnerable. Her head must still ache. Even in sleep her hands cradled the side of her face. But as he touched her cheek, she sighed and smiled. It was sweet.

He scooped her up, carried her through the big house, and tucked the woman who stole his heart into the bed that he never meant to spend so many nights sleeping in. For a moment, he watched her, dark curls fanned across his pillow, her curvy body covered in his sheets.

God, she was beautiful

Then being a good Dark Knight, he behaved himself and took her place on the couch in the living room. Turning out the bedroom light, she stirred. He swore Madison said his name. His real name.

It stopped his heart.

Later, he decided he only wished it.

When he woke on the couch, the morning sun was shining bright, the storms were over, and Madison was gone. But the red lipstick kiss and her message *Thank You for Helping Me* scrolled across the bathroom mirror made him smile.

For once, he did the right thing.

Last night a beautiful woman slept in his bed.

Too bad she slept there alone.

Mind Gone Mad

Regret can tear a man Apart,
Piece by piece, until he has no Heart.

~~ Malcolm Thornbriar

The guilty shadows were growing stronger now. Malcolm could not escape. For years, the dark regret had crept closer in his mind. Shadows of sin that cried out for redemption. There was no redemption for him. Not in this world and certainly not in whatever might come next. His crimes damned him, eternally. Crimes against family and against love. Crimes against his two children.

Seeing Solaris was the catalyst, the one element he had avoided. She reopened all the old wounds. His heart felt raw and overrun by old memories. A guilty conscience knows no sleep. He had slept very little since her return. Insomnia created an imbalance. His mind was unraveling.

He knew it. But Malcolm could do nothing to stop it.

The look in her eyes completely undid him, that raw fearless contempt. She was an honorable woman, no longer a child, she was wise and strong. She looked exactly like her mother did, at that age.

And the way she spoke—it shredded his heart.

Staring out the window of his massive glass office, Malcolm stood perfectly still: a strict white figure of the man he used to be. He missed that man, missed the happy vibrant life he enjoyed so many years ago. Today that man was a stranger.

The San Diego sunset was vivid tonight. Yesterday it rained, but today the horizon burned pink and orange as the summer sun dropped into the western sea. This was the time of day that hurt the most. As daylight took its last breath he was forced to recall another sunset when love had a final heartbeat. Her blood ran crimson on the floor.

This floor. Malcolm shuddered. In his mind, the white carpet was forever stained. But that day, it wasn't white. His neurotic white tower world came later, when the shadows of guilt arrived. That day years ago, the floor was gray marble, polished to a shine that let the blood pool, spreading as fast as his fear. The love of his life died that day. He killed her.

White could never erase his sins. Standing at the place where she died was Malcolm's private daily penitence, his atonement, making his guilty shadow existence barely tolerable.

"Gina," he whispered. A ghost of memory seemed to shift in his mind. "Are you there?" Beside him, Malcolm was sure he felt the air stir. He couldn't look, knew better than to turn his head, for the illusion would end. The air around him felt saturated with disappointment, seemed laden with sorrow, too heavy for life to exist. He felt her anger.

"I'm sorry, Gina."

"You say that every night. Yet you play their game, growing rich on their lies."

"What choice do I have?" He asked the lovely voice living only in his memories. The other one's voice was shrill, a falsetto as fake as her whole stolen existence. "If Solaris and Wyatt knew the truth, they would hate me forever."

This time she didn't answer. Malcolm already knew what Gina would say. His own hardened heart and greed caused their children to defy and hate him, even without knowing their father's horrendous truth. Wyatt simply demanded respect and clung to his sister as family. But Solaris stood strong. Malcolm's guilt made her fear him as a youth, defy him as a woman, and lock him out of her life.

"Our daughter was there that day."

It was true. Malcolm prayed Solaris never remembered. Not that day, nor any of the dark days that followed. Days of ransom and blackmail, days of everlasting heartache. Instead, let her remember the day he found her again, a child walking alone on a sunlit beach. They left her there. That day, she ran to him, grateful to be alive.

Solaris was the price he paid for the life he lived now. It was a heavy price to pay. No one ever said thank you. Why would they? No one knew the devil's deal he was forced to make, the unbearable terms and conditions, how he sacrificed to keep the beautiful daughter innocent and safe. Sometimes he hated her.

Mostly, Malcolm hated himself. A single tear slid down.

"This has to end."

"Then tell the truth. Give her my Heart Stone."

"But your necklace is gone."

"Is it?" Suddenly Malcolm knew that somehow, the precious gemstone still existed. Gina wore it that day. It had been around her neck since the moment he gave it on their wedding day. She had loved him then.

But he destroyed love. Fear was his master.

Malcolm knew who had the Heart Stone. Except the man who found it, who traveled halfway around the world seeking truth for a woman he loved enough to protect from her own father's sins, was dead now too.

"Tristan," he snarled. "Damn you."

Another sin he carried. Tristan's death was his fault, too. When the younger man had called asking for help with the mafia leader, Malcolm was so furious at the reporter for threatening to expose his secrets, he betrayed his promise. He didn't help. He told Navarro exactly where to find him.

He only wanted the Columbian to bring him Solaris. He thought nothing of the consequences. When the kidnapping in Peru failed, apparently Navarro took matters into his own hands. The jet crashing wasn't an accident. Malcolm felt sure it was murder, cold and cruel.

Solaris suffered once again, all because of him.

The dark guilty shadows of his own personal hell were creeping closer inside his twisted mind, gaining strength with the oncoming night. He was terrified of the dark. Across the white room Malcolm thought he saw them, moving like demons seeking vengeance.

The sun had set. He had to run now, run across the expanse of his white world for his shoes and race into the elevator that glared blinding white. No shadows could live here. In the underground garage, he ran to the white Cadillac with the innocent white leather interior. Inside, Malcolm locked the doors and started the engine. As headlights flicked on, he felt safe again.

Suddenly, he had a genius idea. It was a moment of true divine inspiration. Malcolm couldn't give his daughter the Heart Stone, but he could give her every other treasure. He had secretly buried them, one by one over the years, as an act of love. He concealed all of Gina's precious mementos. Pictures, jewelry, letters she had written, even ticket stubs for places they had been.

He had kept her life sacred. Each memory was near a red rose bush. The hidden boxes were a memorial to a good woman who was forever lost, yet who still cruelly lived on inside that artificial shell that he hated. He had buried each precious memory with care, the way he should have buried her. Malcolm would find them. All of them. And give them to Wyatt and Solaris.

The truth would set him free.

Watching Malcolm Thornbriar was usually boring, barely worth his time. The architectural millionaire worked seven days a week, drove the exact same roads going home, went to the same restaurant for dinner and sat at the same table, facing the same direction every damn night. He ate separated by a white linen tablecloth from a wife he barely glanced at or spoke to, yet that vain woman purposely enjoyed the attention of every other man in the room.

Personally, he found the bitch disgusting.

But no one asked his opinion. Or even knew that he watched.

After dinner Malcolm always drove straight home to their La Jolla oceanside mansion, hurrying inside as if running from danger. Once there, he dismissed his wife, changed into white pajamas and sat alone on his white leather sectional under bright white lights and drank vodka martinis until he achieved a blurry-eyed stupor. Then he stumbled upstairs to bed where he tossed and turned in a white on white room all alone, with every light blazing.

The man was terrified of the dark. Obsessed with cleanliness and order. And crazy as a loon. Which made tonight's odd activities even more puzzling. Malcolm was on his hands and knees in the dark, digging around a collection of rosebushes with a shovel. Using a flashlight to see, he sifted through the pile of dirt with his bare hands. He looked desperate, as if searching for his lost sanity.

He had followed Malcolm to a park tonight, a children's playground centered in a neighborhood the Thornbriar Corporation recently developed. Few homes had sold, yet. Lights up and down the streets were spotty and traffic was light. Chances of someone catching the crazy architectural icon digging in the dirt were slim.

But he saw. And took pictures, evidence of the truth he was slowly unraveling, truth that deserved to be told.

This was the third rosebush Malcolm had unearthed. The holes in the dirt were frantically dug. Normally utterly controlled, tonight the man in white was a maniac, obsessed with digging up a rose garden. Suddenly, he stood and let out a triumphant shout. In his hands was a metal box. It was sealed inside waterproof plastic. He broke the seal with a pocket knife. Scrubbing it off with his filthy shirtsleeves, he pried the lid open with mud encrusted fingernails. Under the flashlight beam, he inspected it.

"Yes!" he heard Malcolm hiss.

The box was snapped closed and shoved into the pocket of his jacket; an expensive white business suit that was ruined by the dark damp earth.

"That's one," he proclaimed aloud.

Then running as if terrified, Malcolm Thornbriar left his shovel, clung to his flashlight in fear, and raced toward his white Cadillac. Inside, he gunned the engine and raced away.

Crazy. Nuttier than peanut butter.

The man watching thought about following Malcolm, but decided to inspect the scene left behind. Stepping out of the shadows, he walked toward the garden. Nothing special; just ordinary red rose bushes. They were planted in a park where children would play, a place where laughter and smiles were plentiful and the beautiful roses would bloom and thrive, basking in the warm San Diego sunlight.

For reasons that weren't logical, he decided to fix the holes, returning the shredded soil around the exposed rose roots. Picking up the shovel, he packed it tight around every bush. The garden felt special somehow, as if it had been planted with love. The roses didn't deserve to die.

"Who knew you were such a nice man," a familiar female voice congratulated as he approached his black Ducati hidden in the dark alley. Madison sat on his bike as if she belonged there.

"How'd you find me?"

"I believe the more pertinent question is," she cleverly retorted, swinging those long legs off his motorcycle, "what did Malcolm dig up? Did you see what was inside the box?"

He swore. "No."

"Still a potty-mouth, I see."

"Boston men are above profanity?"

"Lover," she drawled, "our men practically invented profane words." Strolling forward, she met him under the soft glow of a backyard security lamp. Indigo skinny jeans tonight, paired with a black body-hugging tank top and ankle boots. She looked hot as hell.

"You seem to have recovered your normal spark."

"Yep, I'm back in the ring, ready to rumble." Her Boston accent purred tonight. That sassy smirk was the best thing he had seen all week.

"You could call, you know, instead of following me."

"That's no fun. Plus, you'd just lie." She inched closer. Tipping her face up toward his, one hand touched his chest. "You still don't trust me."

"I trust you."

"Liar," she breathed, "now tell me something honest."

Instead, one arm snagged her waist, towing them together. Her curvy body flattened against his. Then he dipped his head and kissed Madison. This stolen moment was his to command. This time he wasn't confined by handcuffs or caught off-guard. He made full use of his hands.

She wanted honesty, this was it.

The woman had slept in his bed. He may have behaved, but his thoughts were not innocent. Remembering how she looked lying on his sheets was torture. Judging by her eager reaction, this kiss would not be their last. When Madison finally stepped away, breathing in funny exhilarated pants, he was pleased to see he had won that round.

"We can't keep doing that," she objected.

"Why not?

"Remember who you are, Thomas."

"I know exactly who I am. Do you, truthfully?"

"Yes, you are a man I should not keep kissing. Good detective work with Malcolm tonight," she added. "Whatever Looney Tunes dug up must be important."

"Tell me the truth, Madie. Why do you keep following me?"

"I didn't. I got here first."

"That's impossible."

She lightly laughed. "Open your eyes, Lover. Nothing is impossible in my world." Then she turned, walked away, and smartly melted into the shadows. He let her go. Wishing Madison had stayed, he listened to her footsteps fade away down the dark alley. Under a large streetlight near the main road he watched her silhouette stride through that bright circle of light. Then she was gone.

Hearing her Porsche roar away, he smiled. Too bad that kiss made her leave. Just then, his phone got a text message:

You let me walk away, secretly wishing I would stay. When the morning clock strikes ten, you'll see me again. Wear your superhero disguise so the bad guys don't get wise.

She also sent an address for a restaurant in bayside San Diego. While he was trying to decide how to feel about this strange lyrical poem, another message came.

Ditch M.T.'s shovel >> dumpster.

A steel dumpster was less than ten feet from where he stood. He had forgotten the shovel in the rose garden. It had both his and Malcolm's fingerprints; prints that would create a million questions and held only one very bad answer.

Swearing at his own stupidity, he turned to retrieve the shovel. How the hell did she know all those things? Tomorrow morning at ten? Hell yes he would be there.

The woman was endlessly intriguing. A mystery he probably shouldn't solve. But still tasting her on his lips and feeling lucky from her hot-blooded reaction to their moments of stolen fire, he decided that he seriously wanted a little Madie Archer mystery in his life.

It was only eight-thirty in the morning but Madison's instincts were wide awake, humming a new tune. Helping the Ducati rider changed things. She got involved in the future, now it twisted into alternate roads with so many different outcomes, it gave her another headache.

"Choose one," she muttered, driving to downtown San Diego, wishing she stayed with Joshua last night instead of checking into a fancy hotel for the week. Becoming someone else took longer than she expected, now things were already happening and she was late.

She wore dishwater blonde hair today with straight bangs, demure eye makeup, and dull gray-blue contacts. Contour shading smoothed away high cheekbones and made her face look rounder, her nose wider. Ordinary. Her character Gloria was a plain woman in a shapeless blue dress that hid all curves and could walk by people unnoticed.

Being inconspicuous was important today. Apparently, the disguise worked. She had walked by Lover Boy twice.

He had followed her advice and was very incognito too.

His gray hooded sweatshirt was loose enough to hide that tightly honed body. The hood was bunched at his shoulders, pulled to lay thick around his neck, hiding a strong jawline. His overgrown hair was darker, damp from morning sea mist and a shower. A blue Boston Red Sox baseball cap was pulled low to shadow his face.

"You're early, Lover." His shocked expression was priceless. "Nice hat," she noted. "Is that secret signal for me?"

"Madison?"

"The one and only, at your service."

"Damn." He scanned her. "You're good."

"Lover, you wish you knew how good." Madison loved making him smile. The man was drop dead gorgeous even on his worst day and that secretive sexy grin was killer. "Did you see anything interesting yet?"

"Besides you," he noted. "Not really."

Offering her hand, she advised, "A couple walking together is boring and safe. A man standing alone watching people looks like trouble."

"True. Thanks."

His hand was strong and slightly calloused. Touching him eased the mental static. She needed to learn to be stronger, to block him. Joshua never gave her pain. The headaches had to stop. As they walked along the waterfront, the alternate futures Madison envisioned finally clicked together into one straight line. She knew she had chosen the right road.

"Where'd you learn to spy on people?"

She explained her job with the hospitality corporation. While she talked they strolled past other people. No one looked at them. But his eyes rarely left her face. The gaze was weighted, questioning.

"Ask me your question," she finally granted.

"Your text message last night was strange."

"Is that your actual question," she mused aloud, "or one of those annoying fill-in-the-blank word puzzles that are impossible to solve. You find the perfect word going across and think it's complete, then discover the word going down is wrong. So, you found a great clue, but you still haven't solved the puzzle."

His unshaven chin turned to hide a grin, but his laugh was deeply amused. "I guess that answers my question."

"But—you never actually asked me anything."

"No, but you like to talk. And I'm very good at solving puzzles." He gave her hand a squeeze. "You're very unique, Madison."

"Uugh. That sounds perfectly awful."

For the very first time, she actually wanted him to like her. Being unique was depressing.

"How'd you know those things about Malcolm, where to find me?"

"Maybe I have great intuition. And sometimes I help people." There. It was simple, but truthful. His reaction was thoughtful, but oddly accepting. If he expected more truth, she offered none.

"Well then, thank you for helping me."

She scoffed, "Who said I was helping you?"

"I'm smarter than you think, Madie. Solving puzzles is my specialty. And I solved your special puzzle." They had stopped walking. She turned to look at him. Somehow his hand lightly holding hers had become two hands firmly claiming her waist. "Tell me what happens at ten o'clock."

"Nothing. I made it up."

"Tell me another pretty lie." His taunt was husky with tempting charm. "It's a great game to play. Who's the Better Liar. But I bet my lies can trump your lies, hands down."

"What's my prize when I win?"

"If you win," he corrected.

"I always win."

"That's because you cheat." It was an open dare. He hoped for the truth, but expected to hear a lie. Instead Madison told him something else.

"Regina Thornbriar just arrived."

"Huh? Where?" He looked around. Over her shoulder, at an angle that was impossible for Madison to see, a black limo had pulled up beside the restaurant entrance. It was ten o'clock, exactly. She watched his face ashen when he saw Regina and another person get out of the car.

"You know that man."

He swore, panicked now. "We need to get out of here."

"Stand still and no one will see you." Then he glanced down and realized Madison wasn't watching Regina and her tall dark Latino companion. She was watching him. His grip on her waist tightened.

"Are you helping me again?"

"Maybe. Who is he?"

"Navarro Altreaz. He's head of a Columbian mafia based in Bogotá. He lived in Florida until the authorities got suspicious. He disappeared to South America. This is the first time he has returned to the States."

"He is also Regina's lover," she judged. "Is he the reason Malcolm was digging up treasures last night?"

"I doubt it. This is a whole new bad-ass problem."

Madison turned, finally looking across the street at the plastic busty blonde and a dark handsome man who emanated an aura of wealth and power. Navarro was extremely dangerous. She could feel it. But Regina had a weird double-image, like looking through a broken mirror. Her other image had tawny caramel hair.

"She isn't the real Regina. I see two women," she honestly revealed," One image looks like Solaris, but it isn't. What's her real name?"

It took him a stunned breathless second. Trust wasn't easy. "Rachel."

"A twin?"

"An evil, hateful twin. The real Gina was a very good person."

He clearly knew more details, but she didn't push. Madison wondered if Joshua could see the truth and wished he were here, but her brother was busy walking Silver Strand Beach with Solaris, making her leg get strong again. Her dream in Boston was right. Joshua had needed her help.

He wasn't drawn to California simply for a mission. He was finding the woman he was destined to love. Without Madison spending time playing detective, he would not be free to be with Solaris. Love was important. Hell, it was everything. Solaris was his future.

First, they had to stop Rachel and Navarro. "We could go inside," she suggested.

"No. I can't be seen." He watched them enter the restaurant.

"Well, now you know Navarro is in San Diego." She chatted. "It's his yacht anchored offshore. That night at the harbor, he gave Rachel those brief cases. He has returned to the States to assert his power. Being seen in the open is a bold move. He must think they are untouchable."

Giving Madison his full attention, he frowned. "You seem awfully well informed. Why does that make me nervous?"

"Doubting Thomas," she grinned, "have faith in me."

He scowled, "Brat." But lowering his head, the kiss he gave was sweet and tender. It was the best thank you note a woman could receive. It ended too soon, but not quick enough to keep that warm caress from touching her heart. Being near him was reckless.

"Don't leave me this time," he whispered.

"I have to. You and I together cannot happen." He looked extremely disappointed. "Stop. The guilt trip won't work." Then he managed to appear truly forlorn. "Fine. Stop pouting. I'll stay, but no more kissing. And if we're not going to sit two tables away from Rachel while you spy and I eat yummy waffles with strawberries, then find us another place. I'm starving."

It made him pause. But he was quick. He realized she had envisioned them being inside the restaurant. "I like eggs, personally."

"Then my name is Gloria. Don't forget."

"I won't."

Being with Madison was interesting and addictive. The woman who normally made an unforgettable entrance melted into her modest librarian disguise as easily as the butter disappeared into her hot waffles. He was impressed. They took a booth with frosted glass privacy panels concealing them from view. Still cautious, he listened to Rachel give Navarro orders. Apparently, here in the States, she was in charge. When he heard enough he forward and quietly told Madie what he knew.

"You are clairvoyant."

Madison's last strawberry was halfway to her mouth. Returning it to her plate, her smooth expression was the ultimate camouflage of emotions. "That's an awfully big word to toss around over breakfast."

"You're funny. I believe that means yes."

She blinked. Today her colored contacts were dull ash-gray. It matched the mousy ash blonde wig and plain blue dress that somehow made her spectacular curves disappear. He liked seeing her natural colors better.

"Are we playing truth or dare?" She coyly asked.

"Sure. I told you the truth sucked."

Pink lips curved. "Yes, it certainly does."

"Then I dare you to tell me the truth."

"One truth?"

"THE truth," he hissed.

"But you're a smart man. You already know THE TRUTH," giving him a naughty rebellious smirk, she ate the last strawberry and licked her lips. "You just want the satisfaction of hearing me whisper it across the table."

"It's why you get headaches."

"YOU give me headaches," she breathed.

"It's how you always find me."

Madison sighed and gave in. "Well fine, now you know and I can," but her attention wandered, her gaze following someone to the door. Concentrating on midair, she silently counted. Finding his face again, she proudly announced, "Okay. It's safe for us to go now."

"Thank you for being yourself that time."

"You figured it out and didn't act like I'm a crazy circus freak," he saw gratitude in her face. "So, I guess we're good."

"Yes, we are." Outside, the morning marine layer had lifted off the bay. The late June sky was a friendly baby blue and San Diego smiled in the warm summer sun. "How fast could you become the real Madison again?"

"I always have clothes in my car. Why?"

"I'm taking a ride up the coast," he planned. "It's a beautiful day and I need to escape this city for a while. I can't think here. I might stop and walk the beach. It helps clear my head. I have an extra helmet at my house. It would be really nice if you joined me."

"No more loaded questions?"

"We'll ride the Ducati. We won't talk at all."

That smile was worth every dollar in his bank account.

Then for one peaceful afternoon he rode miles along the coast with her arms wrapped around his waist, got to watch Madison stroll down the beach in a black bikini, and earned one very tasty goodbye kiss that said what neither had the courage to speak aloud. Some people were a force of nature.

Drawn together, their attraction was almost magnetic.

They were a storm in the making.

Remember Me

Some memories have a deadly price.

~~ Solaris

It was Friday afternoon and Solaris was smiling. All week she had walked Silver Strand beach with Joshua. Today she was finally able to run beside him for almost a mile. The leg was healed. Each step felt like a victory.

The pain was gone.

Joshua did it. He helped her be strong. Since the day they made love and shared secrets, they talked their way through all the tough questions: hers about the Archer family curse and his questions about Tristan.

He didn't judge, had no jealousy, and never said things that made her regret. Instead Joshua said he felt the tragic ending to such an important friendship seemed unfair.

Such a good-hearted man. She felt lucky.

At night as she lay naked in his arms, Solaris knew that he loved her. He never said the words. But his actions did.

They had a pattern now, a routine. Solaris stayed the night, but every morning after their walk on Silver Strand, she returned to Wyatt's house for the day. They may share intimacies, but her vow for space remained. Right now, she was alone. Wyatt rarely came home anymore and dinner with Joshua tonight wasn't for hours.

Solaris was bored. She regularly cleaned the house, but kept avoiding the spare bedroom stacked with her boxes from Peru. For three months, they sat untouched. She only unpacked her clothes, some bathroom things, and her photography gear.

What remained was everything she used to call home in Miraflores.

Avoiding it was silly.

Tristan didn't pack her life in boxes so it could be ignored. They could have walked away from her apartment that fatal day, left everything that she owned behind. But he didn't. He cared enough to make sure she could leave Miraflores without ever wishing she could return.

Life needed to move forward.

She opened the bedroom door. It was time to unpack. The first few boxes held little emotional impact, kitchenware and dishes. Other boxes held ordinary household belongings, decorations, and artwork from the walls.

But the fifth box made her pause.

This was from her bedroom.

While other boxes were hastily packed, everything in this one was carefully wrapped inside red bath towels. Unrolling one bundle, she found the framed picture of her and Wyatt she always kept on her dresser. The next towel held a porcelain Plumeria flower Kianna gave her for good luck.

More pictures, keepsakes from her travels.

Everything Solaris opened was a memory.

She found her oak jewelry chest. Trinkets she collected from around the globe were still inside the three drawers. Opening the fourth drawer, she wondered if Tristan ever guessed that his engagement ring was inside. She had kept it for six years. But Solaris never looked at it. It was simply a reminder of something good.

The drawer was empty. Her heart plunged. The red velvet box wasn't there.

"Oh my god," she breathed.

Frantic, Solaris dug through the remaining bundles of sentimental keepsakes, hoping it fell out and lay among the towels. The moment her hand latched around a long cylinder at the very bottom of the big box, all the air rushed out of her lungs.

"No. He didn't."

Unrolling that last towel, her hands shook. In her palm lay the same ornate jewel case she held that night in Miraflores, a night filled with surprises. Flicking open the tiny leaf latch, Solaris sunk to her knees on the floor.

Inside was her engagement ring.

And a blood-red ruby teardrop pendant. The Heart Stone.

This was a message from Tristan.

Wyatt was starving, irritated at the whole world, and wished for nothing more than a good meal and some time with his sister. Coming home today felt strange. It was as if he didn't belong to this carefree extravagant life anymore.

He never had, not really.

But he pretended the possessions and pompous lifestyle mattered, for a while. Now it seemed the masks people wore in life were being lifted. Old realities had been unearthed as a lie. The secrets were finally solved.

He had a witness.

The truth he found would be monumental.

Digging in the refrigerator he found a cold beer, opened the bottle and took a big swig. Then he leaned in and scrambled around for something edible. His cell phone rang. Glancing at it, Wyatt scowled but continued searching for food with one hand.

"Yeah. What?"

The man on the other end was concerned, "How is she today? Is her leg healing? Do you think Solaris will need surgery?"

"I don't know," Wyatt grumbled at the rapid questions while sifting through salad greens and disgusting fruits in search of something on the red meat list. The pickings for real man food were slim. What the hell? He stays away for a while and the house turned into a health food store.

"Besides," he argued, "Isn't knowing about her your job?"

The man swore at him for being a lousy brother. Finding deli roast beef and cheddar cheese, Wyatt grinned and didn't argue anymore. He knew Solaris was okay. He had kept track.

Pulling sandwich ingredients from the refrigerator, he held the cell phone pinned between his shoulder and ear as he listened to the man fume. Wyatt put the pile of food on the counter. Then reached into the fridge for more.

"Hey, don't yell at me. You called me, remember?"

"Fine," the man griped. "What did you find in LA?"

"Brother," he said with real feeling, "I hit the royal jackpot." Saying it felt so good, Wyatt laughed and felt a little delirious.

"Really? And?"

He started to answer, but turning around loaded down with his second armload of food, he saw Solaris standing in the kitchen entryway.

Something was seriously wrong. Her face was pale and her stance was rigid, but her eyes were bloodshot from crying.

Around her neck hung a teardrop shaped red ruby.

Solaris wore their mother's Heart Stone.

"Oh shit," he softly swore.

"How long have you been playing their twisted game, Wyatt," she yelled loud enough the man on the phone heard, grew quiet, and swore too. "Is that why you follow me on that motorcycle?"

He swallowed hard. "That man isn't me."

"Stop lying." She shrieked, raging. "I'm through with all the lies!"

"Calm down, Laurie."

She wasn't listening. Her angry voice rose to near hysteria. "I thought you loved me!" Her hand touched the red ruby. "I remember it now. Dad paid them blackmail money because of me. He kept me alive that day, but he lost Mom. Our father shot our Mom. I was there. He is still being blackmailed. Because of me, his whole marriage is a lie. Those secrets are why Dad hates me so much. Is that why you hate me too?"

"God, no. I could never hate you. I love you."

Convincing her was impossible. "Whose side are you on, anyway? For weeks, you've spied on me. I thought you were just mad about Joshua," then her eyes settled on the phone, her gaze narrowed.

"Who are you talking to?"

"No one."

"Bullshit. Give me that."

Before he could react, Solaris yanked the phone out of the wedge between his shoulder and ear. The whole exchange was awkward. Wyatt almost dropped glass jars of pickles and mustard before he managed to put all the food down upon the kitchen countertop. Didn't matter. His appetite was gone anyway.

"Who is this," she demanded into the cellular.

Wyatt's heart clenched and went ice cold. The man on the other end could have hung up, but he didn't. Instead, he did the unexpected.

He consoled Solaris.

She should have instantly recognized that deep voice. For some strange reason, she didn't question his identity. Pacing the kitchen, her head was bent as she listened to him talk.

"Why should I believe you," she demanded. Again, she listened.

Wyatt wasn't sure if he should leave or just sit down and cry.

Seeing his beloved sister so livid, clearly recalling the kidnapping when she was a girl, understanding the blackmail that followed their mother's death, and all the terrible reasons their Dad had hardened his heart, his own heart broke into a thousand pieces.

Where did she find that damn necklace?

Of all things to shatter her forgetfulness, their mother's Heart Stone ruby had released the traumatic memories.

"I remember everything," she spat, "All of it."

The man on the phone kept talking. The low male rumble kept Solaris listening.

"Trust him?" Her angry gaze flicked toward Wyatt's face.

He cringed. Never in their lives had she looked at him with that much betrayal and rage. But her gaze gradually softened as the man on the phone talked.

"But he lied. Wyatt knew about this. He looks guilty as hell right now. I can't trust anyone."

The man's next words met with angry resistance.

"Yes, I do trust Joshua. I know he can keep me safe. Don't tell me what to do! Who the hell are you, anyway?"

Then taking the phone in her clenched fist, she slammed it down onto the marble floor and crushed it hard beneath her tennis shoe. The left foot, he noted. It must be healed. "Well. That's one way to say goodbye."

"Shut up, Wyatt."

Fury spent, her backside leaned against the counter. One hand raked through long tawny hair. When she looked at him again, eyes glistened, but she was obviously still thinking about the things the man had said. He must have told her to trust Joshua, that the solemn Archer would keep her safe. That one shocked Wyatt deep.

"Tell me the truth," she spat the ultimatum, "or I'm walking away. I will leave your life. Forever. You will never see me again."

Wyatt swore.

"Mom would have washed your mouth out with soap," she tartly reprimanded. "Our REAL mom. Not that evil bitch twin imposter."

"Sorry," he breathed, "for everything," He ached from the prospect of losing Solaris. She would walk away. "And Queen-zilla's real name is Rachel."

"Rachel," she repeated, turning pale again.

"The man who kidnapped you is Navarro Altreaz."

His sister was listening now. Wyatt had one chance.

"Dad called our real mother Gina, never Regina. He loved our Mom deeply. The Heart Stone was his wedding gift. It's a teardrop because Mom believed only love makes us cry, and good love brings beautiful tears."

"Tristan told me that part, when we were in Peru."

Wyatt nodded, glad she was open to what he had to say. "They were happy, very much in love. But whatever happened that day at his office when our Mom died, it gave Rachel and Navarro power over Dad. They took you. How long Navarro kept you, I don't know. I didn't know any of this. I was in the Navy, on the other side of the world. But recently I learned when you came home, Dad started paying extortion money and partnered with Navarro. Rachel took over Mom's life."

"Yes, I figured that out."

"Until a few weeks ago, I didn't know any of this. Then," Wyatt pointed down at the crushed cell phone pieces scattered on the floor, "that man called me. That one honest call changed everything. Do you know who that was, Laurie?"

"I assume it was your private detective."

"No. That man is our good friend. We are lucky to have him." A brisk urgent knock suddenly rapped on their front door. It saved him from saying more. They ignored it. The doorbell rang over and over. The pounding increased. "You should probably answer that," Wyatt told her, knowing it was time for him to leave again.

Solaris turned away and marched to the entryway. Flinging the door open, Madison rushed inside with a clicking whirl of high heels, wearing a tasteful white business suit and sophisticated platinum blonde curls.

"Oh my lord," she exclaimed, "If you two don't stop this, my head will rupture. Gee, Solaris, nice way to declare war. Sure, be angry. Ask questions. But don't picture yourself walking away, forever. Damn. What about Joshua? He loves you. And give Wyatt a break. He's a good guy."

"Madie?"

"Yeah. Where is he?"

"In the kitchen." They both heard the electric garage door open and a loud engine growl as the Dodge Viper left the house again.

Madison looked extremely frustrated. "Really? Fine. Run away!" She yelled at her disappearing brother. "Chicken!" Yanking off the blonde wig, her own dark brown curls were tamed in a sleek twist. Judging by her

169

polished appearance, she had been incognito as a wealthy elegant lady when life came screaming at her senses.

"So, you saw the future." Solaris surmised.

"Yes, and it was ugly."

"Because I died."

Madie blanched, "At least you aren't naïve to the dangers. Yes, I saw that terrible possibility. One bad decision rolls right into another, Solaris. Truth is an extremely powerful weapon. Use it wisely. Timing with stopping Rachel and Navarro is everything. Do you want to lose the good people you love?"

"No. I've lost enough people."

"Okay. Then call Joshua."

"What should I say?"

"The truth. He is your life now. Dedicate yourself to loving him. Every future where I see you and Joshua together, everything is fine. Justice will come," Madison promised, "but it will take more time. You must stay with him. Don't leave his side. Go to him. Right now."

"Okay. I will."

"I love you, Solaris. You've become family. You know that, right?" She nodded. Giving her a quick hug, Madison flounced out the door. She roared away in her black Porsche, obviously in pursuit of her wayward brother.

Joshua was her future, her life now. Did he want that?

Only he knew that answer.

When Solaris returned to the kitchen, the cellphone she smashed was gone. Wyatt would buy a new one. He left food scattered across the granite countertop. What a mess. Lying beside his half-drank bottle of beer was the yellow notepad she used for grocery lists. He had quickly scrawled a message. Reading it, her stomach knotted.

I'm 99% sure our house is bugged. Rachel heard you. She's dangerous. GET OUT OF HERE. Stay with Joshua. I'm not the Ducati rider. You just talked to him. I LOVE YOU!!! They will pay. I promise. Please don't leave. You are all I have.

She had talked to the Ducati rider. Her heart fluttered. He wasn't the enemy. Wyatt trusted him, even called him brother. Slowly, Solaris slumped down to the floor and wished she paid attention to that deep soothing voice. She was so outraged nothing registered. Memory of the sound of it was lost. Closing her eyes, she tried to recall the things he said.

Fingers rubbed the ruby. Their mother's Heart Stone.

It had a story to tell, truth hidden since she was eleven years old. The Heart Stone helped her remember. It was a story of murder and love, a story both beautiful and damning. It was shaped like a teardrop because you had to care to cry, and only strong love could also bring tears of joy. To the woman who owned it, tears of love were beautiful.

Suddenly, she knew who the man was.

Her heart filled with hope. Solaris smiled.

It took an hour to silently pack everything important from Wyatt's house and decide how to approach Joshua with her problems. First, Solaris had to find courage to face her new truth. Now that she knew everything about her secret past, it became hard to imagine a happy-ending.

Joshua had courage. He'd understand.

But when she parked her red Jeep at his beach house and rang his doorbell loaded down with two suitcases, her precious photography gear, wearing a tattered heart on her sleeve, Solaris felt anything but courageous.

"What's this?" He calmly asked.

"I need to stay with you. Please?"

Grass green eyes flicked toward the ruby necklace on her neck. Instinctively touching it, his fingers cradled the red gemstone in his palm. While sensing its story Joshua looked shocked, then angry, but his final expression was the one she needed to see. She saw love.

"I'm sorry. This is a terrible weight to bear."

"Will you please help me?"

"You already know that I will." Then he drew a slow thoughtful breath and assessed her. "We could leave Coronado and you've considered going somewhere safe for a while, but you've decided to stay," he astutely judged. "To face this. Uncover the truth. Make them pay. Am I right?"

"Yes." She handed him Wyatt's note. He read it. "If the house is bugged they know that I remember," she explained. "But all we have are a child's traumatized memories. They also heard Madison tell me to come here. We never mentioned the necklace aloud. Everyone knows we are together. Staying with you will seem normal."

"So, we stick with our routine, except you don't go back to Wyatt's anymore." She nodded in agreement. "Okay, I'm in."

Taking one suitcase and the photography cases, Joshua ushered her inside. Evening had come. The lights were dim downstairs. He had been in his bedroom getting ready for their dinner date. Most of the lights came from the stairway. That's when reality hit her.

Being here meant they were living together.

He sensed her thoughts and glanced toward the steps going up to the bedroom they would now share. "I could politely ignore what you're feeling. But I won't. Yes, we're living together now. Maybe it's selfish, but I'm happy you're here tonight."

"Am I complicating your life?"

That sexy amused smile curved. "From the moment we met, Babe."

"Sorry."

"I've learned to adapt."

She felt bad.

"Stop thinking that way," Joshua ordered, but she wanted to cry. "You love me," he rationalized. "Your love is stronger than fear. You will release me from being a Guardian. Do you know how I'm sure of it?" Her head shook. "My gifts are changing." He softly revealed. "I used to see the dark shadows and energy from everyone. Now, the only person I can see is you. Your love for me is stronger than darkness or fear. You have chased away all the shadows."

"I made you weak?"

"No, Babe. Love makes us stronger." A tear escaped and slid down her cheek. Joshua caught it with his thumb.

"I love you, Solaris."

Her breath caught. It stung. "You finally said it."

"I should have said it weeks ago."

Lost in his arms, she clung to him and cried. But the tears were beautiful, joyful, filled with love and hope.

Around her neck the Heart Stone gleamed.

Solaris felt lucky. Joshua truly loved her.

A Second Chance

In the moonlight I see a friend,
A man too good to be true
And too damn sexy to be forgotten.

~~ Madison Liberty

Over his shoulder, he saw a shadow move. In one smooth motion, he pulled the 9mm semi-auto from the waist of his jeans and automatically took aim. The black Beretta Storm made an ominous click in the dark. Whoever followed him thirty miles inland to the neglected hillside property east of Spring Valley was either brave or careless. He had no qualms about leveling anyone intent on making tonight his last.

He had plenty of tomorrows coming. At least, he hoped.

There were no city streetlights here. Overgrown grass and shrubbery spread wild. Any form of civilization had long been reclaimed by nature. Aiming at the black spot beneath the canopy of trees, he waited.

Nothing moved. Maybe he imagined it. No, he was being watched. He felt it. Then an image flashed through his mind. Smiling a little, he knew exactly who stood in the midnight shadows and lowered the pistol.

"Get over here before I shoot you."

Madison laughed aloud. She was closer than he thought. She practically stepped out of the air. Her stealth mode was impressive. So, that's what being a ghost looked like. He felt like one, most days. The Beretta was secured and stored at his waist again.

He hadn't seen Madie all week. But she occupied his thoughts. After the day they saw Navarro and rode the Ducati together, she disappeared. Once, she sent a text message saying she learned to block him, that he no longer gave her headaches. He was glad. He hated causing her pain.

The moon was out, casting a soft glow. As she walked toward him, her dark silhouette gained details. Ms. Endlessly Intriguing wore black slim jeans tonight, low-heeled boots, and a dark stretchy shirt that hugged her tempting curves. A leather jacket was slung over one shoulder, held by two fingers. For later, he guessed, when the night air became cooler.

She looked like sweet smiling sin.

Madison was a sleek panther prowled toward him, a huntress with a plan. He had the sneaky suspicion he might be tonight's prey. *Lucky me.*

"Should I be surprised?"

"You tell me. This is your stake-out."

"Only cops have stake-outs."

"And whoa buddy, you are no cop."

He grinned. "Bingo." But he never heard her Porsche. "Where did you park?"

"Guess."

"Way out there by my Ducati?" She smiled wide, laying one hand upon his chest, but the tempting touch was just a game. If he kissed her, she would just leave. "Damn, Madie. You hiked a mile in the dark, all alone, just to find me?"

"Oh, sure," she purred with thick Boston ooo-ahh sounds. "I have eyes like a cat." She blinked wide to prove it.

"Curiosity killed the cat, you know."

That sweet tongue clicked, "Not this pretty kitty, Lover."

He liked the teasing name. Maybe someday it would be true.

"So... what exactly are we watching from up here?"

"People."

"You always watch people." Making a low satisfied chuckle, Madison snagged the binoculars off the brick perimeter ledge, where he had left them. A waist-high wall edged the neglected grassy knoll, keeping people and rocks from tumbling down the rough incline. The area used to be maintained, the hilltop a beautiful lookout point, but years ago someone purchased the whole section, for privacy.

At the bottom of their hill was a five-story building. Faint lights pierced the night. The first three floors were industrial looking with reinforced steel doors and iron barred windows. But the upper two floors had wide glass throughout. Most of the blinds were closed, but the occupant inside seemed confident in their security: three wide windows on the fifth floor were uncovered, giving clear view into the rooms from atop the hill.

"Oh, I see. What is Rachel doing?"

"That is the biggest question of my entire year."

"Has she been there long?"

"A few hours." A grinding motorized growl filtered through the walls. Wearing thick magnifying glasses, blonde hair pulled into a ponytail, the beauty queen was hunched over a steel worktable, examining something.

"What is that thing she's fiddling with?"

"It's a diamond cutting machine."

His answer was casually given, but Madison was quick. "Ahh-ha! That's why she was so damn happy to get those cases from the ship. She's an illegal diamond smuggler! Imagine that. And I thought they were moving drugs. Navarro Altreaz must be her source."

"They've been partners for years."

"That evil-criminal, artificially preserved, money-greedy witch."

It was the finest insult he'd ever heard. Madison certainly had a flair for words. She always made him smile.

Letting her spy on Rachel for a while, he had the luxury of getting a good look at his wildcat companion. Dark brown curls were loose tonight. Much like the woman, they had a mind of their own. She wore very little make-up. This was about as real as he had ever seen her.

"Stop watching me. I can feel it."

"But I like looking at you."

"Look, Lover," her tongue clicked, "but you can't touch."

He huffed. "Why do we have that asinine idiotic rule?"

"You know exactly why, Mr. Anderson."

"I'm not—."

"Yeah, yeah, we covered that. You are not *The One*. What-ev-errr. You are you," she jauntily mocked in a lilting sing-song voice, "and you are here. I know who you are, and you know I am smarter than you. That's all that matters. The rest is just a classic case of bad timing and poor judgment."

It stung a little. "You think I have poor judgment?"

"Time will tell."

Reaching into the leather jacket she laid upon the perimeter wall, Madison grabbed a red apple streaked with green and took a crisp bite. It crunched in her mouth and the night air immediately smelled honey-sweet and slightly tart. It made him hungry. He hadn't eaten today.

"Got another one of those?"

Abandoning her surveillance of Rachel's illegal gemstone operation that had taken him months to find, Madison tipped her head in a coy gesture, sizing him up for apple worthiness. "I might. What do I get in return?"

"You get to hang out with me tonight."

She scoffed, "That isn't a reward."

"Then why are you here, miles away from San Diego? Sheer curiosity, or did you just have the burning urge to see me up close and personal again?"

"I was bored."

"No, you weren't." Snagging one arm around her slim waist, he claimed her. Captured, she didn't fight. Instead she looked extremely pleased. Clever wildcat. She knew he couldn't resist. He negotiated a trade. "One kiss for one apple: deal? You won't be bored anymore and I won't be hungry."

"You drive a hard bargain, but kisses beneath the stars with you, big guy," she patted his chest, "are not on my agenda tonight."

"What exactly is on your psychic agenda?"

"Helping Solaris. Remember her? She's still a target." Pulling away from his arms, she ordered, "No more touching. I mean it." He held up both hands in surrender. Satisfied he wouldn't grab her again, from the other jacket pocket she offered the apple. "Here. Now, behave."

"Thanks." He quirked a smile, "And I rarely behave."

"Believe me, I noticed."

"How is that going; you noticing everything I do?"

"Totally under control. I only see you when I want to."

"I'm glad. I hated giving you headaches."

Hearing he cared about her feelings clearly pleased her deep. But she stubbornly tried to hide it. "Just eat and don't get all sappy on me."

"Okay." The apple was juicier than he expected, sweet like natural candy with a hint of sour. "It's good. What kind is this?"

"Honeycrisp. I found them at the health food store. That, my friend, is the best damn apple you will ever eat."

Starting to take another bite, he paused. "Am I?"

"Are you what?"

"Am I your friend?"

That sly promising smile. Damn. It always kicked at his heart. "Hmm, I'd say friendship is probably tangled up somewhere in the nature of our relationship."

"Oh... so now we have a relationship."

"Shut up and eat your apple."

"Yes, Dear." He obediently took another big crunchy bite. Eating hers with one hand, holding the binoculars with the other, Madison returned to watching Rachel work on gemstones. Elbows resting upon the brick wall, the lenses nestled in her hand with easy confidence.

He probably should care what the devious bitch in her secret hide-out was doing. He didn't. Not anymore. Even after he finished his Honeycrisp and lined up their apple cores to stand together on the brick wall like little orchard people on surveillance, he only had eyes for Madison.

"You're watching me again."

"Is there a law against that?"

"Life always has rules, Hot Stuff. The goal for tonight is to stop the bad guys. Solaris deserves justice. I talked with her at Joshua's. She told me all the things she remembered, about being kidnapped by Navarro. She watched Malcolm shoot the wrong woman. She was only eleven years old, but Solaris saw her Mom die."

He knew that, but hearing it put a knot in his belly.

"Blocking the memories was pure survival," Madison continued, eyes on the blonde bitch who caused so much pain. "Her young mind couldn't handle it. I felt so bad for her, I cried too. She is my friend. Maybe someday, even family. That means," she concluded, "you and I doing anything beyond sharing apples would break the family code of conduct laws, big time."

He disagreed. "I thought we already established this: Solaris is happy with Joshua. I'm happy for her. It's a free world and I am a free man. You are a sexy, smart, sassy woman. You don't take bullshit from anyone. Plus, you decided to find me tonight. You even shared your apples. Life is good."

Madie snickered but still didn't look at him. "If life was so holly-jolly fun we wouldn't be hiding in the dark watching Bimbo Bitch."

"Still. You are here tonight."

"It makes you happy?"

"You know damn well that it does." Maybe Madison could ignore that volatile pull created by two perfectly matched people, but he didn't want to. The appealing angle of her bent waist as it curved down toward those long legs made his mouth water. Reaching out, one hand stroked her sleek hip. She didn't move. That feline body was exquisite.

He leaned in, whispering in her ear. "I could make you happy, too."

The binoculars finally lowered. She whirled to face him.

"Tristan. Stop. I mean it."

His entire world screeched to a halt.

The air crackled. Everything felt too loud, too tight, and too raw. He couldn't even breathe. Hearing his name spoken from her lips made his heart clench. Then it kicked hard, harder than ever before.

It felt like coming to life again.

His existence suddenly became real again, all because sassy Madison Archer had said his name.

"Say it again, like you mean it."

"Tristan, stop flirting or I will—."

He gently placed one finger over those apple sweetened lips, "Just the first part," he softly begged. "Please? Like you mean it." Pale green cat eyes acquired glints of dangerous smolder as Madison understood what simply saying his name aloud had done for his lonely forgotten soul.

"Tristan," she softly purred. Seeing him smile, she touched his at her mouth. Their fingers entwined as if they were lovers.

"Again. Please."

"Tristan," it was a sultry bedroom whisper. She lightly teased his finger over soft lips as she spoke, letting him feel the breath of that one word. Then taking the very tip between her lips, she gave his finger a provocative lick that shocked him.

But then, she was an unpredictable woman.

"Your name is Tristan Thomas Kennedy." She reverently emphasized each part, her focus never wavering from his face. "Your eyes are ocean blue and your hair is actually light blonde. You aren't dead. You are very much alive. And you aren't alone anymore. You have me."

It felt so good to hear those words. A hot shiver zinged along his spine. Tristan was alive again, no longer just a forgotten ghostly shadow. And he had Madison. This beautiful smart sexy woman had stolen his heart.

"You liked that?"

"I like you, Madison."

"Ditto: very very dangerously ditto." His hands gripped her waist. Tristan had no intention of ever letting go. Two lifetimes he had lived, never feeling as alive as he did with this extraordinary clever woman.

"You knew my name, all along?"

"Sure. I knew that day at the Hotel Coronado. Only one man would watch Solaris with that much heartache in his eyes. That day, you could have walked right out on the grass, show her you are alive. But you didn't," she praised. "You walked away. You care enough to let her embrace the good she found with Joshua. You haven't fought for her or caused trouble. You are only trying to protect her. But you're still in danger, aren't you?"

"Yes. Why didn't you say anything?"

"Some secrets should be respected."

Tristan wasn't convinced Madison always knew. "Then why did we go through the whole hardcore interrogation tactics, the night you drugged me and I woke up handcuffed on the floor?"

One shoulder casually shrugged. "I was hoping for a confession. It would have simplified things. But you're a stubborn secretive man. So, I let you play your secret spy game. I only stepped in whenever I needed to change your fate. Keeping you safe hasn't been the easiest job in the world."

"You changed my fate?"

"Yes, Tristan. I kept you from being arrested. I told you to get rid of the shovel. I even showed you Navarro so you wouldn't cross paths with him by accident. Small changes can move lives in a new direction."

"And appearing here tonight?"

"Pure selfishness. I like you, even if I shouldn't." She looked offended that he had doubts. "You really think I would keep kissing a total stranger?"

"I don't know. You're pretty unpredictable."

"Am I?" She reached back at her waist and found his fingers, bringing them to her face. Her lips teased his hand, teeth nibbled at his fingertips. It made him groan. Guiding his hand in a slow trail down the smooth column of her throat, she let go, allowing his hand to drop lower.

"Damn, Madie."

"Now show me that you mean it."

Cupping her generous curves with permission, he felt soft hands rake up through his overgrown hair as she stood on her toes and eagerly pulled their mouths together. It was hot. She was hotter.

Tristan felt stunned by the knowledge that all along, this sassy smart woman had been his secret guardian. Everything about her was shocking. Especially this kiss. Giving and taking, Madison wasn't holding back tonight. Rules were gone. Every brush of her lips and hands stirred up more trouble than he had ever tasted.

And Tristan knew trouble. This went way beyond Santa's naughty list. His hands slid beneath clothes. Her skin was smooth and firm. She wanted his touch, wanted to feel their fire. The way she moved in his arms was like an amazing sensual dance, one only Madison could perform with such untamed enthusiasm. Rules, hell. Rules be damned.

When they finally came up for air, all he could do was smile.

"Why are you grinning?"

"Can't a dead guy smile?"

"Not like that. And not holding me how you are."

Tristan had turned while they made out. Holding her up with one arm, he had pinned her hips against the wall with his. Their overheated bodies melted together. Madison had wrapped those long thighs and calves tight around him. They could make love right here, and no one would ever know.

"We're dangerous together," she breathed.

"Maybe. But we belong together."

"Not like this. Not tonight." Agreeing completely, he reluctantly released her. "How did you fake your own death?" She calmly asked while smoothing half-removed clothes. Her face was serious now, satiny lines of cool composure. Playtime was over.

But Madison knew his name. That changed everything.

"Easy: a parachute, a programed auto-pilot, and a strategic timed explosion that sent the jet plunging into the ground near Bogotá, Columbia. Boom, I made national headline news."

"Then you became Thomas?"

"I already had that alias. As a reporter, Thomas Anderson was useful. The darker hair is just a temporary dye that washes out and the brown contacts help me blend in. Dress a little different, change a few facial features, and you become someone new."

"It's true. I do it all the time."

"Thomas Anderson is totally legit with real bank accounts, passport, and a birth certificate. Since Thomas is my middle name, it was an easy identity to assume. I became Thomas undercover; digging into things famous Tristan Kennedy couldn't."

"That's smart."

"When Solaris was hurt in Peru, I told her goodbye. Then I parachuted from the plane with a backpack of supplies to get me out of the mountains and enough cash to board a quiet cargo ship home to the States. I knew Navarro attacked us just to kill me. I thought disappearing would keep her safe. It took two weeks to walk out of the crash site, to find civilization again. Then I was on the ship for weeks. When it docked in San Diego, I got the Ducati, moved into the house on Diamond Street that I originally bought when I was engaged to Solaris, and became invisible."

"Not to me."

"No," he grinned, "I'm not invisible to you." Soft fingers affectionately stroked across his unshaven cheek. This kiss was tender. He knew she cared. Then Madison laced their fingers together in a compassionate gesture that meant almost as much to Tristan as when she said his name.

"I'm sorry your life fell apart."

One shoulder shrugged, "I needed a do-over anyway. The man I used to be isn't someone I'm proud of."

Compassion warmed her gaze. "Can I ask you something personal?"

"Fire away."

"The house on Diamond Street ... did Solaris live there with you?"

"No. She never even knew about it. I originally bought it as a rental investment, thinking someday if I married her, we'd live there. But this spring when trouble started tracking me across the world, I stopped renting it. Somehow, I knew I'd need a safehouse."

"Do you still love Solaris?"

That made him pause. "Love has degrees."

"And how does she rate?"

Tristan wanted to answer honestly. "Somewhere between friendship and forever, I suppose. When we were younger I thought it was love, but I was too self-involved. You were right. It was all me, me, me. I never really knew Solaris. Until I became Thomas and started watching her, I had no idea how she thought or what she cared about. We were strangers, going through the motions of love."

"That's kind of sad."

"I agree. Walking away from her six years ago was easy. When I went to Peru, I was running from trouble. When I realized Solaris was in danger too, my feelings evolved. We slept together only one time."

"I didn't need to know that."

"Yes. You do," he adamantly declared. "You asked if I love her. The answer is I loved her enough NOT to sleep with her again. Solaris is like special family to me. She never loved me, not with her whole heart. We talked about it. But she found real love with Joshua. He's good for her. Everything I did tore her life apart. She deserves better."

Madison looked relieved. "Thank you for being so honest."

"Honesty is all I have left. Dead men have nothing to lose." She gave his hand a small squeeze. "Now, can I ask you something?" She nodded. "What's the deal with you and Joshua appearing here? I doubt coming to Coronado was just a cool vacation idea. He's obviously fallen in love, but you act more like there is a goal, like you're on some sort of mission."

She licked her lips. "Ask me something else. Anything else."

"I told you the truth."

"This is different."

"Am I important to you?"

Hesitating, her eyes grew wet with unspoken emotions. "Yes, Tristan. You have become very important to me."

"Is there more to us than reckless heat?"

"We may have potential."

"Then tell me the truth."

She balked again. "But it's a family secret."

"I already know you are clairvoyant," he urged. "I've followed Joshua enough to know he's gifted too. Yet you watch over your brother as much as you do me. Why is that?"

"Protecting him is my duty."

"Duty? That's an odd word to choose."

Madison scowled. "Please don't make me do this, Tristan."

"If you can't trust me completely," he honestly warned, "then we have nothing."

She sighed heavily. "I will say the truth one time."

"Once is enough."

Taking a deep breath, she confessed, "Archer's have dreams that guide us to innocent people whose lives are in danger. We've been this way for centuries. It's our family curse. Twelve generations ago, Liam Archer didn't protect Amaryllis Caldwell, the woman he loved. Fear was stronger than love. Life punished us."

"How?"

"Now all Archer's are Guardians. If we turn twenty-five without the dreams of danger coming, it skips us. We get a normal life. Otherwise, once the dreams come, our abilities grow."

"So, Archer's have precognition and a responsibility to use it for the greater good, at any cost."

"Wow, okay. Damn, Tristan." He loved when she said his name. "That is just about the finest summary explanation I have ever heard."

"Thank you. I was a halfway decent reporter, in another lifetime."

Madison rewarded him with a tiny cute smile. "And in this life?"

"It's a whole new game. I'm still figuring it out." Tristan studied his partner in crime. "You are too, am I right?"

She nodded. "In Boston, the night Joshua dreamed of danger for Solaris, I dreamed of him. Joshua's safety became my responsibility. It was my first dream of danger. My birthday is July thirtieth. I almost made it without the visions. I would have been normal." She huffed, shrugged. "But now my abilities are growing and Joshua's are part of his soul. Our only hope for release from our duties to protect others is to find a love that's true, one freely given, a love stronger than fear."

That interested him. "If you find it, what happens?"

"Our gifts remain, but we no longer dream of danger. We only sense the people we love. They are the only ones we protect."

It gave Tristan hope.

"Now you know everything. Until the danger has passed here, we won't return to Boston. Joshua cannot leave Solaris unprotected and I am bound just as strong to guard my brother. Our father tried leaving his calling and he died. I won't suffer the same punishment."

"Then guardian angels are real."

Her shocked laugh burst out, "I am no angel. And Joshua would punch you in the mouth if you called him that."

"No doubt," he agreed. They shared a smile. "Where do I fit in? Am I just another one of your duties?"

Madison seemed puzzled by that. "Not to my knowledge. I have no idea why you are so strong on my radar. Joshua is too worried by you watching Solaris to know who you are. He thinks you are Wyatt."

Tristan chuckled. "That's funny. And ironic."

"Why?"

"Wyatt has been helping me."

Green eyes widened. Tristan had finally surprised her. "Impossible. I've never seen you two together. You are always one place stirring up trouble, and he's off somewhere else digging into the past."

"Exactly. We're both looking for evidence. Two people can work better than one. Why do you think I got the cell phone?"

"I had wondered about that."

"I called him the very first day I arrived." Tristan noticed lights going off in the illegal gemstone cutting operation. They watched. Soon Rachel drove away. The building was dark and quiet now.

"Want to play a game?"

She frowned. "What kind of game?"

"Cat burglar."

For a moment Madison studied the darkened building with that far away expression. Then she looked at him and grinned, "Are we breaking and entering, with intent to prosecute?"

"Absolutely."

Tristan had prepared for this all week. He just hadn't expected company on tonight's adventure. But for some odd reason when he put latex gloves into the pocket of his gray sweatshirt, he had unconsciously grabbed two pair. Weird. He gave a set to Madison. "No fingerprints."

"I wish I had brought my pistols."

Tristan did a double take. "Isn't one gun enough?"

"There are two Glocks in my purse at all times."

That amused him. "And your trusty bag of tricks is where, exactly?"

"It's in my car, along with my phone. I was blocking you tonight, so I didn't get a headache. Damn. I feel dumb."

He gave a light chuckle at her lack of preparation, "But you're the smarty-pants psychic with precognition. Didn't you foresee us breaking in here tonight?"

"No. When I get involved in the future it changes. I can't see myself."

"You are your own blind spot." She nodded, putting on the gloves.

They hiked down the hill. At the front door Tristan handed her his cellphone and turned on the flashlight app. "Here. Hold this so I can see." Watching him enter numbers into the keypad beside the steel entry door, his cat burglar partner looked nervous, wired tight and out of her element.

Red security lights flashed green. The deadbolt clicked.

"Stay right there," he told her. On the interior keypad that disabled the motion detectors, Tristan stood in the only space he knew was clear of sensors and entered the second code. Red lights turned green again. "Now come inside." She did and they closed the steel door. He relocked it.

"Okay. You can move now. This floor is clear."

"This floor?"

"They have each level on a separate security system," he explained. "Navarro and his men can be here, but still keep certain areas protected. Once a floor is deactivated, they can leave the doors open and move around. Or they can lock themselves in tight and be untouchable. It's smart and hard to break into. You need all seven codes. Two for the entry, one on each floor, and one to access the rooftop terrace."

"Do you know them?"

Tristan grinned, "Ahh, my Pretty Kitty Cat, trust me." In answer, she hissed. He chuckled. "Rachel doesn't bother memorizing the codes. They randomly change and she gets them sent to her cellphone."

"You hacked her phone?"

Tristan savored her awestruck expression. It was high time they were on equal ground. Madison wasn't always the smartest cat in the room. He had an occasional flash of genius too. "I cloned it to my laptop, and I've been recording all of her conversations and text messages for the past month. I plan to share that juicy info with the FBI pretty soon."

Madison finally smiled. "Damn. You're good."

"Say it like you mean it," he flirted.

"Don't push your luck tonight, Tristan." She had said his name again. It felt fantastic. Seeing his happy expression in the cellphone light, she giggled. "Are you going to grin like that every time I say your name?"

"Probably. I hated being dead."

Together, they walked the first floor, aided by the phone light. It was plain concrete, open without walls, filled with weight lifting equipment and a boxing ring. Apparently, Navarro kept his men in shape. Good to know. Madison's boots clicked as they walked. Her hand nervously slipped into his. The trust made Tristan deliriously happy.

Opening the second-floor door, they discovered a giant ammunitions vault of guns and explosives. "Damn. He's prepared for war." Tristan exclaimed. "What do you see, if we borrowed one," he asked Madison.

"Bad things. Don't touch anything."

He took pictures with his phone, reset the alarm and motion detectors for the lower level and closed the door, just in case. If anyone came, the locked doors would ease suspicion and buy them time to escape.

The third-floor had long rows of file cabinets, a feminine decorated office, a professional printing press, and two huge copy machines. "This must be where Rachel makes the forged documents for the gemstones."

"Sheesh," Madison was wide-eyed, "forgery too? Where does she find time to manage her designer clothing company? I researched her. Regina Thornbriar Inc sells clothes around the world. Doing both jobs seems impossible. This business looks all-consuming."

"The designer business is a front," he informed as they climbed stairs to the fourth floor. "She launders gemstone money through her dress sales. Rachel doesn't even design anything. She slaps her company name on other people's work. Ninety percent of her recorded income is falsified."

"Wow. I can't wait until she gets caught."

"She was, once."

"What? And they let her go? That was stupid."

"When she was younger Rachel was caught stealing jewels from a vacation house in Miami, Florida. The owner happened to be there. But she was never arrested. She cut a deal, instead. Guess whose house it was?"

Madison thought for a second. "Oh my god, that's how she hooked up with Navarro? Rachel was robbing a Columbian cartel boss' house?"

"Yep. And the rest is very bad history."

The fourth floor proved to be an apartment with plush furnishings, a large gourmet kitchen with a fully stocked bar, and a big mirrored playground bedroom complete with an expensive sound system and a gleaming dance floor with a silver stripper pole.

"Uugh, yuck," Madison snarled as his flashlight illuminated giant mirrors lining the ceiling and walls. "That is the most egotistical bedroom imaginable. Sleazy isn't sexy. Watching yourself in that many mirrors is just plain vulgar. Good lord. Rachel is at least fifty years old."

"Fifty-eight," Tristan informed. "She may look twenty-five, but she's still a middle-aged woman."

"She should respect herself more. And have some maturity. I can understand wanting to feel beautiful, but I can't believe Rachel is so vain she dances for Navarro on a stripper pole. That's just eeww!"

"I totally agree," he said.

They moved on, locking that level behind them. Finally, on the fifth floor, the world of illegal diamonds was revealed. Polishing tables, cutting stones, and lapidary tools of the trade littered the various rooms. Tristan took a hundred pictures. Although they found tiny gem shards and many unfinished raw stones, there were no polished gemstones or diamonds to be seen. As he walked around the farthest corner, Tristan grinned. His light illuminated an entire wall of gray metal. Rachel's titanium safe proudly filled the next room. He had hit the jackpot. He even knew the combination.

Suddenly, Madison froze and grabbed his arm. "Someone is coming!" He killed the phone light. Far below, they heard two cars. Then laughter. One high and giggly, the other was low and drunken.

They were trapped.

"Maybe they will leave," he told Madie.

"Or maybe they will shoot us and toss our bodies into the ocean," she hotly predicted, grabbing his hand to lead them back through the lapidary rooms toward the last stairway. Tristan felt blind, but Madison actually could see like a cat in the dark.

"Please tell me you know the code to the roof."

He did. But that door was a one-way trip. "It only opens from inside and locks automatically again. If we go up there, we will be stuck outside."

"Just do it. We'll find a way down."

Tristan hoped she had a plan. Stepping outside, the fresh night air hit their faces and he took a deep breath. Behind them, the steel door closed and locked. In the rooms below them lights were coming on and music began to blast. They searched along the edge of the flat roof terrace, but there was no fire escape ladder, no way to get down.

It was going to be a long night.

Madison woke blinking, realizing she had fallen asleep nestled against Tristan. They sat leaning against the brick wall with the doorway that had locked them outside. His arm wrapped around her felt nice. Her cheek was tucked beside his heart. It was warm and safe, except for the fact morning had come and they were still trapped on the rooftop of the enemy's hideout.

Tristan's phone had died. It happened just after they realized they were trapped. Apparently, the phone didn't appreciate being used as a flashlight and camera for two hours. They couldn't call Joshua or Wyatt for help. Five stories were too far to jump. After a few hours, the loud music from the lower level had stopped. Rachel and Navarro left again, but they still had no way to get down. Worse, no one even knew they were missing.

Tristan was awake. She could feel him breathing.

"Hey," he huskily half-laughed, "look."

He pointed toward the hill.

Joshua stood by the waist-high retaining wall opposite them, where they had watched the building from last night. Her brother held a crossbow notched with a thick steel arrow. It was aimed in their direction. Powerful arms were held taut as Joshua drew the bow as far as he could.

Now Tristan panicked. "What the hell is he doing?"

She whooped with joy. "Saving us!" Madison had never felt so happy to see such an angry man. Joshua fired. The tri-tip grapple arrow sang in the morning air as it soared and drove deep into the wall, several feet away from where they sat. It made a noisy thunk, a swish whispered as the rope tied to the eyebolt anchor sailed between the hill and their building.

Joshua still held a large loop of rope in his hands.

Madison jumped up. "Yes, yes, yes! We're going home!"

Next, her brother tied a black backpack to the rope. Envisioning what he wanted, she went to work. Unclipping the rope from the grappling hook, she fed it thought the eye, letting the length of it slide through the steel anchor embedded in the wall, Joshua held his end taut. Like a pulley system, she tugged the backpack across the chasm. Finally, Joshua held only the very end, Madison had the pack, and a pile of rope was neatly looped at her feet. Inside the backpack were two rappel waist harnesses and belay locks to keep the rope from sliding too fast.

She gave one harness to Tristan. "Put it on."

"Oh hell no."

"Suit yourself."

She measured the long rope in half, centered on the arrow eyehook, and then tossed one end over the edge of the building. A few moments later, she felt the signal tug. Joshua had hiked down the hill. Madison attached two descender clamps and locking carbineer clips to the other half and eased out to the edge. While Tristan watched, she stood with her back to the hill, toes on the very edge of the building. Then she leaned back and let the rope take her weight. It held nicely.

"Are you really jumping?"

"Sure am. And unless you grow a pair of wings, you'll jump too."

Tristan made a face and didn't look happy. Madison gave him an air kiss and disappeared. One quick belay hop was enough to scare her. Feet braced against the brick building, working the repel locks to inch her way down, she leaned into the ropes and very slowly walked all the way to the ground.

Joshua was there. He held the other rope taut, keeping it from sliding through the ring on the rooftop wall. Her weight balanced the equation. When they were done, the rope could be removed and returned to its owner.

"You are in big trouble."

She didn't care. "I am sooo glad to see you!" He frowned, watching her release the waist harness and locking clips. Unconcerned about how mad he was, Madison threw her arms around him. "I love you, Joshua!"

"Yeah, yeah. Save it." The ropes were moving. Acting as spotter, Joshua held the loose one taut again. Apparently, Tristan had changed his mind about living on the enemy's rooftop for the rest of eternity.

"How did you find us?"

"You sent me mental Archer SOS signals all damn night."

"I did?"

"Loud and clear. I have a headache as big as the Atlantic."

"Sorry." Knowing personally how crippling the pain could be, she felt bad. "You said Solaris has changed your abilities, so I didn't think you would sense me."

"Well, I love you and you were in trouble, so I did."

Madison grinned. "Cool. Now you are my Guardian, too."

"Apparently, I am."

"It's an adjustment, isn't it?"

He swore. "Everything here is an adjustment." Then he angrily looked up at Tristan, who was skilled in repelling despite his reluctance, and had already descended halfway down the building.

"I saw the Ducati and your Porsche hidden a mile away. Wyatt is with Solaris at her gallery, working on her book about the jaguar in Peru, which clears him as being the Rider. Who is your partner in crime?"

"A very good friend, so promise to be nice."

Joshua gave a gruff grunt and made no promises. "Your reasons for camping out on top of a building in the middle of nowhere with the Ducati Rider better be damn good. I had to lie to the woman I love to borrow her climbing gear. Solaris thinks we're rock climbing today, just for kicks. And I don't appreciate being left in the dark about your—friend." he realized the rope he held had gone slack.

He looked. Her companion had reached the ground.

"Hey. Thanks for the help," Tristan said.

Recognition took a second. Then anger exploded. "You?! You're dead!"

"Easy, Joshua." His fists were clenched. "Don't do it," Madison warned, stepping between them. "Just stop and breathe. I should have told you."

"Hell yes, you should have told me!"

"Tristan isn't after Solaris. He has been helping us."

Proving it, Tristan pulled a black USB flash drive from his jacket pocket. "Here," he tossed it at Joshua. "Give this to Solaris."

He caught it. "What's this?"

"Confidential financial files and a diary I stole from her father."

"Give them to her yourself."

"If I could, I definitely would."

Unperturbed by Joshua's temper, Tristan yanked the doubled rope free from the arrow eyehook above, neatly catching the loose end that tumbled down the wall. He had even brought the black backpack and her jacket. Madison was so excited to be rescued she foolishly left them on the roof.

"But right now," Tristan coolly continued, meeting Joshua's narrowed gaze, "the fewer people who know I'm alive, the safer everyone is. Navarro and Rachel won't be free for much longer. Solaris will get her justice. Wyatt too. Lord knows they deserve it. I just need a few more days."

Then he handed Joshua the neatly coiled rescue rope and walked away. Gray hood pulled over his head again, he disappeared around the corner of the building. Madison let him go.

She quickly gathered their climbing gear and harnesses. All that remained as proof of their adventure was a steel grappling arrow embedded deep into the brick wall, five stories up.

"Start talking, Madie."

"Okay, but you can't tell Solaris about him yet."

"I won't lie to her again."

"Waiting a few more days isn't dishonest. In this case, it's the right thing to do. Tristan gave up *everything* to protect Solaris. His whole life is gone. He can never return to it. The world thinks he is dead. He deserves the chance to talk to her himself."

Joshua curtly nodded. But it wasn't until later as they privately talked at home and Madison concluded her long-winded story that she felt certain her brother actually agreed; the truth had a time and place. And honesty should come from the right person.

Tristan had earned the right to tell Solaris the truth.

Dangerous Days

There is only one Trouble I want.
And she kisses like a Wild Cat.

~~ Tristan

Returning to his house on Diamond Street, Tristan desperately needed sleep, but the day was already rolling. The evidence he photographed at Rachel's secret jewel cutting building demanded his attention. He stayed awake all night, sitting on that rooftop, thinking about all the trouble that he had seen.

Madison was the only trouble he wanted to keep.

Life was better with her in it.

He loaded the pictures onto his laptop, saved copies to his secure server, and emailed everything to Wyatt. They had been sharing evidence like this for weeks. It was the safest way to insure the recordings and pictures were never lost. Soon, they would drop the whole bomb in the FBI's lap. He couldn't wait.

In six years as an investigative reporter he learned all the tricks for spying on people and gaining evidence legally. If given to the authorities at the right time and context, every picture and recording would be completely admissible in court. Tristan had successfully tied everyone together. It wasn't easy, but he'd built an airtight case.

Except for Gina's murder.

That one had a unique unexpected twist.

Good thing Wyatt took Kianna to LA with him. She knew how to talk to people, to establish trust. Without the wise diplomatic lady's help, justice might not have come. But it would, soon.

They had found a witness.

By late afternoon Tristan still fought the urge to nap, but ate a ham sandwich, and checked on Malcolm Thornbriar. It was easy. He had hacked his office computer. He was there, adding to his diary. At least the crazy old man wasn't out digging up more rose gardens.

Malcolm had torn up more than twenty now, often in broad daylight since he was so terrified of the dark. Tristan had watched, cleaned up any evidence, and always fixed the plants afterward. The lunatic.

The unearthed boxes must be Gina's. It was the only logical explanation. Malcolm kept them at his white tower office. But Tristan wasn't breaking in again, just to satisfy his curiosity.

Once was enough.

The sun was setting on another day. Tristan got ready for the night. Dressed in black, he slid the black helmet over his head and started the Ducati. The roar was a familiar tone.

It was Trouble Time again.

The waves were smooth tonight. The high-power speedboat cut through the ocean like a shark. Their captain was a skilled navigator. Wyatt's friend was ex-Navy SEAL who owed him a favor. The tattooed man's name was Gator, and he had one inked on his forearm, but Tristan was fairly sure his mother named him something friendlier.

"There it is," Wyatt pointed to lights seen from the luxury yacht owned by Navarro Altreaz. He wasn't there tonight, but someone was. As they drew closer, slowing to ease sound, lights gleamed in the darkness.

Gator nodded. His policy was 'don't ask—don't tell' and never questioned why the two angry armed men needed a safe ride out to sea tonight. Their business was not the SEAL's concern. But Tristan didn't'tice the huge Bowie knife sheathed to Gator's thigh and the pistols holstered over his Kevlar vest. Gator might not ask, but he wasn't naïve.

Trouble was nothing new to this man.

Soon, Gator cut the main engine, let the speedboat coast with the waves, and then quietly trolled to the side of the yacht. All Navarro's men were below deck, except for one, and Wyatt had already shot him with a dart tranquilizer from thirty yards out, in the dark.

Tristan was impressed.

For being just an attorney in the Navy, the man definitely knew how to handle himself with a gun. If Solaris saw her businessman brother now, she'd be shocked. Especially to see them geared up for war, in Kevlar vests, hoods, and black body armor, creeping toward the ship they intended to sink.

Navarro Altreaz was not leaving town.

His name and picture had long ago been posted on the federal aviation 'do not fly' list and FBI considered him a terrorist. One anonymous call to the authorities to inform them the Cartel leader had been seen in California had already set up road blocks the length of the State and closed the Mexico border to Navarro.

Wyatt climbed the steel ladder first and scrambled out of view. Tristan started climbing, but seeing Gator's speedboat silently slide away into the dark, knowing he'd only return when they signaled him, a knot twisted inside. They would catch that ride home.

They were not catching a bullet tonight.

While Wyatt patrolled the upper deck and bridge, pistol raised and ready, Tristan hunted through the interior rooms on the main deck. The silencer on his Beretta was a worthy investment. The first two men he encountered drinking beer in the galley were too slow to react. Checking the VIP Stateroom and salon, it was clear Navarro lived on the ship for long periods of time. Everything was fully stocked.

Finding no one else, Tristan quietly slipped below.

Lower level guest cabins had closed doors. The first room was empty. There were supposed to be five men on board. He found the fourth one and silenced him fast. In the engine room, Tristan planted explosives low on the hull, pocketing the remote detonator for later. Then using his pocketknife, he slashed wires and hoses from the engine, just in case.

If the blast didn't sink it, the yacht would still be dead in the water. Going back upstairs, he searched everywhere, but didn't find the missing man. Tristan silently crept to the upper deck and found Wyatt in the wheel house, quietly destroying the radio and navigation equipment.

"Hey," he whispered, "did you see anyone?"

"Nope. Only the guy I put to sleep with the dart," Wyatt slashed the ship to shore radio wires with a knife. "You?"

Tristan didn't admit he had no hard feelings about using bullets on Navarro's men, instead of tranquilizers. Wyatt was a law-abiding citizen. He'd never been held captive in Columbia, fought guerilla rebels, or escaped death by firing his weapon at men who wanted him dead.

"I found three more. We still have one, somewhere."

"Then let's jump ship and sink this puppy." Wyatt finished his part of the job. "He can swim with the sharks."

Tristan agreed. Cautious, they crept aft toward the water level diving deck where they intended to signal Gator. But coming around the last corner, in the lights they saw legs sprawled out on the deck.

Gun aimed, Tristan stepped into view. And swore.

On the white deck lay a very large Columbian rebel with a giant bowie knife sticking out of his bloody chest. Gator was soaking wet, casually leaning against the steel ship railing. He was surveying his unlucky opponent like a trained hunter.

"Geezus, Gator!" Wyatt loudly exclaimed.

The ex-SEAL grinned. "Hey, I couldn't let you boys have all the fun." His Navy brother in arms swore at him again. "Eeeh, hush up, LawMan. Bad men deserve to die badly. And that was one, was one very bad man."

"What the hell happened?" Wyatt demanded.

"This big barracuda thought he'd sneak up on you two." Gator casually described. "So, I snatched a tow rope, had a little swim, tied our boat to the side of the ship and joined the party." He flashed a grin that proved he enjoyed his skills. "No more barracuda."

"You couldn't have just shot him?"

"Well, now, LawMan. Where's the fun in that?"

It made Wyatt swear again.

And it made Tristan glad Gator was friend, not foe.

Striding over, putting his boot on the large Colombian's bloody chest, Gator yanked the knife out. Then he calmly stepped to the diving deck and rinsed the bloody blade in the seawater. The weapon was returned to his thigh. "You boys ready to get the hell out of here?"

Tristan was. Wyatt nodded, helping Gator tow their speedboat close enough to board. When they were safely half a mile away, Tristan looked at Wyatt. "Ready?"

"Do it." Tristan pushed the detonator. The yacht exploded, fire shooting into the sky. The hole must have been huge. The sea rushed in, tugging down, drowning the fire. As they watched, the yacht slid beneath the waves.

"Let's go home," Wyatt told Gator.

Arriving at the small boats harbor on Coronado long after midnight, they separated quickly. Riding the Ducati again, Tristan felt better. Tonight's raid wasn't pretty, but it was necessary.

Let the countdown begin.

This weekend was the Fourth of July.

Navarro would want to watch the fireworks from the water. Soon, he would realize his precious yacht was missing. Being an international criminal, he would not file a report. But he also could not leave San Diego. He and Wyatt had a few loose ends to tie up, but if all went well, on Monday morning, after the celebrations were over, Tristan planned to give everything he had to the FBI.

Now Navarro was trapped here.

He had no escape.

The house on the hill in Diamond Street was a welcome sight. Feeling too tired to even bother finding the bed, Tristan left on his bulletproof vest and flopped down across the couch. This was the second night he had not slept. Exhaustion was playing tricks on his mind. Driving here he had the paranoid feeling he was being followed.

And it wasn't Madison. It felt sinister.

Tristan had doubled back, changed directions several times, but the warning knot in his stomach stayed. It was spooky. Maybe he should eat. One ham sandwich and one apple in two days didn't do wonderful things for his blood sugar levels. Or mental state.

Later. Right now, lying on the couch felt fantastic.

Throwing an arm over his eyes, Tristan relaxed.

"Just a few hours," he mumbled, fading fast.

Moments later he was almost asleep, but that sound was unmistakable. Tristan flew upright, muscles coiled. Someone was trying to pick the lock on his front door. The living room lamp was still on. Quickly, he rolled off the couch and flipped it off.

The noise stopped.

Hunched down low, crouching down near the floor, Tristan readied the Berretta that had saved his life more than once in recent months. Over his Kevlar vest, he slipped on his black leather jacket.

His phone got stuffed into one pocket.

Waiting in the dark, he listened.

Maybe knowing he was at home would make them leave. If it was just street kids breaking in, they'd run off. But that knot in his stomach shouted he had been found. Navarro's men wouldn't leave. They would enjoy the challenge. And they wouldn't kill him. Yet. Instead, they would hurt him bad enough to make him pray for death. They had questions.

The Columbian wanted his precious ruby back.

Low voices rumbled outside. *Damn.*

Moving quickly through the house Tristan rapidly loaded his laptop and some clothes inside his leather backpack. He had always known this day might come and had prepared.

He wouldn't be returning home to Diamond Street anytime soon. Still crouched low and moving fast but silent, Tristan snagged his black helmet and put it on. The Ducati was parked inside the garage. But if he opened the electric door they would hear the motor and be waiting, guns blazing.

He had an idea.

The stereo and TV came on full blast, rocking the house with monstrous sound. Tristan hoped the distraction would work. Running, he escaped through the side door, into the garage and shoved a heavy tool cabinet against the only entry.

Inside, it was pitch black. Using a broom handle, he shattered the ceiling security light that normally turned on when the garage door opened.

He still wore the dark clothes from their night at sea. Even the Kevlar, which he prayed wouldn't be put to the test. The black leather jacket and helmet made him nearly invisible.

Sitting on the Ducati, he waited deep in the shadows.

Angry voices shouted over the music. The house walls rattled as his front door was kicked in. More voices shouted inside the house.

Tristan pushed the remote. Slowly, the garage door hummed opened. The motorcycle engine rumbled to life.

The house sat upon a small hill. The upward angle gave him the advantage. From the city street lights outside he saw a big blue SUV and a black Cadillac parked in front of the house. One man stood in the sloped driveway, his gun aimed at the darkened garage.

The rest had charged inside the house.

Tristan waited. He was still invisible in the furthest depths of the garage. Getting ready, he revved the engine. The growl blended with the pounding music, making the two sounds into one.

The man boldly stepped forward.

The Ducati shot from the dark, launched straight toward him. Panicked, the man jumped away from the attack and his gun fired wildly. Tires screamed upon concrete as the motorcycle found grip. Tristan hit the arch of the hill going at least sixty. The wheels were airborne as it sailed down the ramped driveway.

Tristan landed in the street and slid sideways, but kept control.

Racing away, he ducked low over the body of the bike. A quick glance in the side mirror revealed men running out of the house, toward the two cars. But the Ducati was already a block away, weaving through the late-night traffic, and he had no intention of slowing down.

As the bike raced, so did his mind and heart.

He couldn't call Wyatt. Tristan refused to endanger one more person like he did Solaris.

He was sure Madison was mentally blocking him. They had spent too much time together last night, had said too many serious things. She was probably freaking out about that now.

Taking a new route away from Diamond Street, he skidded the Ducati around a tight corner, jetting through a narrow dark alley and popped out on another street. But a few blocks later, he looked over his shoulder and swore, seeing Navarro's men were still following.

Tristan was certain this was the hotel Madison chose for this week because of its premium view of the water for the bayside holiday fireworks. He'd been here for a while, but he was getting tired of lurking across the street watching people come and go.

He was hungry, tired, and his patience had run out.

He had spent the whole day running.

Sometime during the long city-wide chase he lost his phone. It probably fell from his pocket when he jumped the Ducati. Finally losing the Navarro's men, Tristan had cruised by the house on Diamond Street, hoping the phone was in his driveway.

He was met with firemen and water trucks working on the billowing blaze that had engulfed the house. They had burned him out.

They sank Navarro's yacht.

So, the Colombian burned down his house.

Payback sucked.

Now, hours later, as Tristan watched the hotel entrance, he kept wishing Madison would do one of her magic appearing acts. A surprise arrival by a long-legged beauty would seriously make his Christmas wish list, right now.

Involving her wasn't his first choice.

But the day was getting older, he was out of options, and it would be dark again soon.

Tristan desperately needed a safe place to hide.

The black Porsche was nowhere in sight, but he knew Madison liked to hide it when the hot sporty ride didn't suit her assumed identity. Another taxi pulled through the entrance driveway of the prestigious hotel. The bellboy hustled to greet the lady with bleach blonde curly hair, tons of it falling to her waist.

Definitely not Madison. Damn.

The woman's white business skirt and blouse looked demure and elegant, like a lady born to money. Black oversized sunglasses hid half her face. As she left the taxi, her hands flashed in the sunlight, showing off a collection of jewels. No luggage, only a white purse.

The staff eagerly welcomed the newest arrival, as if they had met before and liked her, smiling wide and friendly. The woman tipped her hips and sashayed through the lobby glass doors.

Suddenly, Tristan was on the move. He would know that walk anywhere. That sexy, confident walk always kicked him in the heart.

By the time he strode through the chandelier embellished lobby, she was inside the elevator. The blonde was focused on her cell phone, reading something. Polished elevator doors began to close.

Tristan stepped inside. Doors closed behind him.

For a long moment, she simply looked at him over the top of heavy tinted glasses that had slid down her slim nose. Green eyes. No contact lenses today. She made a funny surprised huff. Then pretending she didn't know him, one manicured finger tipped the lenses back up where they belonged and she kept reading her cell phone.

"Madison."

"Sshh, there are cameras in here."

"No one is watching."

"Trust me, at this place they had best be watching us or someone in security will get fired."

Looking at Tristan over the top of the glasses again, she clicked her tongue at him, "a dangerous looking man wearing all black just waltzed right through their uber-secure lobby and he cornered a female hotel guest in the elevator. She is alone and defenseless." Madison described what the elite hotel security should see. "If someone with muscle doesn't meet us the moment this elevator opens, I'm laying down the law."

"You can't have me arrested."

Madison snickered, "Lover, have faith."

"Damn. Don't play this game."

"But I love games, especially with you."

The elevator dinged and the doors slid open. They were already on the top floor. Exactly as she predicted, two fully armed security guards wearing formal black suits and stiff ties waited in the foyer.

The men were professional and polite, but all business.

Hating this, feeling like the unluckiest man alive, Tristan stepped out of the elevator, following Madison.

"Good afternoon, Mrs. Aberdeen," the larger man greeted, keeping a serious gaze focused upon Tristan. He held his Ducati helmet in one hand and had slung the leather backpack over one shoulder. His rough appearance didn't ease their stance. Good thing he put the Kevlar vest and body armor from last night in the bag.

"Hello gentlemen." She sweetly purred.

The guard discreetly gave Madison a smile. "I hope you are enjoying your stay with us. Is everything satisfactory?" His gaze narrowed upon Tristan again, implying he was an unwanted problem. "We pride ourselves on our superior service. Can we help you with anything?"

"Oh no, I am perfect, absolutely perfect," she gushed in a false southern accent. Shifting her hips, she turned, laying one hand upon Tristan's chest in a possessive gesture. "My darlin' husband has arrived. He's such a bad boy," she giggled like a seeing him was a delight. "He drove that scary motorcycle all the way from Atlanta just to see little ol' me. Isn't that romantic?"

Madison offered her hand, jewels on her fingers winking.

Tristan took it. Guiding him past the men, the guards seemed satisfied of her safety.

"Have a good day, Mrs. Aberdeen."

Her throaty reply was sexy. "Oh yes, I believe I will."

Holding hands like lovers they walked down the hallway to her room. Madison slid her keycard through the lock and let them inside. The luxury suite had glass walls from ceiling to floor.

He'd been right, the ocean view was stunning.

Bigger than his entire house on Diamond Street, her penthouse hotel suite had a gourmet kitchen with stainless steel appliances and granite countertops, a creamy leather sectional in the modern furnished living room, and two large bedrooms.

So, this how a pampered princess lived her life.

His backpack, helmet, and leather jacket were unloaded into a plush armchair near the door. Then Tristan turned to look at her. God, that was a ton of blonde hair. But it was a great Southern belle disguise. The only details about her people would clearly remember was a slim lady and all that thick curly hair.

"That was interesting."

"I have the coolest job in the company." She declared, all Boston accent again. Tristan preferred that smart stylish voice. "I can be anyone I choose and if I get bored, I just transform into someone new."

"Who are you today?"

"Julianne Aberdeen, a wealthy antique store owner from Atlanta, Georgia," she introduced, sliding the costume rings off her hands and dropped the dazzling fake jewels in a glass dish on the entryway table. Next, she removed the curly blonde wig, tossing it aside, too. Her dark hair was pulled up into a sleek twist at the nape of her neck. "I have a dozen aliases for spying on the hotels, all with big expense accounts and VIP clout. Julianne is my favorite."

"Why is that?"

"Well, darling," she drawled in the fake southern voice. "Blondes have more fun."

He grinned a little, "That's a myth."

Madison laughed, being herself again. "I believe back when you were *Famous You* with blonde hair," she informed, "half the female population of America lusted after you."

His brow lifted. "Is that so?"

"Yep. That's the naughty rumor."

Tristan moved closer, needing to touch. His hand was upon her waist, pulling them together. She smelled expensive today. Whatever perfume Madison was wearing did amazing things for his libido.

"You smell delicious."

"Thank you," she breathed, green eyes focused on his lips. "And you look like a badass. I do love a man who can wear black with style."

"I'll show you badass..."

Lifting her by the waist, Tristan quickly pinned her body against the wall, kissing Madison with a fierce wild need. It had been a long life and he intended to make every good moment count.

She met him, move for move.

In truth, he might not see another tomorrow. There was only right now. There was only her. Her slim white skirt hiked up around her hips as he held her up. His hands helped, of course.

Long legs wrapped around his waist.

He pressed tighter into her warmth, letting Madison intimately feel how much he needed her.

This kiss wasn't going to end.

Not without some mutual satisfaction. And a fully involved, hands-on, naked demonstration that they were incredible together.

Madison ground against him, doing that slow sexy dance that would steal a man's soul while making love. She clearly enjoyed his uninhibited enthusiasm. Arms clung to his neck as he kissed her deep. She hummed his name, murmuring wordless sounds of pleasure against his lips. His hands gripped and warmed her body, stealing everything within reach.

Fingers cupped her round ass, finding only slender lace panties keeping them apart. Damn, that was sexy.

Her head tipped back, breaths coming faster. Taking that as an invitation, Tristan licked down the column of her neck, working his way down to those enticing D-cup breasts.

Then his unshaven face tickled sensitive skin and she started giggling. "I like this game."

He looked at her. "Me too."

"It's the only game where everyone wins."

"Hell yeah."

Tristan smiled at her rumpled clothes, the elegant blouse pulled loose from the waist of her slim business skirt he's pushed up around her waist, that curvy ass possessed by his hands. She still wore those white heels.

"You look wild, happy, and incredibly beautiful."

The compliment made her body heated, willing. But looking at her sleek hair, he decided to put her down.

She wobbled for a second, making him grin.

"Wait. Stay right there. Don't move."

"Uh, okay. Why?"

While Madison stood in front of him, he slowly removed the pins from her hair to release the cocoa curls. "Here. Hold this." As he removed each bobby pin that secured the tight twist, he purposely placed each one into her open hand. He did it with deliberate sensual consideration. Tristan made Madison his captive simply by the gentleness of his care.

He didn't hurry.

But it made her eyes glaze, breaths tight with emotion. His hand caressed her cheek as he worked, touching like lovers should. Fingers brushed along her neck, beneath the hair as it fell, making the captive woman shiver.

When the last pin lay in her palm and her beautiful hair had tumbled down, Tristan gently raked both hands from her scalp all the way through the long ends that were pressed into soft curls.

Madison closed her eyes and made a mewling whimper that was an odd mixture of pleasure and pain. "Oh god, you have to stop."

"Now tell me how you really feel."

Green eyes opened. Glistening. "Don't make me fall in love with you, Tristan. I can't. I just won't." He didn't answer, simply tipped his head to question why not. Finally, her heart was wide open to him, vulnerable. But he saw fear in her eyes. "We may have incredible spontaneous combustion," she reasoned, "but sleeping with you while Solaris still thinks you died feels really wrong."

"She loves Joshua."

"Yes, she does. But she also believes she lost you. That left an empty place. Maybe Joshua filled that. I honestly don't know. Usually I'm all about committing acts of rebellion and doing as I please. But until she talks to you and can choose which man she loves with an open heart, getting serious with her sexy-Ex is way off my personal Richter scale."

"A Richter scale?"

"You know, one to ten in degrees of carnal sin."

Tristan didn't like the sound of that. In fact, he stepped back and scowled at her. "Is this worse than being on Santa's naughty list?"

"Way worse. Level One equals something silly like holding hands on the school bus in third grade, feeling all grown up and daring. Ten is selling my soul for one night of selfish sensual pleasure. Sleeping with you is a definite twelve, maybe thirteen."

"Wow. Okay, that is—damn." That old familiar knot tightened inside his stomach. Tristan had never heard anything more damning.

"Now you see my moral dilemma. Sleeping with you feels like stealing. You don't belong to me. And I am no thief. You may be fine with pretending that hot sex has no consequences, but I cannot."

Tristan felt deeply offended that she believed he had not considered the right and wrongs of their situation. "I'm not without a conscience, Madison." He scolded, "I do have a sense of decency, you know."

"And undressing my hair so seductively, was what, exactly?"

"I can't say hot sex wasn't priority number one," he teased hoping a little charm would help them return to being playful.

She made a rude scoff and stepped away, creating distance between them. Frustrated hands quickly smoothed down her rumpled skirt, tucking the blouse in again. Madison was serious, defensive about her reasoning, and bordering on being full blown angry. If he wasn't careful, her next words would be to get the hell out.

"But my intentions were honorable," he hastily explained, "There's a big difference between fooling around just to have fun and making love to someone that you really care about."

"Yes, there is a big difference." Hand on one hip, she struck a sassy stance, "I'm extremely interested in hearing the nature of honorable intentions. Tell me, *Ghost*, what are your intentions for us?"

He didn't like the reminder of his status. "I'm not a ghost."

Green cat-eyes rolled. "Your honorable intentions: what were they?"

Tristan knew he owed her the truth. Walking toward her slowly, he chose his words with care. "I believe loving you was my long-term intention," he gently confessed, "although in the midst of everything we have going on, I probably have not made that part very clear."

Lips began to object. She ended up saying nothing.

"I do have a goal. My goal for you is very serious and goes way beyond fun in the bedroom." It was now or never. Today certainly wasn't the day he planned to say this to Madison, but Tristan knew by the mistrustful look in her eyes this might be his only chance.

"You said love could save you from dreaming of danger, that a love freely given, one that is true and is stronger than fear, could release you from being a Guardian."

"I was talking about Joshua."

They were face to face again. "It applies to you, too."

She had no argument.

"We may be just beginning, but my feelings for you are true. Give me a chance. I'm not afraid to love. I can release you from dreaming of danger, Madison Liberty."

Her lips puckered. Eyes filled with tears. She drew a ragged breath. Every secret wish in her heart was clear on her face.

"It's impossible."

Madison stubbornly spun around and marched into the living room. Kicking off her white heels, she held them in one hand and flung them through the open bedroom doorway as hard as she could. Then she flounced down on the creamy leather section and sat there pretending to watch the bayside view beyond the glass windows.

Tristan calmly followed. "Why are you so mad?"

"It's a myth. I don't believe that love can save me."

"You would with the right man."

"And you think you're up for the job?"

"I had hoped."

She made a sad skeptical sound. Bare feet curled up beneath her on the couch. It was a protective move, unconsciously made, like holding her heart in a fist so he could not touch it. A heart she was afraid to give.

"We have no future, Tristan. We only have wild heat. If you believed that I might love you someday, you are wrong."

It seriously pissed him off. "You don't love me?"

"No. I don't. And I will not love you. Ever."

That fierce rejection pushed him to the limit of tolerance. It took a lot to make Tristan angry, and hearing her deny their possibilities struck a match that burned deep.

He raked one hand through overgrown hair, trying to stay calm. "I'm exhausted, Madison. I haven't slept in two days. After sitting on the roof with you and dealing with your extremely pissed off brother, last night Wyatt and I blew up Navarro's yacht."

Her head swiveled his way, green eyes wide. "Why?"

"I didn't sacrifice everything in my life just to let the Columbian escape. But somehow, they found me last night. I spent today running from Navarro's men. They burned my house on Diamond Street down to the ground. If he gets his hands on me, I really am dead."

Her face blanched.

"You'd know all those things," he dryly continued, seething at her stubborn indifference, "and probably more, but we got too close, so you decided to completely tune me out."

"No, I just got stronger." Her tart reply felt false, forced. "It had nothing to do with us."

"Let's not play the denial game. We both know I'm right. But you're too caught up in guilt over Solaris, too worried about consequences of love, too afraid I will break your heart."

That one hit home.

"Go away, Tristan. Leave me alone. Our games are over."

Instead he turned, walked into her bedroom.

"Wait. What are you doing?"

"Refusing to say things we'll both regret."

The luxury bedroom looked soft, safe, and inviting. Tristan decided to take off his clothes. Sitting on the edge of the bed Madison had slept in all week, he let his thick leather riding boots thump on the floor as he took them off, just to make her aware of what he was doing.

If she had any objections, now was the time.

Only silence came from the living room. Good. His shirt came off too. This was one fight she didn't want to have with him. Neither would win. Denying they had a future stung deep. It was a lie.

Yes, he had loved Solaris, but she was not his forever love. She was his special friend, a friend for life.

Madison owned his heart.

Now she kicked a giant hole in it.

He heard her moving around. Tristan braced for a fight. But Madison only went to the kitchen and poured a glass of ice water. Then she flounced down on the sectional again and let out a heartbroken sigh.

The rest of his clothes met the floor.

In her oversized lavish gold and white bathroom, he threw the brown contact lenses into the trash. That felt good. Looking at the blue-eyed man in the mirror, he made a decision.

"To hell with this."

Tristan shaved for the second time in his life with a ladies' pink razor. Soon, the dark stubble was gone and the face he uncovered was familiar. Then he took a long hot soapy shower that left his mind blank, cooled his temper, and made his tired body feel comfortably numb. He even shampooed out the dark temporary hair color. It took five times of scrubbing and rinsing, but the water finally ran clear.

Tristan was tired of hiding. He felt sick to the core of pretending to be dead, waiting for the dark moment when death really would come.

No more.

Wrapping a white towel around his waist, Tristan walked barefoot back into the living room where Madison still sat on the sectional. The sun was setting low in the western sky. She was watching the sunset, thoughts deep and focused. She didn't even notice him there.

"I'm staying here tonight, like it or not."

Her head turned. Her eyes were huge, staring at him. "Oh my god," she breathed. "Your hair is super blonde."

"Yeah, so?" Long damp strands lay upon his bare shoulders.

"It needs trimmed."

"You know what? I really don't care."

She stood, stepping toward him as if drawn. "Wow, you shaved too?"

"It was time."

"Damn. Your eyes are the color of the ocean in Hawaii."

"Yes, Madison. I have blue eyes and blonde hair," he had no patience for allowing her time to absorb his changed appearance. Tristan was still too mad at her. "You knew all of these things."

"Yes, but actually seeing it is, wow." She moved closer, almost close enough to touch. "You look ... good, really good."

The awestruck compliment didn't faze him. "This is me, the real me. If I drop this towel right now, you will see all of me." Madison drew a sharp breath. "Unfortunately, that's a game I am seriously beyond playing with you. What you said really pissed me off."

Her face puckered and eyes watered. "I didn't mean to."

"Yes, you did. You purposely said those things to push me away. Everything you said hurt, Madie. But I'm too exhausted to fight you. If we have no future, so be it. Love can't save you? That's bullshit! You want to deny that we're perfect for each other? Fine. Deny away, baby. I am way beyond caring. Whatever we might have had, we are through."

"Please, don't say that."

"I did. And I meant it. Now live with it."

"I'm sorry, Tristan."

"Now you are. Everyone's suddenly sorry after someone gets mad. But you pushed me too far this time," he coolly informed. "I could have loved you, Madison. I could have set you free from being an Archer Guardian. But here's the secret, Lady Smarty-Pants," he leaned in, a breath apart. "You can't receive a love that's stronger than fear, without giving courageous love in return. That game runs both ways. You're letting fear win."

"I'm not scared!"

"Liar. You are absolutely terrified to love me."

She remained sadly silent.

"Can I get some sleep now?"

She nodded. He'd made her cry. A tear ran down one cheek. Tristan was too tired and frustrated to feel sorry. Leaving her standing there watching him, he walked away. Collapsing on the soft bed, in the only place in the world he knew for certain he was safe, he pulled the sheet and blanket over his body and closed his eyes.

God, it felt good.

So much better than dying.

The nightmare was almost over. On Monday morning Tristan Kennedy would walk into the FBI office and give them every shred of evidence on Rachel and Navarro. Then he'd find Solaris. Apologize. Wish her happiness with Joshua. Thank Wyatt for helping him. He would reclaim his life.

Madison didn't love him? Fine. To hell with endlessly intriguing and amazing heat. Damn it, he deserved a happily-ever-after, too.

Tristan slept deep.

Waking in the dark, hours later, he felt a warm soft woman beside him. How long had she been lying there? It must have been a while. Sleep had stolen the edge off his taut emotions. Comforted by her presence, Tristan wanted to hold her. His hand slid over her waist and found it bare. Madison was naked too. Mostly naked. He felt lace along her hip. Stirring, she curled up on her side facing him and wrapped both arms around him. Now her warm skin lay against his. It felt heavenly.

"Just sleep, Tristan. I love you. I'm so sorry."

"Don't play games."

"I do love you," she sincerely confessed. "You know that I do."

In the dark, he smiled, hearing truth in her words. "Say it again."

"I love you, Tristan Kennedy," her beautiful voice declared.

"Do you mean it?"

"With all my heart. I'm sorry for the things I said. You were right. I was afraid. I won't tune you out anymore. It almost got you killed. I should have known you were in trouble last night, needing my help. I'm sorry they burned down your house. I really liked that house. If I'd been doing my part, things might have been different. I should have been there for you."

"A little help would have been nice."

"I'm here now, to stay. And I really am sorry. Please forgive me."

He already had.

Shifting, pulling her over to lay half across his chest, Tristan kissed her deep. She mewled and that sleek naked body automatically responded, beginning to weave a sensual dance, rubbing all the warmest places. But making love tonight wasn't right. She was sad and sorry. When they made love for the first time, he wanted her feeling happy and playful.

"Soon," he whispered, stroking her pretty face with his hand.

"Don't you want me, Tristan?"

"You know damn well that I do. I've wanted this since the first night you waltzed into that bar on those killer stilettos. One look, I knew I was in trouble. But I want more than one night with you. Much more. Will you give me more?"

She didn't hesitate. "Yes, I will."

He kissed her again. Softer, this time.

"I'm done hiding. Soon, I'll talk to Solaris, show her I'm alive. Then you'll see what I already know: her loyalty is with Joshua. We're only friends. Tonight, just let me sleep beside you. Let's get back to feeling good about us. Can we do that?"

"We can." She sniffed and laid her head upon his shouder, "My mind is wide open. If anything happens, I'll know. Trust me to keep you safe."

"Thank you."

She kissed his neck and he felt tears.

"I love you, Madison Liberty." She made a funny whimper. Arms around him tightened. "Damn woman. You kicked a hole in my heart."

"Stop. You'll make me cry again."

"If we survive this—."

"We will," she vowed, "we have to."

Independence Day

Freedom is born from Courage.

~~ Solaris

Today was the Fourth of July. Independence Day. Solaris hadn't spent the holiday on American soil in six years. She was excited. They planned to watch the annual parade down Main Street in Coronado, then spend the afternoon grilling steaks in the back yard, drink a little, laugh a lot, and watch the fireworks show on the San Diego Bay at night.

But starting her morning walking Silver Strand came first.

It was like a practiced religion now, pushing herself each day to go farther, faster, and get stronger. She no longer needed the ankle brace. There would be no surgery. At her check-up several days ago, the doctor proclaimed it healing well.

Today she was running beside Joshua.

Feet were flying across the wet sand, that thumping rhythm as they raced together down the golden shore felt amazing. He glanced at her and grinned. It was a challenge. They sprinted full out for a whole mile. When he got winded and stopped running first, she cheered.

Solaris did a silly happy dance in the sand. "That was fun."

"You're pretty fast."

She laughed. "Ah, you let me win."

"Maybe. Felt good, didn't it?"

"You bet!"

On their customary casual walk back to her Jeep, talking and looking for shells, a strange early morning fog rolled in from sea. The low-lying clouds quickly blanketed the entire San Diego shoreline in misty white. Coronado Island disappeared from sight.

"Wow, this is a fast weather change," Joshua watched it cut visibility down to just a few yards.

The beach was wall of white. The waves beside them became louder, a strange thunder, rolling just out of sight. The wet mist dampened her running clothes and left dewdrops in their hair.

But Solaris liked it.

Fog rolling in off the sea meant that the summer rains were coming soon. Rain would ease the July heat, clean the air, breathe hope back into the world. The heavy white air wasn't cold, like winter fog. It was humid, clinging to their skin.

The world felt small and safe.

"I hope this fog doesn't spoil the fireworks," Joshua commented.

"It won't. It will lift by mid-afternoon."

"Isn't summer fog unusual?"

"Not really. It happens just before the summer monsoon storms hit." Solaris explained as they strolled along, holding hands.

"The hot air over the land draws the offshore marine layer moisture in from the deeper parts of the ocean. We call it a 'southerly surge', basically a warm air temperature inversion. In a day or two we will have rain."

Enjoying the rare scene, they talked about their afternoon barbeque plans with Wyatt. Keeping in their new habit of staying away from the mansion everyone was sure had been bugged, Joshua had invited everyone to his beach house.

"Do we need to stop at the grocery for anything else?" Solaris asked.

"I think we're good. Wyatt is bringing steaks, I bought shrimp to grill, Madie already had a ton of appetizers delivered from that fancy hotel where she is staying, and you made salad."

"What about beer, or other drinks?"

Joshua laughed, "Why, are you planning on getting me drunk so you can take advantage of me?"

She turned, kissed him. "Funny man."

"I love you, Laurie," he grinned, arms claiming her waist, turning the quick kiss into something far more playful and fun. Then Joshua looked around her and seemed in awe, "Even in the fog, your pink energy shines."

"Pink for love, right?"

"Yes. And passion. I think we have plenty of that, too."

She wholeheartedly agreed. "Then let's go home and shower together. We have plenty of time for us, before everyone comes over."

"I like the sounds of that."

Still holding hands, enjoying the anticipation of their plans for the patriotic holiday, they were almost at the parking lot.

In the fog, Solaris saw the faint line of the brick half wall edging the southern parking lot. The public parking area to the north by the showers was filled with camp trailers and RV's for people celebrating the holiday. But the upper lot where her Jeep waited was completely empty except for the faint glow of red taillights through the mist as a single car drove away.

Then those disappeared too.

Finding the keys from her leggings pocket, Solaris clicked the alarm, expecting to hear the usual electronic chirp and see headlights flash.

Nothing. She pushed the button again.

"That's weird."

Suddenly the rhythmic thunder of ocean waves was joined by a deeper mechanical growl. A black car raced out of the thick white fog and screeched to a halt, sliding sideways. Engine still running, the driver's door was flung open and someone stepped out.

"No, no, no!" Madison ran toward them. She leapt over the brick retaining wall, charged like a sprinter in a race, and grabbed her brother's hand, yanking him with her toward the ocean.

"Run Solaris," she yelled. "Run now!"

Another shadow moved.

It was big and fast, running straight at her. On instinct, Solaris sprinted toward the waterline far down the wide beach, arms and legs pumping just as hard as she could. But before she caught up with Madison and Joshua, something heavy and solid suddenly struck her back, throwing her body sideways onto the sand.

"Stay down," a gruff voice ordered.

Fighting hard, Solaris managed to flip over on her back, but the powerful man pinned her down. He wore a black t-shirt and dark jeans. She screamed in terror, but a strong hand clamped over her mouth.

"Damn it, be quiet."

The voice was so familiar the shock of it silenced her terrified sounds. Her body froze.

She wanted to hear his voice again.

"Just lay still," he ordered in a gruff whisper, head tucked down, his words spoken against her ear.

Then something big and red in the parking lot blasted upward. His head instinctively ducked closer, pressed beside her cheek. Over his broad shoulder, she watched the misty white sky explode into a giant ball of fire.

The hand covering her mouth muffled the scream.

It was Peru all over again.

Except she wasn't falling down a cliff and the gunfire sounds she heard was just her Jeep being ripped apart. The explosion was a bomb, not a rocket launcher. And the man covering her body with his own wasn't dark and evil. He was protecting her. Risking his life, to save hers.

"Shit, that was close," he breathed. Sitting up a little, looking at her lying beneath him, his hand moved away from her lips. His face was a breath away. He had cerulean blue eyes. And pale blonde hair.

"Tristan?"

"Be quiet. We aren't alone."

Proving it, real bullets tore through the air, landing with hard thunk impact sounds on the paved parking lot. Some hit the brick retaining wall. Whoever was firing at them wasn't accurate in the thick marine fog. The gunshots were wild and random.

A few struck the beach throwing sandy shards into the air. Madison ran past where Solaris lay, going toward the danger. She hid behind the brick retaining wall and gripped two black pistols. She took aim.

"Give me one of those," Joshua shouted, running to take cover behind the wall too. The Archers returned fire. Precise, no bullets wasted. In the fog Solaris heard men grunt and bodies fall.

The rain of bullets finally stopped.

"Go Tristan! Go now," Madison shouted at them.

Through the bright orange glow of fire from her Jeep, Solaris watched a man she thought was gone forever rise to his knees above her. He offered his hand. Numb with shock, she took it. Standing together, Tristan pulled her up from the sand.

His warm hand still clutched hers.

It was surreal. "You really are alive."

"So are you. We got lucky. Madie woke up screaming that you two died here today." A large slash was torn into the upper left arm of his shirt. Blood dripped below the black sleeve.

"You got shot!"

It happened when he covered her. That bullet was meant to end her life.

"It's nothing. Let's go."

Then they were running together through the damp fog toward a black Ducati that was parked near Madison's Porsche. The expensive sports car was pierced with bullet holes. His bike was fine. It had been protectively sitting on the sheltering side of her destroyed car.

"Oh god, it's ruined."

"Don't worry about it. It's evidence now."

In the distance Solaris heard shouting from people camping in RV's closer to the public facilities. Further away in Coronado, sirens wailed. The Archer's were prowling the parking lot, pistols aimed and ready, making sure no one else lurked to hurt them.

Joshua looked at her. Then he nodded at Tristan. "Get Solaris out of here," he ordered. "Don't let anyone see her."

"Get on," Tristan ordered, swinging one long leg over the bike. "They can handle this mess. We can't be here when the fire department and cops arrive. I promise I will keep you safe."

She climbed on. They raced away from Silver Strand.

Riding behind Tristan on the black Ducati, both arms hugged his waist, her heart raced too. He really was alive! Solaris tucked her head against his back and wanted to cry.

They didn't have helmets. The wind helped dry wet eyes.

At a long stoplight in Coronado she quickly yanked off her loose white running t-shirt, leaving on a stretchy pink tank and the gray sports bra she wore underneath. She tucked the Heart Stone inside, keeping it hidden. Then she tied the white cotton shirt around Tristan's bleeding bicep, putting pressure on the wound.

"Does it hurt?"

"A little," that shoulder shrugged.

"I went to your funeral."

"Really?" He seemed surprised, "Thanks."

"I locked myself in Wyatt's house for two months because of you."

He swore. "Sorry, Solaris. Really, I am. But sometimes the best way to stay alive is to make everyone believe you died a terrible fiery death. That's exactly what we are doing with you, right now."

"You could have told me."

He seemed ashamed, "I wanted to."

"It was you, that day on the phone at Wyatt's house."

"Yes. I decided if you recognized my voice, it didn't matter. We had bigger problems to deal with."

"I figured it out later," she confessed. "I hoped it was true. Thinking you might still be alive made me really happy."

Tristan glanced back at her and grinned. "Still friends?"

"Always."

Solaris held him tight as they left Coronado. She was glad she wore leggings today instead of shorts. The fabric protected her legs from the hot Ducati engine.

They raced across the blue curved Coronado Bridge and hit the freeway going eighty. Speeding through the white fog was eerie, but Tristan wove through traffic with ease. He finally parked inside the underground garage of a luxury hotel north of the San Diego bay.

Taking her hand, they hustled inside.

Solaris walked beside his left arm, shielding the red stained bandage from view. The shirt was already soaked. Exiting the elevator on the top floor they hurried to the end of the hallway. He had a room key.

"How long have you been staying here?"

Opening the door, his expression became guarded. "Only last night. Get inside. We need to talk."

"You think?"

Inside, the blackout drapes were closed. The oversized luxury penthouse was shadowy as a large cave. Tristan seemed to prefer hiding in the dark, but Solaris flipped on the lights.

He turned and blinked at her.

"You said Madie woke up screaming," she reminded, "which means she was sleeping here too."

"Yes. This is her place."

"Do you love her?"

His jaw dropped. "I return from the dead," he coughed out, "but you only care if I'm in love with Madison?"

"It's a fair question."

"There are better ones," he dryly disapproved.

"Okay. Here's a big one: Joshua ordered you to take me away this morning, which means that he trusts you. Am I the only person you haven't talked to?"

"Pretty much. Sorry."

It stung. But then she realized something else. If Tristan was the Ducati rider, her brother was innocent.

"Wyatt has been helping you."

"Your brother is a very good man. So, yes."

"Does Joshua know that you love his sister?"

"Back to that again?" Tristan swore and scrubbed both hands over his freshly shaven face, then raked them through his pale blonde hair. It made his left arm bleed more. Red dripped down his elbow.

"Someone just tried to kill you. I got shot and right now the Archer's are giving statements to the FBI. Soon your burning Jeep will broadcast on the news. Can we talk about that instead?"

"First let's work on that arm."

Towing him into the kitchen, Solaris hung his wounded bicep over the sink and used paper towels to clean his bloody elbow and upper arm. The white shirt she tied around his bicep was completely red.

"Besides, I know who just tried to kill me. Rachel ordered Navarro to do it." Watching her work on his arm, Tristan said nothing. "Since you failed to question who Navarro is, I assume he is the Columbian who ordered the attack on us in Peru."

"Yes. He is."

Tristan was starting to look pale. It wasn't from their conversation. Solaris realized his arm was worse than he let on.

"You don't look too hot. Let's see how bad this is." She used kitchen scissors and cut away his black t-shirt right up the chest and down the arm so he wouldn't have to lift it away from the sink. He shrugged it off. Then she loosened the makeshift tee-shirt bandage.

Seeing it, he swore. "Damn. I hope it was just a graze."

A harsh bullet wound cut horizontal along his bicep an inch deep. Blood ran freely down his elbow and puddled in the stainless-steel sink. Solaris quickly tightened the shirt again, keeping pressure on the wound.

"You need stitches."

"Dead men can't go to the hospital." He grimly noted, leaning a little heavier against the kitchen counter. "I saw a big medical bag in the bathroom cabinet. Madie's always prepared for emergencies. I bet she has first aid stuff and bandages."

"Okay. Stay right here." She moved away to retrieve it.

"Wait." His voice made her turn. "I have to apologize, Solaris. I thought disappearing would help you. But I never should have left you alone."

"You knew all about Rachel in Peru?"

"I did."

"She's the bad twin, the diamond smuggler you were after?"

"Yes. I couldn't tell you then. But Madison and I found the jewel warehouse a couple of days ago. I have a ton of evidence against her now. Wyatt and I sank Navarro's yacht and warned the FBI he'd been seen in the States, so he can't leave the country. I guarantee they will pay for their crimes and what they did to your family."

His secret life was dangerous, and he did it all for her.

She had to swallow hot emotions.

"I know you struggled to accept Joshua," his thoughts shifted. "Wyatt told me about the morning he found you crying and how upset you were."

Her eyes stung at the memory. "I felt guilty. Because of you."

"Don't. Not now, and not ever. You are my truest friend. But Joshua is the love of your life."

He said it with such adamant honesty, her heart leapt. "Wow, you have no idea how much it means to hear you say that. A thousand times I wished we could talk like this. I really missed you, Tristan."

"Well, I'm back."

Tears threatened to fall.

Solaris hurried to find the bathroom and washed her face to recover some courage. Returning with the professional medical kit, she went to work on Tristan's arm.

"That bullet was meant for me."

He made a rebellious smirk, "Ahh, Sweetheart. Plenty of those bullets had my name on them. Navarro has been hunting me for months. I stole the Heart Stone. It was his most prized possession."

"This Heart Stone?" She revealed the ruby hanging by the gold chain, the gem hidden beneath her gray sports top. Tristan looked relieved to see she wore it. "It helped me remember. Why did Navarro keep it?"

"I don't know. But it meant everything to him. He even knew the story about what the teardrop shape meant. To him, that stone was sacred. When I stole it back, intending to someday return it to you, he vowed to kill me."

Solaris was cleaning his arm as they talked. Tristan groaned agony as she drenched the deep cut with a harsh iodine disinfectant.

"Sorry."

"It's okay. Just fix it. I can't lose too much more blood," he grimly declared, looking at the red puddle in the sink, the lines trailing down, staining his arm. "I probably need that stuff."

"We have more, if you need it." She quickly reassured, hoping it didn't come to that. "I'm type O-Negative. Anyone can use my blood. I had to give Kianna some once, in Africa. Madie's medical kit has everything we need. If you're extra nice to me," she teased, "I just might share."

It made him grin.

"You should marry Joshua. He's the right guy."

Solaris stopped working and gaped at him. "Where the hell did that random idea come from?"

"I've thought it for a while."

"Well, I will. If he ever asks."

"Trust me, he's a smart man who knows how lucky he is. When you two are ready, he'll ask."

"What about you and Madison?"

Cerulean blue eyes studied her face. He searched for the right words, honest words. "You may have found your forever with Joshua, but Madison thinks because I loved you first, my love for her isn't stronger than fear and I can't break their family curse."

"Is it?"

"Not to trivialize anything that we had, but everything about that sassy smart woman completely kicks my ass."

Solaris grinned. "I say you better marry that wild tigress."

He found that amusing. "Then we'd become in-laws."

"We always were family," she reasoned, preparing medical supplies to stitch the bullet wound. "I think some people are destined to walk through life together. We sure are. But until now, we couldn't find our proper place. We didn't have all our puzzle pieces. Now, we do. Everyone fits."

"That's a beautiful way to see it."

Hearing him agree made her smile. "Wyatt just needs his special puzzle piece, then everyone will be happy and loved."

Tristan choked on a shocked laugh.

"What's so funny?"

"Nothing," but those ocean blue eyes said he lied.

"You doubt that he'll ever find love?"

"Oh, it could happen," he nearly grinned. "But she'd have to be a very unique puzzle piece, a strong trustworthy woman."

"True. Now hold still. This is going to hurt." Solaris closed the wound with slow precise stitches. They had nothing to numb the pain. But he never said a word.

"There," she finally breathed. "I'm done."

Tristan inspected it. "You should have been a doctor."

"No way. I hate hospitals." She carefully cleaning the rest of his blood and iodine stained arm. Soon, his skin looked normal again, except for the place where he was shot, which was bruised and swollen. Then Solaris covered the stitches with a thick bandage, wrapping his upper arm with sterile white cotton.

"How's that feel?"

"It's good. Thanks." From his backpack on the chair, he grabbed a clean shirt while she sanitized their kitchen mess.

"There's blood all over the front of your pink tank top," he observed.

Solaris looked down. "No offense since it's your blood, but yuck."

"None taken. Let me see what we have here." Tristan went into the bedroom and borrowed a red button up blouse and slim jeans from Madison's closet.

"Thanks. Hope she doesn't mind."

"She won't. Madie loves you."

After Solaris changed too, they migrated into the living room. She opened the living room drapes. It had been more than two hours since her Jeep blew sky high. Fog still lingered along the coastline. Thinning now, patches of sunlight gleamed between the low-lying mist.

Soon, it would be gone.

Cradling his arm like it hurt, Tristan lounged on the creamy leather sectional. His skin was pale and he looked weak from losing so much blood. Solaris brought him a pillow from Madison's bed. He stretched out and looked grateful. She curled up in the opposite corner.

"Tell me what you remember of the past."

"You mean about the day Mom died?" He nodded, waiting for her to begin. "Rachel picked me up after school, pretending to be Mom. She dressed and talked just like Mom. She fooled me completely. We went to Dad's office. He knew who she was. They started fighting, yelling about twins and lies. I remember feeling dumb for thinking Rachel was my real Mom. I started to cry. Suddenly, Navarro and his men came in with Mom. She fought against him and he hit her. Her cheek was bleeding. Rachel had me, holding me tight. But I bit her hand and ran."

Tristan listened intently. "Good for you."

"Mom and Rachel both chased after me. Dad yelled to leave me alone, pulled a gun from his desk and fired. But he shot his own wife."

Saying the next part was hard.

"Mom fell on the floor by the windows. Rachel laughed. It was so evil. Dad made this awful heartbroken sound. He dropped to his knees and cried. Then Navarro scooped me up. His men carried Mom away. We left Rachel there with Dad. In the elevator, I screamed at her to be okay. Mom opened her eyes and looked at me. Then, she died."

"Good lord, Solaris. That's awful."

"I think that's why my mind suppressed everything. A child shouldn't see death, especially a parent. I was kept on a big yacht for a while, fed and taken care of, but I was locked inside a room all alone."

"No one touched you—like sexually?"

"Never. Navarro was extremely protective. He read to me, talked to me. He claimed if this plan didn't work, he'd sail for Columbia and raise me as his own daughter."

Tristan looked lethal at that news. "Oh hell no."

"But Dad paid the ransom. Rachel won. They dropped me off at the pier, on the south end of Silver Strand Beach and told me to walk toward Coronado. Halfway up that long beach, Dad found me. When I came home, I was sick and slept a lot. I ran fevers. Somehow during that, I forgot everything, so we pretended life was normal. But Dad hated himself for shooting Mom, hated me for growing up to look just like her, and hated that I managed to forget things that haunted him day and night, forever."

Tristan looked at her, questioning. "How do you know that?"

"You were the one who gave Joshua the zip drive with the bank account files proving that Rachel launders diamond money through both hers and Dad's businesses and that Dad is financially partnered with Navarro, right?"

"I broke into his office a few weeks ago."

"You also copied Dad's personal journal."

"Yeah, I didn't read it."

"He wrote letters to Gina, apologizing, begging her forgiveness. He sees ghosts, these dark evil shadows he believes will send him to hell. He covers his sins with a world of white."

"Your Dad will go to jail too, you know."

"He's far from innocent. Wyatt read the financial records. Dad started out paying blackmail, but got greedy after he saw how much money Rachel and Navarro were making from gemstones. He wanted in. Now he takes a cut of every dollar they make. I know he'll go to prison. International conspiracy and embezzlement laws are strict."

Her cell phone rang. Solaris jumped up. She forgot it was in her leggings pocket. She scrambled to get the folded pants off the chair and find the phone. It was Wyatt.

"Hello?"

"Solaris! Oh god. Thank god," he breathed.

"I'm okay. I'm with Tristan."

Her worried brother fervently thanked the heavens again. "I tried calling him a dozen times. Where are you?"

"We're at Madison's hotel room."

"Stay there. Don't let anyone see you. Your jeep exploding is headline news. Everyone wants to know who killed the famous photographer."

"Damn. It's on the news already?"

"Yeah. The Archer's are helping the FBI. I told them everything, turned in all our evidence. They raided the jewel warehouse, but no one was there. For your own safety, the news is reporting two unidentified bodies were inside the Jeep when it blew."

"Oh, wow."

"Agents already informed Dad, but they can't arrest him without getting Rachel and Navarro, first. For now, Joshua is keeping a low profile too. We want everyone to think you guys are dead."

"No one knows that I left there with Tristan?"

"Only us and the Feds. Please stay hidden. I love you! Tristan deserves to get his life back. I'm working on it. You'll be safe with him. This will all be over soon."

"I hope so." Then he was gone.

Malcolm knew today was the day. His heart had burned to ashes for the final time. Seeing the remains of his daughter's bombed out Jeep on the news, hearing the attack was by Colombian men, was too much. The stern federal agents who appeared at his office only made it worse.

Silver Strand, of all places.

That long strip of golden sand was the same place he had found Solaris, so many years ago. That day, Malcolm got his daughter back from Navarro, but lost himself instead.

He stood at the office windows, where he had stood for several hours. The fog was burning off, moving out to sea. Sunlight peeked through.

It was a sign.

Solaris was the reason he let Rachel rule his life.

Now that reason was gone.

It was time for justice: time to pay for his sins. Everything was in place. Returning to his desk, Malcolm sat down and wrote the last journal entry.

It was to his children this time, apologizing for every crime.

Then he arranged the unearthed boxes and precious photographs of their mother in chronological order. It created a massive memorial of Gina's life, perfectly displayed on the giant white floor of his tower office.

She died here.

The tribute to the true Regina Thornbriar should be in this room. If only he had the Heart Stone. Then his penance could be complete.

Driving home, for the first time in years Malcolm didn't race. He was no longer afraid. Guilty shadows had no power.

Somewhere during this awful day, he realized that all along, he was one too. Just a shadow of a man. He had been walking in darkness, living with fear, avoiding his fate. Sunlight stopped touching his soul the day that Gina died. Today he embraced his fate.

Malcolm knew what he would find when he walked through the door of his home in La Jolla, but seeing the reality was shocking.

Rachel was celebrating her victory with Navarro and his friends. Loud music blared. She wore a slutty silver outfit that revealed every falsified curve. Dancing like a stripper in heat, she flaunted that artificial youthful body, fanning the flames of desire with every lusty man in the room.

All the men greedily watched.

She was in shameless self-centered bliss.

His daughter's brutal death had ushered forth a drunken carnival of intoxication. Cocaine lined a mirror set on the glass table, alcohol flowed with abundance, and laughter rang throughout the rooms. It was debauchery and carnal sin.

Solaris deserved better.

Their attention was completely focused on Rachel. The loud rock music made it easy to walk right into their gluttonous party undetected.

A silencer was hardly necessary. Malcolm used one anyway. When the first shot split Navarro's forehead wide open, everyone froze. There was no sound. Just an abrupt explosion of flesh.

Life seemed to move in slow motion.

It was a surreal moment, almost a perfect moment. One Malcolm had envisioned happening for years, had practiced over and over in his mind.

The reality of it felt wonderful.

Empty gaping dark eyes stared in shock, but saw nothing. Blood flowed down Navarro's thick neck and chest. He was a big muscular man, but that shot made every muscle in his powerful frame useless.

As the lifeless body dropped to the floor, Rachel screamed.

Five quick shots finished the other shocked men. They were too high on drugs, wasted on alcohol to think clearly. They only knew their boss was dead. Normal reaction time was slow, giving Malcolm the edge.

Quickly, fallen bodies covered the wild party scene, turning it into a bloody morgue.

Now Rachel was hysterical.

"Shut up, you Bitch!" Malcolm lunged.

Screams were silenced as his vengeful hands found her soft throat. It wasn't fast and it wasn't pretty. He had never touched her skin before, not even in passing. Her beauty was lewd, vulgar, and obscene.

His desire to touch any woman died with Gina.

Touching her now, his fists clenched tight. Choking. Creamy flawless flesh tore beneath his fists as she fought. His pure white world became splashed with vengeful red. They fought, struggling through the house. Throwing Rachel down on the marble floor, the sound of her skull striking stone was beautiful.

He did it again. And again. It was the sound of freedom, of justice long overdue. Redemption was sweet.

Stillness finally came. Now Malcolm smiled. Blood had stained his hands. He laughed at the mess he made, the trail of blood, and wiped red streaks across his neatly ironed white shirt.

Standing over her body, he was pleased to see that Rachel now looked as ugly on the outside as she had been inside her cold silenced heart.

She stole everything good.

Today he had revenge. He had never been happier.

Opening the French doors to the back yard, Malcolm flung them wide open and took a deep breath. The sea air was moist, clean smelling. It felt invigorating, left him energized, as if he had not taken a breath of fresh air in years. He looked up at the afternoon sky. The fog was completely gone.

Summer sunlight now touched his whole California world.

It was another beautiful sign.

Laughing with delirious joy, Malcolm stood on the grass and listened to Rachel's party music fill the warm July Fourth air.

It really was a day to celebrate independence and freedom. He danced a little. His movements were awkward at first, but his celebration of freedom gained enthusiasm until he was dancing like a lunatic, completely manic with happiness.

Sweating and smiling from his own private party, Malcolm finally decided to take a walk on the path going down the hill, to the beach far below. Blue waves rolling toward the peaceful shore reminded him of days he'd spent playing in the water with Gina.

She always smiled. And held his hand.

It was time to swim in the ocean.

The scene was hard to swallow. Bodies lay where they fell under the bullets, except for Rachel. The trail of her blood was spread across the house, ending in a pool beneath her sprawled out beaten body. It was barely recognizable.

The FBI had stormed the house, coming to arrest people. They were handed a scene of cold murder, instead.

"We found him," someone solemnly announced.

Federal agents gathered outside. Standing on the grassy hilltop lawn, they gazed down at the beach. On the ocean a hundred yards from shore, a man dressed in white floated face down upon the blue water.

His clothes drifted loose around his body like a shroud.

Justice is Served

In one move of madness, he ended the lies.
He must have loved us.
He gave his children a clean slate.

~~ Wyatt

"Kianna," he called out from the front courtyard. Wyatt was in a hurry, striding toward the gated estate house in the San Diego foothills that had become his secret refuge in recent weeks. It was a safe quiet place, secure from danger. Today he flung the front doors open wide. "Kianna? Hey, where are you?"

"Up here, Ku`u Lei." Leaning over the brass banister that edged the landing upstairs, the beautiful woman put one finger up to her lips, "Shhh, my noisy bull. Your sweet Makuahine is sleeping."

Wyatt didn't care.

Taking the stairs two at a time, he raced toward Kianna. Her long black hair was loose to her waist today, neatly tucked behind both ears. The diamond studs he bought winked with jeweled light as she moved. Tiny stars, she called them, always wearing his gift of love. Her simple flowered sundress looked graceful. Wyatt liked her exotic elegance.

He had secretly loved Kianna for six years. Until Solaris came home to stay, he never said a word. Now, he wanted to shout it from the rooftops.

"It's over," he declared, hands taking her waist.

"I'm so glad." Arms wrapped around him. "And our Ohana?"

"Solaris is just fine. Tristan has her."

Kianna drew back to look at him. "Auē, my god. Imagine her surprise. Dead men walk and talk. That bad boy even rides a hot bike," she teased, proving how much she liked Tristan. He had been here several times in the past few weeks, always sneaking in so they could talk. Their trip to LA had brought home something important. "How did this reunion happen?"

"Madison, I think. Somehow she and Tristan got there just before the Jeep blew."

"And Joshua is okay? Solaris loves him."

"He's safe too."

She looked relieved. "We are lucky, Wyatt. Life has blessed our family." He felt grateful for Kianna's good and loving heart. She had watched over Solaris, traveled the world by her side, making his sister's dreams into her own. The assistant he had hired became family.

And that was only one reason why he loved her.

It was just shocking to learn that she loved him too. Coming home changed everything. But for him, talking on the phone every day for six years was more than business. There were days Wyatt called just to hear her melodic voice and the funny Hawaiian words she tossed into her speech.

Work was foreplay, their prelude to love.

One real date was all they had needed to find honesty.

"There's more. Dad delivered his own kind of justice today. I just came from the house in La Jolla. The FBI had to inform me first."

"FBI? What did your father do?"

Before he could tell Kianna about Malcolm's brutal revenge, down the hallway a bedroom door opened. Someone appeared.

The woman was slender and anxious, as if life had not been kind. Her long tawny hair had silver-gray streaks at the temples. Her right shoulder was held rigid, as if broken once and the bones never healed right.

But those amber brown eyes were all Solaris.

She had been crying.

"Wyatt," she barely breathed though her sorrow. "I saw the news."

He had hoped they wouldn't turn on the television today. "Solaris is with Tristan. No one was inside the Jeep. The story on the news was reported wrong to protect her from Rachel."

"Oh, thank god." Her skin had paled and golden-brown eyes gratefully gleamed with tough emotions. She took a labored breath as if the air felt too thin. Emotions were tight. One hand clutched the wall. Gasps were raspy. He took quick strides toward her.

"Easy, Mom. Everything is okay."

The name made tears of love fall down her cheeks.

Wyatt caught her up just as she dropped to her knees and cried like his sister often did. Strong arms held her tight, cradled against his heart. Gina clung to her son.

"I'm right here," he assured the woman he thought they had lost forever. But two weeks ago, he and Kianna found her in Los Angeles. Hiding from the past, powerless to change it, Gina had lived her life in fear, invisible to those who loved and needed her the most.

Her children.

The bullet Malcolm fired tore through her right shoulder, breaking the bones. She wasn't dead, only unconscious. But Malcolm had reacted, believing he killed her. It set everything else in motion.

Navarro lied to Rachel about disposing of the body. He kept Gina hostage upon the ship too. Solaris was locked inside a room and never saw her mother. They were kept apart. The Colombian kept Gina as his personal insurance policy, if things went wrong. But Malcolm paid the money. Rachel took power. Navarro was free to smuggle illegal gemstones.

When Solaris was released and the lies began, he had no further need for the Gina. But she had one thing he coveted.

A priceless ruby: a gemstone of luck and love, a jewel so extraordinary it deserved his reverence. The Colombian had a weakness for pretty things. Navarro had talked to Gina, heard her story. He swore financial allegiance to Rachel, but the gentler twin earned his respect.

The woman wearing the Heart Stone was special.

Over the following weeks that he held her on the ship while he decided what to do with her, they spoke every day. In time, Navarro agreed that tears shed because of love were indeed beautiful, something sacred to cherish. He wanted the Heart Stone. But the teardrop ruby could not be stolen. He firmly believed Life would curse such a man for his greed.

It could only be given, freely.

Gina bought her freedom with the Heart Stone.

Two million dollars to live on and he gave her a fresh start, but in their deal, she lost Wyatt and Solaris.

All love for Malcolm was gone. His fear killed it.

Gina boldly told Navarro, even if she had died when Malcolm shot her, allowing Rachel to take her place in the world was despicable. Her husband owed it to his children to give them a life of truth.

She was released at the Marina Del Ray harbor.

And then she completely disappeared.

"It's over, Mom. No one can hurt you or tear us apart. You're safe now. We can be a family again."

"Malcolm will never allow it. He likes the money he makes."

"He's gone." Telling her about Malcolm's revenge was hard. "You're finally free. We all are. He took Rachel and Navarro with him." Then Wyatt sat with his mother and Kianna, telling them everything that he knew about those final moments.

Listening, Gina trembled with relief. "It really is over."

"Yes. Would you like to see your daughter?"

This time, his mother smiled. It was a familiar sunny smile, one that lit his life every time his sister blessed him with one.

"Yes. Please."

Their safe hotel suite had become an intolerable prison. They waited hours with no word from anyone. Tristan wouldn't let her turn on the television, Joshua and Madie hadn't called, and Wyatt wasn't answering his phone. In her heart, Solaris knew something big had happened. She felt it.

That paralyzing fear inside of her was gone. It had been there chilling her heart and stealing all her courage since the moment she fell down the cliff in Peru. Now that fear had disappeared.

Danger had passed. It had not touched her. She was safe. It was a calm knowledge inside. Even her lost courage was back, warm and familiar. Her mind kept returning to that moment in Peru when she lay on the ledge, staring up at the blue eyes of her truest friend.

Tristan had rescued her courage.

It had been stuck on that ledge, all along.

"We should call Wyatt again."

Stretched out sleeping on the long leather sectional couch, his bandaged arm was cradled against his chest to ease the pain. Hearing her request from where Solaris was pacing the floor, Tristan opened blue eyes.

"We're not bothering your brother."

"But I need to talk to him."

"Why? I'm here. Talk to me."

She hesitated to say what she sensed. "Maybe I'll just tell Joshua."

"Good idea." He closed his eyes again.

Pacing wasn't helping. She kept it up for a while, but felt trapped here. "Please can I call someone? The silence is killing me."

The injured blonde looked at her again and let out a huff. "Wyatt is busy. The Archer's are busy. The Feds are busy. Navarro and Rachel's hours of freedom are limited. Even your lunatic Dad will have his day in court." He grumpily stated, "Now chill out, take a seat, and stop making me crazy."

"You didn't used to be so crabby, Tristan."

"Bullet wound, Solaris." He reminded, shrugging the arm. "Remember stitching it without painkillers? I didn't say anything, but that hurt like hell. A few shots of tequila would improve my attitude. But, we have none."

"Sorry. I could find a store for you."

"Nice try, Sweetheart. You aren't leaving here."

"Room service?"

"No. This is Madie's penthouse. We'd be questioned."

"I could—"

"Sit. Breathe. Stop thinking so damn much. I'm fine."

Giving up, she sat down. Tristan sighed and relaxed again. Looking out the windows, the afternoon had turned sunny warm gold and the ocean rolled in friendly shades of liquid blue. The morning fog had melted away. It was another beautiful day in Southern California.

"We should order a pizza."

"Wish for one. I bet Madie brings it to you."

She though his nonchalance was funny. "Like a genie, just make a wish and she it comes true?"

"Usually."

"I want pepperoni and sausage with a big iced tea."

"Then Magic Madie will deliver your pizza."

She laughed at the idea. "Soon?"

"Yeah. Soon."

"How do you know for sure?"

Tristan's grin was mischievous and playful, "Because a pepperoni pizza sounds great. I haven't eaten anything but a ham sandwich and an apple in two days. I was too busy chasing down evidence and running from Navarro's men. Now I'm starving. I need food to recover from all the blood that we washed down the sink. Trust me, Madie will know. She's tuned into me."

"She also loves you."

"It happens," he teased. "I'm irresistible."

They shared a playful grin. It felt fantastic to have her friend back.

Solaris didn't have long to wait. An hour later, the penthouse door burst open in a noisy rush of talking people. Tristan sat up, looked over the back of the leather couch and smiled wide.

Madison carried three large boxes of pizza and Joshua's arms were filled with grocery bags. Drinks, snack chips, and fresh salad greens were unloaded on the granite kitchen counter. There was even a bottle of tequila.

"Ha. Told you," he whispered.

"Brat." While Tristan casually helped Madison in the kitchen, Solaris ran ahead, meeting Joshua's open arms with a deep grateful rush. He buried her face against his chest and held her tight. It felt like home, the only place she belonged.

"Something happened, didn't it?"

His expression was serious, "Yes. How did you know?"

"I felt it."

That sly knowing smile. "And?"

"Whatever happened, I know the danger is gone. You're truly. You never have to be a Guardian for anyone, ever again."

He was shocked. "Your thoughts were only for me?"

"Of course: I love you."

"You're glowing," he whispered against her ear. His kiss was soft and beautiful. It promised a lifetime more.

They finally turned toward the noisy commotion happening in the kitchen. Madie was fussing over Tristan, giving him a big plate of pizza, a gallon of orange juice, and the whole bottle of tequila. She ruled that he had to drink the juice first to help his body recover: then a little alcohol for the pain. Tristan argued that he could mix the tequila and orange juice together; then everyone would be happy.

Madison won, of course. Orange juice now. Tequila later.

While they all sat at the table and ate, Joshua and Madison told them the details of Malcolm's final act. It was hard to hear.

Maybe this was the best ending for her father, the only way his suffering would end. He was already broken. The media would have torn him apart while Rachel and Navarro fought in court. Shooting their mom was an accident. But news reporters would have found his faults, discovered the money he made in the scandal, and ripped the truth wide open, exposed it raw and cruel for the world to see.

He died a man driven to madness.

Simple closure. His sad story ended today.

The world would never see his fears, the weakness, or his hard heart. His legacy as a businessman would stand and the tales of years of extortion by Navarro would find sympathy in the community.

She and Wyatt would not endure speculation by reporters, or explain their lives to anyone. Malcolm took all the insanity with him. In one bold move, one man changed everything.

The danger really was gone.

A brisk knock sounded on the penthouse door. "Expecting someone?" Joshua asked.

"No." Madison studied the air for a second. "Oh. My." Her eyes quickly focused upon Tristan. "You knew about this."

"Probably," he dryly agreed with a half-smirk. "Whatever it is. I do know a few things I probably shouldn't."

Her tongue clicked at him. "You are so bad." But her lips curved as if she approved. "Solaris, you have company. You should get that."

Wondering who waited on the other side, Solaris opened the door. "Wyatt!" Powerful arms enveloped her.

"It's over, Laurie."

"I know. Madie and Joshua just told me."

"The FBI said we all need to lay low for a few days."

"I have no problem doing that."

Her brother hugged her so tight and for so long that she couldn't breathe. "Stop, stop," she laughed. "You're squishing me."

But he was too emotional. "You could have been inside that Jeep. I'll hug you all I want. I'm glad I can still squish you."

"I love you, Wyatt." Her smile changed him, like a world of worry lifted off his shoulders. Solaris had never seen him happier.

Seeing everyone else, Wyatt nodded his unshaven chin at Tristan. "Looks like you took a bullet, Bud. How's the arm?"

"I'll live."

"Did Laurie patch you up?"

"Yeah, we played doctor."

Joshua suddenly laughed aloud. "I did not just hear that."

"Not THAT kind of playing doctor," Tristan quickly clarified.

Joshua snickered again and sent her a sly sexy smile that always worked magic in her heart. Solaris felt his trust and his love. He accepted Tristan as her friend. There was no tension, no jealousy or worry.

It was a wonderful moment.

Solaris suddenly realized Wyatt wasn't alone. A beautiful Hawaiian lady politely waited in the doorway. "Kianna!"

"Aloha, my sister." She smiled. But her gaze fluttered past and found Wyatt's face. Her serene expression changed to one of love. She adored her brother.

"Ah-ha! So, that's where he has been staying." Solaris laughed. "Strong women need strong roots," she quoted her friend's wise words. "Have you found your roots, my kaikua'ana?"

"Ae, I did. Very strong roots. Like an oak tree, Wyatt is."

Solaris embraced her. "Ho'omaika'i 'ana."

"Mahalo," Kianna thanked her for the congratulations. Taking her hand, she stepped into the hallway. "Come, we brought you a gift. She is scared. Can't breathe, just like you do when emotions are too big. Maybe you can help our sweet Ohana. Please?"

"Can't breathe?"

She followed Kianna.

A woman stood in the hallway. One hand clutched at her chest. She was hyperventilating, gasping at air that felt too thin to breathe.

It was a mirror of her future self. Same tawny hair and amber eyes. Solaris drew a deep breath. It burned with truth. A tear fell down her cheek.

"Mom?"

Gina tried to speak, but words were caught in her throat, trapped beneath deep emotions. Solaris gently laced their fingers together, laying their joined hands over her mother's rapid beating heart.

"I do that too. I do it all the time."

Later that night, standing on the wide penthouse balcony with all the people that she loved, Solaris felt truly lucky.

Fireworks burst into the starlit sky. The city was out in force, witnessing a vibrant celebration of freedom, a tradition of independence from oppression and tyranny. The fireworks were a tribute to the courage of men in America's past who had the strength to stand up for the things they believed were right.

But it paled compared to the silent celebration of freedom inside the hearts of every single person who stood beside her. They were a somber group. But extremely grateful.

She looked at the faces of the people she loved. Joshua beside her, then Wyatt with his arms wrapped around Kianna, and at the end of the terrace Madison leaned against Tristan.

Their eyes met.

The trustworthy blue eyes of her greatest, most loyal friend. A knot caught in her throat. He gave his life away, risked everything in search of the truth. Her truth. His actions set in motion the wheels of justice, rippling outward, drawing the Archer's to San Diego as Guardians.

He had changed their fate.

And along the way, they both found real love.

She knew the days ahead would be hard. The FBI had called Wyatt, warning him of the memorial of keepsakes their father left in his office. The things they would see and learn about Malcolm would probably hurt. But she had these people.

Her family. They were her strength.

Solaris held her mother's hand.

Looking into amber brown eyes that mirrored the gold tones of her own, their tawny warm blonde hair fluttered in the night ocean breeze. Even the tears of love were reflected back at her. The Heart Stone now hung on Gina's neck, where it always belonged.

It was given in love, worn now to honor a love strong enough to overcome fear, love that brought tears. They had certainly shed their share.

Someday, many years from now, Solaris might wear it again. Eventually, the precious gemstone would be worn by her own daughter, if she and Joshua were lucky enough to have one. It would become their family legacy for a belief in love. Its story would be told for generations.

Solaris touched it. Her Mom smiled.

It was a perfect moment. A beautiful moment.

That sunny smile was the one from her childhood, the one her heart still remembered, beautiful and sweet.

"I love you, Mom. Welcome home."

I Choose You

Fate is not written. Every moment is a choice.

~~ Madison Liberty

It was almost midnight before Madison watched Tristan say goodbye to everyone, then close and lock their penthouse door. It had been a wonderful evening filled with laughter, a few happy tears, and lots of love. Since the FBI advised them to avoid reporters for a while, Wyatt and Gina continued to stay at Kianna's house in the foothills. Joshua took Solaris home with him, of course.

A few days behind closed doors would be good for everyone.

She certainly needed it.

Madison already knew the next week or two would be spent healing, recovering from everything each person had experienced. By the time they were all together again as a family, hearts would be whole and hope for their new life of safety and freedom would have strengthened every tattered soul. This would be especially true for Solaris and Gina.

Mother and daughter were like beautiful mirrors, one set further in time than the other. But while Gina had loved a man and knew the burning betrayal of that love, Solaris would never walk that painful road.

Joshua would love her, honor and protect her until they were both very old and very gray.

Next spring, they would have a wedding to attend.

Madison could already see it.

These people deserved happiness. She felt proud that she had played a small part in righting all the wrongs in their lives.

It took moxy.

Madison had finally done something to make a positive difference in the world. She listened to the signs, had chosen the right actions. Today when Fate shouted that death was in the air, she and Tristan raced to Silver Strand, changing that future.

Solaris and Joshua had lived.

Shooting Navarro's men in the fog had not left a warm fuzzy feeling inside, but there had been no other choice.

Now she planned to use that courage one more time.

Madison still worried that Life would always send her dreams of danger. She might always be called to become someone's Guardian. But that fear wasn't stronger than her love. It didn't matter if she dreamed. What mattered is the man who stole her heart with their very first kiss.

"You look tired," she told Tristan.

His backside leaned against the granite breakfast bar counter in the dining area where he stood drinking the last of his orange juice. "I'm okay." But his bandaged left arm was held rigid, that shoulder tight. She knew it was killing him.

"We could go to bed."

He hesitated, giving her a skeptical look. "Am I sleeping with you, or on the couch?" His recently shaven chin nodded toward it.

"Do you think you should sleep alone?"

"I don't know. You saw me with Solaris tonight. I think we clearly proved that she loves Joshua and I love you. But if you want space and time, I'll respect that."

Madison clicked her tongue. "You disappoint me, Mr. Kennedy," she teased, "I had decided you were The One."

That clever sexy smile was hot. "As in: I am The One for you?"

"Precisely. And I have a present for you, Lover."

"Is it a nice present?"

"Ooh, very nice. You will thank me."

She liked how those blue eyes followed every step as she padded barefoot across the floor to retrieve the white paper pharmacy bag from inside her giant black leather purse.

"My brother Lincoln is a doctor. Did I tell you that?"

"No." His gaze stayed with her as she returned to him.

"I called him today. He ordered you a prescription."

"Is this legal?"

"Perfectly." Facing Tristan again, she set the white bag on the counter beside his hip. "Now let me help you to feel better."

"What are you going to do?"

"Just relax and trust me, Lover."

Madison slowly lifted his shirt over his blonde head and carefully slid it off the sore arm. She dropped the unwanted cotton barrier on the floor. Seeing his bare chest sent heat through her core.

She wanted him. Needed Tristan. Never again would she let fear keep them apart. Her hand slowly stroked across his taut skin.

"Mmm," he sighed. "That feels really good."

"Lover, you look really good."

He was a beautiful strong man.

Unable to resist the wild beauty of him Madison tasted his neck, slowly kissing the small sensitive places that no one ever casually touched. Tristan let her.

The tender shell of his ear was loved, the side of his throat knew her touch, and the wonderful place where his pulse raced beneath her mouth grew warmer. Her lips slowly worked down the firm planes of his bare chest and taut abs until it made him groan.

"You will only sleep with me. Ever." She declared, "Got it?

His hands were fisted in her hair. He wanted her close, needed this too. It wasn't tight. His grip was loving, as if he couldn't bear to be apart.

"Agreed," he breathed. "That rule cuts both ways."

"Absolutely. You will find that Archer's are eternally loyal." Looking at him, fingers affectionately caressed through the side of his long blonde hair. "Tomorrow we're going downstairs to the salon and this is getting cut. You deserve to look like a respectable man when the world is told you are still alive and your gorgeous picture covers the internet and every newspaper in America."

"Sounds good, but I have a few terms you must agree with too."

"Oh? You have conditions to our relationship?"

"Yes I do, and you won't like it." The intensity in his blue eyes made her belly tighten. "You must promise to stay in San Diego. This is my home."

The knot inside disappeared and Madison gave him sweet smile. "I like it here. Joshua lives here. That's an easy promise to keep."

"Good." But he wasn't finished negotiating. "After we get my hair cut tomorrow, I want you to come with me to see my family. They deserve to be the first ones to hear that I am alive."

"Yes, they do. I'd love to meet your parents."

"And no more living in hotels," he added. "I want us to live in a house, like normal people. We can rebuild the one on Diamond Street, together."

"Can I bring Captain Morgan?"

"Sure. Bring the goofy looking pirate."

It made her extremely happy.

"I'd like having a real home with you. My job as company spy is blown anyway. I raced out of here this morning looking like myself. Joshua and I had to meet with the hotel manager to explain why a team of FBI agents were suddenly assigned as additional security in the building. The whole hotel staff knows that Madison Archer is staying in the penthouse. People will talk. Our other hotels will know I have brown curls. My anonymous identity is gone."

"What will you do now?"

"I'm sure Victoria can find a west coast job for me. What about you? Will you become an investigative reporter again?"

His short laugh vibrated the chest lying beneath her hands. "Hell no. That crazy life is over. Wyatt already offered me a partnership at the architectural firm. Since Malcolm is gone, Wyatt is the boss now. He owned it all, anyway."

"You don't know anything about building houses."

"No, but I'm smart. I can learn. Wyatt proposed I handle public relations and marketing. I think I can do that."

She nodded, knowing he would do it, too. Whatever Tristan decided to become now, she knew in her heart it would be good.

"Is that the last of your demands?"

"Yeah. I think I've covered it."

"Then let's look at your arm, see if it needs anything."

Madison carefully removed the thick sterile bandage. The bullet sliced left bicep was bruised, uncomfortably swollen, and it had bled a little, but the stitches looked good.

"Solaris did an excellent job. It will heal nicely." Playing nurse, she put antibiotic cream on the cut and wrapped his upper arm with fresh gauze, to keep the wound clean. Then she reached into the pharmacy bag.

Tristan objected when he saw the needle.

"Oh hell no. What is that?"

"A tetanus shot. You're due. If I don't give you this, you will get sick, sick, sick. I see it happening and it isn't good."

He didn't look happy, but Tristan let her prepare it and inject the tetanus booster into his upper right arm.

"Now both shoulders will be sore," he griped.

"Don't be a baby."

He pouted a little. "That was my present?"

"No silly," she giggled at his disappointed frown. "That was simply prevention. These are your real gift." Reaching into the prescription bag again she gave him two brown plastic bottles: an antibiotic to take for a week and Dilaudid, a powerful pain killer. "Lincoln said these pain pills and alcohol don't mix. Since you didn't drink any of your tequila today, you can safely take these now."

"Why didn't you give me these pills earlier?"

"You wanted tequila." She smirked, "Your wish is my command."

He chuckled, "Yeah. Right."

"Plus, the pain pills will make you sleepy and I knew you wanted to spend time with everyone tonight, so I waited."

His hands had been busy untucking her shirttails. Curious fingers found her skin and slid around her bare waist, then up her back. With one deft flick of his thumb and fingers, he unfastened her bra.

"Right now, I want to spend time with you."

That pleased her.

"You don't want a pain pill?"

"Not if it makes me sleepy. I need time with you first."

Those were the words she had hoped to hear. "You want all of me?"

"Yeah, I want all of you. Tonight. All night."

"Just for tonight?"

"No Madie." His expression became serious. "You and I are living together now. You are not going back to Joshua's house. You will sleep every night in the same bed with me. Deal?"

"For how long will we play house?"

"Years. Marriage might even be on the table, someday. I want you to see that future, choose it, and commit."

His stern gaze meant he expected resistance. It made her smile. "Okay. I choose that future. With you. I commit myself to you, Tristan."

Shocking him, Madison stepped just out of reach and pulled off her shirt and black bra in one smooth motion. They landed on the dining room floor. All the lights were on.

Her breasts were fully exposed to his cerulean blue gaze.

He cleared his throat. "Those are for me?"

"Could be. Are you feeling lucky?"

"Right now, I sure am."

While he watched, staying just out of reach of those busy hands, she shimmied out of her jeans. Only black lace panties remained.

Tristan was breathing faster, a capture audience.

She knew he was dying to touch. Not yet.

"Do you like what you see?"

"Hell yeah."

Pleased with herself, feeling playful and happy she had Tristan to love, Madison hummed a tune and turned in a little hip shaking circle, letting him enjoy the full effect of her naked body.

He swore and lunged for her.

But she lightly danced away and laughed.

"Damn, Madie. Don't play games. Let me have you. Please?"

"First, close your eyes."

"But I want to look at you."

"You can, in a minute. Now, close your eyes."

He let out a resigned sigh, leaned his very fine backside against the counter again and obeyed.

"Now hold very still."

The warmth she injected into his upper left bicep muscle must have burned. Blue eyes popped open and Tristan was mad.

"What the hell?"

He saw the needle and tried to snatch it out of her hand. But she jumped back, Then the small dose of localized morphine kicked in, numbing the aching wound.

"Oh god," he groaned in relief, "that feels so much better."

Madison capped the syringe, tossed it back into the white bag.

"That shot, Lover, was my real present," she purred, enjoying the smile slowly curving on his face. "Linc only prescribed one. I would have saved it, if you wanted to sleep tonight. You'll feel numb for about four or five hours. Then you can start taking the pills, if you need them."

"Thank you."

"I love you, Tristan."

He looked incredibly happy to hear those four words, even happier than the moment she had first said his name aloud.

"You're going to make me say that over and over, aren't you?"

His grin was wicked. "Baby, you're gonna scream my name."

A strong arm quickly snagged her naked body, towing them together. Firm bare breasts pressed against his warm taut skin.

"You own my heart, Madison Liberty."

His kiss was hotter than she anticipated. The slant of his mouth taking hers was possessive and needy. This kiss enveloped her, overwhelmed all her senses, and involved every inch of her warm willing body.

Madison wanted to dance.

In Tristan's arms, she did.

They eventually moved into the bedroom, falling together onto the soft welcoming bed without ever losing contact. His hands and mouth devoured her. The man was famished, alive like never before in his life.

He was an extremely skilled Lover, earning that name completely. Later, she did cry out his name.

Madison declared her love over and over.

And Tristan smiled.

Continue to follow Tristan & Madison in: Dream of Danger

About the Author

Leslie D. Stuart is a romantic suspense author, the creative director for Destiny Whispers Publishing LLC, and the executive editor for Destiny Rose Editorial Services. Book, reading, and writing are her passion.

She is happily married and lives in Tucson, Arizona with her husband, two adorable little dogs, two chirpy birds, and two spoiled cats. Their home is a busy place, especially with two beautiful granddaughters who call her Nana. She feels lucky.

Leslie loves roses. More than 120+ bushes grow around their home and bloom nearly all year in the warm Arizona sun. Her favorites are red Don Juan, purple Heirlooms, and a black-red damask rose called Oklahoma. She has every color from white, all reds, to bright Tropicana orange.

As a child Leslie moved frequently and was always the "new-girl" in school. It made her appreciate the wonderful home life she has now. She has lived in Oregon, Montana, Minnesota, California, and various ranching towns in Arizona. She still loves to travel and has visited nearly every state in the nation, including two of the Hawaiian Islands, plus Mexico and Canada. Her favorite cities are San Diego, Boston, Portland, and the Monterey Bay. She has seen amazing places that stay in her heart. Some are fictionalized in her books.

Leslie and her family have walked many miles on Silver Strand Beach, watching the dolphins play and gathering shells. When sunlight hits the sand just right, it really does glisten gold with mica flakes. The sand dollars they have gathered there are very special treasures.

The dolphin moment witnessed by Solaris & Joshua really happened to Leslie and her husband one warm summer day on Silver Strand. Unfortunately, they were not fast enough to capture any photos. The only pictures of that beautiful moment are the ones saved in their memories and written in this book.